'COME HERE, MY ANGEL . . .'

With an audible cry of ecstatic delight she buried her face into the warm strength of his naked chest, feeling she had finally come home to rest. She breathed deeply of the male fragrance of him, and he felt her tears trickle down and tickle his taut belly. 'How is it you're obedient now?' he asked tenderly, cupping her chin and lifting her face so he could look into her overflowing eyes.

'I shall always obey you when you order me to do things I agree with,' she sniffed, and Benedict laughed and kissed the salty stream that ran freely down her smiling cheeks . . .

Angelica murmured appreciatively and returned his kisses, opening her mouth hungrily to the domineering pressure of his tongue . . .

Also by Aleen Malcolm from Futura

CHILDREN OF THE MIST

ALEEN MALCOLM

Futura

A Futura Book

Copyright © 1988 by Aleen Malcolm

First published in Great Britain in 1989 by
Futura Publications, a Division of
Macdonald & Co (Publishers) Ltd
London & Sydney

ISBN 0 7088 4254 2

Reproduced, printed and bound in Great Britain by
Hazell Watson & Viney Limited
Member of BPCC Limited
Aylesbury, Bucks, England

Futura Publications
A Division of
Macdonald & Co (Publishers) Ltd
66–73 Shoe Lane
London EC4P 4AB
A member of Maxwell Pergamon Publishing Corporation plc

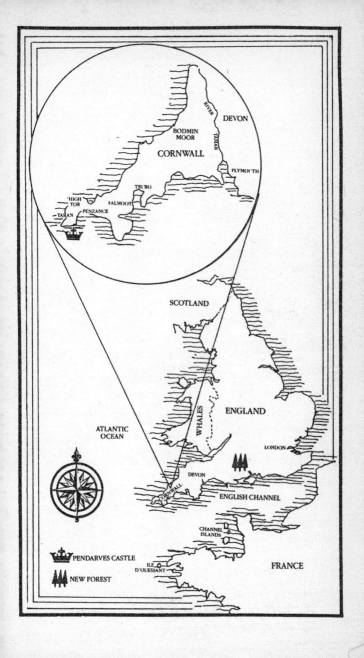

SCOTLAND

DEVON

RIVER TAMAR

BODMIN MOOR

CORNWALL

PLYMOUTH

TRURO

FALMOOT

'HIGH TOR

PENZANCE

TARAN

WHALES

ENGLAND

ATLANTIC OCEAN

LONDON

DEVON

CORNWALL

ENGLISH CHANNEL

CHANNEL ISLANDS

ILE D'OUESSANT

FRANCE

PENDARVES CASTLE

NEW FOREST

PART ONE

ANGEL

Cornwall

Go and catch a falling star,
Get with child a mandrake root,
Tell me, where all past years are,
And who cleft the Devil's foot.
Teach me to hear mermaids singing . . .

John Donne

PROLOGUE

How could a gloriously vivacious woman such as Catherine Pendarves have been created within such a dismal pile of rocks, mused Dr. Simon Carmichael, suppressing a shudder as the massive studded door crashed shut. The ominous sound bounced off the cheerless walls to echo jeeringly through the myriad catacombs of corridors. Mischievous blobs of light danced around him as he stared about the vast central hall, accustoming his eyes to the grim dimness after the bright sunshine of the golden blossomed moor. Furtive whispers hissed and mingled with the wailing skirl of the wind trapped high in the jagged turrets and the hollow booming of the sea in the caves far below. He gazed up at the cruel teeth of a suspended portcullis and hastily stepped to one side, colliding into a suit of armour. Instruments of torture and gruesome etchings depicting horrendous punishments lined the walls as though warning all who entered Pendarves Castle to beware.

The doctor's boots rang sharply on the stone floor as, with medical bag in hand, he dutifully followed the rustling skirts and jangling keys of the housekeeper. He started with terror as the shadows suddenly seethed with hissing black-garbed beings, their faces appearing unearthly in the dusty rays of light that stabbed down from the high slit windows of the Norman fortress.

It had been more than fourteen years since he had set foot in Pendarves Castle, yet it seemed that time had stood still. Nothing had changed. Even the housekeeper appeared exactly the same; as grey and timeless as the cold Cornish slate, her chiseled face as expressionless as it had been that bitter winter

3

night when she had silently ushered him into the comfortless chamber where Catherine Pendarves lay dying after giving birth to a stillborn child. She had been little more than a child herself, he recalled sadly. No more than seventeen or eighteen, even younger than his own daughter, Angelica, who was now so far away in London making her debut into society under the auspices of her maternal grandmother. At the thought of his beloved child's serene face, he felt the oppressive gloom lift a trifle and he smiled wistfully, wishing he could see her dressed in the fine gowns his doctor's salary could ill afford.

Poor Catherine Pendarves. She had been so tiny and fragile in the enormous bed, her exquisite face pale and framed by her flaming auburn hair that sparked with the wavering candlelight. Radiantly beautiful Catherine, breathtaking even in death. It was difficult to believe she was guilty of the wantonness that was attributed to her, for surely wickedness would mar such perfection.

"Dr. Carmichael?" The housekeeper's chiding voice brought him sharply back to the present, and with a shock he looked down at the shrivelled body that was dwarfed by the black-canopied bed.

Sir Godolphus Pendarves glared malevolently, and Simon was awed and repelled by the strength that emanated despite the frailness and apparent paralysis that froze one side of the skeletal face. It was as though the merciless cruelty of the inner man was now imprinted for all to see, and the good-natured doctor felt his rage rekindle.

"And of what service can I be to you, Lord Pendarves?" he asked cuttingly. "Make your last moments on this earth more bearable than your daughter's?"

"She was a whore! Like her mother before her! A whore like all mothers! Like Lilith! Eve! Mary! Whores!" rasped the cadaverous old man.

"You let your only child bleed to death! Let her scream in agony for three days and three nights," accused Simon, still unable after all the years to comprehend such inhumanity.

"No more than the innocent lamb of God upon the cross! And unto woman God spake thus . . . 'I shall greatly multiply thy sorrow and thy conception. In sorrow shall thou bring forth children,' " pronounced Godolphus Pendarves, the spittle bubbling on his dry pleated lips.

"You are not God!" retorted the doctor. "You are a vicious, punitive, unforgiving monster who denied himself both daughter and grandchild as comfort for his old age," he blustered impotently, unable to feel a shred of compassion for the pathetic shell of a man.

"And your ungainly daughter is a comfort to your middle years?" challenged Pendarves after a maniacal screech of laughter. "All daughters are whores! Even yours, whom you misguidedly christened 'Angel,' you fat fool! You obese, complacent idiot! All whores! All profane! All unclean! It states so here in the Bible . . . in Leviticus!" he crowed, clawing at a large leather-bound book on the shiny black counterpane beside him. "Your daughter is a whore!" he brayed loudly before a paroxysm of coughing left him gasping for breath.

Simon ignored the streaks of blood that now bubbled with the spittle from the sunken mouth. He gazed about the forbidding bedchamber that appeared to be more like a burial vault as he tried to control the rage that pounded his pulses. He had been summoned to Pendarves Castle in a professional capacity, he reminded himself as he resolutely opened his medical case and fumbled about, knowing there was nothing he could do for the man except ease his suffering.

"No! Suffering cleanses!" spat Pendarves, stabbing a boney finger to indicate the bottle of opiate that Simon was about to uncork.

"If I cannot be of service to you, why was I fetched?" asked the doctor, wishing he had the means to prolong the spiteful man's life so he could increase the suffering he felt Pendarves deserved.

"To witness my death and witness . . ." and the old man sucked in his breath noisily as pain caused him to stiffen. Simon waited for him to continue and gazed about uneasily as the hair on his neck prickled in warning. He sensed there were other witnesses avidly awaiting Lord Pendarves's demise, lurking behind him in the thick shadows. But he saw nothing tangible, just an elusive ruffling of the drapes that shrouded the windows and furnishings, and the silent wisps that rippled across the high vaulted ceiling from the smoking candles.

"Devil Tremayne, child of shame. Devil Tremayne, child of shame," intoned the old man, and Simon spun about, hearing a sharp scrambling of nails on the stone floor. "Are you there Devil-Child?" called Pendarves eagerly, but there was no answer.

"Devil Tremayne, child of shame?" repeated Simon, his eyes aching as he tried to penetrate the dense blackness.

"Quiet!" hissed the old man. "Is that you, Devil-Child? Is he here?" he whimpered, frantically clutching at the housekeeper's skirts. An animal growled menacingly and Simon gasped and ducked as something screamed shrilly and fluttered by, brushing his head before flying wildly around the chamber. Pendarves chortled delightedly. "Come to your grandsire, Devil-Child," he wheedled. "Come to your grandsire, child of shame."

"Grandsire?" exclaimed Simon, gaping in stupefaction at the enormous shadow of a bat that was silhouetted and distorted by the dancing candle flames.

"The whore Catherine's child didn't die!" rejoiced the excited old man. "It didn't die! Just ripped her whore's body in two."

"But I was here! I saw!" protested Simon. The man was obviously senile, demented, believing a bat to be his daughter's offspring. He frowned, trying to recall the tragic night more than fourteen years before. He had stood at the foot of a similar black-shrouded bed in a frigid sepulchral chamber, staring helplessly at the advent of death.

"You saw what I wanted you to see! You saw the whore die!" snarled the vicious old man, and Simon nodded sorrowfully.

"It seems her cries still hang in the air," he whispered, acutely remembering the horror and impotence he had felt. Catherine's fingernails had been ripped and bleeding from where she had clawed at the carved bedposts, trying to loosen the black silk cords that had bound her slender wrists.

"How very . . . very poetic, Dr. Carmichael," mocked Pendarves. "Had the filthy whore seduced you, too?"

"You are despicable!"

"Silence!" shrieked the old man as once again an animal growled deep in its throat. "Show yourself to me, Devil-Child!" he ordered, his jaundiced eyes flickering wildly from side to side as he tugged frantically at the housekeeper's skirts, unable to lift his head from the pillow. "Is the Devil-Child here?" he whimpered, and the woman silently nodded. Simon turned, following her intense gaze, and caught his breath at the sight. A slight graceful figure stood with one small hand on the massive head of a huge wolflike creature. A profoundly mystical feeling seemed to emanate from the child, causing inexplicable emotions to surge through the pragmatic doctor. "Come to your grandsire, Devil Tremayne, child of shame," rasped the dying man.

"That cannot be Catherine's child!" uttered Simon. "You said the babe was dead! I took you, a magistrate and Christian, at your word! What was the point in such a wicked lie?" he demanded, watching the elfin figure who valiantly approached the bed. The child kept hold of the enormous animal, who bristled and bared menacing teeth, warning all to keep a respectful distance.

"Revenge, sweet, sweet revenge!" snarled Godolphus Pendarves. "Benedict Tremayne of Taran killed my daughter with his unnatural spawn! Made her his whore and then flung her out, so she came crawling on her bloated, shameful belly back to me!" Blood bubbled up with the ferocity of his fury, choking his frenzied words. For several moments his gnarled hands flailed the air as if to ward off death. Then there was an awful rattling in the knotted throat, a long diminishing hiss, and the old man froze in a grotesquely twisted position.

"Grandfather is dead!" remarked the Devil-Child flatly.

"And none too soon," added the housekeeper irreverently. The hound bayed eerily. As though it were a signal, the rustling and whispering in the corridor grew in intensity and a procession of black-garbed people shuffled in. Simon recollected himself and quickly moved to shut the staring eyes and cover the hideous features that grimaced so derisively in death. The housekeeper stayed his hand, and he was amazed at her strength. "No! Let the poor unfortunates see that he has finally left this earth! He made our lives a living hell! Let them see that we're finally free!" she declared, her face gleaming with a frightening fervor.

Simon numbly stepped back and watched as one by one each person silently and thoroughly scrutinized the motionless Lord Pendarves before filing from the room. He frowned, noting the emaciation and suffering that marked each ancient servant. There had to be twenty or more, all dressed identically in shapeless black clothes like some harsh religious order, he mused. He looked thoughtfully at the back of the glossy ebony head of the Devil-Child, wishing he could see the face, wondering if the exquisite features of Catherine had been inherited.

Catherine Pendarves had stolen a small corner of his heart, he admitted, remembering her as an enchanting maiden of sixteen with her glorious mane of fiery hair rioting in the sea-wind as she raced her fleet mare across the rolling moor. He had reined his horse and watched, enjoying the fluid sensuousness of her lithe, budding body. In those moments he had forgotten he was a staid, respectable doctor, comfortably married to a loving generous woman. He had forgotten that he was over forty years old and more than slightly overweight. In those precious heady moments he had been young, handsome, and supremely athletic as he answered her taunting challenge. He had kicked his docile gelding into a wild abandoned canter in pursuit of the entrancing woman-child. Of course she had left him far behind, panting for breath and feeling more than a little silly. He could still hear her mischievous giggle wafting on the sea-breeze.

"There is nothing more to keep you here, Dr. Carmichael," clipped the housekeeper, again bringing him sharply back to the reality of the deathbed room. "Yeoman, show the doctor to his horse," she added, and one of the black-garbed servants silently held the door open, signalling his dismissal. Simon kept his eyes pinned to the slight figure, who stood staring at the dead man, one small hand still clutching the shaggy mane of the large hound.

"Devil Tremayne, child of shame," he repeated pensively. The youngster spun about and Simon stared into one of the most arresting faces he had ever seen. A pair of enormous dark eyes looked into his, and he gasped audibly at the depths of suffering he saw mirrored there. Compassion surged through him, and he instinctively reached out in comfort. But the animal snarled threateningly, and with a low sob the youth eluded him and fled from the room, followed by the formidable pet. The bat swooped down with a piercing scream and the rotund doctor ducked, covering his head.

"I am sure there are sick people in need of your attention," reproved the housekeeper, as though corpses, bats, and enormous dogs were part and parcel of her mundane duties. Simon stared at her numbly as though waking from a dream.

"Devil Tremayne, child of shame?" he questioned dazedly.

"Devlyn Pendarves, heir to the Pendarves quarries and mines," corrected the woman.

"The quarries and mines have been shut down for years," stated Simon harshly. "Another of that bitter man's crimes," he added, thinking of the many families that had relied on the steady employment who now lived in utter poverty gleaning what little they could from the rocky beaches and barren moors.

"Lord Godolphus was a very pious man. He didn't want to lay up for hisself treasures upon this earth, where moth and rust doth corrupt," sneered the gaunt woman bitterly before spitting into the leering face of the corpse. Simon opened his mouth to protest, but the housekeeper turned and glared at him, daring him to remark on her crude action. "This way, Dr. Carmichael," she directed cordially.

"What is your name?" he demanded, but the woman swept past without a word. Simon shrugged and followed the rustling starched skirts and jangling keys back through the grim corridors. In each arched doorway huddled two or three black-garbed servants. Like watchful crows, he thought wryly. "What of the child?" he asked as they descended the wide stone staircase to the central hall.

"None of your affair!" was the unsatisfactory reply.

"The next of kin must be informed. It will be awhile before he reaches his majority." Simon frowned, thinking the youth's stature was small and frail for a nearly fifteen-year-old.

"There are no next of kin," snapped the housekeeper. Simon noted the spasm of unease that flickered across the inscrutable features.

"I beg to differ," he contradicted mildly, idly watching the bony fingers nervously fidget with the long silk cord that held her ring of keys. A cord that painfully reminded him of the bonds that had cut so cruelly into Catherine's tender wrists.

"What do you mean?" she hissed.

"That there are certain relatives, namely Sir Torrance Pendarves of High Tor."

"A grandchild inherits before a cousin several times removed."

"Inherits?" queried Simon, not comprehending the housekeeper's seeming change of subject.

"You were summoned here to witness Lord Pendarves's solemn deathbed acknowledgment of his heir," she insisted urgently.

"I was?"

"You cannot deny that you heard Lord Pendarves claim his grandson and admit he lied about Catherine's baby!" cried the woman vehemently.

"What is your name?" snapped Simon, feeling for the first time that he held the upper hand in light of the housekeeper's obvious agitation.

"Peller. Rebecca Peller," the woman answered reluctantly.

"Well, Miss Peller, I was more concerned with the boy's immediate welfare, but if it is solely a question of inheritance that you are disturbed about, I suggest Lord Pendarves's solicitors in Falmouth are better qualified than I. I wonder if Biddles, Biddles, and Penrose'll be as surprised as the rest of the area to learn that Catherine's child lives?" he added dryly, keeping his seemingly unconcerned eyes pinned to the woman's drawn face.

"I have not the faintest notion of the correspondence between Lord Pendarves and his solicitors," protested Miss Peller defensively.

"And yet you appear to . . . run this establishment?" remarked Simon, indicating the vast, bleak interior of the castle with a sweep of his hand. "And from the condition of Lord Pendarves it would appear that he has been incapacitated for a very long time? May I venture to hazard at least a year if not more?" The woman refused to answer, her mouth firmly closed in a thin hard line. "Why did he lie about the existence of his grandchild?" probed Simon after a long tense moment where they locked eyes in a battle of wills.

"His lordship informed you!"

"Ah, yes, revenge . . . sweet, sweet revenge," acknowledged the doctor. "Which brings up another next of kin."

"Who?"

"Sir Benedict Tremayne of Taran. Devil Tremayne, child of shame?" he reminded her sarcastically. "I am certain that Lord Taran will be most interested to learn he has a son."

"The Devil-Child is not Taran's son!" crowed the woman emphatically, and to the plump doctor's amazement the gaunt lines of the dour female's face softened and she gurgled with amusement. "I swear to you on my mother's grave that the Devil-Child is definitely not Tremayne's son," she sputtered before throwing her head back and roaring with mirth. Simon spun about as her insane laughter was joined by a chorus of hoarse voices and echoed hollowly through the grey fortress. "Devlyn Pendarves is not Tremayne of Taran's son!" she repeated before slamming the heavy studded door, leaving him blinking dazedly in the blinding sunlight.

Simon stared thoughtfully up the sheer impenetrable walls to the forbidding black ravens that roosted in the narrow slit windows. He shuddered as a mournful baying moaned with the sea-wind that whined in the turrets.

"Not a very cosy home for a young orphan," he remarked aloud as he gazed over the edge of the sheer cliff to the expanse of rough sea that rhythmically surged against the jagged rocks far below. Conscious of being scrutinized, he turned and surveyed the wild, rolling moor that stretched inland as far as the eye could see. He walked awkwardly to his carriage, eager to be away from the brooding desolation of Pendarves Castle.

Simon reined his horse after a mad canter of about half a mile and stared back at the stark fortress on the bleak promontory above the grey sea. His mind swirled with the bittersweet golden memories of Catherine; the enormous dark eyes of her child tortured him. As a doctor he had seen suffering, but he had never before seen it so silently and eloquently mirrored. Bloodless wounds of abject misery, he fretted, not knowing whether he should return and insist that the youth accompany him home. If only Angelica weren't in London. With her no-nonsense practicality, she would know what to do. How he missed his daughter, he sighed, knowing his wife, Emily, would just absently pat his hand and chatter about herbacious borders, not listening to a word of an unpleasantness.

"That dark boy is none of your business, Simon Carmichael," he admonished himself, resolutely slapping the reins and continuing on his way. "Seventeen years ago you were foolishly infatuated with a female young enough to be your daughter. That poor unfortunate girl has been dead for nearly fifteen years, so there is no sane reason for you to get embroiled in what does not concern you," he ranted. Then he sighed deeply as he frankly admitted to himself that in all the intervening years, just the thought of Catherine caused his sluggish blood to pulse and his plodding step to lighten. She had been his only excitement, his only madness, his only magic in what was otherwise a routine, exemplary life. Oh, he could not complain. He had the proper conventional love of a loyal woman and three obedient, unremarkable children, but Catherine had been a beam of golden enchantment that illuminated his dull unimaginative days. He sensed that same intangible energy sparking from the Devil-Child. How could a delightful, joyous sprite like Catherine have arisen from that ugly pile of rocks? he pondered for the umpteenth time as he gazed sorrowfully back over the barren moor. How could such a humourless, cruel monster like Godolphus Pendarves have sired such a precious vital being? Hot angry tears poured down his face and he felt the pain of his loss as though it were very recent.

"Am I crying for Catherine or for the youth I could have enjoyed if I had been as brave as she?" he questioned aloud. The summer heat shimmered the inland false horizon, yet he felt an uneasy chill and the memory of the dark child's haunted eyes dug into his bones. He urged his horse to a faster pace, eager to be ensconced in the unremarkable cosiness of his modest home, watching his wife putter about her garden.

Messrs. Biddles, Biddles, and Penrose, wearing outdated long frockcoats stiffened with buckram and identical high beaver hats perched on their thickly powdered periwigs, leaned on their silver-knobbed malacca canes, gaping incredulously at the small caped figure silhouetted against the blood-red sky. An enormous wolflike creature paced back and forth, occasionally throwing back its massive head to bay mournfully as an accompaniment to the child's carefully intoned Latin prayer. Several smaller creatures suspiciously resembling bats flittered about on jerky wings emitting shrill shrieks. The oldest Mr. Biddles was convinced he was dreaming. He was apt to doze off in the most inappropriate of places, but never in his nearly eighty-nine years had he observed such an unearthly scene. The younger Mr. Biddles kept his eyes pinned firmly on the more comforting sight of the grave where Sir Godolphus Pendarves resided in his coffin. He refused to surrender to the terror that thumped through his body as eerie bent shapes detached themselves from the shadows of the surrounding tombstones to spit curses along with the handfuls of dirt they threw at their recently departed master. Mr. Penrose was paralyzed with fear. He stood in his accustomed dignified pose, but his knees trembled and his black gloved hand clutched his walking cane instead of resting on it elegantly.

Devil shivered at the frightening sight of the three fearsome strangers whose coat-skirts stuck out starkly against the striated sky. Three faceless, black-clad bodies in descending order, from very tall to tiny and shrivelled, each with an intimidating high hat and cane. They were faceless, yet their hidden eyes burned with judgment; censure crackled through the dusk so the Latin words were nervously jumbled and mispronounced, convincing Mr. Penrose that he was in fact attending a Black Mass and a small demon was reciting the Lord's prayer backwards.

Finally the interminable service ended and the last of the long line of black-garbed servants had shuffled past the open grave, and the last rattlings of dry earth and pebbles had rained against the coffin, leaving a pause filled by the usual continuous noise of crickets, surf, and marauding owls. Devil put one foot in front of the other, not looking to either side, eager to be free from the company of strangers. The rhythmic ring of a spade cutting into the arid soil kept pace with each measured step.

"What is the name of your . . . um . . . er . . . pet, young man?" joked the exceedingly terrified Mr. Penrose, furtively fingering his rosary beads and warily eyeing the enormous black animal as the funeral procession returned to the castle from the graveyard on the barren moor.

"Bucca-Dhu," replied Devil without looking up at the tall thin man.

"Bucca-Dhu!" gasped Penrose, recoiling and lifting his cane to indicate the huge hound. "The black demon from the sea?" The large animal growled a deep warning and caught the brandished cane in teeth that glistened macabrely in the moonlight. Mr. Penrose yelped and gawked helplessly as his malacca cane, passed carefully down through four generations of legal Penroses, was snapped and cast aside. Devil glanced up miserably at Miss Peller, expecting to see disapproval, and was shocked by her malicious glee.

"Did the young man say that his puppy dog was called Bucca-Dhu?" queried the very ancient Mr. Biddles.

"Yes, father," answered the younger Mr. Biddles, who was at least seventy years old. "Now, young sir, why would you use such a blasphemous name?" he demanded pompously. Devil didn't acknowledge him but kept walking toward the castle that loomed ahead. "I am addressing you, young man!" postulated the solicitor, reaching out to detain the disrespectful youth. Miss Peller hastily interceded as the massive animal snarled and tensed to spring.

"Begging your pardon, sir, but I wouldn't be touching Sir Devlyn Pendarves if you value your health," she warned as the child soothed the giant hound and several bats flickered about, mirroring the youngster's agitation.

"For God's sake, get away!" screamed Mr. Penrose, losing his tall beaver hat and his elegant demeanor as he flailed about, trying to scatter the twittering animals. They fluttered about his white powdered wig like moths around a candle.

Devil whistled and to the solicitor's consternation the small rodents flew to the child's beckoning arms and disappeared under the folds of dark cloak.

"Filthy, unnatural creatures that carry disease and can turn a sane man into a crazed beast who foams from the mouth," chattered the younger Mr. Biddles.

"There are over eight hundred species of bats ranging in size from a mere inch with a five-inch wing span to more than a foot with a six-foot wing span," informed the oldest Mr. Biddles conversationally, still convinced he was in the midst of a most remarkable dream.

"You will entertain your grandfather's solicitors," hissed Miss Peller, sensing the youth was about to escape to the sanctuary of the north tower. "And if you value our lives you will have a care as to what you say," she added. "if you gentlemen will follow Yeoman, he'll lead you to the small dining room, where you may partake of refreshments," she stated loudly, keeping her sharp eyes pinned to the upturned face in order that her threats could be well felt. The child's delicate nostrils flared with trepidation and the Bucca-Dhu growled his evident dislike of the harsh woman.

"Where are those rodents?" ventured Mr. Penrose, sidling past the youth and into the draughty central hall that at that moment appeared more welcoming than the eerie moonlit causeway. Devil stared mutely, not knowing what to do or say as somehow the least thing caused shock and disapproval. Strangers were infinitely difficult to be around.

"Come along, young man," wheezed the very ancient Mr. Biddles, leaning heavily on the youngster's shoulder. Again the huge dog growled menacingly and the younger Mr. Biddles hastily removed his father's hand, nearly toppling him in the process.

The "small dining room" seemed misnamed as a vast hall yawned, the very end disappearing into deep shadows. Despite the summer month, a fire had been lit. It didn't do much to warm the cold grey stones, only adding an acrid smoke. Several large thronelike chairs had been set in front of the hearth, and Devil waited hesitantly for the solicitors to seat themselves before sitting.

"Who taught you Latin?" barked Mr. Penrose, relieved that the uncanny child was seated farthest from him.

"My grandsire," answered Devil after a long pause, hoping it wasn't a secret. Listening intently and not detecting any sharp intake of Miss Peller's breath, the child relaxed slightly.

"Your grandsire?" repeated the younger Mr. Biddles, and Devil nodded, wishing that Yeoman would hasten the pouring of the brandy as the three strangers silently scrutinized, disapproval oozing from every pore.

"My grandsire," concurred Devil as Yeoman slowly tottered across the uneven flagstones balancing a salver where the goblets teetered precariously. Once again there was a pregnant silence while brandy was swirled thoughtfully and sniffed appreciatively.

"By Jove, remarkably fine," rejoiced the oldest Mr. Biddles after a very noisy slurp.

"Yes, indeed," agreed his son, raising his eyebrows conspiratorially at Mr. Penrose, who in his nervousness had foolishly drained his cup and was trying to smother his paroxysm of coughing. "From your grandfather's cellar?"

Devil stared hollow-eyed.

"Tastes like excellent French stock," chuckled the ancient Mr. Biddles. Devil hoped that Yeoman, who had nearly reached his dotage, hadn't opened the wrong cask. "Are you into smuggling, young man?"

"My grandsire taught me Latin," offered the youth, hoping to divert the conversation. The only answer was a resounding snore as the ancient Mr. Biddles's wigged head slowly sank between his high starched collar points.

"Do you go to school?" whispered the younger Biddles, putting a long pale finger to his bloodless lips and fondly indicating his slumbering parent. Devil shook a dark head. "Do you have a tutor?" Again Devil shook a dark head and then, at a frantic movement and sharp intake of breath, nodded affirmatively as Miss Peller advanced, followed by black-shrouded figures bearing trays of food. "You do have a tutor or you don't have a tutor?"

"I have a tutor!"

"What is amiss?" loudly demanded Miss Peller, and the ancient man popped out of the starched wings of his collar with his periwig at a rakish angle.

"Where was I?" asked the oldest Mr. Biddles.

"My father was attempting to ascertain whether the young lord was being properly educated and what provisions his grandfather has made as to guardianship," pompously stated the younger Biddles, straightening his father's attire and getting his hand smacked for his efforts.

"Young master Devlyn is too delicate to be sent off to school," informed Miss Peller. "You'd never believe he is in his fifteenth year, would you? Looks more like a child of nine or ten if that, wouldn't you say? Curate Pomfrey tutors him," she added, and Devil smothered a grin as a picture of the senile old curate prancing on the moors flashed into mind. "But why are you worrying the poor bereaved child's head with such things? He is puny and delicate and his only relative has just been buried . . . He is but a sickly young orphan. Surely you have all the legal papers and such in your offices in Falmouth?" she ranted self-righteously.

"Well, actually, we have nothing at all save some land leases, and those are long since void," replied Penrose, offering his goblet to Yeoman for a refill. Devil caught the fleeting flash of satisfaction cross the housekeeper's stony face.

"Nothing about the young lord, his grandson?" she enquired innocently. "No last will and testimony or the like?"

"Nothing," answered Penrose, insensitive to the younger Biddles's frowns, squints, and gyrations as he tried to warn the rash sixty-year-old junior partner to button his loose lips.

"But I was witness to such a document," stated Miss Peller. "Jonty Pengelly, too."

"Pengelly of High Tor?"

"No, his brother. Jonty Pengelly, Lord Pendarves's valet for nigh on thirty years."

"When did you witness such a document?" demanded Mr. Penrose, forgetting his previous terror and posing affectedly by the hearth with one buckled shoe on the copper fender. The Bucca-Dhu growled ferociously from the deep shadows, and the solicitor hastily resumed his seat, accepting yet another refill of brandy.

"More than two years ago," recalled the housekeeper. "Everything he owned on this earth was for his grandchild, Devil."

"Devil?!" the name chorused from hoarse throats.

"The master's little joke, I think. But Lord Godolphus was by no means a frivolous man, so maybe he knew something," explained Miss Peller enigmatically.

"Devil?" the name caught painfully between Penrose's dry lips, and he stared at the slight dark youth with awe.

"Sir Godolphus had me fetch Simon Carmichael," the gaunt woman continued brokenly, weeping and wringing her hands in a most convincing fashion. "That poor sainted man on his deathbed," she sobbed, and Devil was mesmerized by the housekeeper's uncharacteristic manner. "His dying words were to Dr. Carmichael, claiming his daughter, Catherine's child as his heir. He was too good for this wicked world!" she ended with a very dramatic wail and then blew her nose loudly.

"This is a very sorry state of affairs. I wonder where the document is?" pondered the younger Biddles after a respectable pause to allow the loyal servant time to compose herself.

"And the next of kin?" chimed Penrose.

"Sir Torrance Pendarves of High Tor has made his home in London these past years since the demise of his wife. He has three young sons, I do believe. One of an age of this lad," mused young Biddles.

"The oldest son ran off to fight the French. Word is that he's missing and presumed dead," chattered Penrose, avoiding sight of the demon child and solicitously straightening his sagging hose so the stripes followed the pronounced curve of his thin bandy legs. "I know of no other next of kin."

"What of the boy's father?"

"I am sure that you, just like the rest of Cornwall, not to mention the whole of the West Country, are aware of Miss Catherine's reputation?" Miss Peller hissed acidly. The three lawyers awkwardly cleared their throats and stared pointedly into their goblets.

"Quite so, quite so," muttered the oldest Mr. Biddles. A lecherous smirk stole over his wrinkled face and he closed his eyes to dream lasciviously of the vibrant beauty.

"Simon Carmichael did mention Tremayne of Taran as being the possible sire," murmured Penrose.

"And there was a rumour of a marriage between the two," whispered the younger Biddles as his father once more snored peacefully.

"Rumour, rumour, rumour," spat Miss Peller waspishly. "Food for idle tongues. There was no marriage! The Devil is definitely not Tremayne's son! Heaven knows who fathered the unfortunate . . . unnatural! Has terrible fits, he does . . .

like one possessed! As for Torrance Pendarves, I seem to recollect something in the will about that man never setting one foot across this threshold.''

"Fits? Possessed?'' squealed Penrose.

"Madame, that is all academic!'' postulated the younger Biddles.

For a moment Miss Peller seemed at a loss.

"With no will in our possession everything you say is academic,'' he enlightened.

"But there's a copy up in Sir Godolphus's bedchamber. I'll send for it. Yeoman?'' she called imperiously, and the old man shuffled up with the brandy decanter. "He is mute but he can hear. His tongue was cut out for speaking untruths,'' she chattered. "Yeoman, go up to his lordship's bedchamber and bring down the mahogany chest that he kept beside his bed. The one with his Holy Bible on top,'' she directed, but the black-clad man just stood dejectedly, holding the brandy decanter and shifting his weight from one leg to the other. "Fetch the master's strongbox, Yeoman!'' she shouted harshly.

"I'll fetch it,'' offered Devil eagerly, seeing the heavy tears slide down Yeoman's face and splash on the dusty stone floor. Devil also needed to be free from the frightening strangers. Miss Peller nodded assent and then smiled with satisfaction as the small lithe figure whirled away amid a cloud of twittering bats who complained shrilly at the disturbance of their refuge. With an answering bark the huge hound bounded from the shadows to follow.

"Fits? Possessed?'' gasped the younger Biddles, and Mr. Penrose mouthed a prayer as he frantically fingered his beads.

"More brandy, gentlemen?'' asked Miss Peller.

"What a very strange young man,'' muttered the oldest Biddles, sinking deeper between the protective points of his starched collar.

"Paternoster cui rescat in cielum,'' fervently prayed Mr. Penrose.

CHAPTER 1

ANGELICA CARMICHAEL was squashed between two very fat, unwashed women, feeling extremely nauseated. This was one morning that eating a substantial breakfast had been a decidedly bad idea, she thought miserably, wishing she could crane her neck out of the carriage window and gulp some fresh air.

"Luverly bitta clorf yer wearin', luvey," rasped one of the women, greedily stroking Angelica's velvet riding habit with plump, greasy fingers. "'Ere Flo, 'ave a feel o' this," she ordered, her stale breath puffing hotly into the girl's face. "Wotcha 'ave ter do to get it?"

Angelica tried to ignore the offensive odors and derisive insinuations of the two women. Think of something else, she pleaded with herself as the coach swayed sickeningly from side to side. There wasn't much of a happy nature to think about, she acknowledged wryly. She was leaving London before the season started. She was fleeing from her maternal grandmother's house unchaperoned, without baggage and virtually penniless. She clutched her reticule, which contained the three gold sovereigns her father had given her for unforeseen emergencies more than a year before, when she had left the peaceful Cornish countryside to embark on the most exciting adventure of her life. It had turned into a most degrading nightmare, but she had dutifully written merry letters home, not wishing to worry her parents or younger brothers. They would be surprised to have her appear on their doorstep without warning, but she had no other recourse. She had been determined to take nothing of her grandmother's

21

grudging largesse, but unless she had wished to return home naked or in her night attire, she had been forced to wear the riding habit. It had been the least conspicuous of her inappropriate and unflattering new wardrobe. What had her grandmother done with her sensible Cornish clothes, seethed Angelica, desperately trying to block out the sweating women on either side of her. Don't think of London or pink dresses, or Grandmaman, or the lecherous Lord Carringdon. Think of Cornwall. Think of the high rugged cliffs and the invigorating salt spray as the waves dash against the granite rocks. Think of rolling stone-girt fields and lush hedgerows. Think of childhood friends and picnics on the moor and beach. A bleak shadow doused the golden memory. She would never see young Torr Pendarves again. He lay dead, cold, and so alone beneath foreign soil. High Tor would never be reopened; the graceful rooms and halls would never ring with music and happiness as they had done when Lady Felicity had been alive. Don't think of childhood, it can never be recaptured. Don't think of being a plain old maid, think of father, who'll be so pleased to see you that his chubby tummy will jiggle with delight. Think of mother, who'll not want to hear anything of an unhappy nature. She'll be so distressed that she'll bury herself in her herbacious border for a week or busy herself in the kitchen baking mounds of cakes so that father will get even fatter. At the thought of the buttery, sugary food, Angelica broke out in a cold sweat.

"Goin' far, little lady?" enquired an oily voice from an unsavoury character sitting opposite with his legs spread wide. Angelica was too immersed in her own misery to realize she was being addressed until a scuffed boot sharply kicked her ankle. She looked into the unappetizing face of a middle-aged man who diligently picked his broken teeth, smacking his loose lips with relish at each morsel he dislodged. Angelica shook her head helplessly and covered the mouth with both hands as waves of clammy faintness swirled her.

"Hey, hey, hey! Pull up, coachie! Pull up, I say!" bellowed the seedy man, thumping urgently on the ceiling of the carriage with his cane at recognizing Angelica's wan countenance as belonging to a person about to be violently ill.

"Pull up 'fore we 'ave a stinkin' mess in 'ere!'' screeched the fat women, drumming their heels on the floor.

Angelica used every scrap of her strength to suppress the spasms that heaved her body as hands clutched and pushed, pinching and pulling her to the door, finally shoving her so roughly that she fell several feet to the ground. She felt so very wretched that she was unaware of the sharp knife that expertly cut through her purse strings leaving loose empty cords to dangle from her wrists. She felt so very sick, she was unaware of the sharp rocks that cut her forehead and cheekbones as she was pitched out face down onto the dusty thoroughfare. She felt so very ill that she wasn't the least mortified to find herself in the undignified position of being on her hands and knees in the dirt. She didn't hear the roars of derision and impatience from the coach and its passengers, or the arrival of a very elegant curricle pulled by perfectly matched greys and housing a very tall, dark saturnine man dressed in an expensive careless style. All Angelica felt was the exquisite relief of finally ridding herself of the coaching station's special bargain breakfast.

Angelica almost cried with the wonderful feeling of deliverance and she rocked back, breathing deeply of the fresh, albeit dusty, air. Her head pounded painfully, so she kept her eyes firmly closed and massaged her temples. It was several long moments before the excruciating thunder had mercifully receded to a distant rumble, and she opened her eyes to the awful realization of her abandonment. The fearsome throbbing had been due in part to the coach wheels that were now continuing to Cornwall without her. She opened her mouth to protest but, aware of the futility, just gave a plaintive wail and collapsed face down in the gravel.

"I would be extremely obliged if you would continue your vapours in the hedgerow as you are quite blocking the thoroughfare," pronounced a deep, almost bored voice. Angelica heard but felt too fatigued and wretched to respond. She lay in the gritty dust, waiting for whoever it was to ride roughshod over her. Anything was preferable to the situation she was in. Maybe a quick death was the solution, she mused as she drifted off to sleep, the rough grimy road feeling like a welcome pillow to her aching head.

Benedict Tremayne stared down at the limp figure with extreme impatience. He had had the dickens of a weekend with his current mistress and was in no mood to be thwarted by a chit who had thrown herself dramatically from a common posting coach a scarce two feet from his horse's pawing hooves. He was in such a foul humour he actually seriously deliberated galloping over the stupid female. He justified the base thought by maintaining that all of her gender were a curse to men. He was about to exercise some restraint by guiding his horses around her so she could continue sleeping peacefully in the dust when a coach and six came barrelling down the turnpike. Without thought he whipped his pair so they successfully moved forward to protect the prone figure.

Benedict snorted with impatience as he reluctantly dismounted. He noted the expensive cut and material of her habit. He frowned at the leather thongs that splayed from one limp wrist. Had the girl been attacked and robbed before being thrust from the coach? he wondered as he expertly turned her over and felt for broken limbs.

Angelica smiled dreamily as she felt pleasant sensations caress her body. She didn't open her eyes or expend energy to question the situation. She was too tired; too drained emotionally and physically. She was home, she decided. She was a little child again and her father was holding her tight, making her feel safe and secure beneath his large strong hands. She grunted appreciatively as she felt herself swung up and cradled in male arms. She nestled against the broad expanse of chest, delighting in the firm muscles and steady heartbeat beneath her ear. How many times had she stayed up waiting for her father to come home from tending his patients? She sighed happily, recalling the strong hands that would pluck her gently from the nest of couch cushions to carry her upstairs to bed. Now she rejoiced as the comforting jolts lulled her, and she reached out a hand to stroke the warm fragrance of her father's coat before letting go of all her worries and drifting into a deeper sleep. She knew she was safe and being carried in strong arms.

Benedict Tremayne scowled down at the battered, bleeding face that grinned contentedly and at the grubby but well-shaped hand that clutched his coat. Whoever she was, in her expensive habit and boots she was no ravishing beauty, but her bones were good, he grudgingly admitted. Her hair was a glorious shade of chestnut, thick and well-groomed, he noted as he evaluated her much as he would any pedigreed live-stock. She was tall for a female, probably five seven or eight with long limbs rather like an ungainly colt, he assessed, his six feet three inches of well-honed masculinity easily lifting her into the high curricle. He propped her none-too-gently on the seat and uncorked a flask of strong spirits with the hopes of reviving her.

Angelica protested sleepily at the uncomfortable position and tried to snuggle back against the fragrant strong chest, but soon she was choking, as burning liquid was forced between her lips to dribble down and sting her chin and neck. The fumes caused her to gasp for breath as tears flooded her eyes.

"Open your mouth, you stupid female," ordered a deep voice, and she stared blearily into quite the darkest eyes she had ever seen.

Benedict was not prepared for the extraordinary colour of Angelica's eyes. He had never seen such a tone before except mirrored on the ocean in that dangerous calm before a storm where yellow, grey, and green mingled and hung suspended.

"Please, I do not . . . I cannot . . . I am most sorry," she lamented brokenly, shaking her head and pushing the flask away as vestiges of the bargain-breakfast once more churned her stomach. "So sorry," she wailed before quickly thrusting her head over the side of the curricle with such haste that Benedict instinctively grabbed her to stop another crashing descent to the ground.

"What in heaven's name am I doing being nursemaid to a leggy chit on the London Road?" he muttered, keeping one hand firmly on her neck and the other arm curled intimately about her belly.

"So sorry," gasped Angelica for perhaps the seventh time as he hauled her back unceremoniously and handed her a large handkerchief.

"Are you sure a good swig of this wouldn't settle you?" he offered.

"I think I am dying," moaned the girl, pushing the flask away.

"Who are you?" he asked roughly as her eyes closed and he feared she would pass out again.

"Angel . . ." she murmured.

"Angel?"

Angelica smiled serenely. "Angel," she whispered. That was the pet name her father used. "Angel," she repeated and drifted back into unconsciousness. Benedict frowned, noting the dark circles beneath the closed eyes and the beads of perspiration amid the cuts and bruises on the wan face. He felt her forehead and groaned at the heat. Determined to catch up with the public stagecoach and transfer the responsibility, he wrapped her in a horse blanket and laid her on the floor. He braced her with his feet as he whipped his horses into a spanking pace and set off in pursuit.

It was midafternoon when Benedict drove into the yard of the Blue Feathers Inn, where the London coach had stopped to change horses. Angelica moaned as the cobblestones reverberated through her despite the superior springs of the curricle.

"Coachman, I believe I have one of your passengers," hailed Benedict, casually blocking the exit. "You mislaid her about twenty miles back."

"I am full. No more room!" shouted the driver. "Now move yourself. I have to get to Portsmouth by nightfall."

Angelica raised her aching head and stared blearily out from between a pair of gleaming jockey boots. She shuddered and groaned as she saw the leering faces of her former traveling companions.

"Where is her baggage?"

"She 'ad none," answered the coachman.

"That's right. Come as she was, she did. With her fancy clothes. Got on at Wimbledon Common, she did," informed one of the large unwashed women as she stared lasciviously up and down the young man's virile body from his broad shoulders to his well-formed legs in their tight riding britches. "No baggage. No chaperon, and 'er clothes cost a pretty penny, I can tell yer," she embellished.

"Some fancy buck threw 'er out when 'e found out she 'ad the pox, I wager," suggested Flo. "So wotchit, me 'andsome young cock," she teased, eyeing his groin suggestively.

"Could be she 'as the plague.'' The seedy man offered his opinion as he continued picking his teeth.

Angelica shook her aching head with disbelief. It was a horrible nightmare brought on by sickness, she decided before collapsing back limply on the curricle floor.

"Get outa the way!'' roared the coachman, and Benedict resignedly guided his team into the yard and the Cornish stage barrelled past at a clipping pace.

"What in hell's name am I going to do with you?'' hissed Benedict Tremayne, ten minutes later after the proprietor of the Blue Feathers Inn had catagorically refused to allow Angelica on his premises. He had plaintively begged the young peer to understand that he ran a clean, decent, highly virtuous establishment; and although he had the utmost respect for Lord Taran and his wealth, he would not and could not in all conscience allow a diseased female of questionable character to enter his hostelry, unless of course there was to be considerable remuneration. Benedict had listened, his thin sculpted lips sneering in a most quelling manner, before curtly whipping up his team and quitting the Blue Feathers without a backward glance.

"I am so sorry,'' repeated Angelica inadequately. "So sorry. Oh, why do you bother with me?'' she muttered before drifting back to oblivion.

"I haven't the slightest notion why I bother with you,'' wondered Benedict, determined to rid himself of the bothersome female at the first opportunity. "Where are you from?'' he demanded loudly. She didn't answer but just murmured fitfully and wound a lissome arm about his left boot.

"Blackfield, one mile,'' he read aloud from a passing sign as they trotted through Hampshire. He had been on his way to a friend's hunting lodge in the New Forest for several days of much yearned-for solitude away from all people, most notably women, with the possible exception of an unobtrusive servant or two to see to his comforts. This proposed sabbatical had been the bone of contention between him and his current mistress, Lady Isabella Bonny, who clung to him so possessively that even her perfume was in danger of suffocating him, he seethed, recalling the unnecessary scene the previous evening that had robbed him of a night's sleep. "Women!" he snarled aloud, savagely tearing Angelica's arm from his leg. "Women," he repeated in a gentler tone as he felt the heat of her high temperature through the soft velvet sleeve. He released the limb so it immediately recurled about his calf as the girl writhed and chattered deliriously. He urged his tired team faster as he silently prayed that his highly polished boots would not be splattered.

"Where on earth is the moon?" he hissed irrationally, and to his relief the full moon sailed impishly out from behind a cloud, illuminating the narrow path that snaked across the treacherous marshlands. He reined his horses and gazed across the wild flatness that stretched to either side, dissected by shimmering gullies between hillocks of spiky grasses. He breathed deeply, enjoying the aroma of the salty mud. His eyes embraced the still tranquility as he listened to the nocturnal sounds of the marsh inhabitants.

"I'm home!" squeaked an excited voice. "I smell the sea. It's the sea, not disgusting perfume covering dirty bodies," she gabbled, flailing her arms as she tried to get up. There was a sharp crack as she bashed her head against the heel of his right boot and collapsed in a limp heap at his feet.

"Ouch," sympathised Benedict, reaching down and feeling through her thick hair to ascertain how badly she might have injured herself. His hand came up sticky with blood and he wondered what other catastrophe could possibly happen before he could palm off his unwanted passenger on the servants of the hunting lodge.

"Hallooo," he hailed as he pulled up in the courtyard of Stephen Bellinger's modest retreat. A tiny wizened figure scurried down the front steps chattering like an indignant squirrel.

"Willie? Willie? Where are you, Willie?" he screeched.

"Good evening," greeted Benedict. "I am Lord Taran."

"Yes, sir. I know, sir. We've met before, sir. I am Alsop, sir," informed the frazzled manservant. "But I am afraid that Willie is off again, sir. The moon is full, as you can see, sir. And when the moon is full, Willie takes off, sir. It gets in his blood, sir."

"Quiet!" roared Benedict, sorely out of patience. "Send out some other servants. I have a sick woman here."

"But I'm all there is, sir," replied the little man unhappily. "You see it's the full moon, so I shall have to see to your horses while you see to your baggage. Or I shall see to your baggage and you'll see to your horses . . ." he trailed off, staring with fascination as the angry young lord leaped down from the high curricle with a limp female in his arms. "I shall see to your horses, sir."

"And I shall see to this baggage," sighed Benedict testily, striding up the front steps as the old manservant called plaintively for Willie.

"What on earth do you mean, 'it's against your religion'?" thundered Lord Taran, fifteen minutes later.

"Just that, sir," confessed the terrified Alsop. "Females are against my religion, sir. I took an oath, sir. You can ask Mr. Stephen, sir. He'll tell you 'tis the God's truth, sir."

"What the hell is going on here?" shouted Benedict. "Was I or was I not expected?"

"Yes, sir. You were, sir," stammered Alsop.

"Then where are the servants, and don't give me that nonsense about Willie and the full moon."

"No, sir, but . . . well, sir. Mr. Stephen says as how you didn't want to see a female, so it was just Willie and me, and now with the full moon . . ."

"Enough!" roared Benedict, striding back and forth making sounds of pure unadulterated fury. "Tell me, Alsop. What do you propose I do with her?" he pronounced, stabbing a finger to indicate the door of the bedroom where he had deposited Angelica. The tiny old man shrugged dismally. "Is there a doctor in the vicinity?" and the man unhappily shook his head. "Do you know anything about sickness?"

"Willie's grandmother has a way with herbs and the like, sir, but she's off somewhere because it's the full moon."

"Probably cavorting with her coven," snorted Benedict.

"Aye, and that's the truth of it, sir. 'Tis why I swore off women, sir. They are all witches, sir. Wicked, blood-sucking demons sent to tempt us, sir. It's all in the Good Book, sir. 'Tis women who've caused Willie to stray, sir."

"Get me a drink, Alsop," demanded Benedict after a long searching look at the bandy-legged little man whose eyes burned with a fanatical fervor. "A very large brandy."

"Yes, sir." Benedict watched the tiny manservant scurry away. What should he do? he pondered, turning to stare balefully at the closed bedroom door.

"Women!" he hissed, throwing himself into an overstuffed chair by the cold hearth. What was there about a cold hearth that was so depressing? he brooded. "Alsop? Light a fire!" he shouted as the man scampered in with a very large brandy snifter which was at least one third full.

"Light a fire?" echoed Alsop, looking at the young lord as though he were mad. "It is a very hot and humid September evening, sir," he chastened.

"I am very aware of the climate and the date," replied Benedict in a most chilling manner.

"Yes, sir. I must get some wood, sir," chattered Alsop, backing out of the sitting room. "What about the . . . er . . . young woman, sir?" he asked as he hovered just outside the door.

"What about her?"

"Do you think she's all right, sir?" worried the old man.

"Why don't you take a look?"

"Oh, I couldn't possibly do that, sir," he returned before he scrambled away.

Benedict breathed deeply of the warming fumes before taking an appreciative sip of the brandy. He snorted with wry amusement as he heard Alsop's lamenting voice outside calling desperately for Willie. He tried to ignore the closed bedroom door as he wished he had deposited her in one of the small back bedrooms instead of the large master chamber that led directly from the central living room. Alsop returned, staggering under the weight of a great many logs. He puffed and panted, making sure the indolent young lord was quite aware of his exertions before painfully bending on cracking knees to put in the most unnecessary blaze. Unable to abide the irritating sounds of the hard-done-by manservant, Benedict took a generous swallow and resolutely stood.

"I took the liberty, sir, of putting a basin of hot water and some towels on the stand," informed Alsop. "The female had a decidedly mucky face, sir,'' he answered the silent scowling question on the young peer's face.

Benedict quietly opened the bedchamber door not knowing what he hoped to see. If she had recovered, he was stuck with a woman to entertain. He couldn't very well turn her out in the wilds of the marshes and forest in the middle of the night. If she was dead, it was going to be an incredible nuisance disposing of her body with the hours of time-consuming questions involved, he thought callously, quietly approaching the large bed. Fortunately, neither condition was the case, he mused, watching the girl whimper and writhe as she fought the uncomfortable binding clothes.

"May I suggest a cooling rag, sir?" offered Alsop from the doorway. "Maybe you should loosen her clothes, sir. They seem a trifle restricting."

"May I suggest, as you seem to be so knowledgeable as to what is needed in this situation, that you do the honours?" replied Benedict quellingly.

"Oh, no, sir, 'tis against my religion," gasped the little man. "I shall see to your dinner, sir," he added hastily, closing the door behind him and bustling to the kitchen.

"Hot . . . very, very hot," moaned Angelica, clawing at the lacy stock at her throat and crying with frustration at not being able to loosen it.

Benedict also groaned as he resigned himself to the task at hand. It wasn't as if undressing women was unfamiliar to him. On the contrary, it was all too usual, almost mundane, he thought savagely, as his large hands joined her frantically eager one in undoing the long line of buttons and hooks.

"Aaah!" sighed Angelica, relaxing into the cool pillows and spreading her unencumbered limbs wide to embrace the chill sheets. Benedict gazed down dispassionately at the leggy female in her small clothes. He had had the dickens of a time with the whalebone corset, which she obviously didn't need as it was quite apparent his broad hands could easily span her small waist.

"Women," he hissed, shaking his ebony head. Why they had the need to encase and bind their bodies in such instruments of torture was beyond his powers of reason. He covered her with the fluffy eiderdown, but she ranted wildly and flailed about until it slipped to the floor. Beautiful legs, he remarked to himself, much as he would if he were examining a horse he proposed to buy. She was obviously of pedigree stock, he surmised, capturing a long fingered hand as he attempted to carefully sponge the dirt and blood from her face. An ugly gash accentuated one of her prominent cheekbones, and he idly wondered if it would leave a scar.

Angelica opened her eyes and squinted up at the dark man who loomed above her. She passed her tongue over her dry cracked lips and swallowed painfully. Where was she? It didn't matter, she decided, closing her burning eyes to sleep and block out the acute discomfort that wracked her body from head to toe.

"Your meal is ready, sir." Alsop's deferential tones from the open doorway caused Benedict to start awake, and he stared down with stupefaction at the long graceful fingers that curled about his own. He must be more fatigued than he thought, he mused, releasing himself and frowning at the small whimper of protest from the girl who nestled into his side. "I am sorry to disturb you, sir. I did knock and when there was no answer, I took the liberty of opening the door, sir. I was quite unaware, sir, that the unfortunate female was an intimate acquaintance, sir," babbled the servant, intrigued by the sight of Sir Benedict Tremayne lounging on the broad bed with an unclad woman cuddled provocatively against him.

"Thank you, Alsop," dismissed Benedict, unable to extricate himself gracefully as Angel seemed to have wound her long lean limbs about his in the most intricate way.

"Would you like your dinner served in here, sir?" asked Alsop, seeming infinitely fascinated by the gyrations on the bed.

"No!" roared Benedict. "Out! Go and find Willie!" he ordered as the small man hovered, his eyes popping at the sight of so much naked female flesh. "My God, it seems the full moon affects both of you! Out, Alsop!" Reluctantly the manservant slithered out of the room and shut the door. "Now, Angel, let go," he hissed, prying her hot fingers from his forearm. "There." He sighed with relief as she released him and stretched with a mournful cry. Before he could clear the bed, she rebounded back and curled into his side, firmly hugging his left thigh with her head pillowed on his hip in a most suggestive manner.

Too weary to engage in a wrestling match, Benedict leaned against the headboard and sipped the brandy he had the foresight to bring in the room with him. What a strange set of events, he sighed, gazing bemusedly at the lustrous hair and lithe bare arms that entwined his muscular thigh. The tasteless shouting match with his mistress the previous night combined with the long ride from London and the brandy soon caused Benedict Tremayne to fall back into a deep restful sleep. The brandy snifter fell with a crash to the floor, but it did nothing to disturb the young man from his sound slumber except to cause him to find a more comfortable position. He enfolded the hot restless female in strong arms so she could nestle more securely into the arc of his body.

Angelica's sleep was not as peaceful as Lord Taran's. In her dreams she found herself back in a grossly exaggerated replica of her grandmother's hothouse amid the cloying perfumes of the prize orchids and Venus's flytraps, fighting off the advances of her grandmother's fiancé Lord Carringdon. The spiteful man's powdered and patched face zoomed into her vision, grotesquely contorting as he mouthed a long litany of all her faults, the hurtful words spitting and hissing through his broken yellow fangs.

"Look what you've done to me!" he screeched with his bulging eyes inches from her face. "Look, you've broken my fingers. I shall never play the harpsichord again!" he wept, stabbing splintered talons at her eyes. "You are everything everyone says you are! Ugly, enormous, ungraceful, disgraceful, ungrateful, stupid, unfeminine, clumsy, an old maid, a hopeless case." The list continued, each painful label stabbing home with a sharp poke from the rigid digits. Angelica whimpered as her grandmother's lined face, hideously covered with thick white powder joined Lord Carringdon's.

"You gawky, spiteful, ugly lump, why did you injure my precious Carry-boo? You nasty, nasty girl, why did you hurt your soon-to-be-grandfather?" shrieked the little old lady, punching and poking her granddaughter, who stood like a helpless giant watching the tears spurt down the ancient painted cheeks. They muddied the powder and oozed into the wrinkles, widening until the porcelain facade cracked into hundreds of pieces.

"I'm sorry. So sorry," sobbed Angelica, trying to sweep up the brittle shards.

"Why, you ungrateful lump, why?" spat the red-painted mouth from the floor.

"Look what you've done to your poor grandmaman!" screamed Lord Carringdon, stabbing a pointed finger at the broken face. "Look what you've done, you ungrateful lump!" he continued, pinching her buttocks and breasts.

"I'm sorry. So sorry," she whimpered.

"Shush," soothed Benedict sleepily, enfolding her tightly. Angelica gave a long shuddering sigh and cuddled closer, trying to avoid the tormenting hands and the nightmarish faces that continued to berate her.

"Whore! Slut! Harlot!" screeched the strident voices. Angelica cried and writhed under the onslaught of stinging blows.

"I'm sorry. So sorry," she sobbed, clinging to the strong body beside her.

"For God's sake, Isabella!" shouted Benedict, awakening to the incredible reality of his infuriated mistress with horsewhip in hand, forcibly restrained by three snickering dandies while Alsop, dressed in nightshirt and cap, cowered in the corner with lantern in hand. "What the hell is the meaning of this?" he thundered, looking with horror at the welts that crisscrossed Angelica's back, so deep that blood beaded through the silk chemise.

"So Lord Taran needs solitude to commune with nature," jeered a voice that positively shook with loathing. "Romping in the New Forest with little furry friends? Rather large for a squirrel, isn't she, Taran? Looks more like vermin!" Once more the whip snaked out, cruelly slashing Angelica's bare shoulder and Benedict's cheek before he caught it in his bare hand and jerked it from the infuriated woman's grasp.

"Get her out of here!" he pronounced in a low, dangerous tone as he purposefully wound the supple leather about his palm, and the three dandies backed away, giggling nervously as they plucked and pulled at Isabella's vermilion riding habit.

"Let me alone, you simpering fops!" she hissed, blindly raking at their faces with her long painted fingernails in an attempt to free herself. She stared at the intimate scene, her voluptuous breasts heaving with rage. Her lover, Benedict Tremayne of Taran, reclined on a broad bed, cradling a nearly naked female. The fact that he was dressed in tight riding britches, high boots and an unbuttoned, rumpled shirt somehow made it even more provocative to her jealous eyes. In the two years of their alliance, he had never held her so protectively, nor had he appeared so dishevelled and vulnerable. He was a sardonic, brooding man whose iron control and contempt for women was legendary. There was a rumour about a woman who had broken his heart when he had been a callow youth, but in the ten years that she had known of him in London, he had kept himself scrupulously free from all but financial entanglements, terminating those when the mistress became too possessive. Now Isabella cursed herself for making such a stupid mistake. A graceless animal howl burst from her mouth as she remembered the humiliating scene the previous night when he had ruthlessly severed his connection with her.

Lady Isabella Bony seethed impotently as she watched Benedict give his undivided attention to the leggy female who writhed and moaned incoherently. She stalked haughtily to the bed and sneered down. "What on earth has happened to your usually discerning eye, darling? Why, she's as ugly as sin!"

"Alsop, throw these intruders out and fetch more cold water and cloths," ordered Benedict from between clenched teeth as he felt the girl's temperature rise even higher.

"Come along, Isabella, we're all a trifle bosky, and I think we've gone a titchy bit too far," whined one of the dandies, tugging at her sable-trimmed sleeve like a worrying puppy.

"Ugly as sin. Ugly as sin," chanted Angelica. "So sorry, Grandmother."

"Grandmother?" snarled Isabella.

"Well, she's certainly a babe in arms compared to you, Lady Bonny," clipped Lord Taran, alluding to the sensitive subject of Isabella's age, which topped his by at least ten years.

"I wasn't aware you were interested in unfledged children," she returned furiously. "My God, she's mad with fever!" she gasped, backing hastily away from the frightening sight of the girl who started to tremble violently.

"Fever?" yelped one of the fops. "There's rumour of plague in London," he chattered, rushing out, followed by the other two terrified men.

"But, Taran, what if you catch it?" wailed Isabella from the doorway.

"Someone else will have to pay your last month's dressmaker bills," he replied tersely, piling blankets on the shivering girl.

"Plague?" queried Alsop.

"You'll pay for this!" screeched the spurned woman lamely, clattering after her travelling companions, her high-heeled boots skidding on the wooden floors.

"I have for years," sighed the young man as he thought of the woman's expensive and acquisitive nature. "Alsop, where the hell are those blankets?"

"Plague?" repeated the man numbly.

"Nonsense. The wrenched chit has in all likelihood eaten spoiled food," he improvised. "Now I need blankets and more water, if you please."

"Plague!" screamed Alsop as the awful realization finally penetrated. He backed out of the room, his eyes bulging with terror.

"Come back at once, you silly little man!" roared the young peer, battling the wildly kicking limbs as Angelica tried to dislodge the restricting covers.

"Plague!" Alsop's voice spiralled back with the sound of his scurrying feet on the graveled driveway. "Willie, 'tis the plague!"

"Hot, so hot," panted the girl. Benedict stared down wearily at her battered face, which was thickly beaded with perspiration. He had managed to swaddle her like an Egyptian mummy with her arms firmly imprisoned at her sides. He sat uncomfortably with his back braced against the headboard, cradling her across his lap. "So hot. So very, very hot," she whispered hoarsely.

"The fever has to break," he muttered as she banged her head wildly from side to side.

"Hot, too hot," she sobbed piteously, her body bucking frantically.

Benedict sighed with relief as she lost consciousness and relaxed in his arms. Every muscle ached with fatigue. Carefully he eased her onto the bed and stretched out beside her as his weary mind pondered his predicament. This most certainly was not the autumnal retreat he had planned for himself, he mused—stranded in the middle of nowhere with no servants and a battered, sick female called Angel who had been soundly horsewhipped by his cast off mistress. Realizing the ludicrousness of the whole situation, he gave a sharp bark of sardonic mirth and drifted off to sleep, only to be rudely awakened less than an hour later as once again the girl thrashed about deliriously.

CHAPTER 2

LADY MELISANDE Moreby-Wentworth-Fowler was propped up by a mountain of lacey pillows on her pink satin bed, nibbling delicate toast fingers.

While she nibbled, Lady Mellie watched herself critically from every angle in several shell-shaped mirrors, seeing in the dim, pink-tinged recesses the exquisite debutante who had taken London by storm more than fifty years before. She had captured more hearts than any emerging butterfly then or since, she mused, gazing with affection at the portrait of Sir Lumbleigh Moreby, her late first husband, hanging dutifully beside his also late successors, Sir Cyril Wentworth and Lord Humbert Fowler.

"How could you all leave your little Melisande?" she reproached the trio petulantly. "I'm so sad and lonely." She sighed, pouting prettily in the mirror. "Even my only daughter ran off and left me. I was too, too much for her, poor little mouse. She took after you, Lumbleigh. And now I am expected to turn her great lumbering daughter into a fragile, graceful lady," she lamented.

It was barely noon and although Lady Melisande was just partaking of her meager breakfast, she had already spent more than three laborious hours on her toilette. She absolutely refused to be seen by anyone, except her personal maid and housekeeper, Maud Smithers, without full makeup and wig, and then only at a discreet distance in a diffused light.

"Enter!" she sang out in answer to a rapping at the bedroom door. She was very mindful to modulate her voice as, to her horror, she had detected an involuntary quaver entering

38

her speech due, no doubt, to the strain of trying to hone her bucolic granddaughter into some passable facsimile of a well-bred female. She must remind her secretary to add Sir Torrance Pendarves's name to the list of guests for her next midnight soiree, she planned. Seven years was more than an adequate length of time to mourn the death of the silly chit he had foolishly married in his semi-dotage. Once he had been smitten with her, but now maybe he would serve her ungainly granddaughter. The rapping continued. "Come in!" she screeched peevishly with a decided vibrato, and a uniformed young maid sidled in and stood just off the carpet at the required distance of at least eight feet from her mistress. "Well, what is it, Wilkins?" she annunciated carefully and nodded with satisfaction to her image in the glass at hearing her steady tone.

"She ain't back, yer ladyship."

"I beg your pardon?"

"Miss Angelica, yer ladyship," explained Wilkins.

"And what about my granddaughter?" pronounced the peeress.

"She's run off, yer ladyship."

"Alone?"

"Yes, yer ladyship."

"That is utterly ridiculous!" trilled Lady Melisande. "Well, isn't it, Wilkins?" she asked of the silent maid, who didn't know whether to shake her head or nod. "My granddaughter may be sadly and most unfortunately deficit in beauty and grace, but she would never go anywhere unchaperoned!"

"She's run off and she 'asn't slept in 'er bed for three nights . . ."

"How dare you! This is more than enough, you impertinent little guttersnipe! Disturbing my breakfast with such absurd lies!"

"I'm ever so sorry, yer ladyship," apologized Wilkins, terrified she was about to lose her job.

"Now, run along and remember I shall not tolerate any more of your insolence, Wilkins."

"No, yer ladyship. I mean thank you," mumbled the maid, blindly reaching behind her back for the doorknob. She turned and yanked it, and the heavy door cracked her head painfully. Slightly dazed, she scrambled from the room as quickly as she could.

Lady Mellie hoped the aggravation hadn't wreaked havoc with her complexion. Leisurely she finished her sparse repast and conversed graciously with the portraits of her three deceased husbands before ringing for Maud Smithers.

"Enter, Maudie-Louise," she sang out merrily, her good humour resolutely restored, as she fervently believed that misery caused premature aging. "I have had such a wonderful idea. I have decided that Sir Torrance Pendarves may call on Angelica. He's seventy if he's a day, so he'll overlook my granddaughter's gross imperfections. Well, isn't that a good idea?" she demanded of the woman, who was as old as she but used no artifice to disguise the thin grey hair and sagging wrinkled flesh. "Are you getting deaf in your advanced years?" she teased when the woman didn't answer.

"Didn't Wilkins speak with you earlier?" ventured Mrs. Smithers.

"We shall not discuss any unpleasantness. Why I let you talk me into hiring such a chit to be Angelica's abigail is beyond me."

"Lady Em," Maud Smithers started firmly. "Your granddaughter is not here!"

"Where is she? Off with one of her many beaux?" asked her ladyship innocently, primping her wig, which itched unbearably.

"She doesn't have any beaux, as well you know!"

"That's why Sir Torrance Pendarves is such a good idea. It will help take his mind off his son!"

"She's run off with just the clothes on her back, poor little wench," sighed Mrs. Smithers.

"Little!" exclaimed Lady Melisande. "She's certainly not little."

"Angelica Carmichael has run off and at this very minute could be in the hands of cutthroats . . ."

"Mind you, I still have an awful long way to go, but my granddaughter shall be the talk of London despite her size and having been buried in the wilds of Cornwall with that ghastly bonesetter of a father," continued Lady Mellie.

"She's certainly going to be the talk of London if she ends up in some brothel!" returned Maud tartly.

"I will not have you clouding my sunny day, Smithers," reproved the painted old woman, keeping a smile on her face with great difficulty.

"You didn't want it clouded yesterday, either, did you?" snapped the housekeeper, snatching up the breakfast tray. "All I can think of is that poor innocent girl."

"Innocent? Innocent? I should very much hope she's innocent," quavered Lady Mellie indignantly. "But she has a nasty streak. She broke poor Lord Carringdon's fingers."

"If he kept his fingers off young ladies' posteriors . . ." muttered Smithers. "I should have spoke my piece months ago about the way you was treating that poor child."

"Smithers, you are really disgustingly old," remarked her ladyship spitefully.

"Miss Angelica is not what you'd call headstrong or spirited, so she had to have been sorely tried to run off like that without a penny with just the clothes on her back," scolded Maud, ignoring her employer's attempts to divert.

"She has not run off! I forbid it!"

"She *has* run off!" stated Maud loudly. "And what is more, I am sending word to her father, Dr. Simon Carmichael. When you wouldn't listen to us, Mr. Smithers and me had a long heart to heart and decided what was best for Miss Angelica. . . ."

"You are what?" interrupted Lady Melisande. Maud Smithers realised that finally her employer had accepted the news of her granddaughter's decampment; and being intimately acquainted with the vagaries of the peeress's violent temper, she scurried swiftly to the door. She just managed to dodge into the corridor when the first crash splintered against the wall.

"Mrs. Smithers, does 'er ladyship know about Miss Angelica yet?" ventured Wilkins, who hovered nervously.

"Just take a listen to all that pandemonium and tell me the answer, you stupid wench," panted the old lady as the house reverberated with Lady Melisande Moreby-Wentworth-Fowler's fury. "Let's trot down to the kitchen and have a nice cuppa tea."

"But what about the mistress?" asked the young maid, staring with her mouth agape at the closed bedroom door, which shook with the ferocity of the raging woman inside.

"There's nothing like a little temper tantrum to keep a person young. Gets the blood running like tree sap in spring. Come along, Wilkins, we won't have peace for long. Soon as she's finished her snit, we'll be run off our feet picking up the pieces and trotting to the apothecary's to replace all the powders, paints, patches, and perfumes she's splattering up the walls."

They entered the large kitchen, and Maud sat at the scrubbed table.

"Well, finally sounds like the missus admits that our Cornish luvey 'as flown the coop," chuckled the cook as she poured generous mugs of steaming tea and the crockery rattled on the wide kitchen shelves.

"Whopsy, there goes her bedroom window again," sighed Maud as they heard a particularly loud explosion followed by glass raining onto the paving stones of the terrace.

"Oh, nearly forgot," said the cook. "Your mister Smithers says 'as 'ow the Barnstable's Charlie saw a lass what looked like our Miss Angel up on the common at the postin' stop."

"When?"

"Three nights past. She didn't have a cape nor a scrap of baggage," continued the cook.

"Had to have been the Cornish stage. Where else would our Miss Angel go but home?" whispered Maud. "Takes days and days. How will she sleep? How will she eat?"

"Terrible, ain't it?" sighed the cook. Wilkins stared at the two older women, who gazed dejectedly into their nearly empty mugs. The house still shook with Lady Melisande's tantrum, although not quite as furiously. Above the ruckus, they all managed to hear a loud hammering at the front door.

"If it's noon it'll be Lord Carringdon," trilled Wilkins, smoothing her hair and straightening her uniform. "What are you both lookin' at me like that for? I didn't listen at the key'ole, I 'eard 'im . . . when I was showin' 'im out yesterday."

"Someone better get the door, 'cos all the men are out lookin' fer news of Miss Angel," observed the cook.

"I'll go," offered Wilkins eagerly.

"Tell his lordship that her ladyship is indisposed and there's a bit of carpentry being done upstairs," said Maud after a loud crash, and Wilkins rushed out of the kitchen.

"What's goin' on there? 'as that old lecher bin in her knickers already?" chuckled the cook. Maud Smithers shook her head resignedly, knowing better than to remark on the woman's crudity.

Wilkins scurried to the marbled entrance hall. She took a quick peek at herself in the mirror before opening the door to Lord Carringdon.

"Good afternoon, your lordship," she greeted, giving him a provocative dimpled grin and a curtsey. "'er ladyship ain't up ter snuff today, I'm afraid, yer lordship."

"Don't be afraid of me, my little poppet," replied Lord Carringdon, reaching out with his uninjured hand and tweaking her pert young breast.

"Oooh, my Lord!" giggled Wilkins, pressing provocatively against his hand as she licked her lips invitingly.

"So, her ladyship is indisposed and I am sadly disappointed."

"Oh, we can't 'ave you bein' disappointed, can we?" murmured Wilkins, gyrating her hips sensuously. "You wasn't disappointed last time, was you?" she asked, stroking his stiff, splinted fingers.

"Were you?" he panted, and she shook her head and grinned, thinking of the tidy stack of coins hidden under the floorboards of her attic room. "You delicious little wanton," he muttered hoarsely as she brushed her hand against his silk-clad thigh.

"Wilkins?" chided a sharp voice.

"It's Mrs. Smithers," hissed the maid.

"Ah, Mrs. Smithers," greeted Lord Carringdon. "I have just ridden a considerable distance only to be informed that my fiancée is ailing. I should appreciate a light refreshment before returning to Grosvenor Square," he stated, handing his hat, quirt, and gloves to the young maid and striding pompously into the front salon.

"Very good, sir."

"Is there news of Miss Angelica Carmichael?" he asked.

"No, it's just like she vanished . . ."

"That's quite enough, Wilkins," scolded Mrs. Smithers. "Go and help Cook."

"I should like Wilkins to stay," countermanded Lord Carringdon, and Maud bit her lip and nodded disapprovingly.

"I want her to see to my . . . er . . . comfort," he added suggestively. "Bring me a simple omelette, fruit salad, and a bottle of sauternes," he ordered, dismissing the older woman with a careless wave of his splinted hand.

All was tranquil above stairs when Mrs. Smithers returned to the salon. She listened at the door, and hearing the telltale rhythmic thuds and rasping grunts of exertion, she sighed and placed Lord Carringdon's luncheon on a table in the hall and walked thoughtfully back to the kitchen.

"What's up?" asked the cook. "Is the missus asleep? Where's Wilkins?" she added suspiciously at receiving no answer. "You don't mean ter say they are 'at it'?"

"Better Wilkins than Miss Angelica," muttered Smithers under her breath.

"Stinkin' old cock! 'e has ter be fifty if 'e's a day! Wilkins ain't more'n eighteen; the old sod could be 'er grampa, couldn't 'e? And if the missus is this side of seventy, I'll be a monkey's uncle." chattered the cook.

"It is not our place."

"What's not our place?" asked Wilkins as she entered the kitchen.

"Well, that was a short nap," sighed Mrs. Smithers, trotting out of the kitchen to answer the bell that rang incessantly from Lady Melisande's bedchamber.

"Sit down and 'ave a bite of lunch. You 'ave it good 'ere, Wilkins, why do you want to muck it up?" asked Cook.

"'o's muckin' it up? If I say no to Lord Carringdon, I'll lose my job, 'cos 'e'll tell 'er ladyship that I was rude or something. That's what I'd call muckin' it up!" shouted Wilkins. "I arsk you, 'ow's a person to win, aye? If I say no, 'e'll just 'ave 'is way anyhow, and I'll not get anythin' but bruises. What's wrong with gettin' a few coppers?"

"Keep yer 'air on! I didn't say there was nothin' wrong with it," laughed Cook, slamming down a plate of bread and cheese in front of the bristling young maid.

"I just don't let no one take nothin', and I don't give it away for nothing no more," said Wilkins vehemently with her mouth full.

"You ain't so tough," jeered the cook.

Wilkins tried to look belligerent and not burst into tears.
"'ow old are you?"

"Fifteen," informed Wilkins. "And I can take care of meself an 'ell of a lot better than Miss Angel!"

"Yer right there," sighed the cook.

"She's nearly twenty, you know. A regular old maid but nice. Poor sod, she'll probably bin raped by 'alf of London by now," Wilkins mused.

"Oh, get along with you! What an imagination! Raped by 'alf of London indeed. Gentlemen 'ave other things on their minds, you know."

"Now who's talkin' twaddle?" hooted Wilkins. "I ain't never met a bloke who didn't want to toss me skirts up and poke 'is dick in."

"Really?" queried the cook incredulously with a touch of envy. "Oh, get along with you and don't let Mrs. Smithers 'ear you talkin' like that. 'ow old was you when you first got goin'?"

"Nine or ten," answered Wilkins. "and it weren't my idea, I can tell you," she added with a wry laugh as she remembered the terror of being raped.

"Well, 'ere's Mr. Smithers and Riggs now," said the cook, heaving her great shape out of the chair as the clatter of horses' hooves was heard outside in the courtyard. "I 'ope there's news about poor Miss Angel. She ain't used ter 'avin' it hard and livin' by 'er wits like you and me. She's one of them. It ain't the same fer gentry, you know."

"She's probably lyin' dead somewhere unless she got lucky and landed in a nice warm bed with an 'andsome duke," mused Wilkins.

"I ain't never seen an 'andsome duke, 'ave you?" the cook asked, peering out of the kitchen window.

"Nah, they're all old and ugly like Lord Carringdon," replied the young maid, clattering the empty plates together.

"Poor Miss Angel, I don't think we're goin' ter like what we 'ear from the looks of Mr. Smithers' face," lamented Cook.

CHAPTER 3

ANGELICA OPENED her eyes as bright warm sunlight flooded across her face. She lay in a rosy suspension looking at the beamed ceiling. Where was she? she mused as her nostrils filled with the comforting fragrance of flowers mingled with a salty sea breeze. She turned her head and winced at a sharp pain that shot through her body. The mullion-paned window was wide open, and she could hear the familiar soothing hum of bees in the tall hollyhocks whose showy flowers were visible above the sill. She didn't think she was home, she reasoned, even though the wonderful perfumes and sounds were nostalgic. Carefully she turned her head to look at the rest of the chamber and she froze, seeing the large rangy man who lay sprawled intimately beside her in the wide bed. She swallowed painfully and smothered a gasp at the sight of clothes piled untidely on a chest at the foot of the bed. Her pulses pounded with panic, and she was terrified they would awaken the man. Slowly she reached down under the covers and to her horror found she was practically naked, wearing only a thin silk chemise. Furtively she looked at him, shocked by the sight of his bare tanned chest. Was he naked all the way down? she wondered frantically.

"How do you feel?" asked a deep, very resonant voice that reverberated right through her, chilling her blood. A very large hand covered her forehead for a moment and then felt her neck and naked shoulder in a very personal manner. Angelica kept her eyes pinned to a beam in the ceiling. The man gave a grunt of satisfaction, and she felt the springs of the bed jostle her tense body as he swung his legs onto the

46

floor. She didn't dare look, but to her absolute horror she felt him stride barefoot around the bed. Suddenly he loomed above her. She stared into his black eyes and found not the slightest trace of comfort in his forbidding features. "There's no need to be afraid," he barked harshly, noting the frantic pulse in her neck and taken aback again by the unusual colour of her wide fearful eyes.

Angelica shrank back against the pillow, holding the sheet high about her neck as she thought frantically about what she was doing in the strange bed with the strange man. Where was she? Who was she? At the second thought her eyes grew even wider and she gasped audibly. Her mind was a blank.

"Oh, no . . . no," she whispered as the full horror swept in.

"For God's sake, this is no time for false modesty," snapped the man impatiently. "I have played nursemaid for nearly four days and am quite aware of every inch of your body . . . and all its functions," he added harshly. "I am, however, vastly relieved to find my administrations have at last had some effect and you appear to be on the mend."

Angelica relaxed slightly as he strode out of the room and the door slammed shut behind him. She waited a few minutes as his footsteps faded and then crunched on the stones outside before carefully sitting up, unable to muffle whimpers of pain as it seemed the skin on her back and shoulder was stiff and tight.

Half an hour later Benedict entered the bedchamber quietly and gazed at the girl who stood unsteadily, staring at herself in the glass. Women and their vanity, he snorted to himself.

"Who am I?" mouthed Angelica, looking at the reflection of the wild-haired, battered girl. "I don't recognize myself," she muttered as the image copied her movements. She found nothing familiar in what she gazed upon. She was so immersed in her terror, she felt she was drowning in the mirror, unaware of Benedict's approach until he, too, was reflected. He watched her frantically moving lips as she fearfully demanded an identity of the strange woman. "Who am I?" she screamed, and her alien facsimile mocked her.

"Hysteria will solve nothing," he stated quellingly, picking her up and carrying her back to the bed. Angelica held on to him as his strong arms gave a familiar feeling of safety. Benedict was about to contemptuously pry her clinging hands off him, but the obvious deep terror that shook her body awoke a shred of compassion in him. "Now compose yourself and tell me what you're afraid of," he asked coldly, his tone in direct contrast to the warm, strong arms that held her close.

Angelica shivered as the censuring, harsh voice cut through her. She pushed away from him and looked searchingly up at his face, hoping to recognize him. She traced his nose and his cheekbones. She must be married to him, she deduced; that is why they slept so intimately in the same bed and she was nearly naked in his arms. But why didn't she recall either him or herself? What had he done to her? she wondered, remembering the wheals and bruises she had seen reflected on her body. The hard black eyes stared back at her as she assessed the stern, almost cruel face. "Did you beat me?" she asked.

"Regardless of my reputation, I am not in the habit of horsewhipping females no matter how deserving they are of such discipline," he remarked cuttingly, depositing her on the bed and throwing the covers about her. "I shall now attempt to concoct a passable repast with the sincere hope that you will rapidly regain your strength and stop being such a liability," he added sardonically, loathe to inform her that his jealous mistress had inflicted the damage upon her person. How did one explain such an absurd and outrageous occurrence? he mused as he strode to the well-stocked kitchen.

He sat at the table and drank deeply from a quenching bitter ale as he thought over the previous few days. He had discovered a new dimension to himself, he acknowledged wryly as he sniffed the remains of a savoury stew that he had put together with an assortment of dishes he had found in the pantry. Keeping the fire going had been the most difficult of the menial chores, he observed as he threw on several logs and stoked up a cheerful blaze before putting the pot on to warm. There was something oddly purging about having to survive without servants and the clamour of London society, he thought as he sawed through a loaf of stale bread, wishing he knew how to bake. There was also something oddly satisfying about having nearly healed a helpless female, he mused. He was the one who had felt completely helpless at the outset, he admitted, remembering the horror that had consumed him after Alsop had abandoned him with the delirious girl. His main instinct had been to get back in his curricle and return to his London house. Why hadn't he fled, especially with all the talk of plague and the pox? he asked himself. He shrugged, not knowing the answer, and not caring particularly that he didn't. He had been dissatisfied with his life of late, he realized, irritated with the round of social and political functions that were expected of him, being a Whig within a Tory government and a close associate of the Prince of Wales. He was so tired of intrigues, especially those of the spoilt young prince, that despite his own cynical view of females, he had to admit feeling sympathy for Mrs. Fitzherbert, the unfortunate mistress of the sybaritic heir to the throne. Seven years before, he had been part of the cruel farce of a marriage where the twenty-three-year-old prince had married the young widow knowing such a ceremony was illegal, as the heir apparent was underage and had not received permission from Parliament. Since the mock ceremony Mrs. Fitzherbert had given birth to a son who could never be called legitimate. Taran stretched his legs and sighed as he admitted to himself he felt more than a little uncomfortable being a guest in Mrs. Fitzherbert's home knowing how false the prince played her and their child.

"Women," he hissed aloud as an old wound stabbed and he thought of his first and only love. Only love because he had sworn that he would never be so hurt and vulnerable again. Maybe it was time to return to his home on the rugged coast of Cornwall and settle down with an undemanding, docile wife who'd ensure his family name continued, he decided. He was tired of the tension in the capital between the Tories and Whigs, between the staid, groping monarch George III and his hedonistic son, between England and France as the two countries moved closer to war. Benedict was thirty-three years old and it was time he settled down, he determined.

Angelica stood in the shadows by the kitchen door watching the tall dark man drink his ale and mutter to himself. Unable to find the courage to approach him she clutched the bedsheet tighter about herself and tiptoed away in search of a door that would lead outside. She was sorely in need of relieving herself. Quietly she opened the front door and smiled with satisfaction, seeing the dense woods either side of the overgrown driveway that would afford privacy. She stepped gratefully into the bright sunlight and was immediately assailed by a wave of dizziness. She sank to her knees trying to clear her light-headedness.

"What the hell do you think you're doing, you stupid chit?" bellowed an extremely angry voice.

"I have to . . . I'm all right, I assure you," struggled Angelica, trying to push him away.

"Where do you think you're going dressed in nothing but a sheet?" he demanded, picking her up.

"Please, you don't understand," she whispered miserably.

"No, you don't understand. There's marsh and quicksand to either side. It's dangerous," he snapped, carrying her back into the house. "What did you think you were doing?" he asked. Angelica shrugged and flushed hotly, unable to admit her urgent need. "I have spent four days chained to this house caring for you; I am not going to let my efforts go for naught," he continued, seating her at the kitchen table and ladling a generous bowl of his stew.

Angelica stared at the food and shook her head weakly as her stomach churned, not well enough to partake of such richness. "I'm sorry, very sorry, but I cannot. It's very kind of you but . . ." she stated carefully as she pushed herself away from the table and stood. "No, don't stop me!" she shouted, holding her hand up threateningly. Benedict raised his thick, dark eyebrows at her display of spirit. "And don't follow me!" she added, opening the kitchen door and swaying on the steps. With a muffled curse he snatched her up and she burst into tears.

"Women!" he lamented, not knowing what to make of her pendulum swings. "One minute showing your teeth, the next wetting my shirt front," he ranted irrationally as he was bare chested.

"Please, I have to . . ." wailed Angelica as she was deposited back in the bed. Benedict frowned for several moments as he tried to fathom her strange behaviour.

"Have to what?" he asked. "For heaven's sake, you

stupid chit!'' he roared impatiently before storming out and reappearing a split second later with a chamber pot. Angelica gave a muffled squawk and hid her face beneath the bedcovers, hoping he would remove himself. ''What on earth do you think I've been doing for the past four days and nights?'' he announced, much to her further mortification.

''Are you going to leave me any vestige of pride?'' she challenged, goaded beyond good reason. Benedict laughed mirthlessly before striding out and slamming the door.

A little while- later and very much relieved, Angelica surreptitiously emptied the chamber pot out of the window onto the hollyhocks, and then she climbed back into the bed absolutely exhausted. She had no idea who she was or who he was or why she was so beaten and bruised, but she was too depleted to care. She drifted into a soundless healthy sleep.

Benedict heard the serene rhythm of her breathing, and he nodded proudly as he noted her cheeks were not as flushed and the dark circles were fading about her eyes. Who was she? he wondered, grinning as he remembered her small defiances which were so unexpected and rather endearing. He quietly closed the bedchamber door and, humming happily to himself, returned to the kitchen to eat his stew. Now the chit was better and obviously in no danger of doing damage to herself in a delirium, he could leave the house and go for a cleansing swim. And that evening when she was well rested, he would find out all about her, he decided, dunking the stale bread in the spicy gravy.

Angelica slept soundly all day and awoke as the sun dipped low in the sky, turning the marshland into a blazing web of molten rivers. She opened her eyes to the red-hued light that bounced off the mullion circles of the windowpanes and made patterns on the walls. She lay without moving as the horrific memories of the morning flooded into her mind and then stopped, leaving her in a terrifying vaccuum. Nothing existed before that morning. She clutched at the covers, winding them about her fingers, trying to hold on to her sanity and not be swept away with the panic that threatened.

Benedict quietly opened the door and watched her, seeing the light of the fiery sunset reflect off her open staring eyes.

He walked to the bed and gazed down at her. She stared back and he frowned at the hollow misery he saw.

"I . . . I don't know who I am," she said in a tremulous voice. "I can't remember anything. Who am I?" she asked. He didn't answer but just expelled his breath, making an exasperated noise. He sat heavily so her prone body bounced up, coming to rest against his muscled thigh.

"Angel," he said gruffly as his mind tried to grapple with the new complication. Could her high temperature have caused amnesia? he wondered. Or maybe when she hit her head on his boot?

"Angel?" repeated the girl, her eyes luminous with unspilt tears. "Like someone who's dead and gone to heaven?"

"That's what you said your name was," stated Benedict.

"That's what I said? I said my name was Angel?"

"You said your name was Angel," he agreed.

"It sounds as if you don't know who I am, either," whispered Angelica after a long pause where she sought desperately to be calm, knowing how he abhorred hysteria.

"I don't!" snapped the dark man harshly, and the girl tried unsuccessfully to stifle the choking sobs that burst out of her heaving chest.

"I'm sorry!" she wailed as the terror clawed in and she felt herself swept away. "But I feel like I'm being sucked down by the quicksands you were warning me of. Nothing is stable; everything's shifting. There's nothing to hold on to." Without a second thought Benedict wrapped his arms about her and rocked her as though she was a small child. What was it about this ungainly girl, he mused as her very real horror released emotions he felt had been a long time dead. How long he held her, muttering incomprehensible noises of comfort that he must have learned on his own nanny's knee, he had no idea, except the room was pitch black without a trace of light when he felt her raise her head from his chest. He cupped her hot wet cheek in his broad hand as she gazed up. "Who are you?" she asked softly.

"Taran," he replied huskily. "Benedict Tremayne of Taran," he further supplied.

"Where's Taran?"

"Cornwall," he said, and waited for her reaction. She had

a soft melodic voice, cultured but with a faint West Country lilt.

"Benedict Tremayne of Taran," she repeated, testing each word for familiarity, and he became more certain that she was from the West Country as the syllables rolled. "What else did I tell you?" she asked after a dejected sigh.

"Well, just before you cracked your head against my boot, you smelled the sea as the tide came in filling the marshes and thought you were home," he informed her softly.

"So my home is by the sea," she mused. "When I awoke this morning and heard the bees in the flowers and smelled the salty mud, I thought I was home, but then . . . then . . ."

"Then what?" he prompted.

"I couldn't . . . couldn't remember what home was," she said, trying to hold back the tears.

"You will," he comforted. "But not if you try too hard. So I propose we do something about dining and getting dressed for dinner," he teased. He grinned in the darkness as he conceded it had been a long time since he had felt so young and full of life. He laid her carefully back against the pillows. She shivered, feeling cold and abandoned. "It's all right, Angel," he soothed as he rummaged about in the dark. "Let there be light," he proclaimed as he located his tinder-box. Soon the chamber was bathed in the warmth of two swinging lanterns. "Now to find the appropriate gown for Lady Angel," he muttered, disappearing into a large armoire and reemerging several minutes later with an armful of strange garments. "Not very fashionable, I'm afraid," he lamented, holding up several large shirts and an enormous multitiered cape.

"Shush," hissed Angel as she heard a clatter from another part of the house. "Someone's out there," she gasped.

"Alsop," supplied Taran as he perused the large shirts and decided on one that he thought she should wear.

"Alsop?" giggled the bemused girl.

"Alsop has returned. While you were peacefully sleeping, all day, I might add, I was very industrious. I had an invigorating swim and rode into the nearest village to inform the general populace that . . . er . . . my wife did not have the plague or the pox."

"Your wife did not have the plague or the pox?" repeated Angel in a very dazed manner.

"It occurred to me that I had read somewhere that one of the symptoms of the plague was swelling beneath the arms and at the crease at the top of the legs, and after ascertaining you had no swelling in either place, I was able to reassure every one," informed Benedict.

Angelica slid down the bed as a flush suffused her whole body. His large strong hands had felt where even she had never dared to touch. How did she know that? she brooded. She could remember shameful dos and don'ts but not who she was? What did she recall about her own body? She forced herself to strive to remember. A naked body was indecent. It had to be covered hastily and touched as sparingly as possible and then only for the act of cleansing, never for pleasure. Even cleansing was a subject of much contention.

"I would like to have a cleansing swim," she murmured aloud. In her mind's eye she could recreate drifting in buoyant water that rhythmically swelled about her.

"When you are healed, Alsop shall heat water for a bath," Benedict said harshly as a sudden picture of a wanton, golden-haired siren, laughing in the white horses of the sea, flooded into his head, causing a sharp pain. Angelica shuddered as the bedchamber door slammed shut and she was left alone.

Who was the strange dark man who one moment could hold her so tenderly in comforting arms and the next be so cruel and aloof? She knew more about him than she did herself, she acknowledged ironically. She knew his name and where he was from. Two facts she was hopelessly unaware of about herself. The confusing mass of bits and pieces of the day jumbled in her mind, and once more she swung her long legs from the bed and hesitantly walked toward the mirror, hoping this time to gaze upon a familiar image. She stared solemnly at the shadowed figure for several long minutes before fetching a lantern, which she placed resolutely on a bureau so it illuminated one side of her face.

Angelica stared objectively at the strange reflection. It was by no means a pretty, adorable face, she conceded. It was too angular, too well-defined but luckily the nose wasn't big and obtrusive, she noted. With a stretch of the imagination it could possibly be described as classical, as the neck was long and graceful and the cheekbones high and aristocratic. On what was she basing her judgment? she puzzled. Why had she remembered her taught standards of beauty just like well-bred propriety and yet was unable to remember her own identity? What did she recall of other things? she strove to recollect as the eerie call of a prowling owl hooted across the marshes.

"Predators," she said aloud. "Owls, hawks, foxes, rats," she listed. "Animals. Horses, dogs, cats," she recalled, picturing them as she named them.

"Predators?" queried Benedict, who, returning, had been watching her for several moments. She stood motionless with her eyes glued to the mirror.

"Man the predator, woman the prey," she quoted quietly. "Who said that?" she asked, watching his shadowy image. He appeared hawklike and merciless, she observed.

"Put on the shirt or you'll shock Alsop's sensibilities. He has sworn off women. They are against his religion," he stated harshly as she seemed like a graceful young deer in the warm lantern light.

"Religion?" repeated Angel thoughtfully. "When you lit the lamps, you said, 'Let there be light.' That has something to do with religion, doesn't it?"

"It is from the Bible, the book of Genesis, which is the basis of both the Christian and Judaic religions," informed Benedict.

"The Bible," iterated Angel as she obediently buttoned the very large shirt over her chemise. "It is so frustrating. I can remember everything except anything to do with me."

"You'll probably awaken tomorrow remembering things you wish had remained forever forgotten," he snapped sardonically.

"I hope so," retorted Angel angrily, furious with his cutting manner. "It is probably extremely ill-bred and ill-mannered of me to say, but I find your sarcasm very boorish and hurtful."

"It is extremely ill-bred and ill-mannered but even more ill-advised," returned Taran harshly. "There is nothing I detest more than domestic squabbles in front of servants, so I suggest you be serenely silent or very prudent."

At a discreet rapping at the door, Angelica gasped and stared aghast at Taran.

"Enter," he called out, and she instinctively moved close to him for protection. Alsop popped his head around the door.

"So happy to see you up on your own two feet, my lady," he gushed, staying well away from her in the darkened doorway. Angel held on to Taran tighter as the little man seemed more like a gnome or wicked troll than a human being.

"What is it, Alsop?"

"Dinner is served, sir. As you requested, sir. By the fire, sir," stated the servant, ogling the girl's long lithe legs.

"That'll be all, Alsop," dismissed Benedict.

"You wanted me to clean and press her ladyship's clothes, sir?" whined the servant, craning his neck to better see more of Angelica's bared skin.

"Later, Alsop!"

"My lady? Ladyship's clothes?" queried Angel as the door was shut hastily by the little old servant, who heeded the implicit warning in the peer's tone. "Who's that?" she squealed as sudden shrill calls for a Willie were heard echoing through the still night.

"Willie is the stable boy," replied Taran, unwilling to admit the lengths he had gone to protect his unknown charge's reputation. He had entered the small sleepy village of Blackfield that afternoon to find it a seething pit of gossip. News of Lady Isabella Bonny's prowess with the horsewhip was rampant. The innocent scene in the bedchamber had been expanded to an orgy, with Angel playing the starring role.

"Why did Alsop call me 'my lady'?" repeated Angel after a silence where she perused his dark features.

"I thought I explained that," stated Taran carefully. "I went to the village to reassure the people that you did not have the plague. I described you as my wife in order to protect your reputation," he recounted, preferring not to inform her of his chivalry in appearing the blackguard to the villagers, who now thought Angel was a poor wronged wife who had suffered cruelly at the hands of his evil mistress.

"How did you know I had a reputation to protect?" asked Angel bravely as she remembered waking up beside him in the bed.

"I didn't," answered Lord Taran cuttingly, expecting an indignant reaction, but to his surprise Angel just gazed up at him thoughtfully with her amazing sea-green eyes, which sparked with amber lights in the lantern glow. What was it about the female that intrigued him so? he tried to fathom.

"I don't have the appearance of a whore, do I?" she asked, looking back in the mirror.

"How is a whore meant to look?" laughed Taran, in spite of himself.

"Pretty and little. Kittenlike, I suppose."

"The way Alsop has been ogling you, I think you had better wear this," he said, taking the enormous, multicaped driving coat out of the armoire. "On second thought, a blanket will be more practical," he added, plucking a cover off the bed and wrapping it about her shoulders before picking her up in his arms and striding out to the central room, where a cosy fire blazed in the hearth.

What was it about the unknown Angel? he mused as he watched the reflection of the flames play on the planes of her face. She was by her own admission no beauty—she was too coltish and awkward—but there was something that caused a catch in his throat. A certain quality that made him instinctively want to protect and comfort her. A certain undefinable quality that made her very dangerous, he decided as he ate ravenously of the sumptuous meal that Alsop had provided.

Angel watched Taran's face as he stared into the fire, noting the play of emotions. One moment his face seemed almost boyish and approachable and the next it hardened into a severe merciless mask.

"What if I never remember?" she said aloud to herself.

"Eat something. You need to regain your strength," he said coldly as similar thoughts roiled in his mind. What was he going to do with her?

"I've had enough."

"Drink this," he ordered, handing her a glass of rich burgundy.

"Thank you," said Angel, accepting the glass, thinking it more diplomatic than to refuse.

"Drink it," he repeated as she tried to furtively put it down, and she obediently took a little sip. He laughed harshly as he recognised an angry glint in her eyes and knew she longed to throw the contents in his face. "It is a medical fact that red wine helps strengthen the blood," he informed her as she walked over to a full bookcase and perused the titles. "You can read?"

"Apparently," she answered, raising her glass to him in a mock toast and taking a large gulp. She grinned mischievously at him. "This is very pleasant tonic. It warms all the way down," she added before draining the glass and holding it out for a refill.

"I would prefer you to savour the wine and not drink it like lemonade. I dislike inebriated females."

"You have a great deal of dislikes," sighed Angel, raising one well-shaped eyebrow at him before continuing her scrutiny of the books. "*The Works of William Shakespeare*," she proclaimed, reaching up for the large volume. A great shower of sooty dust was dislodged and she sneezed and coughed, flapping her hands about trying to clear the air. " 'Would it not grieve a woman to be overmastered with a piece of valiant dust?' " she chuckled when her choking fit had abated.

" 'To make an account of her life to a clod of wayward marl'?" supplied Taran, finishing the quotation.

"Well, I am most impressed. It would seem you know your *Much Ado About Nothing*," praised Angel. "Is it vanity because the name Benedick is used?" she quipped. "Benedick the married man?" she teased.

" 'What! my dear Lady Disdain,' " quoted Taran. "Just a moment, there is a perfect piece of prose I learned at school," he muttered, holding up his hand for silence as he concentrated, trying to remember. " 'She speaks poniards, and every word stabs: if her breath were as terrible as her terminations, there were no living near her; she would infect the north star.' "

Angelica shivered at the contempt that rang with the words. She shook her head sadly as she tried to recall a lighter, happier passage, but the carefree banter of a few minutes before was shattered. She replaced the volume and crossed to the wine bottle. She poured herself half a glass and sat on the couch looking into the dark-red liquid morosely. Taran watched her silently.

"How did I get hurt?" she asked softly, not daring to look up at him.

" 'The venom clamors of a jealous woman, poison more deadly than a mad dog's tooth,' " he cited savagely, filling his own glass to the brim.

"*Comedy of Errors*," she whispered.

"It is a comedy of errors all right." He sighed, throwing himself into a chair by the hearth and gloomily staring into the glowing coals.

"What has that to do with the whip marks?" Angel ventured after a long ticking silence.

"They were inflicted by a jealous woman," Taran stated harshly.

"Why?"

"You were ill and I was tending to you. The situation was misread," he explained tersely.

"I don't understand. Do I know this woman?" floundered Angel.

"No!"

"Have I done something wrong?"

"Enough of your whining questions!" shouted Taran, feeling guilty at the sight of her stricken face. Angel froze at the incredible rage that emanated from him. She wanted to escape from the room and hide under the covers in the bed, but she couldn't move. She stared into her wine glass as she fought the aching tears that welled and desperately tried to stop her hand from trembling. Taran groaned as he watched her brave attempt to control herself. He felt as though he had just hit a defenseless fawn, kicked the shakey legs right out from under her.

"I am angry at myself," he confessed as a large tear plopped into Angel's wineglass. She nodded as a sign she had heard, not trusting herself to speak. "Angel, look at me," he begged, but she kept her eyes lowered, remembering how he despised hysteria. Taran groaned as another tear plopped into the glass.

"I am quite all right," she started in a strange jerky voice, and she resolutely drank from her glass.

"Salty?" he teased, and she gave a sobbing gurgly laugh that he found so endearing that without a second thought, he had her clasped in his arms. "What am I going to do with you, you absurd Angel?" he murmured into her chestnut hair. She didn't answer, but she cuddled close to his warm strength not wanting to think of anything.

Alsop entered to clear the supper things and clucked disapprovingly at the sight that met his eyes. Lord Taran lay fast asleep on the large couch in front of the hearth with the long-legged female clasped in his arms. The indecent shirt she was wearing had ridden up exposing naked thighs and calves. Alsop sucked in his breath; just the sight of a well-turned hosed ankle usually had an arousing effect. This was too much for a God-fearing, religious man, he seethed. What the gentry got up to was not fit for decent, simple folk to see, he fumed, tiptoing about the room and peering at the sleeping couple from every angle.

CHAPTER 4

"SHE'S 'ERE! Mr. Smithers 'as gone and found 'er! Our Miss Angel's 'ome!" screeched Wilkins, getting herself entangled in the layers of lace curtains that swathed the windows of the front parlour.

"Stop screaming like a common fishwife," panted Mrs. Smithers as she and Cook trotted out of the kitchen. She sighed and rolled her eyes heavenward as Lady Mellie's bell rang imperiously. "Now, seeing as you have gone and woke up her ladyship, you can see what she wants."

"But I ain't 'er maid, I'm Miss Angel's," whined Wilkins.

"You do as you're told or you won't be anybody's anything," threatened the old lady, giving her a shove before straightening her cap and apron and opening the door.

Wilkins sullenly backed towards the stairs, craning her neck to catch a glimpse of her young mistress while Cook stood unobtrusively in the shadows by the kitchen door wiping her hands on a dishcloth.

"Yoo 'oo! Miss Angel!" trilled Wilkins saucily through the banister rails, but seeing Mrs. Smithers's furious look, she scampered out of sight to answer the incessantly ringing bell.

"Oh, Miss Angelica, it does my old heart good to see you. You had us worrying ourselves into an early grave, you did," scolded Mrs. Smithers as she ushered the dazed young woman into the dim hallway. "What are you poking me for, Mr. Ess?" she snapped, turning furiously on her husband, who shook his head warningly at her. "What's wrong?" she demanded.

61

"Miss Angel's 'ad a long, very tiring journey and what she needs is a nice 'ot cuppa tea and to be tucked into 'er own cosy bed away from a lot of questions," informed the wiry old man. "This is Mrs. Smithers, your grandmother's housekeeper, Miss Angel, she'll show you to your room," he said gently, seeing the panic flare in her green eyes.

"What are you talking stuff and nonsense for, Mr. Ess? Miss Angel knows her own Mrs. Smithers, don't you luvey?"

"She's lost her memory," whispered her husband. "The poor girl can't remember a bloomin' thing."

"Oh, my! Well, we'll find it for you, just you wait and see. There's nothing what a good cuppa tea and a good night's sleep can't do," she soothed, leading the girl up the stairs. "Your poor battered little face," she chattered, not knowing how to deal with the situation except to fill in the somehow oppressive silence.

Angelica felt like she was in a nightmare as she was led through the strange house. Everything seemed shrouded in clouds of pink netting, muting the colours and the light. An army of alabaster busts on marble pedestals lined the walls amid powdery arrangements of dead grasses and bleached dried flowers. The predominant colour and feeling was of a vague cloying pink, a perfumed, suffocating atmosphere that choked her nose and throat.

"That's the way, Miss Angel. Everything's going to be as right as rain. You're home all safe and sound," crooned Mrs. Smithers as they reached the second landing of the winding staircase which was carpetted in a thick pastel rose. "You'll feel better after a good night's sleep," soothed the old woman, ushering the girl into a large bedchamber that was cluttered with alabaster busts and Dresden ornaments and shrouded with yard upon yard of suffocating pink netting. The voluminous gauze smothered the windows, the bed, the overstuffed love seat and chairs, looping across the ceiling and about the door.

"Is this my room?"

"Don't you remember it?"

Angel shook her head and recalled Taran's sardonic words about remembering things better left forgotten. This was a room that screamed to be forgotten. "Please, I must open a window," she whispered, feeling she was being strangled by the filmy draperies.

"Oh, no, Miss Angel, you're forgetting yourself!" exclaimed the old woman. "Oh, dear, I'm so sorry," she added, realizing her unfortunate choice of words. "But your grandmother forbids it. She's old, but don't tell her I told you, and she's susceptible to chills," she chattered. "Oh, my lor', there goes her bell again. Wilkins must have told her you were home. Here's your nightgown," she added, laying a frothy pink robe on the shiny pink bed and trotting to the door. "I'll be right back, luvey."

Angelica sat on the bed trying to control the panic that pounded through her. The sickly scent of stale powder and perfume choked her and the cloying heat of the cluttered room made her nauseated and faint. Did she really belong in this thick, pink environment? she wondered, trying to find suitable adjectives to describe her surroundings and wishing she were back in the rustic retreat in the salt marshes.

"Miss Angel?" hissed Wilkins, popping her pert little face right into Angel's line of vision so she gave a startled gasp. "Sorry about that but I knocked and knocked. You must've bin daydreamin'," she conversed. "Cor, look at yer poor muggins! 'o 'it you?" Angelica looked at her blankly. "Are you all right?"

"Who are you?"

" 'o am I? Me?" Wilkins laughed, pointing at herself. "I'm Wilkins, yer own personal maid, at yer service! Don't yer remember?" Angelica shook her head sadly. "Oh, my lor', yer poor ole thing. 'ere, let's 'elp you off with yer ridin' 'abit and get you all tucked inter yer pretty bed. Ain't this a luverly room . . . like bein' in the clouds . . . just the right room fer an Angel," soothed the younger girl. "What the bloody 'ell 'appened to yer back?" she asked inelegantly, seeing the whipmarks. "Cor, you didn't 'alf get a wallopin' from someone," she observed. " 'ad an 'ard time of it, 'ave you ducks?" she asked, gently touching the cut cheek where a tear trickled slowly. "Life ain't kind ter females on their ownsomes, is it? Well, yer 'ome now and Iris Wilkins won't let anybody else raise an 'and to you again. 'ere, in you pop,'' she ordered, pulling the bedcovers back.

Angelica listlessly obeyed, her thoughts miles away as she wondered what Taran would do when he returned to find her gone. He had left for London to fetch clothes and his own servants prior to driving her to his family seat in Cornwall. He had hired a good-natured village woman to keep Alsop true to his religious convictions and then had ridden off, promising to return within the next three days. He would probably be entering their rustic retreat that very evening and be exceedingly relieved to find himself free of her, she decided sorrowfully, staring tearfully up at a host of fat pink cherubs who floated merrily on the ceiling.

"You should see 'er back! She's bin flogged! 'orsewhipped!'' recounted Wilkins to her rapt audience of Cook and two scullery maids named Simms and Sykes. "Terrible it is! 'er poor face 'as bin bashed up, too.''

"You think 'er memory's really gone?'' gasped Sykes. Wilkins nodded solemnly. "Cor blimey!''

"She can't even remember 'er own room! Not even 'er own Granny. Cor, you should 'ave seen when she went in ter see 'er ladyship. Poor thing walked right up to the old girl! 'Get back! Get back!' screams Lady Em and then when Miss Angel don't understand, 'er ladyship threw 'er eidie-down over 'er 'ead,'' giggled Wilkins with her mouth full. "Give us more bread, Cook?''

"What 'appened then?'' asked Cook.

"Mrs. Ess dragged poor Miss Angel outa the room. Ooh, you should 'ave 'eard her ladyship's language. Every dirty word I know and a few more.''

"Ain't no wonder she's lost her memory from what I 'ear,'' observed the cook with a smug look of victory on her fat face.

"What did you 'ear?'' challenged Wilkins.

"I 'eard that there was fine goins-on in Blackfield, enough ter curl yer ears.''

"What?'' mouthed the enraptured Sykes.

"Orgies.''

"Go on!''

"Really. Orgies just like them Romans with the grapes and sheets," pronounced Cook, and Sykes and Simms sat with their full mouths agape.

"Miss Angel at an orgy? Come off it!" laughed Wilkins.

"Cross me 'eart and 'ope ter die!" swore Cook. "I 'eard Mr. Ess tellin' Mrs. Ess. 'e says the 'ole of the New Forest was scandalized by the goins-on. Our Miss Angel as naked as the day she was born rollin' about on a big bed with—"

"You 'ave ter be 'avin' us on!" interrupted Wilkins, getting irritated with the fat woman, who now had Simms and Sykes holding on to her every word, not taking their wide eyes off her as they shovelled the food into their slack mouths.

" 'ard ter imagine, ain't it," chuckled the fat woman. "Don't look the type, do she? Looks like butter wouldn't melt in her innocent little mouth. Oh, she might look like an old vinegar maid, but seems as like our Miss Angel ain't no better than an 'ore."

" 'ere, 'ere, Cook! That ain't no way to talk! I thought you liked 'er!" protested Wilkins.

"I did but it makes me bloody angry ter think of all the worryin' we did and all the time she was 'avin' a fine old time of it."

" 'avin' 'er face bashed in? 'avin' her back and tits flogged is 'avin' a fine old time of it?" spat Wilkins.

"Well, she arsked fer it, didn't she? Runnin' off like that without a chaperon?" goaded Cook. "I wager she was 'avin' a fine old time with Lord Carringdon, too."

" 'ere, that's enough filth outa your gob!" hissed Wilkins.

"Oh, deary me, I think Wilkins is jealous," stated the cook, picking up a large carving knife. "Now, where was I?"

"Miss Angel was stark naked on a bed," prompted Simms.

"Right, she was as naked as the day she was born with about four men."

"Four men?!" chorused the scullery maids.

"And there was another woman dressed in flamin' red with an 'orsewhip," related Cook with relish.

"Disgustin'," breathed Sykes, so entranced she leaned forward putting both elbows into her supper.

"I think you lot are disgustin'," spat Wilkins. "One minute yer all blubberin' cos you think Miss Angel's dead, but as soon as she turns up, yer stabbin' 'er in the back and sayin' filthy things about 'er!'' she screamed before slamming out of the kitchen.

" 'ere maybe we was bein' a bit 'ard on Miss Angel,'' said Cook. "Let's keep it to ourselves. I wouldn't want Mrs. Ess 'earin' about it.''

Wilkins stormed up the carpeted stairs to Miss Angel's room, not knowing why she was so furious. Very quietly she opened the door and peeked in. Angelica lay with her eyes wide open.

"Miss Angel? It's me, Wilkins,'' she whispered.

"Come in.''

"Do you remember anything yet?'' asked the maid, sitting on the edge of the bed.

"No and I'm finding everything somehow terrifying,'' confessed Angelica.

"Like what? Oh, you mean yer granny? She's 'armless,'' comforted Wilkins. "Leastwise, I think she is. A bit strange, that's all,'' she added, unwilling to admit the old woman gave her the willies. "Yer 'ome now. There ain't nothin' ter be afraid of 'ceptin' some mean mouths.''

"What do you mean?''

"Nothin'. 'ere tell us what else scares you?''

"Everything.''

"Yeah, it must be somethin' not bein' able to even remember yer own name,'' sympathized Wilkins.

"Tell me about myself?'' asked Angelica, sitting up and moving closer to the maid.

"Well, like what? I 'aven't bin 'ere that long. Just a few months. Mrs. Ess 'ired me from the work 'ouse after you got 'ere.''

"After I got here?'' repeated Angel. "Where was I before?''

"I don't know . . . in the country somewhere with yer family,'' answered Wilkins.

"Family?''

"Yeah, yer mum and dad. Yer granny and yer mum don't get on from what I 'ear. Seems yer mum run off . . . eloped with yer dad, so yer granny didn't talk to them until you was eighteen.''

"I'm eighteen?"

"Nineteen."

"So I've been here for a year?"

"More! 'er ladyship 'as bin tryin' ter turn you inter a fine lady so you'll marry an 'andsome duke or something, like she wanted yer mum ter marry."

Angelica digested this piece of cryptic information and had to laugh at the way Wilkins stressed the word *trying*.

"I gather my grandmother wasn't very successful," she remarked wryly.

"With what?"

"Turning me into a fine lady?"

"It ain't that, Miss Angel. It's cos she's tryin' ter turn you inter 'er, if you see what I mean?"

"I can't say that I do."

"Well, it's like this. 'ave a look at them dresses," said Wilkins, shimmying off the bed and opening the armoire door to exhibit a row of frilly gowns in various shades of pink. "I don't mean ter be forward or nothin', Miss Angel, but they are ever so pretty and would look very nice on me, bein' little and dark, but you're another story altogether. Yer tall and . . . well . . . regal. . . . Now, don't laugh. You are. That's why some think yer 'aughty but you ain't. I know you ain't. You got all this luverly dark red 'air what don't look good with pink and that's a fact all right. The only clothes you 'ave that show you off proper is yer green ridin' 'abit," chattered the girl, watching Angelica examine the contents of the armoire.

Angelica stared about the room at the numerous alabaster busts. Each white profile was identical. She had a furious desire to sweep them off their marble pedestals, and at the thought a nightmarish image clawed into her mind. She saw a smashed painted mask that her trembling hands tried to reassemble as the garish disembodied mouth berated.

"That was yer granny when she was young. Some say she was ever so pretty, but it ain't to my taste," said Wilkins seeing Angelica's intense fascination with the alabaster busts.

"They are all the same?"

"Yeah, every larst one of them. There's fifty-three. One of yer granny's 'usbands 'ad about an 'undred made. Some are in 'er town 'ouse in London and the others got broke, I suppose. They give me the creeps, if you wanna know.''

''I agree with you,'' laughed Angelica, finding the thought of a hundred identical alabaster busts of her grandmother more than a little ludicrous and intimidating. ''Now, tell me more about myself.''

''Well, there ain't really much more,'' confessed the girl, not knowing quite what to say.

''When did I leave here and why?''

''You run off about a week ago,'' she said unhappily. Angel silently pondered this new piece of information.

''Why did I?'' she asked in a small voice.

''I dunno,'' shrugged Wilkins. ''You left a note but I can't read. But I think it must 'ave 'ad ter do with 'ow 'er ladyship nags and picks at you all the time . . . and then there's 'is lordship.''

''His lordship? Do I have a beau?''

''Not likely!'' exclaimed Wilkins. ''Oh, I didn't mean it like that, Miss Angel, but there ain't been no beaux. 'er ladyship 'as these awful midnight soirees cos she don't want ter be seen in the daytime, and it seems there ain't many eligible lords who care for midnight soirees in Wimbledon. Leastwise not at Lady Em's.''

''Lady Em?''

''That's yer granny. 'ere, let's see if I can get it right. 'er name is Lady Melisande, I think it's really a fancy way of sayin' Millicent, yer know. Lady Melisande Moreby-Wentworth-Fowler. 'ow about that fer a monicker? Moreby, Wentworth, and Fowler were 'er 'usbands. All dead.''

''Who's Lord Carringdon?''

''Yer granny's fiancé. Maybe it's a good job you've forgot 'im,'' informed the maid.

''Why?''

''Well, you broke 'is fingers. Oh, it weren't your fault. 'e 'ad it comin', the 'orney old geezer.''

''I broke his fingers?'' repeated Angel.

''Four of 'em,'' Wilkins informed her with gusto.

''So I ran away about a week ago?''

''That's right. Mrs. Ess thought as 'ow you was trying ter

go 'ome ter yer mum and dad cos you got a coach up on the Common at the postin' stop.''

Angelica frowned, trying to picture herself, but nothing Wilkins said was familiar. "Where is my home?''

Wilkins shrugged. "My geography ain't there. If you say the name of the place, I'll know it though,'' she offered eagerly, and then laughed at herself for her silliness. "If you could do that, you wouldn't 'ave any need fer me to 'elp, would you?''

"I can't tell you how glad I am to have your help,'' whispered Angelica, giving the younger girl an impulsive hug. "Now, tell me about the 'mean mouths' you mentioned earlier?''

"I can't,'' answered Wilkins, shaking her head. "Honest, I can't. It weren't nothin', Miss Angel. Just spiteful, lazy sluts who ain't got nothin' better to do.''

"Maybe you had better tell me so I can protect myself,'' said Angel after a long silence.

"Well, the talk in the kitchen is that you weren't found alone. That there was . . . er . . . men,'' recounted Wilkins awkwardly. Angel nodded, thinking of Taran and Alsop. "There was?'' gasped Wilkins. "Oh, well, they ain't too broadminded and well think you're a . . . well . . . what do they know, aye?''

"It wasn't very circumspect, was it?''

"I wouldn't know, Miss Angel, 'cept it ain't what a person would expect of you,'' struggled the maid.

"What would a person expect of me? Describe me, Wilkins.''

"Well, you ain't—or at least you wasn't—what a person would call . . . er . . . flighty. You like books and museums. Oh, you got me inter 'ot water a coupla times when yer granny found out. Mind you, some of them statues were a bit . . . well . . . you know. All them bodies with tits and dicks.''

"Not on the same statue, I hope,'' giggled Angel, and at that Wilkins went into peals of laughter.

"You ain't like the rest of them. I told Cook that when you was gone, I did,'' gurgled the maid.

"Like the rest of what?''

"You know, gentry?"

"Why did I break Lord Carringdon's fingers?"

"Never let go, do yer?" giggled Wilkins. "You was just teachin' im ter keep 'is 'ands to 'isself."

"But how?" questioned Angel, not able to imagine herself snapping anybody's fingers no matter what the provocation.

"' e did 'is usual. Put 'is 'and on the seat of the chair just as you was about to sit down. That way 'e gets a bit of a feel, if you see what I mean? Well, I suppose you sat down 'arder than usual and what with the buckram they're usin' in corsets these day . . . well, you must 'ave ground yer bum a bit and what with your boney backside and the whalebone—crack! And there you 'ave it! Four busted fingers!" She snickered.

"Oh, Wilkins, I am so glad you are here," sighed Angel when she was able to stop laughing. "Do you have another name?"

"Iris. I think it's a flower."

"It is, a very beautiful one."

"Me mum called us all names like that. There was me sister Rose and me sister Daisy."

"Was?"

"Dead. So's me mum. 'er name was Gladys Williams. She was from Cardiff, that's in Wales, yer know."

"And your father?"

"Never 'ad one. Me name's meant ter be Iris Williams, but there was another Williams at the work'ouse so they called me Wilkins instead. Don't make no difference ter me now. At first I didn't know 'o they was talkin' to," she tittered. "They must 'ave thought I was deaf or potty," she added, remembering the many beatings she had received for not instantly obeying.

Angelica caught the momentary vulnerability that was quickly covered with a cocky bravado. "I think we need each other," she said softly, feeling great affection for the indomitable little maid.

"And you need yer sleep," retorted Wilkins brusquely, not used to sentiment.

"How old are you, Iris?" asked Angel as the younger girl tucked her into the awful pink bed.

"Fifteen."

"I should be tucking you in," whispered Angelica, staring about the strange cluttered room.

"I could sleep in yer dressin' room if it'd make yer feel better," offered the maid, recognising the fear in the wide green eyes. "There's quite a comfy cot in there. I just 'ave ter pop down and tell Mrs. Ess so she don't think I'm out on the tiles," she chattered.

"Are you sure you don't mind?"

"If you could see the leaky rat 'ole that I share with Simms and Sykes, you wouldn't arsk such a potty question," giggled Wilkins.

"Simms and Sykes?"

"Scullery sluts and they don't 'alf snore," she snorted. "Now don't you fret none cos I'll be back in two shakes of a lamb's tail."

The door closed behind the vivacious little maid and Angel's head span with nightmarish glimpses of her brittle painted grandmother, whose numerous alabaster effigies seemed to stare accusingly from all corners of the shrouded room, and the dark brooding features of Benedict Tremayne of Taran.

Iris was about to knock on the Smitherses' parlour door, but hearing the intensity of the raised voices within instead pressed a keen ear to better hear the heated conversation.

"Tremayne of Taran and you didn't tell Lady Em?" shrieked Mrs. Ess for about the tenth time. "Why, Mr. Ess? Just tell me why? Lord Taran hisself, the richest, most eligiblest in London and you didn't think it fit or proper to tell her ladyship!" she continued, not giving her poor husband a chance to answer. "Well, why? Go on, Mr. Ess, tell me why?" she demanded.

"I told you," grumbled the old man as he buttoned his nightshirt.

"You told me! You told me!" spluttered his enraged wife. "You told me you didn't think it your place! You told me it weren't fit or proper! Well, was it fit or proper for Lord Taran to take advantage of our Miss Angel?"

"It ain't fit nor proper fer it to be told. It could damage 'er reputation, so I'm warnin' you Mrs. Ess to keep yer trap shut," hissed her forbearing husband.

"How dare you talk ter me like that, Mr. Smithers! Keep my trap shut indeed! I'll have you know that . . ." she ranted, following her husband into their bedroom and slamming the door with such violence Iris felt the concussion reverberate through her. She swore softly as she strained to hear more of the conversation. Realizing it was impossible, she knocked sharply.

"Who is it?" demanded Mrs. Smithers crossly.

"Me, Wilkins."

"What are you doing hanging about at this time of night?" asked the old woman suspiciously as she opened the door.

"I've bin wif Miss Angel," informed Iris, sidling into the room. "Cor blimey, seems there were some fine goings-on in the New Forest." She sighed cunningly, hoping to glean additional information.

"Like what?" snapped Mrs. Smithers.

"I ain't at liberty to say," replied Wilkins. "'ceptin' my mistress is fair done in and can't be alone, poor luvey."

"Oh, I'll go right up," fussed the old woman, patting her grey hair, which was tightly tied up with screws of rags.

"Ain't no need. She wants me ter sleep in 'er dressin' room. So you just pop inter yer cosy bed wif Mr. Ess. Men! Gawd! I'd like ter shoot the 'ole bloody lotta them!"

"Here, sit a bit," offered Mrs. Smithers, patting the sofa and settling herself.

"Well, just fer a bit, cos my poor mistress needs me," confessed the girl, sitting herself next to the old woman, who was bundled in a grey flannel nightgown and winter coat.

"What has she told you?"

"I told you that I ain't at liberty, but I'll tell you this, if I 'ad my way the bloody bastard would be made ter marry 'er, lord or no lord! 'o the bloody 'ell do men think they is, aye? Take advantage of a refined innocent lady and 'spect ter get off scot free?" ranted Iris. "I think Lady Mellie should see to it. Should move us to the London 'ouse, throw a big ball and announce our Miss Angel's engagement to 'is lordship. 'ere, why are you lookin' at me like that, Missus Ess?"

Mrs. Smithers exchanged a long look with her husband,

who stood at the bedchamber door glaring suspiciously at the two women.

"Go see to yer mistress, Wilkins," growled the old man.

"Yes, sir," replied Iris. "That poor Miss Angel don't even know 'er own name nor 'er own face in the mirror," she said, closing the door behind her and then pressing her ear to the wooden panel.

"Wilkins has a very good point," observed Mrs. Smithers. "I think her ladyship should know."

"I don't! Knowin' 'er ladyship, she'll make a great to-do. Cause an 'elluva scandal and the bloody man won't marry our girl and what'll we 'ave gained? Aye?"

"Yer right, Mr. Ess. What we should do is somehow convince Lady Mellie it's time ter move to the London house. Then we can plan a few parties at a decent hour and send Lord you-know-who an invitation," plotted the old woman.

"And 'ow do you 'ope ter convince 'er ladyship? You know she 'ates London," laughed Mr. Smithers, pouring himself a generous mug of stout.

"Just leave that to me, old man. Now that winter's on its way, this old house can get quite uncomfy what with the draughts and faulty flues belchin' dirty smoke all over Lady Em's lovely alabaster busts," chuckled Mrs. Smithers wickedly. "Her townhouse in Moreby Gardens will seem ever so inviting after all the horrible little catastrophes that are going to happen, just you wait and see."

Iris pursed her lips together to stifle her giggles of excitement as she crept away from the Smitherses' door and scampered up the stairs to Miss Angelica's room. She knocked gently and at no reply carefully opened the door and popped her head in. "Miss Angel? Are you awake?" she hissed eagerly, nearly bursting with the exciting news she wanted to share. "Miss Angel?" she whispered as she approached the bed. She gazed down at the tear-stained sleeping face feeling a mixture of disappointment and protectiveness. "Oh, Miss Angel, everythink's goin' ter be all right," she crooned softly, gently wiping the salty drops from her mistress's .smooth cheeks. "Iris Wilkins is goin' ter take care of you and we're goin' ter London ter see the King and the Queen and the palace . . . and we'll 'ave parties and fancy balls . . . and get you married off to the richest, eligiblest lord in all of London . . . and we'll never 'ave ter be cold or 'ungry . . . never 'ave ter 'ore fer a few coppers again . . . we'll live 'appily ever after,'' she rejoiced as she turned the wick down on the bedside lamp so the cluttered room was bathed in a warm softening glow.

Iris undressed and neatly folded her maid's uniform before curling under the thin scratchy blanket on the hard narrow cot in the adjoining dressing room. "Yeah, everythink's goin' ter be roses. We'll live 'appily ever after in a big posh 'ouse in London. Gawd, I 'ope Lord Taran ain't an old fatty with stinkin' black teef,'' she sighed as she fell asleep.

CHAPTER 5

TORR PENDARVES was suffocating in dense darkness. Excruciating pain knifed through him, and he was unable to move, yet a rhythmic rolling pitched him from side to side. He strained his eyes, desperately and vainly trying to pierce the blackness. Panic threatened to tip him over the brink into madness and he forced himself to reason carefully. Where was he? He smelled salt, brandy, and decaying flesh, he noted as he was smashed against a hard object. He clawed at it and damp wood left stinging slivers down his torn nails. A barrel, he surmised, groping at the splintery slats and metal bands, and the rhythmic keeling caused by a rough sea. He was on a boat buried beneath a shelter of some kind, because he couldn't see the sky nor feel the sharp salt spray. Not a breath of air stirred the fetid atmosphere, although he could hear the whining howl of a furious wind. It was raining or sleeting, he deduced from the thunderous drumming on taut material.

Where was he? Was he finally going home? The last coherent thing he remembered had been the deafening rumble of iron wheels over cobblestones that had painfully jarred through his damaged body. He had bitten his lips to keep the screams locked within him, because somehow he was aware that he was a secret. Whatever happened it was imperative that he be silent or they all would die. They? Who were they? He had drifted in and out of consciousness, welcoming the crescendoing agony, knowing it heralded merciful nothingness. Now he was blind and virtually paralyzed; smothered by darkness being cruelly buffetted on a stormy sea. Suddenly he sensed that he was not alone. His skin prickled. He listened intently, his noisy heart pounding painfully through his rigid body, joining with the tempo of the battering wind and the rise and fall of the waves. The suspense of listening stretched his nerves as taut as the ropes and canvas that twanged in the driving gale until he couldn't hear. He couldn't see. He couldn't breathe. The thick night air was seeping inexorably up his nostrils and down his throat, stopping the passages and weighing his chest so it couldn't expand. He was swimming blindly through deep molasses, desperately trying to reach the surface . . . to break free of the stickiness that dragged him down. There was no surface . . . no air in which to throw back his head and gulp the life-giving coolness. Summoning all his energy, he opened his mouth and tried to scream, but a laboured grunt burst from his exploding lungs.

"Shut him up, there's a revenue cutter close," hissed a harsh voice. The pressure on his nose and mouth increased, further shutting off his breathing. He fought, mindless of the agony that stabbed through his whole body; he was unable to scream. He forced his mouth open and sank his teeth into the object that pressed against his face and had the fleeting satisfaction at hearing a muffled cry before he again lost all sense of time and place.

The impenetrable blackness had lightened to a monotonous grey. Above him the black-winged gulls wheeled and wailed against the dreary sky. He shivered violently as the rain beaded thickly on his clothes and slowly seeped through causing his bones to ache. Everything was so cold and misty. He felt that he was floating on icy clouds. Would he ever be warm again? The boat rocked at anchor and noises filtered into his drifting consciousness. A clatter and rumbling reverberated along the wooden planks, getting sharper and sharper until the clamour cracked into his brittle freezing body. He moaned but the sound was mocked by the screeching gulls, drowned by the pandemonium of roaring voices, trundling barrels, and staccato bootsteps. Each sound shattering through until he brutally bucked his head against the hard deck, preferring to be the master of his own torture. In the midst of his agony he stared into a very beautiful face. He lay still, mesmerized by the enormous expressive eyes. Eyes so very dark and profound that they appeared almost purple. Eyes fringed with thick curling lashes where raindrops, or tears . . . or even precious jewels . . . hung suspended. He was entranced by the exquisite features.

"Is the poor sod alive?" growled a rough voice, and the beautiful young being nodded a tousled ebony head. "What about the others?" This time the dark head shook sadly, and with great difficulty Torr turned his aching head to see what caused such sorrow. Two men lay partially covered by a heavy tarpaulin, the rain streaming off the stiff material onto a motionless, marbled profile, and splashing over the busy rats that availed themselves of the barely cooled flesh. There was something about the rag-wrapped shoes and soiled striped trousers that caused his stomach to convulse. He felt as though he were drowning in a seething mass of rats and vomit.

He awoke again, seeing giant shadows darting up and down sheer wet rocks. The reflection of a fire sent flaming tongues across the frightening features of a witchlike crone who stirred an iron cauldron and intoned unintelligible incantations. From the surrounding darkness, he heard furtive rustles and the rattle of chains. He was neither hot nor cold, yet he lay naked on a long stone slab. His head was propped so he could see the length of his lacerated body and the horrendous gaping wound in his upper thigh. He stared at his manhood lying curled and relaxed. It was still there. There had been so many days and weeks of excruciating pain shooting through his groin that he had been firmly convinced of his own castration. He reached down to touch himself and the old hag cackled.

"E'en on his deathbed a man has lusty thoughts! E'en on his deathbed a man holds on to his own root like maybe 'tis the key to heaven's gate!" she chortled. He heard a husky mischievous giggle. Torr turned his head and once more gazed into the poignant little face with the incredible luminous eyes. He smiled at the beautiful vision, feeling happy and euphoric, free from all pain and worry. He breathed deeply of the unfamiliar but not unpleasant aroma of medicinal herbs, which relieved the heaviness that had painfully restricted his chest.

"Is this England?" he managed to ask, his tongue feeling thick and tangled as though he were drunk.

"Nay, 'tis Cornwall," was the crone's terse reply. He gurgled with delight, knowing that to the Cornish, Cornwall was no part of England but a country separate and superior. He chuckled, feeling a golden happiness, longing to tell them that he was also Cornish and that his middle name was Tamar, for the river that divided Cornwall from England, but he couldn't stop laughing long enough to formulate the words.

"Make thyself useful, Devil-Child. Tie the hot poultices about the wound. Thy young hands are more nimble than mine," ordered the hag. The exquisite little face frowned and stared down at a splayed palm.

"I cannot, Granny-Griggs."

"What is et? Show me, Devil-Child."

Torr's happy euphoria fled as the small hand was raised exhibiting cruel teeth marks across the heel. He ran his tongue across the sharp edges of his teeth, feeling them ache and pulsate. He wanted to say he was sorry, but he could make no sound. He sat up and reached to comfort but there was a sudden threatening growl and a huge black creature leaped out of the shadows and onto the stone slab, pushing him back with an immense paw. Torr lay gaping up at the gleaming fangs and the fiery eyeballs, feeling the beast's hot breath and warm saliva drip onto his face and chest.

"No, Bucca-Dhu!" screamed the Devil-Child.

"Oh, God," mumbled Torr. He had been shot, stabbed, burned, and dragged countless tortuous miles only to find himself home in Cornwall, lying naked like a sacrificial lamb on a pagan altar about to be devoured by the Bucca-Dhu. The absolute ludicrousness of the situation surged in and he shook with helpless laughter; his voice sounding high-pitched and maniacal, which served to increase his mirth.

"Down, Bucca-Dhu," repeated the Devil-Child, and the monster gave Torr a slobbering lick across the face before bounding obediently to the floor of the cave.

"Who bit thy hand?" hissed the hag. The child exchanged a rueful grin with Torr and shrugged narrow shoulders. "Thet's no fourlegged creature's bite," and again there was a careless shrug. "Well, whatever has done et has left its claiming mark on thee for the run of thy life! 'Tes bit clear to the bone!''

Again the child smiled reassuringly, and Torr felt guilt like a thousand ants crawling just beneath his skin. His bodily pain was numbed, yet somehow his senses were heightened and raw. The sight of the small hurt hand throbbed achingly, looming larger and larger, the twin crescents from his jaws forever printed, each tooth wound stabbing at his eyeballs.

"So sorry, Devil-Child. So sorry, Devil-Child," he mouthed, unaware of the tears that poured down his unshaven cheeks.

"All right, thee Living-Dead, make thyselves useful here. The lad's going to need strong hands to hold him down and more potion to ease the agony of his healing," spat Granny-Griggs as she dipped a wooden stick into the bubbling cauldron and hauled out a steaming poultice of boiling mud and leaves. The darkness of the vast cavern came alive with hissing shadows that shuffled closer.

Torr gazed at the wetness on the Devil-Child's smooth cheeks as he obediently drank the euphoria-producing elixir. Why was the beautiful demon crying? he wondered abstractedly, forgetting all about the cruelly bitten hand and the dark shades that moved to surround him, their chains clinking. One moment he was suspended in rosy happiness and the next his body arched against the unbelievable pain. He heard his own voice howling, joined by the eerie baying of the Bucca-Dhu as he was whirled away into circles of darkness.

"Devil-Child! I'm sorry, Devil-child," he screamed. How could he possibly have forgotten the terrible hurt he had inflicted? How could he have felt so carefree and elated when such grievous misery streamed from the luminous, fathomless eyes in the exquisite little face? "Devil-Child?"

Sir Torrance Pendarves gazed down helplessly at his oldest son, who writhed and screamed upon the bed, caught in the throes of yet another horrendous nightmare. In the week or so since his golden-haired namesake's miraculous return, his London house had rung with the young man's anguished voice that desperately summoned the macabre spirits of darkness, causing consternation amongst his superstitious servants. Being Londoners, they were blessedly ignorant of the Bucca-Dhu, the Cornish monster from the sea, but they were all too aware of demons and devils, witches and the living dead.

Mrs. Goodie, his housekeeper, gently sponged the suffering young face.

"Ain't no wonder the lad's half out of his skull what with that pagan concoction wrapped about that nasty wound. 'Tis a wonder his leg weren't crawling with maggots! 'Tis a wonder his leg didn't just drop off! All that filthy mud and weeds! 'Tis a wonder there was no putrefaction . . . not a sign nor smell of infection! Doctor Baldwin says as how 'twas a wonder and no mistake," chattered the apple-cheeked woman.

"Yes, it surely is a wonder. I never thought to see my son again in this life," wearily answered the tall old man, holding his child's sunburned hand in his. "He's a man now, isn't he? Four years ago he was a gangly callow youth . . . now look at him," he directed, his voice breaking with emotion as he surveyed the heavily bandaged but virile young man who filled the bed. "He's grown taller than I and I'm no bantam . . . filled out, too," he continued.

"A young god and no mistake," agreed Mrs. Goodie, tenderly brushing the thick golden hair back from the drawn but tanned face. Torr's eyes fluttered open and he stared silently at his father.

"You were dreaming again, son," stated the old man.

"Devils and demons and the like," sniffed the housekeeper. Torr silently gazed at his father, remembering his nightmares. The pulsating wound caused a sharp recollection. He attempted to move his limb, but there was just a paralyzing heaviness.

"Well, my boy, you're looking a hell of a lot better," remarked Sir Torrance awkwardly, not knowing what to say to the silent young man.

"Thanks to Goodie, the lice, fleas, and filth have fled this useless flesh," remarked Torr bitterly. The thought of living in a crippled state was unbearable.

"There's nothing amiss with your body that rest, good food, doctoring, and time won't heal," chided Mrs. Goodie.

"Be patient," comforted Sir Torrance. "You'll not be

gallivanting with the ladies for a while, but you must thank
God that you have a leg at all.''

"Aye, from what we hear, much higher and you'd be no
further use to the ladies at all," gurgled a mischievous voice,
and a blond youth sidled into the room followed by a younger
boy.

"Now, Master Ajax, is that any way to talk around an
innocent woman like me," scolded the middle-aged housekeeper, suppressing a chuckle as she bustled about smoothing
the bedcovers.

"You have to admit that that ugly scar across his cheek
gives rather a satanic sneer that I'm sure the ladies will find
positively irresistible," giggled the youngest boy.

"All right, Master Felix and Master Ajax, that's it. You
shouldn't be in here," stated Mrs. Goodie, noting the ticking
tension in the lean jaw and how the invalid looked pointedly
away from his younger brothers.

"No, let us stay. We'll be as quiet as mice," begged Felix.
"Won't we, Ajax?"

"You want us to stay, don't you, Torr?" cajoled Ajax,
but there was no response and the fourteen- and eighteen-year-
olds shrugged and sadly left their brother's room. Mrs. Goodie
bustled after them, closing the door, leaving father and son
alone together.

Torr felt the burden of his father's hands clutching his. He
wanted to pull away, to isolate himself in his own misery, but
he was too cowardly to behave so monstrously. He kept his
gaze averted, knowing his father's eyes never left his face.
The silence ticked.

"I thought you were dead," sobbed Sir Torrance, una-
shamed of the wetness that streamed down his lined face.

"There were . . . there are times I wish I were," stated
Torr, his eyes fixed blindly to the patterned wallpaper as he
remembered the preceding weeks of excruciating pain, hidden in farm carts, barns, cellars, and smuggling boats to
escape from France, only to arrive home as a useless cripple.

"You are safe now. Don't think of the horrors."

"And if I never walk again?"

"We'll deal with it," returned the old man huskily after a
pause, taken aback by his son's bitter ferocity.

"*We'll* deal with it?" asked Torr, and laughed sardonically.

"*You'll* deal with it," emended Sir Torrance, gently tracing the jagged scar that crossed his golden son's prominent cheek and sorrowfully noting the hardness that ruthlessly set his firstborn's handsome features on prematurely cynical lines.

"War is a bloody nightmare!" snarled the young man as the awful memory of screaming men and horses ripped into his mind. His aquiline nose flared, recalling the acrid stench of gunpowder and seared flesh. He closed his blue eyes tightly, trying to block the remembered sight of exposed entrails glowing a horrendous shocking pink against the thick brown mud.

"War is hell," agreed his father.

"Why didn't you tell me?"

"I tried."

"You tried and I wouldn't hear. All my life, ever since my first memory, I wanted to be in the cavalry. To ride into glorious battle to the rousing beat of the drum. I would fall asleep dreaming of a gold and red uniform, a gleaming sabre at my side . . . astride a proud stallion," confessed Torr. "Oh, my God! I thought war was a majestic parade!" he swore, and Sir Torrance looked into his son's steely eyes wishing there were tears to melt and soften the bleak cruelty. "Pegasus is dead!" stated the young man bluntly.

"Aye, son, I know," answered the old man, thinking of the magnificent bay stallion that he had given his boy six years before for his sixteenth birthday, the very same year Felicity had died. "I know. Major Forester told me," he added huskily as his own grief welled.

"Poor wretched animal. He didn't deserve to die so unmercifully for my selfish vanity. He writhed and thrashed until his golden coat was caked with his own saliva, blood, and excrement."

"Don't think on it."

"He screamed and screamed, begging me to end his misery, but I was helpless . . . impotent! I could do nothing but lie in the mud, blood, and shit and witness his agony!"

"Try to sleep, my son. The horrors and pain will fade with time if you let them. When your mother, Felicity, died, I thought I would go insane from the agony of it. And as well you know, for a while I was insane, selfishly wrapped in my own grief, unable to comfort you and your younger brothers for your great loss. I sincerely thought I wanted to die because I was unable to live without her . . . but here I am . . . and there you are, a precious part of her.'' He squeezed his son's hand but there was no answering reassurance, no acknowledgment. "I suppose a part of me did die . . . that part that was intricately and inexplicably entwined with your mother . . .'' The old man's voice trailed off unhappily, unable to reach, to connect with his embittered son, his rheumy eyes gazing into space as though to somehow summon help from the vivacious spirit of his young wife, who lay beneath the Cornish earth several hundred miles away.

"I should like to sleep,'' dismissed Torr, wrenching his hand away from his father's tight clasp.

"Oh course. I do so apologize,'' stammered the old man distractedly, patting his son's clenched fist. "Sleep is by far the best healer,'' he added, backing to the door, keeping his concerned gaze on his son's averted face so that he was unaware of Ajax standing at the open door, where he had witnessed the exchange.

Sir Torrance walked blindly past his eighteen-year-old son and into his study, where he poured himself a large whiskey.

"I don't think Dr. Baldwin would approve of you drinking with your bad heart,'' chided Mrs. Goodie, trotting in and placing several letters on his desk.

"Don't think, Goodie, just join me in a drink,'' snapped Sir Torrance, carelessly splashing more of the amber liquid into a glass and thrusting it at her before taking a long punishing swallow. "Go on, woman, drink up! Drink up!'' he barked.

Mrs. Goodie sighed, sat and smoothed her apron over her ample lap. Her mouth was pursed, refusing to take even a sip. "You know what I think of spirits! You know what Dr. Baldwin says about you and spirits!''

"Drink!'' he roared. Mrs. Goodie opened her mouth to remonstrate indignantly but, recognizing a kindred anguish in his eyes despite the grim expression on his lined face, obediently raised the glass and took a ladylike sip.

"Well," she sighed as the burning liquid spread a comforting glow in her belly, "there's a letter there from Lady Melisande Moreby-Fowler-Wentworth," she informed, waving a dimpled hand toward his desk. "And you still haven't opened the letter from Biddles, Biddles, and Penrose."

"Lady Moreby-Wentworth-Fowler," he corrected absently.

"Looks like an invite of some sort. You don't suppose you've been invited to one of her awful midnight soirees, do you?" The plump housekeeper giggled.

"I doubt it. Lady Melisande has never forgiven me for repulsing her advances, and that was more than fifty years ago," remarked Sir Torrance without a trace of humour or rancor, taking another long gulp of whiskey. "He's changed, Goodie, he's changed. I don't know my own son anymore," he mourned. He drained his glass and poured himself more.

"Well, 'tis no wonder! What did you expect? And getting yourself bosky isn't going to set anything to right. Nor is giving yourself another funny spell," fretted Goodie.

"He's angry. Angry and cynical but not a tear . . . even telling me about Pegasus's death . . . not one tear."

"Give the lad time. He's been to hell and back."

"Will he ever walk again?" hissed Sir Torrance. The housekeeper shrugged and stared miserably into the golden liquid, remembering the sight of the horrendous wound in the muscular thigh.

"Funny that he has not mentioned Cory." She sought to change the subject somewhat by mentioning the young man's personal manservant. "Has he to you?" The gaunt old man tersely shook his head and the two fell silent, not knowing how to comfort each other.

Each day Sir Torrance patiently sat with his son, but the clear blue eyes never acknowledged him and the young man made no attempt to get out of the bed. One afternoon Sir Torrance dozed and was awakened by anguished cries.

"Devil-Child? Where are you, Devil-Child?" screamed Torr. "Help me, Devil-Child!"

"Wake up, my son. Wake up. You are safe at home in your own bed," comforted Sir Torrance. Torr opened his eyes to see his father bending over him as his younger brothers raced into the room.

"I apologize if I have disturbed your rest, Father," clipped Torr coldly.

"Your pain is mine, son. I should just like to help," said the old man gently, making no attempt to hide the hurt he felt at his oldest son's rejecting behaviour.

"I should like to help, also," offered Ajax.

"Me, too," sang out Felix.

"And I should appreciate my privacy," responded Torr curtly. "Please close the door when you leave."

"Very well," sighed Sir Torrance, standing stiffly and shepherding his younger sons to the door.

"I am very sorry you got wounded and that Pegasus was killed!" shouted Ajax angrily, breaking free from his father. "But that does not give you the right to be so bloody cold and insulting! Snarling and snapping at anyone who tries to help you! Well, if you want to just lie there feeling sorry for yourself . . . do so! Have a bloody good time of it!"

"That's enough, Ajax!" remonstrated his father.

"No, let him speak," countermanded Torr. "You were saying, Ajax?"

"You were my hero," whispered the eighteen-year-old, unable to hold on to his anger. "I looked up to you. . . ."

"And now I've fallen off my pedestal? Why, because I'm not dead? Buried like a hero in some stinking foreign soil? I'm not a glorious memory?" derided Torr. "No, I am just a broken, crippled relic! What did I ever do that was so heroic?" he demanded when Ajax just stood tongue-tied, shrugging unhappily. His father ushered Felix from the room, leaving his two older sons alone.

"You were my big brother . . . that was enough," Ajax finally whispered.

"Enough for what? To be a hero?" challenged Torr.

"Enough to emulate you. I leave for France after Christmas."

"War isn't a parade," protested Torr.

"I know that."

"How?"

"I helped cut the clothes off you. I saw your body . . . your wounds. I hear your nightmare screams," replied Ajax.

"You are too young!"

"I am eighteen, the same age you were when you left," stated the youth before quitting the room and slamming the door.

Torr stared morosely at the walls of his room. He wanted to call his brother back, but what could he say to him? He sighed and closed his eyes, hearing his steady heartbeat pulse, much like the sea surging into the hollow caverns deep in the bowels of the earth. Where had he been? Had the Devil-Child just been the product of his fevered brain? And Cory? where was Cory?

"Oh, my God, Cory!" he gasped aloud. How could he possibly have forgotten so important a person as Cory. "Cory?" he shouted, blindly fumbling for the handbell beside his bed to summon his sprightly little valet. The bell was knocked to the floor, where it rolled, the clapper muffled by the thick carpet. "Cory?" he screamed, fighting the waves of madness that twirled him. He tried to fathom the last time he had seen or heard his chipper manservant's voice. He recalled the monotonous trundling tumbrell and the comforting cockney crooning.

"Hits alroight, littall guvner, 'ang on hin, littal guvner," the optimistic, singsong voice played in his ears. Cory had been with him most of the long painful journey, not so much as a well-defined personage, but as a cheerful, courageous spirit amid the swirling mists. "Cory!" he bellowed.

His door was slowly opened and Torr watched his father tentatively peek into the darkening room as though summoning courage to address his son. Torr was detached, noting the old man's awkwardness and discomfort but feeling no responsibility for it.

"Are you awake?" whispered Sir Torrance, not knowing if his son was once more in the throes of a nightmare. There was a sardonic bark of laughter. "I apologize for Ajax. Youth is an impatient time," he stated as though his twenty-two-year-old son had left childhood behind eons before. Torr didn't answer, he just stared silently. This tall, fragile old man was his father. When had he got so old? he wondered vaguely. He had always been old, older than the fathers of his school chums, but never this old. . . . Four years had certainly weighed heavily on them both.

"How did I get home?" he asked roughly, unable to voice Cory's name out loud for fear of what he might hear. "I don't know if what I remember is real or delirious fantasy," he continued. "I recall various modes of extremely uncomfortable transportation . . . and a boat. A smuggling vessel I'd gather, from the barrels and stench of brandy."

"It was a Cornish vessel," supplied his father.

"So I was in Cornwall?"

"Yes. I received word that you were alive and hidden in a farmhouse on Ile D'Ouessant just off the coast of Brittany."

"Received word from whom?" asked Torr. "Word from Cory?" he demanded harshly when his father didn't answer.

"I wondered when you would speak of Cory."

"What sort of monster am I that I could just go and forget him? I owe my life to him! How could I just put him out of my mind like that?"

"We do what we have to do to cope, I suppose . . . anything to hold on to our wits," awkwardly comforted the old man. His son refused to meet his eyes and a silence yawned between them. "Yes, I received word from Cory, and arrangements were made to smuggle you into England."

"Where is Cory?"

"Dead. Apparently he died aboard the smuggling vessel . . . an infection of the lungs. You have no recollection?" questioned Sir Torrance gently. "Major Forester was told that there were eleven of you . . . all badly wounded or very ill. You were the only man to survive."

"I recall just two other men. They were dead. I saw rats feeding on their bodies." Torr closed his eyes and once again he felt the rhythm of the sea, once again he saw the profoundly haunted eyes of the Devil-Child, once again he saw the rag-wrapped feet and the familiar striped trousers. "One of those men was Cory and I was too full of myself to care!" he lamented.

"You mustn't blame yourself."

"Where is he now?"

"Buried at sea."

"But he hated the sea! Hated water of any kind . . . to

drink . . . to bathe in! He got seasick at just the thought. Oh, poor, loyal Cory fated to swim for all eternity,'' laughed Torr. "How the bloody hell could I have forgotten him? How could I? He wiped my nose and my backside . . . polished my boots, nursed me like a baby, bawled me out like a staff serjeant, and dragged me out of my first whorehouse.''

"I know,'' replied Sir Torrance inadequately.

"Did you know the smugglers?'' asked Torr after a weighty silence.

"They are good Cornish people eking out a living the only way left to them,'' sighed his father. "What do you remember of Cornwall and High Tor?''

"Nearly everything. I was grown when we left. I remember the moor and the sea . . . and especially mother's garden.''

"That is why I couldn't bear to stay and why I cannot return. I should hate to see my Felicity's garden ravaged by the cruel ocean winds and full of weeds. You were sixteen when your mother died, but your horizons had expanded further than High Tor. You were away at school most of the time, so perhaps you don't remember the Cornish people . . . the simple hard-working Cornish people. The miners, the fishermen, the farmers . . .''

"I'm not very adept at remembering people am I?'' laughed Torr cynically. "I just use them and dispense with them. I remember Angelica Carmichael and the plump doctor. I remember lined weatherbeaten faces often without teeth. Old men mending their nets, puffing on their pipes, telling me fantastic stories about fairy creatures . . . mermaids and the Bucca-Dhu, goblins and knockers, piskies and trolls. Maybe they weren't fairy stories after all.''

"What do you mean?''

"I was taken from the smuggler's vessel into an enormous cavern. I could hear the roar of the sea and the crackling of a fiery furnace . . . and the clanking of chains. The shadows turned into black-garbed creatures. I lay naked on a pagan altar, and a witch stirred a cauldron full of mud and leaves . . . and I was watched by the Devil-Child and the Bucca-Dhu. I was given something to drink that stopped my pain and jumbled my tongue so I could only giggle like an idiot.

When I asked where I was, I was told I wasn't in England but Cornwall.''

"And this is what you repeatedly dream about?'' asked Sir Torrance. "This Devil-Child and the Bucca-Dhu? Describe them to me.''

"The Devil-Child is the most exquisite being . . . a face that defies description, more poignant and expressive than I have ever seen or imagined. The Bucca-Dhu is an enormous black wolf. . . .'' Torr struggled impotently.

"Your fevered brain probably played games. A fisherman's son and his dog?'' soothed Sir Torrance.

"Perhaps . . . but the beautiful Devil-Child somehow took Cory's place, taking care of me—saving me from myself. I first saw the Devil-Child on the boat,'' he recounted, omitting how he had bitten the small hand, omitting reference to Cory's striped trousers and rag-wrapped feet.

"Just a fisherman's son helping his father make extra money,'' repeated Sir Torrance. Torr frowned, desperately trying to put his recollections in perspective.

"What about the moving shadows of the Living-Dead? What about the witch?'' he demanded angrily, unaccountably infuriated at having the Devil-Child reduced to nothing more than a smuggler's son.

"You were ill . . . fevered. The mind can play strange tricks.''

"Who were the Cornish men who brought me from France?''

"Jonty Pengelly, brother to Jago of High Tor and manservant to my fanatical cousin, Godolphus Pendarves, who incidentally went to meet his maker last year.''

"I have a vague recollection of our distant cousin, Catherine, although I couldn't have been more than six or so when she died. I distinctly remember the talk. She was reputed to be devastatingly beautiful but totally unprincipaled. In fact a wanton, the siren who broke Tremayne of Taran's heart.''

"Poor wench,'' sighed Sir Torrance. "She was as you so aptly put it 'devastatingly beautiful.' Most of Cornwall fell in love with just the sight of her. She was an exquisite mermaid, a joyous siren cursed with a humourless, merciless father. Cousin Godolphus believed that all females were whores, and Catherine apparently sought to prove his conviction.''

"So the old fanatic's dead. . . . Who's next in line for that Norman folly?" laughed Torr, remembering the stark fortress that loomed out of the barren moor on the lonely promontory that jutted into the churning sea.

"Heaven help whoever it is," agreed Sir Torrance, shivering at the thought of the cheerless, unhappy place. "But let's hope whoever it is reopens the pits."

"Reopens the pits?" queried Torr, thankful to have his mind off his own problems.

"Godolphus—we called him 'God-awful' when we were boys because he was the most God-awfullest bore—was mean and vicious and so rigidly judgmental. Do you know as magistrate for the area that he sent more men and women to the gallows than any other in the history of the West Country?" recounted the old man. "For a while as an idealistic young man, I believed that my cousin, although a disagreeable person, was much maligned. I truly believed him to be a sincerely religious person until one day I happened to leaf through his Bible. Every derogatory reference to females was underlined in red!" Mrs. Goodie sidled into the room and beamed with pleasure at the apparent communication between father and son.

"What has that to do with the mines?" asked Torr.

"Well, a number of years ago, Cousin Godolphus had a funny spell. Terrified that he was going to die and wouldn't be able to fit through the eye of the needle, he closed the mines and quarries, putting more than a hundred men and their families out of work. Cousin God-awful was so terrified of being too prosperous to enter the Kingdom of Heaven he caused such abysmal poverty that I sincerely pray he got firmly stuck in the eye of the needle . . . or preferably stuck right on the point," chuckled the old man, delighted to be conversing with his son at long last.

"Abysmal poverty?"

"The land about Pendarves Point and High Tor is windburned and just suitable for sheep grazing . . . and except for the odd parcel of bottom land a man can't scrape much of a living."

"There's the sea."

"Yes, there's the sea, but she is like a woman . . . she has her moods. She can be very generous and also very stingy,'' explained Sir Torrance. "By closing the mines and quarries and all the related industries, he stopped the steady wages that had been depended on for many generations by many, many families.''

"And here we are at war with France, needing all the resources we can possibly muster!" Torr responded hotly.

"War has not been officially declared as yet."

"Not officially but it's just a matter of time. France is at war with Austria and Prussia—and is laying siege, attempting to stop and block all trade with the British Isles. France means to conquer the whole of Europe, and there's that slow-witted, plodding monarch—''

"You are a Whig!" interrupted his father as footmen entered with wine and food, followed by Mrs. Goodie.

"And what is wrong with that? Aren't you a Whig?" challenged his son roguishly, allowing himself to be lifted and propped against the pillows and accepting a brimming glass of rich red wine.

"When you marched out of here just four years ago, you were a dyed-in-the-wool Tory. 'Twas Pitt this and Pitt that, King George this and King George that, if you recall?" chuckled Sir Torrance, happily, waving the footmen away. "Drink up, we'll not be enjoying these superb French wines much longer if what you say is true."

"Unless your smuggling Cornishmen oblige," laughed Torr.

"Stop all this nattering and imbibing or you'll never regain your strength and your own two feet," scolded Mrs. Goodie, uncovering the platters on the tray across the young man's lap.

"Run along, run along, we're eating, we're eating," snapped Sir Torrance, noting the hardening of his son's expression at the reference to legs and shoving a piece of roast pheasant into his mouth and washing it down with a thirsty gulp of wine. "Eat up, my boy or we'll never be free of this pestering harridan," he teased as the housekeeper tucked a serviette into the neck of Torr's nightshirt and put a fork in his idle hand. Mrs. Goodie plunked herself down in a chair and stubbornly refused to leave the room. She watched the motionless young man.

"Is that pheasant all right? I told the cook it smelled too gamey for an invalid," she chattered, reaching and snatching a morsel from Torr's plate.

"It is delicious! Eat, boy, eat," coaxed Sir Torrance, and his son started to pick absently at his meal.

"All this talk of Cornwall brought to mind that letter what's been gathering dust on your desk. It's from Corn . . . wall. From Fal . . . mouth. From Bid . . . dles, Bid . . . dles and Pen . . . rose, Sol . . . ic . . . it . . . tors," declared Mrs. Goodie, reading haltingly from the envelope she withdrew from the pocket of her apron. "Well, aren't you surprised, Master Torr? Your old Goodie can read! Master Ajax and Felix taught me," she announced proudly.

"As my cousin Godolphus would no doubt quote, 'Tis not only a folly but a sin to teach females to read,' " said the old man dolefully, refilling his glass and drinking.

"How much have you drunk today? You know what Doctor Baldwin says?" berated the housekeeper.

"What does Doctor Baldwin say?" enquired Torr, coming out of his own brooding thoughts.

"What is that letter, woman?" demanded Sir Torrance, pointedly changing the subject.

"It's that letter from Cornwall."

"I'll get to it," snapped the old man, waving the housekeeper and the letter away. "Now off you go! You're forgetting your place!"

"He just doesn't like to deal with anything to do with Cornwall . . . brings up sad memories," confided Mrs. Goodie to Torr, who took the letter. "And he'd had three funny spells now. His heart," she gossipped, ignoring Sir Torrance's apoplectic glares.

Torr cleaned his knife and broke the seal on the envelope.

"Cousin Catherine had a child, a son, Devlyn Pendarves," he stated after a pause where he had quickly perused the enclosed document.

"Impossible! She's dead! Has been for more than fifteen years!" snorted Sir Torrance.

"Apparently the boy is older than fifteen."

"Would have to be!" agreed Mrs. Goodie, determined to be part of the conversation.

"This is a letter from Cousin Godolphus's solicitors apprising you of his demise and the contents of the will, which leaves everything to his grandson," stated Torr. "Apparently you are in line to inherit if anything happens to the boy."

"Let us hope that the boy has more sense than his grandsire, but I doubt it, raised by that perverse, twisted man. Poor youth, being raised in that bleak pile of stones. Fortunately, he was probably sent off to school," sighed Sir Torrance, staring moodily into his wineglass. "So Catherine birthed a child? My, that was a well-kept secret, but I suppose a child was a natural result of all that gallivanting she did! But 'tis strange . . . 'twas said she died in childbirth and the wretched babe also died," he mused distractedly.

"Then she must have had another child in a previous year," suggested Mrs. Goodie. "Does it say how old the boy is?"

"No," replied Torr, scanning down the single sheet of paper.

"Couldn't be more than a youth. Catherine wasn't much more than seventeen or eighteen when she died, poor lass," remarked Sir Torrance, discarding the empty wine bottle and reaching for another. "Wonder who the father was?"

"Devlyn sounds Irish to me," volunteered the housekeeper, shaking her head with disapproval at her employer's drinking. "Oh, those Irish are a randy lot and no mistake!"

"Well, if cousin Catherine's reputation has validity, any number of mature males in the West Country could've spawned the unfortunate offspring. She didn't have to go to Ireland," remarked Sir Torrance dryly. Suddenly he belched loudly and clutched at his chest, his face grimacing in pain. "Indigestion," he panted, pressing both hands to his ribs.

"Another funny spell!" squawked Goodie in alarm.

"No, no. 'Tis just what we Cornish call 'a-rizin' of the lights,' it'll pass," he groaned. "Ah, there, that's better," he said as the initial sharpness lessened and he released his pent-up breath with relief.

"Maybe you should lie down, Father," suggested Torr, horrified by his parent's bluish pallour.

"No need, my boy. Just wind. I ate and drank too fast. You know, Goodie, I do believe that pheasant *was* a trifle gamey,'' gasped Sir Torrance, stiffening as once again he was caught in a fierce vise of pain. He bucked back in his chair, his hands frantically scrambling at his neck as though to loosen his cravat before collapsing and sagging like a limp rag doll. Mrs. Goodie stood with her back pressed against the wall, both hands stuffed into her gaping mouth, her eyes bulging with panic. Unable to move or speak, she emitted jerky screams as she watched the twenty-two-year-old try to swing his useless leg out of the bed. The tray crashed to the floor, food and drink splashing and soiling the covers and carpet. The young man crawled through the wreckage, tumbling heavily off the bed and dragging his body through the messiness towards his motionless father. There were graceless grunts of exertion as he painfully hauled himself to his knees, using the rungs of his father's chair to lever himself.

"Shut up!" he ordered the hysterical woman. Mrs. Goodie jammed her hands farther into her mouth as the youth listened for a heartbeat. Hearing nothing, he savagely ripped open his father's coat and shirt, laying his golden head on the too-white skin.

"He's dead," he stated bluntly. His knees buckled and he sprawled on the carpet, gazing up at his father's peaceful expression, unable to conceive of how quickly life had fled. "He's dead," he repeated matter-of-factly.

"No! 'Tis just one of his spells!" protested the woman, tears spurting and sliding down her round, rosy face. "No! No! It can't be!" she wailed loudly.

The thud of racing feet reverberated through the house. The door flew open, and in streamed maids and footmen followed by Ajax and Felix.

"What is it?" demanded Ajax as everybody just stood, shocked by the sight of the motionless old man in the chair and the young man lying at his feet, his white nightshirt soiled with food and garish splashes of red wine.

"Our father is dead," sighed Torr, his blue eyes fixed to the ceiling.

"Oh, my Lor'!" screeched an upstairs maid, never having seen a corpse before and unnerved by the sprawled young lord who spent his nights screaming for demons and devils. Further frightened by Mrs. Goodie's lack of control and not

knowing how else to behave, she added her piercing screams.
The other maids followed suit.

Ajax was unable to cross the room. He tried to ignore the
screaming women as he focused on the still figure of his
father. The sight of Torr, his hero, obscenely wallowing in
wasted food sickened him.

"Our father is asleep," he pronounced carefully, terrified
by the rage that raced his pulses.

Felix pushed past the clustered servants and slowly approached his father. He stroked the lean, parchmentlike face
and the iron-grey hair.

"Our father is dead," he stated, his voice treble and
bell-like, seeming much younger and more vulnerable than
his fourteen years.

"No! It isn't true!" shouted Ajax, his voice cracking like
an early adolescent's. "It isn't true!" he glanced frantically
about, searching for confirmation, but the maids screamed
louder and the men stared at their feet. Felix wrapped his thin
arms about his father and sobbed, and Torr lay on the floor
amidst the nauseating mess of food, hating himself, knowing
this was the time he should be standing tall, taking charge. A
sharp kick into his healing ribs caused him to gasp, and the
assembled servants were shocked into silence by Ajax's cruelty.

"Our father is dead because you killed him!" screamed the
eighteen-year-old, lashing out with grief and fear, feeling so
very orphaned, so very alone. "You killed him! It's your
fault!" he howled, pushing past the stunned servants and
rushing from the room.

"You know he didn't mean such a wicked thing, Master
Torr . . . I mean Sir Torr. Oh, I don't know what I mean,"
sobbed Mrs. Goodie. "Master Ajax is out of his head, poor
lad. Come along, Master Felix, come to your old Goodie,
young fella-me-lad," she sniffed, pulling herself together and
disentangling the grieving child from his dead father. She
enfolded him against her ample bosom. "And what are you
lot just standing about goggling at? Send for Doctor Baldwin!
Carry his lordship to his own chambers! Get Master Torr
cleaned up and into a freshened bed!"

Torr watched the busy commotion bustling about him,
unable to feel or connect with anything. The body of his

father was removed, along with the remains of their last supper together. Torr was plucked from the floor, stripped, washed, redressed, and tucked into a clean bed just like a puling babe. He lay, hearing Felix's hiccoughing sobs and Ajax's wild bellowings, helpless to contribute anything. There was the sound of voices remonstrating with Ajax and then a door slammed, echoing hollowly, ominously. A detached sense of doom shrouded the ensuing silence and then he nodded his head in time with the approaching footsteps.

"Master Ajax has gone to his barracks!" cried Mrs. Goodie, bursting into the room without a seemly knock. "Says he's never coming back! Says as how he taking the very next boat to France! You must stop him!"

Torr continued nodding his head, unable to feel or formulate anything except numb despair. His face felt stiff, tightly bound with unshed tears. His father was dead and he couldn't weep. His father was dead and he was supposed to be in charge.

"What are you going to do?" implored the distressed woman, but the young man just continued nodding cynically at her, his golden hair sparkling in the candlelight like a halo about his hard, chiseled face.

CHAPTER 6

"I DUNNAW 'bout you, Miz Hitchins, but ees lordship scares me some'at awful," declared Peg Hatch. "All theze years I heard tell Lord Taran wuz proper handzome but ee's more like Awd Goggie weth them terr'bul black eyebrows and ee's some muggety."

"Stop up thet runnin' mouth of yourn, you coxy 'aythen and thank ees lordship fer an honest day's work and a Christmuz gobbler ter put some mait on yer bones," scolded Mrs. Hitchins, noisely slapping her large mound of dough so flour puffed up in white clouds. "Now go clear ees lordship's breakfast dishes."

"Ee fair scares me and I don' scare easy."

"Good, 'tis right fer you ter be scared. Ees lordship owns Taran, so if you wanta stay you'd better do a fitty job. You wuz the one what wheedled and craaked, wantin' ter work in the big house."

"That wuz 'fore ee come back," returned the sulky girl.

"Oh, the hard work wuz too much fer you? Aye, the place wuz in proper cruel shape most of the rooms having bin shut up fer years but, 'tis all done in time fer Christmuz and 'ted'nt no good t'git all hurried up about et now," purred the cook-cum-housekeeper proudly.

"What if ee gits after me?"

"Oh, my dear life and days! How you do go on!" chortled the woman flouring the well-scrubbed table and her rolling pin.

"I've heard tell about 'ee's orgies in London Town weth

the Prince of Wales and all 'ee's fancy painted wemmen,'' recounted the girl indignantly.

"Then ee won't be thrusting 'tween yer spindly shanks, will ee?" answered the woman sharply. "Now do ee git on weth the job 'stead of fricking 'round? Or do I take this to ee?" she added, brandishing her rolling pin.

" 'Tedn't my job, 'tis Jenny Mullet's!'' whined Peg. "I'm scullery and I have the scroff ter put in the pig's bucket."

"Jenny went home to the cottages fer Christmuz. Awd Mother Mullet's right poorly and ent expected to larst 'til the New Year."

" 'Tedn't jonnick thet Jenny Mullet got off fer Christmuz and I uv ter work," complained the maid.

"I'll tell ee what ent fair and thet's you oways craaking and crowling. I's hed quite enough uv yer emperance!" thundered the older woman, crashing her rolling pin on to the oak table. "Go see to Lord Taran!"

"All right. All right. Keep yer hair on. 'Tedn't no need ter get all hurried up about it," remarked the girl, pertly smoothing her hands down her scrawny chest and sashaying out of the kitchen.

"Keep my hair on?" sputtered Mrs. Hitchins, her rosy face mottling with purple rage. "Keep my hair on?" she repeated, furiously punching her pasty dough. "Some happy Christmuz this bodes ter be!''

Benedict Tremayne stared out of the window at the infinite greyness, feeling nostalgia wash through him. He had forgotten the majestic vista and the sharp cleansing scent of the sea.

"Merry Christmuz, yer lordship," greeted the maid. "I's Peg Hatch, Hezekiah Hatch's daughter. Hezekiah who be your foreman in the clay pit 'fore he wuz hurt in the slide what kilt yer own father. Lost his leg ee did. Ee speaks well of you, ee does. I knocked but seeing as there wuz no answer I come in," she chattered, unnerved by the tall shadow of the man who neither turned nor acknowledged her presence. "I den't think no one wuz in here, yer lordship. I come ter clear yer plates," she explained, waving her hands at the remains of the meal on the table. "Be it all right ter clean up?" she asked, intimidated yet fascinated by the virile broad shoulders that loomed against the wide bay window overlooking the sea.

Taran nodded without turning and continued to gaze over the grim expanse that mirrored his disposition. The furtive clatter of the gathered dishes jangled his nerves and he breathed heavily, expressing his exasperation. The girl dropped a pile of crockery in her nervousness. The plates smashed noisily on the granite floor. There was a shrill shriek and then silence. Taran sighed deeply and turned to reassure her, but the frightened maid stood gracelessly frozen with her loose mouth agape, staring with horror at him as though he were an ogre capable of inflicting some form of unspeakable punishment. Her expression increased his extreme fury, especially as there seemed to be an almost excited gleam in the popping eyes and the slack lips drooled wetly. With another snort to indicate displeasure he strode out of the room and slammed the door behind him, determined to see to it that Hezekiah Hatch's daughter was relegated to some hidden part of the house.

"Christmas," he murmured aloud as he poured himself a snifter of brandy. "Merry Christmas, Taran," he toasted, raising the glass to his reflection in the mirror before turning back, drawn once again to the ever-changing endless sea. A storm was brewing. The clouds gathered, shifting and deepening their colours to various hues, from eerie sulphurous yellow to a startling green, until they attained the indescribable blending of converging tones . . . of a taut calm . . . a muted violence . . . an anticipation. That breath-held moment when all strength had been gathered. That incredible time before the heavens opened and energy was released. As imperceptibly as the grey clouds had shifted and subtly changed into that suspended moment, so did Angel's eyes seep into his mind. Those strange sea green–grey eyes. He smiled softly, remembering her unexpected flashes of spirit, and he wondered why he was haunted by thoughts of the awkward, gawky female when he should be thankful he had been relieved of the responsibility. Where was she? he wondered, gazing about at the stony greyness of the Cornish slate and remembering the warmth and intimacy of the wood-panelled house in the New Forest.

"Taran. Taran," he sighed. "You are getting maudlin and sentimental now you have left your carefree twenties far behind and are firmly entrenched in middle age. "Carefree," he whispered, staring down at the rain-lashed cliff path where he had raced in his youth. "Was I ever carefree?" he said as another face haunted his mind. "Catherine," he intoned, waiting for the searing pain to engulf him, but he felt nothing. "Catherine," he repeated, but all he felt was a soft regret, a bittersweet sadness. Gone was the white hot anger and burning pain. He chuckled wryly and refilled his glass before settling into a comfortable chair. He overlooked the white-capped water that surged furiously against the jagged cliff on which his house was perched. "Catherine," he repeated, leaning back and travelling back in time.

To state that Catherine Pendarves had been his first woman would have been incorrect, but she had been the first woman he had loved. From the age of fourteen or fifteen, he had rolled in the grass, the haylofts, coves, and boats with many willing country lassies. It had been a golden release, uncomplicated and joyous until Catherine. There had also been older women who had taught him all manner of delightful variations in an assortment of boudoirs, gracefully accepting expensive trinkets for their enjoyable lessons, until Catherine.

When had he first loved Catherine Pendarves? he strove to recall. He laughed softly, admitting that he had loved her for as long as he could remember. Sir Godolphus Pendarves had stalked into the village chapel one dreary Sunday in winter, his forbidding face set on its usual disapproving lines. He had dragged a tiny, elfin child, whose vibrant auburn hair sprung rebelliously from beneath the hideous black bonnet that was crammed on her little head. To seven-year-old Benedict seated with his parents and two-year-old brother, Michael, in their family pew, the child was like a vision that lit the gloomy dark interior. Even though her tiny arm seemed pulled out of its socket, Catherine smiled sunnily at all she passed as she was marched down the central aisle. From that moment, she had captured a tender place in his heart. She completely fascinated him, and throughout his boyhood he observed her much as he did rock-pools and baby birds, transfixed by the miracle of nature. Such a glorious, fearless little being, darting this way and that like a little sunbeam in a dusty room; constantly changing and exploring, growing into an even more tantalizing young woman. A work of exquisite art to be observed from afar, to be appreciated but never touched. She was a matchless, perfect object that took his breath away and continued to amaze him much like his prism, which refracted a beam of light into an incredible rainbow; like the poetic power of a stooping hawk; or like the gleaming, clean curves of the porpoises arching through the surf. Just the sound of her voice caused his emotions to well, as when he heard the bursting exultation of the lark on a lazy summer day.

"Oh, Catherine, what happened?" he asked aloud, seeing her tawdry and tarnished in the arms of another man. Into his mind flitted his first remembered sadness. He could not have been more than four or five, still dressed in frocks and chasing butterflies through the long dry grasses that tickled his chubby hot cheeks and successfully hid him from the nurse's watchful eyes. He smiled wistfully as he recalled reaching carefully for the monarch as it gently vibrated its multicoloured wings. He remembered the wonderful triumphant crowing that had burst through his pursed lips as his hands finally closed about his prey. He felt the terrible enormity of his horror when he showed his father the prize, only to discover mud-coloured dust sticking to the sweat of his grubby palms. One minute a vibrant trembling butterfly and the next an ugly squashed insect. He had been responsible. He had been the killer.

"You are getting maudlin, Taran," he repeated harshly, finding himself staring intently at his broad palm. "Did you expect to find the mark of the monarch etched?" he asked himself cynically, before clenching his fist as though to quash the memory.

Benedict leaned back in his chair, listening to the hollow loneliness of the howling wind and the thunderous rhythmic roar of the sea as it surged against the sheer cliff with such ferocity the salt spray misted the windows.

"Christmas at Taran," he said aloud, remembering the happy clamour of his childhood when the heavy velvet drapes would be drawn, hiding the vast cold sea, and an enormous fire crackled in every hearth throughout the huge rambling house. The air would be redolent with the fragrant aroma of brandied puddings, roast geese, mince pies, and hot cider. Excited voices would chatter and carol from the servant's hall, where festivities would be organized for the children from the estate and mines. From the formal dining hall came a steady hum of activity as maids and footmen rushed up and down the fifty-foot-long banqueting table preparing for the Tremaynes' Christmas feast. The ghostly echoes of those happy times lamented with the wind, seeming to berate the empty cheerless house. Christmas at Taran and there was no frantic chaos, no preparation, no carolling, no mouth-watering bouquets, no anticipation, but just a faint lazy clatter from the dim recesses of the kitchen. There was no father's gruff teasing or mother's tinkling laughter. They were both long dead and dutifully interred in the Tremayne family crypt beside his younger brother, Michael, who had drowned more than seventeen years before. He had died less than a year before his own rash marriage to Catherine.

Benedict sighed. It had been so very long since he had thought of the terrible day that cruelly marked the end of his happy childhood. From that day everything had changed. His mother never smiled at him again in that special way—the way he had first seen her smile as he lay in his cradle. She somehow blamed him for Michael's death, and although it was never really said, he had read in her eyes that she wished her firstborn had died and not her most carefully nurtured baby. Taran let his mind drift back to that fateful summer day. He had just finished his first year at Oxford University and was home for the holidays, delighting in all he had achingly missed. Not even stopping at the main house to greet his parents, he had raced his weary horse across the moors to dispell the academic cobwebs, and at Taran Cove had stripped off his clothes to plunge into the chill sea, eager to scour away the city soot. He had swum out towards the horizon, not knowing that his brother, Michael, had plunged in behind him.

"Poor Mother," he whispered, gazing out at the vast unyielding ocean. She had watched her son die and had been powerless to do anything. She had watched and screamed, but her voice had been drowned out by the surging sea. Taran shook his dark head and refilled his glass. It had been so many years, yet he was still in awe of the horrendous event. Death had been so silent. There had been no clap of thunder, no fork of lightning, nothing to herald such a terribly definitive act. He had swum through the choppy waves, feeling exhilaration after the long months of study. He stroked strongly, his muscles stretching and tingling in the icy salt water. Reaching the calm, out of the pull of the shore, he flipped onto his back and floated, appreciating the clear infinite sky after the town's grimy greyness. He had closed his eyes and listened to the mewing cries of the gulls and the steady flap of the cormorant's wings as they flew just above the surface. Why hadn't he heard his brother drowning? Why hadn't he heard the terrible screams of his mother? How could he have been so blissfully unaware?

Michael's body had not been found for nearly a week. Taran took a long punishing swallow as he tried to block the grisly memory of his brother's remains that bore little resemblance to the earnest boy who had followed him, copying his every move since babyhood. The senseless death on that balmy summer day not only marked the end of childhood but also the disintegration of his parents' happy marriage. Just as his mother blamed her older son for Michael's death, so his father blamed his wife for the overprotectiveness that he felt caused the boy to emulate the independence of his big brother. Everything had become muted after that—everything except Catherine, who became more vibrant in contrast. The usually fleeting summer days dragged painfully, and he had eagerly returned to Oxford to continue his studies, relieved to be rid of the oppressive grief. Within a year, he married Catherine, hoping to bring happiness back into his life.

The storm had passed and streaks of golden sunlight burst free of the gray horizon, limning the angry waves with bright undulating bars. Benedict flung the windows wide and breathed deeply of the brisk cold breeze that surged into the room. He needed to clear away the depressing traces of the past and the effects of the brandy. Why had he returned home? He mused as he made his way to the stables intent on a bracing gallop across the moors.

"Weell, weell, weell," hailed an ancient bandy-legged man who held his sides and chuckled gleefully at the sight of him. "Ooh, ah, et's bin a braave spur since larst I see'd thee, Master Benedict, zurr! Merry, merry Christmuz, your Lordship, and I's hoping' th'eez home ter stay," he wheezed, pumping the young man's hand up and down, loath to let go.

"Silas Quickbody!" exclaimed Taran, losing his brooding expression and grinning with delight. "What on earth are you doing here? I was informed by Angus Dunbar that you'd retired and were living a life of ease in Penzance."

"Ent no peace fer the wicked," returned Silas, staring up into the young lord's face, his shrewd old eyes noting the harsh lines of cynicism and dissipation. "I come back ter Taran when I heard as how thee wuz home. Edn't none what knows good horseflesh like Silas Quickbody. Well, thou 'tedn't think I'd let zum lazy slocum tend these pretties, ded thee?" chortled the old man, rubbing the velvety nose of a spirited stallion. The horse stomped impatiently, wanting to be out of the confining stall, and the old man nodded his approval of the proud butting heads of the perfectly matched greys, who vied for attention. "Ef'n thee wants a job done fitty . . ."

"Must do it thyself," laughed Taran, finishing the old adage.

"Or get Silas Quickbody ter do et fur thee," crowed the groom. "Oooh ah, I taught thee well, Master Benedict. Them's fine steeds, my lad," he praised, hobbling past the stalls and admiring each of the horses. "Is thee glad tur be home at Taran after all the years?" he asked after a pause, bending to pat a golden retriever bitch.

"It is my home," answered Benedict evasively.

"Ah, thou still feel some bitter about et?" Silas stared at the young man's stern profile. " 'Bout Master Michael and Miss Catherine?" he probed.

"How's Mrs. Quickbody?" asked Benedict curtly changing the subject and referring to Silas' bossy little wife who had efficiently run the estate's large kitchens from before his father's time.

"Just like Master Michael and Miss Catherine, Mrs. Quickbody is dead and gone and her clothes all washed up so 'tedn't no good ter be bitter about et," sighed the leathery old man as he saddled the dark stallion. " 'Tes going ter be a harsh winter," he stated sagely, filling in the long sad silence. "Thee knows what is said? Frost enough 'fore Christmuz ter hold up a duck . . . ?"

"Rest of the winter will be muck," supplied Benedict. "It is good that you're back at Taran, Silas."

"Aye, et is good thou art back, too. 'Tes time ter put grief away and fill up thy great big house with childers," suggested Silas, tightening the cinch. "Be thee riding far? The weather still looks a mite tender," he asked solicitously.

"Just need to clear my head," reassured Benedict, mounting the impatient animal, who pranced sideways.

Silas Quickbody watched the dark horse and rider as they cantered across the enclosed courtyard and out to the steep cliff path. He had been the one who had thrown the boy up on the high back of his first horse. He smiled, remembering how the three-year-old toddler had adamantly refused to be mounted on a pony. "Not a baby, Silas Quick," he had stated. Silas shook his head dolefully at the change in the open shining face. The man who had returned home was not the gentle-hearted charitable youth of before.

"Enything amiss, Silas? 'ee looks proper doomful?" screeched Mrs. Hitchins through the kitchen window. "Bring thy awd bones next ter the fire 'fore 'ee steeve ter death weth cold. 'Tedn't fit weather fer a dog," she said, shivering.

"Be that emperant skinamalink, Peg Hatch in there?" demanded the old man, tempted by the fire but preferring the company of the horses to the acid tongue of the impudent maid.

"Nay, I couldn't take her craakin' so I thought ter give myself a Christmuz present. I give thet spiteful flink the day off," chuckled Mrs. Hitchins, pouring two steaming mugs of tea as Silas made himself cosy in a large armchair to one side of the wide kitchen hearth.

"I remember when each hearth held a great spitted joint turned by the kitchen lads, who'd reach out to steal a taste of pork crackle or crispy lamb's fell. A whole juicy lamb there, a piglet turning here, and perhaps a milk-fed calf over there. . . and one big sniff of the fragrant air and thee would drool. . . and after weth the juices still running down thou'd set back feeling fuller than a tick and content weth the world, knowing there was still plum puddings and tipsy-cakes to come—but there wuz no hurry. Happy voices singing, snoring, and belching—not this heavy silence.'' The old man stared sadly into the glowing embers, remembering his energetic little wife with a booming voice, running hither and thither from spit to spit, scolding and laughing.

"I dunnaw what Taran wuz like afore, all I know ez there's no pleasing 'ees lordship these days. 'Oways proper maggoty and scowling like there'll be no tomorrow. Never a smile nor gentle word in the six years I hev worked here. I come from High Tor after Lady Felicity died, when Sir Torrance packed up and moved to London. Now there wuz misery for thee. If thet poor man could hev painted his young wive's flowers black, he would hev. So I come to work here, hoping fur a spot of sunshine, but the place is as dolefu' and doomfu' as High Tor what weth her ladyship locked in her chamber fur nigh on nine years, weeping and awailing fur her drowned son and his lordship working the pits like a common navvy.''

"Afore Master Michael's drownding, there wuzn't a more cheerfu' young scamp than thet Benny,'' mused Silas sorrowfully.

"Sir Benedict Tremayne, Benny?'' giggled Mrs. Hitchins, the pet name seeming ludicrous when applied to the tall, formidable Lord Taran. "Well, awd man, thee must know better, for I've not seen him more'n two or three times in all the years. First there wuz his poor mother's funeral and then four years ago when that great missment in the pits killed his father amongst others,'' she added. "But thee must know best . . . e'en though tes said thet 'thet cheerfu' young scamp' near killed Catherine Pendarves weth his two bare hands when he found her futting weth a stable hand—''

"Tes not our place, woman!'' chided the old man. "Tes just suffice ter say thet there wuz them sorely, sorely hurt . . . and the poor lass dead and buried these past sixteen years.''

"But her clothes by no means all washed up!'' snapped Mrs. Hitchins.

"And what do 'ee mean by thet?"

"Thee know as well as me, awd man. There's strange happenings at Pendarves Castle. Has been since a year—maybe two—before Sir Godolphus died. Just this last month, two vessels smashed out on Wolf Rock, and the poor sailors hearing dreadfu' bayings of a phantom wolf 'afore the ship sank like a stone. Tes said ghostly wreckers haunt Pendarves Point, guiding ships to their doom. Perhaps the ghost of Catherine Pendarves?"

"Silly pratings! Tes the season fur storms and wrecks," dismissed Silas.

"There's them what's seen black-garbed witches dancing around the nineteen stones of the Merry Maidens . . . and tes said thet the Bucca-Dhu prowls the moors weth a Devil-Child atop a giant fairy horse thet breathes fire!"

"Tes Christmuz day, a Christian time, so stop thy pagan prattle!"

"Aye, tes Christmuz day but who'd know et?" sighed the woman, suppressing a shudder as the wind whined about the large hulking house, rattling the windows. "A spot of Christmuz cheer is what ez needed," she determined, heaving her girth out of the soft cushions and trotting across the stone-flagged kitchen to a cabinet. "A mug of Christmuz cheer," she declared, fumbling with the large ring of keys that hung from her thick waist. She gleefully unlocked the door and reverently removed a large earthenware jug. "Rhubarb wine," she proclaimed. "Four years old," she embellished. "Put up weth my own two hands thet sorrowfu' spring when awd Sir Benedict met his maker in the pits and Hezekiah Hatch lost his leg," she chattered as she uncorked the jug. "Ooh aah, my dear life and days!" she exclaimed, wrinkling up her nose at the strong aroma that caused her eyes to stream. "Oh, my, my! Et don't smell a mite pindy, do et?"

"Oooh ah! tha' should put the spirit uv Christmuz into our awd bones," agreed the groom, rearing back as the powerful fumes assailed him and eagerly holding out his empty tea-mug for a jot. "Whoa there, woman! Doo 'ee think ter get me meazy-mazy?" he said as Mrs. Hitchins filled the cup to the top with her potent brew.

"Ded the master say when he'd be coming back?"

"Just a ride ter clear 'ees head, he said, but it looks like there's a sea fret coming in," worried Silas, frowning at the swirls of mist at the kitchen windows.

Sir Benedict Tremayne of Taran reined his horse at the crest of the sea-scarred cliff that marked Land's End and stared out at the awesome breakers that smashed their wild fury with all the might of the Atlantic Ocean behind them. The ferocity of the vast pitiless sea never ceased to amaze him. He gazed towards the hidden razor-sharp reefs known as the Longships, hearing the ghostly moans of the drowned sailors who for centuries had lost their lives on the jagged teeth, howl with the lonely wind. The haunting cry of "Wreck on the Longships!" screamed in his memory, and he recalled the many exciting but terrifying nights when rough urgent voices barked orders over the thunderous roar of the surf, and biting wind and rain stung his face and numbed his hands in the raging darkness as he worked alongside of his father and other Taran men. They had formed a human chain through the churning water to rescue the survivors of the floundering ships. And in the watery morning the limp bodies had floated gently in and out with the tamed waves . . . and the busy scavengers had been like scuttling crabs poking and searching amongst the seaweed for a stray treasure from the wreck. He as a boy would stand with the men trying not to shiver with fear and cold, trying not to cry as tired muscles hurt and a dead man's staring eyes seemed to curse. His hands had grasped steaming mugs of soup, or else the icy cold of a silver flask that with a swift tilt could pour burning spirits to heat the belly and chase away the terrors.

Taran frowned, seeing the telltale black ring of muddy charcoal on an outcropping of rock. "Wreckers," he pondered aloud. Ever since he could first remember, there had been talk of "wreckers." People who deliberately lured unsuspecting vessels onto the lethal rocks so they could salvage the cargo for their own gain. Wreckers, like the legendary mermaids who, with voluptuous promises, tempted the woman-starved sailors to their watery graves. "Not so legendary," he muttered, thinking of the long-haired siren who had tantalized him on those very cliffs and moors. He kicked his horse into a brisk canter along the perilous path, oblivious to the thick fog that snaked tapering fingers just above the rolling sea. The boom of the surf and the salt spray filled him with bittersweet remembrances of his lost childhood and youth. The horse's hooves skittered, and loose shale clattered down the treacherous escarpment, and with a rough curse Taran yanked the reins, sharply changing directions so he galloped over the bleak moor. How had it become so colourless and cold? he wondered, remembering the moor emblazoned with golden gorse and purple and pink heather . . . a welcoming, warm haven, hot and sultry and wild and free. Now sad bedraggled sheep huddled beneath shelves of rock and between craggy crevasses, their very greyness mirrored in the stark granite cairns that studded the bleakness and the low threatening clouds that cast long confining shadows. He closed his eyes, remembering the blaze of summer and the fire of his youth as the freezing dampness seemed to seep into his bones, making them ache with a premonition of age. He felt old, he admitted as his horse slowed his pace and picked his way across the barren heath. A sudden fleet movement caught his eye and he gasped as an enormous black animal bounded from one rock to another before being lost in the swirling tendrils of the sea fret. The sound of rapid hoofbeats followed and out of the mist appeared a small rider perched upon the high back of a large black horse. Taran noted the shocked surprise that widened the arresting eyes of the child as they met face to face. The small nostrils flared and the boy dug in his heels, causing his stallion to rear before galloping away, becoming lost in the thick fog. Curiosity overriding his better judgment, and excitement in the chase putting youth back in his blood, Taran urged his horse after the swarthy trio. He knew he was rash and expected a rabbit hole to bring his wildly galloping mount to a painful halt. But he laughed aloud, throwing his head back so his thick, black hair streamed in the wind. He gasped as Pendarves Castle loomed out of the fog and an eerie baying chilled his spine. He slowed his horse to a walk and approached the formidable, hollow-eyed fortress, his keen eyes searching for a sign of life. Vaguely he recalled hearing that Godolphus Pendarves had died a year or so before, but he had purposefully ignored the news, not wanting to disturb old wounds. Several large ravens circled the turrets, seeming to warn him to keep his distance, and the uncanny howling of a wolf echoed from deep within the grim granite structure.

"Why ez the Bucca fretting?" hissed Granny-Griggs, ceasing her stirring and lifting a gnarled hand to her ear to better hear over the bubbling and hissing of the cooking; hear above the crackling of the blazing hearth and the thunderous roar of the waves in the caves below.

"What is it?" demanded Miss Peller, staring at the wildly gesticulating Yeoman, who turned various shades of purple in an effort to make unintelligible strangled cries.

"Halleluja!" chanted Curate Pomfrey, lifting his grubby threadbare cassock and prancing merrily into the kitchen on spindly legs.

"There's a stranger outside," chorused the Three-Marys, clutching each other in fear.

" 'Tis the Magi!" rejoiced the senile curate. "For it is Christmas and the wisemen have come to greet the child."

"What is it?" asked Miss Peller, sharply clapping her hands to silence the muttering Marys and chanting curate.

"The Magi!" cackled Granny-Griggs. "Pomfrey's abin in the brandy kegs agin!"

"Pengelly, who's there?" repeated the housekeeper to the old man who hovered in the arched doorway. "What's causing the hound to take on so?"

"Tes none but zum poor stranger lost in this thick sea fret. Cannot see the nose on yer face in some parts," answered Jonty Pengelly, and the chattering old people hissed to a sudden silence as a violent hammering shuddered through the cold stones of the castle.

"That's imperious knocking for a poor stranger," observed the gaunt Miss Peller.

"Because it is the Magi!" pronounced Curate Pomfrey.

"Sounds more like excise men," snorted Granny-Griggs, and the three Marys shrieked with alarm.

"Jonty Pengelly, look out of the spy-hole. I have a sour

forboding about who our Christmas visitor might be,'' hissed the housekeeper. ''Yeoman, is all hidden and locked up?'' she asked sharply, and the mute nodded frantically as he leaped up and down with fear.

''Dominus Christos,'' chanted Curate Pomfrey happily.

''Where's the Devil-Child?'' worried one of the Marys.

''Where the Bucca be,'' laughed Granny-Griggs. ''And from the sound of thet howling, I'd say they be up high on the ramparts.''

''Well, who is it?'' demanded Miss Peller as Pengelly entered.

''Tes Tremayne of Taran. I heard as how he were back,'' answered Jonty.

''Tremayne of Taran!'' gasped the housekeeper. ''I expected bad but not this. What do you think he wants?''

''Shall I let him in so we can find out?''

''Are you mad, Pengelly?'' retorted Miss Peller, pulling her black shawl tightly about her long thin body and sitting in her straight-backed chair. ''He'll go away,'' she added as the loud knocking echoed through the hollow corridors. The Three-Marys huddled together to one side of the large cooking hearth, watching Granny-Griggs's constantly moving gnarled hand stir the cauldron. Yeoman jiggled up and down with terror and the curate chanted merrily in Latin, prancing from square to square on the kitchen floor as though playing hop-scotch. Furtive whisperings and scurrying feet heralded more of the black-garbed old people, who clustered, fear shaking their bowed shoulders as the heavy iron knocker was crashed against the massive door.

''There's nothing to fear if we just sit tight and bide our time. He'll get tired and be on his way,'' stated Miss Peller.

''Tremayne of Taran alone?'' enquired Granny-Griggs, and all eyes looked anxiously at Jonty Pengelly, who nodded silently, his thoughts high up on the turret where the dark child stood with the giant hound looking down at the black-haired man. It had given his old heart a curious twist seeing Benedict Tremayne's distinct features. The large expressive eyes and the sleek ebony hair were so much like the child's. It was imperative the two should not come face to face, worried the old man because the relationship was so obvious.

Taran let the heavy iron door knocker fall again as he thought of the split second where the child's face had loomed out of the fog. The wide dark eyes below the thick riot of black hair reminded him of his brother, Michael. The same fine sensitive features, the slight bones. Had his imagination been playing him tricks? he wondered. He sat his horse and walked him slowly about the stone fortress. Except for the mournful baying that skirled with the mist and the ravens who ponderously roosted in the deep slit windows, the castle seemed deserted. Yet he couldn't shake the strong sense that he was being watched.

"Anyone about?" he roared, and a sudden twittering cloud of bats flickered out of the steamy tendrils of fog and the howling lament increased in fervor. Thoughtfully he dismounted again and examined the soft ground, noting fresh hoofprints. "The moor abounds with wild ponies," he told himself, knowing the prints were too large for the shaggy little animals. He followed the trail around the castle until he came to the barbican, an exterior gatehouse that protected the entrance, where the hoofprints ended. Interesting that the portcullis was well-oiled and free of dust and rust on the winding gear, he noted. Why would the occupants of Pendarves Castle keep themselves so secure from intrusion? he pondered as he rode slowly away determined to return at another not so inhospitable time.

"He's gone?" asked Miss Peller sharply, and Jonty Pengelly nodded, and the long hiss of relief whistled through the pleated lips of the old huddled mass.

"Time to eat our Christmas meal," announced Granny-Griggs. "Sit thyself down, Devil-Child," she ordered, catching sight of the child in the shadows. "There's a marrow bone for the Bucca-Dhu," she chattered, turning back to her steaming cauldron, but the child made no motion to join the others, who scrambled eagerly for a seat at the long bare table.

"That was Tremayne of Taran?"

"Yes, Devil-Child, thet was Sir Benedict Tremayne of Taran," answered Granny-Griggs, cackling triumphantly at Rebecca Peller, whose gaunt face was enfused with fury and fear.

"Silence!" screamed the housekeeper and the Living-Dead huddled together.

"That was my father?" whispered the child, remembering the dark, hawklike features of the tall rider on the bleak high moor.

"That was the man that caused your mother's death!" stated Miss Peller. There was a silence as all eyes were pinned to the slight shadowy figure of the Devil-Child; a silence broken by the brittle crackle of the fire and the rasping purr of a one-eyed cat who rubbed against Granny-Griggs's legs.

CHAPTER 7

"WOTCHA GRANNY put you on the third floor for?" panted Iris, entering Angelica's room after a perfunctory knock and collapsing against the closed door. "This bloomin' comin'-out ball of yourn 'ad better be a good 'un," she puffed. Angelica looked up from her reading and smiled absently before gazing out of the window at the River Thames, ruffled and pitted by the constant rain. "Is that a letter from yer dad?" asked Iris eagerly. The tall girl nodded and sighed. "Then wotcha so grumpy for?"

"I wish I could remember the people he mentions. Maizie Skinner and Caleb? Whoever Sir Torrance Pendarves is or was, isn't anymore because he died and his sons, one, badly maimed, have reopened High Tor, whatever or wherever High Tor is . . . and my mother is happily doing what she is most happy doing . . . and I haven't a notion what it is my mother is most happy doing!"

"Where does it say that?" enquired Iris, hanging over Angelica's shoulder and perusing the letter. "I dunno 'ow you can read that! It's all scribblin'. I ain't ever going ter be able ter read grown-up writin'!" she wailed.

"Of course you will. You've learned the whole alphabet since Christmas," encouraged Angelica.

"We all got fitted fer our new uniforms terday. Even Mister Smithers and the footmen. Talk is it ain't going ter be black no more."

"What colour?"

"It's a big secret, just like you not knowing nothin' about yer own ballgown. Mr. Ess 'as wagered that we're all goin'

114

ter be in purple and puce ter match Lady Em and the pink wallpaper. And Mrs. Ess says 'as 'ow she 'as this 'orrible feelin' in 'er bones about the ball!'' recounted Iris gleefully, but Angel didn't even manage a faint smile.

"I also have an uneasiness about this ball. Every day the modiste marches in followed by her grim little seamstresses . . . measuring and draping . . . with sly smiles and knowing little pokes and I have to stand still for hours on end . . . and they never say a word but keep long lines of pins pressed between their lips in case they snicker," stated Angelica bitterly. "It is as though they know an excruciatingly funny jest that is to be played on me."

"Don't be daft! It's goin' ter be the grandest, most poshest ball in the 'ole world," declared Iris after a long pause. "And you, Miss Angel, is goin' ter be the grandest, most poshest debutante in the 'ole of London town."

"Probably dressed in purple and puce, too!"

"Mrs. Ess and me 'ave bin droppin' big 'ints to 'er ladyship and 'er dressmakers sayin' as 'ow you look ever so much better in green, so I betcha buttons ter bulldogs yer dress ain't pink," soothed Iris. "Oh crikey, will it ever stop bloody rainin'?" she lamented, dashing into the dressing room and reappearing with her black cape and a large black bonnet.

"Where are you going?" asked Angel, eager to be out of the stuffy house.

"Just a coupla errands," dismissed Iris, tying the enormous hat on her small dark head.

"In that bonnet?" exclaimed Angel.

"Fetchin', ain't it? Some old lady give it ter me fer me mum's funeral."

"It's awful! You're all hat and no Iris!"

"It does the job then," returned Iris, nodding with satisfaction at her reflection.

"I need some fresh air. I'll help you with the errands," said Angel, placing a bonnet on her own head.

"I don't need no 'elp!" cried Iris. "I mean ter say it ain't yer place. You could get me inter trouble."

"I understand, Iris."

"You don't wanna get wet so you 'ave a nasty cold fer yer fancy ball, do yer?"

"I said I understood, Iris," snapped Angel crossly.

"We 'ave ter keep you nice and 'ealthy fer yer comin' out next week," chattered the maid as she backed out of the door, clutching her small ragged reticule that held some money and Lord Taran's London address. Furtively she crept down the back staircase and let herself out of the servant's door. She scurried along the cobbled mews by the stables unaware of Lord Carringdon, who was about to step out of his enclosed carriage. He watched her thoughtfully before sitting back and signalling his coachman to follow the bustling little figure.

By the time Iris reached Tremayne House, the rain was sheeting down with such ferocity she could barely see her hand in front of her face. She was weighed down by her sodden wool cape, and the enormous bonnet had lost its formidable stiffness. It had collapsed about her small face, the black dye streaking her cheeks and neck. She clutched at the wrought-iron palings that surrounded the tall impressive mansion and stared blearily at the dark windows, looking for a sign of life. She made her way around to the back past the stables, which also seemed empty and deserted, and bravely knocked at the servants' entrance. As she waited she blew on her cold hands and stamped her numb feet, humming a tuneless ditty at the same time to keep her spirits up. She knocked again and still jiggling about tried to peek into a window, where she saw a glimmer of lantern light escaping through a space in the drawn drapes. She got a foot-hold on the iron-railing and heaved herself up to better see into the house when the door was abruptly opened. Iris quickly jumped down, nearly leaving her wet boot wedged between the palings and painfully wrenching her foot in the process.

"Did'nt fink no one was 'ere," she muttered, swallowing hard and gazing up at a sturdy young man who stood coatless with his shirt rolled up to his elbows.

"Yes?" he boomed impatiently, and Iris tried to appear at her most vulnerable and helpless. "There's no use putting on any lost dog airs wie me, wench. You look like a drowned rat anyway," he said tersely with a Scottish brogue.

"Is this Lord Taran's 'ouse?" she whispered plaintively,

squelching the acid retort she longed to let fly at the brusque man.

"And what if it is?"

"Well, I'm Daisy, sir," she answered, bobbing a curtsey and liberally spraying the man with rain. "So I'm 'ere."

"Why?" barked the laconic man.

"Why? Fer the job, of course."

"You've been misinformed. There's no job here!" snapped the man about to shut the door in her face.

"Misinformed?" screeched Iris, lurching heavily so she stepped into the hallway, her soggy boot firmly stopping the door. "I walked all the way from 'ammersmith in this 'orrible rain!"

"What's going on?" enquired a woman's voice.

"It's all right, Mrs. Perkins," replied the man, about to forcibly remove Iris so he could slam the door.

"No job!" wailed Iris piteously as a great roar of thunder crashed and lightning flashed. Using the elements to her advantage, she gave a shrill scream and threw herself into his arms.

"Mrs. Perkins, keep an eye on her, and when the worst of the storm is over, send her back to Hammersmith," growled the man, firmly putting Iris from him. She stifled a giggle at seeing that the black dye from her bonnet had liberally splotched his snowy shirt front. She stood with the water puddling at her feet as he strode away.

"Don't mind Angus Dunbar, his bark is worse than his bite," laughed Mrs. Perkins, leading the way to a cheerful kitchen, where a small fire blazed merrily. "Put yer shoes at the hearth and drape yer sopping cape over here," she directed.

" 'o is 'e?"

"Mr. Dunbar? He's his lordship's businessman . . . runs the estate and this house, but what with packing everything up he's just about doing everything."

"Cor, way 'e acted I thought 'e was 'is lordship isself, 'cept that 'e opened the back door," said Iris, removing the limp dripping bonnet.

"Pretty little thing you are even with all that black dye dribbling down your face," observed the elderly woman, pouring a steaming mug of tea.

"Did somebody die?" asked Iris, curling her cold hands about the hot cup and sipping the tea gratefully.

"Die? Nobody that I know of. Why?"

"You said the 'ouse was bein' closed up."

"His lordship has gone back to his estate in Cornwall, and I'm retired with a pension."

"Forever?"

"I hope so . . . well, at least until I die. It's a very generous stipend, it is."

"No, I mean 'as 'is lordship gone ferever?"

"What a funny question. What's Lord Taran to you, my girl?" snapped the woman suspiciously.

"Nothin' . . . I was just talkin' . . . tryin ter be polite and 'ave a conversation, that's all," said Iris quickly. "Luverly cuppa tea," she added, sipping noisily and staring about the kitchen. "Not a very big kitchen fer a great big 'ouse, is it?"

"Big kitchen's all shut up."

"Shame, ain't it . . . empty 'ouses always give me the shivers. Don't you get the shivers with empty 'ouses?" struggled Iris.

"Can't say that I do."

"Why would anybody leave such a big posh 'ouse like this? If it was mine I'd 'ave every room full of candles and music and 'ave lotsa parties. Bet 'is lordship 'as a big family? A beautiful wife and lots and lots of little nippers to fill up the 'ouse?" she probed, but the woman sat staring silently, her thin mouth tightly closed.

"Can I 'ave some more tea, please?" she asked, smiling innocently and holding out the empty cup.

"The storm's nearly over," said Mrs. Perkins curtly, making no move to lift her teapot.

"You don't say," replied Iris as an enormous roll of thunder rattled the windows. "Look, missus, I dunno what I 'ave done ter make you nasty . . . and I appreciate yer 'ospitality and the tea, but 'ow would you feel if you was me? Aye? Comin' all this way in this weather on a wild goose chase? 'ere, feel my cape, it ain't warm enough fer winter . . . look at my boots. . . . you know why I was wearin' that black 'at? Go on, guess!" she insisted as the elderly woman shrugged. "I come 'ere straight from my sainted mother's funeral. That's right. Some mean-mouth played some 'orrid trick on me by tellin' me there was a job ter be 'ad 'ere at Lord Taran's 'ouse . . . so I left me poor dead mother even before they put the coffin in the ground, and do you know why? Go on, tell me why," hissed Iris, caught up in her heartrending story and thoroughly enjoying herself.

"Why?" enquired a gruff voice, and she stared across at Angus Dunbar lounging in the kitchen doorway.

"It don't matter . . . I'm on me way. Sorry fer wastin' yer time," dismissed Iris, running a hand through her wild wet curls.

Angus looked thoughtfully at the bedraggled young girl.

"I am fascinated. Why would a dutiful daughter leave a puir dead mother before she had been placed under the earth?" he asked, making himself comfortable at the kitchen table and pouring a cup of tea. "Would you like some more?" he offered, holding up the pot and gesturing towards her empty mug. Iris stared at the tips of her stockinged toes. Three years before she had rushed away from the pauper's graveyard, where they had been burying her mother and two sisters. "I am waiting with avid curiosity," urged the Scot. Iris's eyes ached with unshed tears. Why had she left the funeral? She didn't know. Silently she shook her dark tousled head, remembering that she had found herself running. Just screaming and running. One minute she had been standing with her head bowed at the graveside, and the next all that existed had been the jolting rhythm of her legs and the strange cries that burst from her mouth. She had run until she had dropped and had never gone back to see the mounds of earth.

"I 'ave ter be off," she answered, truculently reaching for the sodden boots. Not a word was spoken as she crammed her cold sore feet into the restricting wet leather, draped the heavy saturated cape about her thin shoulders, and crammed the hideous dripping bonnet on her head.

Angus Dunbar's eyes narrowed as he watched the girl march defiantly across the kitchen, her boots squelching. He stretched his legs and leaned back, wondering what ruse she would use to delay her exit. Would she stagger and faint? Bend double with a sudden agonizing spasm? Sob pitifully? All those ideas and more darted through Iris's agile brain.

Deciding on a pitiful sob, she emitted a shuddering sniff and spun about on her heel, but on catching his cynical expression changed her mind. What was the point in hanging about the warm dry house except for shelter from the storm? She had obviously found out all she was going to, she reasoned, looking from Mrs. Perkins's suspicious face to the young man. He stared at her indulgently, as though reading her very thoughts and finding them amusing.

"Well?" he asked as she stood poised on the threshold.

"Well, seein' as 'ow there ain't no job as 'is Lordship ain't 'ere and ain't ever hexpected, I should be on me way. Just one more thing. Does Lord Taran 'ave a wife?"

"He's sworn off women and weren't ever interested in little snips from the gutter like you!" hissed Mrs. Perkins scathingly.

"Shove it up yer arse'ole!" answered Iris with a saucy curtsey. She slammed the outside door behind her and instantly regretted her rudeness as the thunder still crashed unceasingly. She shivered, wrapped the sodden cape tighter about her slight shoulders, and bowed her head against the driving force of the icy wind. She did not see Lord Carringdon, who stepped down from his carriage directly into her path.

Angus Dunbar stood at the dark library window watching the girl being helped into the carriage. He frowned, recognising the gaudy crest emblazoned on the door.

"What would that ostentatious bore Carringdon want with Taran?" he muttered as the showy but inferior horses took the carriage out of sight.

Angelica gazed out at the storm, feeling a vague nostalgia as the Thames was whipped and the boats creaked and strained against their moorings. Her warm breath frosted the cold panes of the window and she rubbed them clear trying to see something that would spur her memory. She felt so very near to remembering. The storm-tossed waters of the river, the rattle and whine of the wind, the constant drumming of the rain, the hollow cry of the gulls who rode the spars of the bucking vessels . . . all of these were trying to unlock memories. She threw open the window and leaned out, breathing deeply, trying to connect with an unknown element. But what she expected to smell wasn't there. She sobbed aloud with frustration as tantalizing whisps of memory elusively floated through her mind, not staying long enough to be grasped and identified.

"Crikey, shut that ruddy winder or we'll both catch our deaths!" gasped Iris, rushing into the room and slamming the door. Angel turned and stared at the little maid, whose face was pinched and blue with cold and whose clothes streamed with water. "Shut the winder," repeated Iris, shivering uncontrollably.

"What happened?" Angel exclaimed, latching the window and following the girl into the adjoining dressing room. "Where have you been? Mrs. Smithers has been turning the house upside down looking for you," she demanded as she helped the shaking girl remove her sodden clothes.

"Oh, Gawd, there goes me job!" wailed Iris, her teeth chattering painfully.

"Calm down. I lied for you. I told Mrs. Smithers that you were running some errands for me," snapped Angelica, briskly rubbing the girl with a dry towel, trying to restore circulation into the thin mottled limbs. "Now everyone is convinced I am a veritable ogress for sending you out in this inhospitable weather," she teased as she tugged a cosy homespun night dress over the quaking wet head. "Get into bed and I'll try and salvage my reputation by getting you some hot broth and some hot bricks."

As the dressing room door shut behind her mistress, Iris dived under the covers of her narrow cot. She curled her thin knees up to her chest and wrapped her arms about her legs, still shivering violently as the nightmarish ride home with Lord Carringdon played over in her head.

"Iris Wilkins, yer a rotten lot . . . sell yer own granny fer a loaf of bread, wouldn't yer?" she sobbed angrily. "Carn't keep yer big gob shut, can yer? Oh, Gawd!" She cried in a way she hadn't done for years. Angelica was just going out of her bedchamber when she heard the furious muttering followed by a muffled howl and then frantic sobs. "Bloody little coward, Iris Wilkins! Don't 'urt me! Don't 'urt me! yer whined like a snotty-nosed baby! What's a little 'urt, aye? Oh Gawd, Gawd, what 'ave I gone and done?''

Angelica stood at the door listening to the hysterical words as Iris berated herself. "Iris?" she said softly, entering and sitting on the bed beside the heaving mound. The girl froze, swallowing her sobs, trying to control herself.

"What's the matter?"

"Nothin'! Just let me alone!" snarled Iris, suddenly throwing back the bedcovers and glaring hostilely into her mistress's concerned face. "Get out and leave me alone!"

"Tell me, Iris!" urged Angelica gently, reaching out to smooth the tangled hair from the tear-streaked cheeks. Iris savagely slapped her hand away.

"Feel sorry fer yer own self, Miss Goody-Two-Shoes!" she spat venomously. "Oh, Miss Angel, I'm sorry. . . . Oh, Gawd, I'm sorry," wailed Iris as she saw the shocked hurt in Angel's eyes. "I didn't mean nothink . . . I'm ever so sorry," she sobbed.

"It's all right, Iris," soothed her mistress.

"It ain't!" keened the maid, diving under the blankets again and hiding her shame. "It ain't ever goin' ter be all right again! I thought I could 'andle 'im, but I couldn't . . . and 'e's ever so mean . . . and 'e don't want you 'avin' none of yer granny's money . . . and 'e'll stop at nothink . . . Oh, Lor, what 'ave I done?" lamented Iris.

"There, there," crooned Angelica, unable to make sense of the long woeful tale. "You stay all bundled up and I'll bring the hot broth. We'll talk when you're calm. I won't be long," and she quickly and quietly left the room.

"I didn't mean ter tell 'im but 'e was goin' ter 'urt me somethink awful . . . said 'e'd sell me ter an 'ore 'ouse where blokes wif the pox went . . . said 'e'd 'urt me in my private parts . . . so I told 'im 'ow Lord Taran was goin' ter marry you . . . and then 'e says about it bein' Lord Taran with you when you run off . . . so some one else 'ad to 'ave told 'im about that cos I didn't . . . I swear I didn't.''

Angelica and Mrs. Smithers bustled in with hot bricks wrapped in yards of rags and a steaming bowl of chicken broth to find Iris curled into a prenatal position sound asleep but hiccoughing and mumbling at the same time. They stood silently staring down at the grubby little maid, whose face was streaked with black dye and tears.

"Poor little luvey, she don't look no more'n a child," clucked Mrs. Smithers.

"She isn't," added Angelica.

"In years she isn't, but in experience she has us both beat," sighed the old woman, tucking the hot bricks around the thin shivering girl.

"I wonder what happened?" said Angelica, smoothing the covers.

"What ever it was, Lord Carringdon had a hand in it," stated Mrs. Smithers tersely.

"Lord Carringdon?"

"Wilkins came back in his carriage. Look, it may be none of my business, Miss Angel," sighed the old woman as they quietly left the dressing room. "And I know you're very fond of Wilkins . . . I am, too . . . but she's had a hard life. Had to look after herself and she does what she has to do . . . that's the way of it," she continued.

"What are you trying to tell me?"

"Wilkins and Lord Carringdon have . . . well, it isn't proper for a well-bred young lady like you to know of such things. I should have seen she got her notice as soon as I knew for sure, but I confess I had a soft spot in my heart for the girl . . . and it really isn't her fault. I know it isn't my place to say so . . . but Lord Carringdon isn't a very . . . nice gentleman."

"He isn't a gentleman at all," agreed Angel, remembering what Iris had told her. "But I am sorry I don't understand what you are saying, Mrs. Smithers."

"Lord Carringdon has bin . . . using Wilkins."

"Using Wilkins?"

"Like a whore," enlightened the old lady, and Angel's eyes widened with shock.

"Like a whore?" she repeated, and the old woman nodded. "No . . . ."

The next week passed in a hive of frantic activity, and Mr. Smithers's worst fears were realized when the servants' satin uniforms for the ball were completed and delivered.

"Pink wigs?" he intoned, wondering why he wasn't the least surprised. Purple frogged uniforms from a bygone era and pink periwigs that had yet to be in fashion.

"If the servants are to wear pink perukes, I shudder to think what my secret ballgown is like," mourned Angelica on hearing the news.

"Some of the footmen 'ave threaten' ter walk out," trilled Iris, ignoring the searching look her mistress gave her and scampering into the dressing room to hang up her new dark purple dress. Angelica shook her head. The morning after Iris's damp excursion, the irrepressible girl had bounced up as though nothing untoward had occurred. Any attempt to find out where she had been was met with a pert evasive answer such as "I went ter see a man about a dog," or "I went ter see a man about a cat."

"Ternight's the night," chanted Iris. "Better 'ave a little nap after tea so yer don't fall asleep in the middle of yer ball."

"Strange that Lord Carringdon has not visited this last week," remarked Angel, staring very pointedly at Iris.

" 'e'll pop up like a bad penny, so don't wish 'im on us fer Gawd's sake," returned Iris airily. "Anyways, I 'ear that 'e is part of the reception line, seein' 'as 'ow 'e's nearly yer grandpa and yer granny don't 'old wif yer mum and dad."

"Reception line?"

"Yea, yer know . . . you, yer granny and 'is Lordship will be standin' up on that sorta tentlike thing in the 'all greetin' all the guests . . . ain't you excited?"

"Frankly I am terrified."

"The 'ole 'ouse looks somethink, don't it? Redecorated from top ter bottom, must 'ave cost a bloody fortune. Well, I'm excited. I ain't ever bin to a ball before . . . or seen one," she corrected. "Ain't you even a teeny bit interested ter see what yer ballgown's like?" she asked impishly.

Angelica Carmichael shook her head in disbelief as she stared into the rose-tinted mirror. She sighed dismally. "There is nothing for it but to kill myself," she decided after a silent deliberation.

"Oh, don't take on so, Miss Angel. You don't look that

bad,'' soothed Iris, smoothing the skirts of her new purple uniform. "Nah, it ain't no use. I carn't lie ter you. You look gawd-awful and that's the truth!''

"Thank you, Iris.''

"I thought them sorta ballgowns was worn 'undreds and 'undreds of years ago?''

"They were. When Grandmaman was a debutante.''

"And what wif that bloody great cage underneath and all them panniers and tassels, 'ow the bloody 'ell are you goin' ter sit down?'' asked Iris, walking around the elaborate structure that housed her young mistress. Angelica shrugged morosely.

"Hopefully I shall die of mortification before my legs get tired.''

"And you ain't goin' ter wear that bloody great wig wif all them jewels and feathers, are you?'' giggled the maid.

"I don't think I have a choice,'' lamented Angel as Lady Melisande's bell tinkled insistently. "I could throw myself off Battersea Bridge into the Thames and drown myself, I suppose.''

"Wouldn't do no good! Yer'd float! Oh, I can just see yer bobbin' up and down like some pink frilly cork,'' chortled Wilkins. "You carn't jump out the winder neither cos the wind'll catch you and yer'll fly away like some bloomin' great bird!'' she added, collapsing across the bed and howling with merriment. Angelica tried to look severe, but imagining the ludicrous picture she would make sailing across London with a cloud of pigeons garbed in the multitasselled, over-beribboned, frilly ballgown was just too much. She staggered backwards and sat, her giggles increasing into whoops of uncontrollable laughter as the enormous skirt flipped over her head.

Mrs. Smithers knocked several times on Angelica's bed-chamber door. Hearing nothing but infectious snorts and chuckles, she popped her head around just as Wilkins managed to haul her mistress upright and try to calm the wildly wobbling tiers of gaudy fabric.

"You look like the curtains in a tart's boudoir,'' choked the irrepressible maid with her legs entwined. The two girls crumpled back into helpless convulsions.

"That's quite enough, Wilkins!" declared Mrs. Smithers in outraged tones. "How dare you speak to your mistress like that?"

"It's . . . it's . . . quite all right, Mrs. Smithers," gasped Angel when she could speak, dabbing at the tears of mirth that streamed down her cheeks. "I did ask Iris's opinion."

"Your grandmother is dressed and ready for the ball and wishes to see you," informed the old woman, gasping with ill-disguised horror at the tall young woman in the old-fashioned, over-decorated gown. "Wilkins, help Miss Angel," she ordered, distractedly waving her hand towards the very high pompadour wig. Iris gingerly approached the enormous powdered and plumed headpiece.

"Crikey, there's a real dead bird in there!" she exclaimed. "Stuffed and dyed pink," she added after giving it a poke.

"Unfortunately it is even worse than it appears," admitted Mrs. Smithers, sitting heavily and shaking her grey head morosely.

" 'Ow can anythink be worse than that?" declared Iris dramatically, pointing to the farcical image of her young mistress in the rose-tinted shell-shaped mirror. "Yer right, Mrs. Ess, it ain't 'umerous, it's a bloomin' tragedy!"

"Thank you, Iris," acknowledged Angel, inclining her head sarcastically and nearly falling flat on her face as the heavy wig unbalanced her.

"Your grandmother, Lady Melisande, is wearing the very same gown and wig," informed Mrs. Smithers. A stunned silence followed the dire pronouncement.

"The very same gown and wig?" repeated Angelica after a lengthy pause.

"You are to wear this domino," sniffed Mrs. Smithers, holding out a gaudy bejewelled mask edged with pink egret feathers.

"Well that's a mercy! Nobody'll know 'o you are!" comforted the maid.

"Is my grandmother also wearing the identical domino?" asked Angel, and the old woman nodded unhappily.

"What's 'er ladyship's game?" asked Wilkins at a loss, but noting the knowing look that passed between Angel and Mrs. Smithers.

"Oh, she's a wily old woman. She doesn't often get the better of me, but she has this time. Oh, I am so sorry about all this, Miss Angel. If I had known what she had up her sleeve, I'd have put a stop to it quick sharp . . . but I didn't have an inkling . . . not an inkling," ranted Mrs. Smithers. "Well, don't just stand there like two great lumps, get to it. Find another gown!"

"There ain't none," declared Iris, opening the wardrobe with a flourish. "See? Two ridin' 'abits and a dressin' gown. We went out fer a breath of air this mornin' and come 'ome ter find Simms cartin' them all away . . . says 'er Ladyship told 'er to. Somethink about moths or fleas or maybe lice!"

"Ooh, that naughty old lady!" hissed Mrs. Smithers, shaking with rage. "I've a mind to have Mr. Ess turn up all the lamps so the house is lit as bright as day. Oooh, that'd show everyone who is the young lady and who is the old fool!" The door slammed behind the irate woman, and Iris and Angel exchanged gloomy glances.

"I'm going to disguise myself," decided Angel.

"What the 'ell for? You don't know 'o you are anyway . . . so yer won't know anyone 'o comes unless you knowed them after yer lost yer memory, and all gussied up wif the bird's nest and the mask stuck on yer face, yer own mum aint goin' ter recognise yer!"

"There was one person I hoped would come," whispered Angel, sadly thinking of Benedict Tremayne's handsome features.

"He ain't comin'," stated Iris sharply. "Lord Taran ain't in town," she added bluntly.

"How did you know?"

"I'm a witch . . . I 'ave me ways," replied the maid evasively. " 'e weren't an old ugly one, were 'e?" she asked, seeing Angel's shoulders slump dejectedly. The girl shook her head and the wig teetered precariously.

"Help me to pin this on more securely; I don't want to appear more incongruous than necessary," said Angelica, clutching at the ornate headpiece.

"Was 'e 'andsome?" probed Iris, standing on a chair so she could reach the top of her mistress's head.

"Who?"

"Lord Taran?" she asked, and Angel dreamily nodded.
" 'ere, wotchit! Keep yer 'ead still. I just got a feather up me
nose! Oh, Lor! there goes yer granny's bell again. I tell you
this is one day I'm 'appy ter be Iris Wilkins. I wouldn't
change shoes wif you fer the crown jewels. 'Ere, ere, chin
up. Look on the bright side," cajolled Iris.

"What bright side?"

"Well, wot wif all that whalebone and wood, tassels and
frills, Lord Carringdon ain't goin' ter get 'is filthy 'ands
anywhere near yer private parts!" declared Iris triumphantly,
and on that comforting note Angelica affixed her domino,
clasped her fan, and tried to make a dignified exit. But she
had to bow her head because the wig was too high and shuffle
sideways because the doorway was too narrow for the enormous hooped skirt.

"Chin up," chirped Iris, blowing a kiss. "You look . . .
very . . . very . . ."

"Pink?" suggested Angel wryly.

Angelica kept her chin up and tried to ignore the snorts and
titters that exploded, she assumed, at the ridiculous sight of
her very tall pink figure, her very diminutive pink grandmother, and Lord Carringdon in violent canary yellow under
a pink tasselled canopy. A thousand pink scented candles
snaked sooty perfumes, heating the ballroom to suffocating
proportions. The smoke distorted the awkwardly hovering
guests and the pink-wigged, purple-clad footmen who stood
like miserable statues balancing loaded trays. Seven harpsichords tinkled slightly out of tune. From the conservatory
could be heard tortured squeaks and wails as thirteen gypsy
violinists warmed their instruments.

Overhearing a conversation between Lord Carringdon and a
decrepit old man, Angelica learned that Lady Melisande was
seeking to recreate her own triumphant entry into society
more than fifty years before. She had duplicated every detail
down to the pink periwigs on the servants' heads. One after
the other, each appearing more ancient than the next, the
guests filed, or rather, tottered by, peering through an assortment of pince-nez, monocles, and lorgnettes. Angelica couldn't
remember one face or name. Each seemed nightmarishly the

same, devoid of any distinguishing feature or gender. The same trite phrases were repeated until she found herself mouthing the words as the perimeter of the ballroom was filled with a mass of mumbling people.

"And which of these two lovelies is our little debutante?" was continually, echoed followed by a gurgle of delight from behind Lady Melisande's pink feathered fan. If a guest was remiss and the question not asked, Lord Carringdon gallantly obliged.

"I am sure you are wondering just which of these two ravishing beauties is . . . ?" he prompted. Or "Simply everyone has been asking which of these two exquisite young ladies is our little . . ." Fortunately, as Lord Carringdon was neither very intelligent nor a witty conversationalist, the guest usually hobbled away in midsentence, being too well-bred to laugh outright, reasoned Angelica. Her head pounded from the weight of the wig and her legs ached unbearably. She idly debated lifting both her feet off the floor to see if the cagelike structure under her voluminous skirts could bear her weight when a strident nasal voice caused her heart to race with panic.

"Lady Isabella, how simply delightful," gushed Lord Carringdon, and Angelica felt her tiny grandmother stiffen. "Melisande, I took the liberty of inviting Lady Isabella Bonny, knowing you would be as overjoyed as I am to see her," he expanded, kissing the proffered hand. It was exceedingly obvious that her grandmother was anything but overjoyed, observed Angelica, as pink feathers flew in all directions from the frantically waving fan. Why did the woman make her skin crawl? puzzled Angelica. What was there about the voice that made her instinctively want to run away?

"Miss Carmichael?" snarled the malevolent-looking red mouth. Angelica chided herself for her uncharitable thoughts and smiled bravely at the haughty beauty, who seemed to stare at her contemptuously.

"Lady Bonny," replied Angel in acknowledgment. "Have we met before?" she asked, during an uncomfortable silence.

"How dare you!" shouted Lady Isabella so loudly that the hum of conversation abruptly stopped and all eyes turned to the dais.

"I beg your pardon?" whispered Angel at a loss.

"Have we met before, you ask?" repeated Isabella in ringing tones when she was absolutely certain she commanded everyone's attention. The harpsichords finally played in unison—one clashing chord—and then tinkled to a stop. The ensuing silence was deafening as each ear strained and Angelica's heart thumped painfully. "You *know* we have met before and *where*! You were naked in my fiancé's bed!" dramatically accused the woman, stabbing a pointed finger. There was an audible gasp of outrage.

"What did she say?" warbled a very old man.

"This . . . this . . . so-called innocent debutante, Angelica Carmichael, was naked in the bed of my fiancé, Lord Taran!" cried Isabella obligingly.

The resulting chaos became a blur in Angel's mind. She raised her chin and affixed her eyes to a sweetly smiling cherub on the handpainted ceiling. Her grandmother had one of her most unbridled tantrums to date and stormed to her suite of rooms, wreaking havoc on her numerous alabaster busts on the way. Once locked in her boudoir she proceeded to scream obscenities and smash every breakable object she could lift. Lord Carringdon chivalrously escorted the wildly sobbing Lady Isabella to her carriage, where he paid her the handsome promised sum and they enjoyed a triumphant laugh. The ballroom hummed happily as the juicy tidbit of malicious gossip was savoured and devoured along with the caviar, lobsters, pheasants, sides of beef, hothouse fruits, and other delectables. It was then washed down with the very best champagne before the sorely offended guests angrily demanded their capes and wraps, refusing to spend one more minute in the debasing company of such a brazen, shameless hussy. The sated harpsichordists, tucking whatever food they could into their bulging pockets, followed hard on their heels, shaking their heads with disapproval at the tall proud female. Angelica stood on the high dais framed by the pink tasselled canopy looking like an unrepentant Madame Pompadour. The thirteen gypsies strolled by, nodding their appreciation of the dignity of the shunned young woman. At a signal from their leader, whose keen sensitivity felt an aura of misery emanating from behind the haughty demeanor, lifted their instruments and played a haunting air as a tribute. Iris hovered in the shadows, sniffing miserably as she watched her mistress, who slowly looked down at the thirteen violinists in a bemused fashion.

Angelica peeled the domino from her face and wrenched the high powdered wig from her head, allowing her own thick chestnut hair to cascade about her shoulders. It caught the leaping lights of the flickering candles like a fiery halo. She smiled tremulously at the musicians. The leader bowed and grinned, satisfied to see that the girl's eyes held a bright spark of spirit, though they brimmed with unspilled tears. He signalled to his men. Still playing, they strolled out of the house. Angelica listened until the melody fused with the night breeze. Then she sighed and gazed about her at the wreckage of her debut into London society.

"Oh, Miss Angel, what are we goin' ter do?" wailed Iris, staring with fear at the ceiling, which shook with the violence of Lady Melisande's fury. There was a particularly rude word caterwauled, a sudden thud, and then silence. "Oh, Lor! I 'ope she ain't bust a gut!" gasped Iris.

CHAPTER 8

SIMON CARMICHAEL was oblivious to the sweet-smelling spring morning. He padded backwards and forwards across the damp springy lawn with his brooding gaze pinned on the undignified vision of his wife, Emily, squatting in a flowerbed, busily planting.

"Emily, I demand your attention," he stated, coming to an abrupt halt before her. He hoped his tone was quelling enough to muster her obedience, but Emily Carmichael continued to putter, humming happily as her hands darted in and out of the plants, prying, patting, and pulling. Muddy splotches and streaks decorated her cheeks and brow, and the front of her gown was liberally plastered with fertile Cornish soil. "Emily, I am quite aware of your predilection for avoiding the least unpleasantness, but this time I absolutely demand that you be cognizant of what is happening. . . . including your mother's demise!" he bellowed, suppressing a strong desire to stamp his foot in an infantile fashion.

"I cannot bring her back, Simon," answered Emily mildly, primping a primula and dousing the vibrant velvet petals with a thick layer of mud. "And even if I could bring her back, I wouldn't. Mother was a most unpleasant person," she added thoughtfully.

"What about our daughter?" roared Simon, indulging his rage by stamping his foot and generously spraying his clean hose with mire.

"You've made a hole in the lawn," chided Emily, crawling to the wound and gently patting the sod as she crooned comforting phrases.

132

"Our daughter is more important than the damn lawn!" spluttered Simon.

"Benedict Tremayne will marry Angelica, as he seems willing though loathe to do. Gossip will die down and that will be that." Dr. Simon Carmichael snorted with exasperation at his wife's ability to be detached and yet succinctly aware of all that was going on about her.

"Angelica has apparently lost her memory."

"Very sensible of her, especially with all the unpleasantness she seems to have been subjected to living with my mother for the past year or so," praised the ardent gardener, busily snipping the dead flower heads off the daffodils.

"So you categorically refuse to accompany me to London for your own mother's funeral?" fumed her incensed husband.

"Yes, darling," cheerfully trilled his uncompromising wife. "If it was winter I might consider it a little, but it is spring and there is too much to do. The herbaceous border is a disgrace, and the vegetable garden is too wet to plough."

" 'scuse me, Dr. Simon but et ez Sir Benedict Tremayne of Taran, the dark defiler of innocent lambs," hissed a middle-aged woman dressed in a large pinafore, gloves, and stout farm boots.

"Oh, goody, Maizie, you're all dressed to combat the stinging nettles," rejoiced Emily.

"What about Sir Benedict?" snapped Simon impatiently.

"The mucker ez in the parlour. My Caleb ez keeping ez eye on him," informed the woman, picking up a scythe and advancing purposefully on the thick tangle of weeds. Simon looked towards his house, wishing he could somehow yank his dishevelled wife out of the perennial flower border and force her to accompany him for moral support. Even her decidedly mucky presence could make the encounter a little easier.

Taran glowered out of the lattice windows of the Carmichaels' cosy parlour, feeling icy fury course through his veins. He had been trapped and manipulated. News of Lady Isabella Bonny's shattering announcement at Lady Melisande Moreby-Wentworth-Fowler's ball for her only granddaughter. Angelica Carmichael, had spread like wildfire through the bored British society from John O'Groats to his remote estate at

Land's End. No less than seven separate acquaintances had driven from London to apprise him of the scandal, and it seemed that serious bets had been placed as to when, where, and to whom his freedom would be finally lost. Apparently his spurned mistress Lady Isabella was so confident that her public declaration of their betrothal would spur his chivalry, she had foolishly placed their engagement announcement in the newspapers. This had the opposite effect on him. He promptly published a retraction and news of his marriage to Angelica Carmichael, even going to the rash length of stating the ceremony had already occurred more than six months before. He now stared out at the pastoral scene in the Carmichaels' garden and cursed his hasty action. There had been a moment of sheer joy at learning the identity of his ungainly Angel, but it had been quickly squelched by the bitter suspicions that immediately followed. All his adult life he had been fending off scheming females who attempted to trap him into marriage, not for any affection for himself but for his considerable fortune and title. It was just too coincidental that a girl, the daughter of a country doctor who lived a scant ten miles from his family seat, should just happen to fall out of a coach right in front of his team of horses on the Portsmouth road.

Simon entered the parlour and inclined his head noncommittally at the tall dark young man. "May I pour you a drink?" he offered, in need of such sustenance himself. Taran nodded assent, the scowl on his swarthy face deepening. "Brandy?" asked the doctor, and again a curt nod. Both men drank, ignoring each other and glaring out of the window at the two women, one who scuttled about on all fours in and out of a regiment of bright red tulips, and the other who ferociously attacked a patch of stinging nettles. "Lord Taran, it is not convenient for me to discuss the . . . the . . . unfortunate . . . occurrence right now. I am leaving for London on the afternoon coach," struggled Simon.

"It would be more expedient if we travelled together," replied Taran tersely. "My coach is faster and I keep fresh horses at several posting inns on the way."

"I have no wish to inconvenience you."

"I am already inconvenienced," remarked the young man sardonically.

"There is a patient I must see before I leave," snapped Simon, colouring with anger at the barb.

"I am sure there are other doctors."

"There are, but I'm worried about young Pendarves," replied Simon, stressing the Pendarves name and staring pointedly at the arrogant man.

"I heard the boys were back at High Tor. I shall accompany you and pay my respects for their father's death," stated Taran autocratically. "I shall be here within the hour. Be ready," he ordered after draining his glass. Simon glared after the dictatorial young man who waved Caleb aside as though he owned the place.

"Arrogant young bugger, ent 'ee?" snorted the old servant. "Ye should hear what my Maizie's threating ter do if'n the man don't do right by our Angel and marry her," chortled Caleb, pointing a gnarled finger at the sight of his wife wildly swinging the scythe and levelling the nettles.

"I don't know if I want my daughter married to that man," sighed Simon, thinking of his gentle unassuming child and the scowling young peer. He frowned as an eerie jingle repeated itself in his mind. "Devil Tremayne, child of shame," he mouthed aloud, remembering the large haunting eyes of the small boy.

"The Devil-Child of the moors and the Bucca-Dhu," shivered Caleb. "Them awd Pendarves pits be haunted with witches and demons."

"Is my portmanteau packed?" asked Simon sharply, not willing to be drawn into a debate on Cornish superstition.

"Aye. Ooh ah, tes going ter be a real treat fer you seeing yer Miss Angel agin after all thes long time, ent it?"

"Yes, Caleb, it is going to be wonderful." Simon smiled. He thrust all thoughts of darkness and worries away as he concentrated on the joy of seeing his only daughter again.

Three hours later Simon leaned back in the comfortable seat of the well-sprung carriage much relieved that Benedict Tremayne preferred to ride his spirited stallion with the outriders. His head ached from the effort of preparing himself to deal with the close company of the harsh sardonic man. Now he sagged with relief and idly watched the young man, who rode his horse as though he were a part of it. Over the years he had heard about the peer's conquests of most of the female population of the court and English society, whether married or single. The exploits of Taran and his constant companion, the Prince of Wales, were well-known throughout the land. Simon conceded that he could understand how many women could be smitten by the handsome though somewhat forbidding features and the virile muscular build of the indolent young peer. But not his Angel. His daughter had a rare gentle feyness that could be extinguished by such bitter cynicism. He would not allow a match between the two, he decided, closing his eyes. He determined to borrow a leaf from his wife's book of rules and block out all unpleasantness by sleeping, but instead he found himself rehearsing all the conversations he was likely to have with Benedict Tremayne when they stopped to change horses or partake of a meal. An hour or so later he drifted off to sleep with his hands entwined across his rotund belly, but his dreams were fraught with unpleasantness. He trotted breathlessly through a vast catacomb, lost in a labyrinth of cold corridors, searching for his Angel. In each arched doorway roosted giant ravens with ancient human faces. He screamed his child's name, but the word *Angel* bounced off the hard rocks. "Devil . . . Devil . . . Devil" echoed back to mock him. Frantically he fought through the living shadows that cackled and clawed, black feathers flying, until a door was flung open and Angelica lay in an enormous four-poster bed shrouded with black curtains. She was spread-eagled, her slim, delicate wrists and ankles cruelly bound with silken cords that cut into her flesh. Her glorious chestnut hair fanned across a snowy pillow, the tresses trailing into bloody tendrils that webbed the sheets and dripped thickly to the floor, draining her of her life's blood. From between her legs, in labourious spasms, emerged the ghoulishly leering face of a demon who imitated Angel's rhythmic cries with an eerie baying.

Simon awakened with a start, sweating profusely despite the chill air, as the coach rumbled to a stop in the cobbled yard of an inn on Bodmin Moor. He gazed about blearily in the pitch darkness trying to orient himself when the coachman opened the door and unfolded the steps. Patterns of warm light pierced the night and raucous voices sang and laughed from the public saloon of the tavern.

"I apologize for the rudeness of this establishment, but it is clean and the food fairly palatable," stated Taran witheringly, assuming the doctor's inertia was due to distaste. He dismounted in one lithe movement and strode loosely as though he hadn't spent more than seven hours straight in the saddle. Simon groaned and admitted to pure unadulterated jealousy of the athletic younger man as his own overweight body positively screamed with pain.

In a small private room the two men faced each other across a table laden with a plain but satisfying meal. After accurately assessing the young peer's closed expression, Simon devoted himself to eating and decided to forgo any attempt at even the most innocuous of conversations.

"What are the chances of Pendarves recovering completely?" asked Benedict idly as he stood leaning on the mantel and staring into the glowing embers of the fire. Simon sipped his brandy and watched the nubile young wench who cleared the table of the remains of their repast casting appreciative eyes at Taran's well-shaped thighs. He made it a practice never to discuss his patients with an unrelated third party. "Ugly wound," remarked Taran, turning his gaze to the doctor. Simon acknowledged he had heard but did not commit himself. "But it is not the wound you're worried about," stated Taran. Simon waited for him to elaborate. It was true that he was more concerned with Torr Pendarves's state of mind than with the sabre wound in the thigh; the younger man's keen observation irritated him, somehow violating his mind.

"I am worried about my daughter," he snapped testily.

"Rather late for that, wouldn't you say?" returned Taran quellingly.

"How dare you," choked Simon.

"I am turning in and suggest you do the same. We shall leave at first light, so I shall settle our accounts with the innkeeper now," he informed dismissingly. The rotund doctor, still shaking with barely suppressed rage, stood to accompany the insolent man. "There is no need to disturb yourself."

"There is every need!" barked Simon. "I insist on paying

my share!'' Taran bowed, sarcastically indicating the portly doctor should precede him.

"As you wish," he said softly. There was something disquieting about the unexpected flash of pride from the undistinguished country doctor, he admitted.

The following days of travel passed in much the same manner. Neither man gave the other much quarter. Benedict rode, acutely conscious of the doctor's eyes. Against his better judgment he was drawn towards the chubby seemingly unpretentious man, and he savagely reminded himself that appearances and manner most often were deceptive. Catherine Pendarves was a good case in point. Angus Dunbar had arrived at Taran hot on the heels of the first bearers of the scandal, and he had immediately ordered the exhausted travel-stained man to make copious enquiries about the Simon Carmichael family. He had felt quite nauseated with the glowing accounts he had received about the upstanding, almost sickeningly saintly doctor, who apparently gave of himself unstintingly to the poorest of the poor. These services were paid for with no more than a glass of water or cup of tea. There was a Mrs. Emily Carmichael, daughter of Lady Melisande, who was known to be a lovable eccentric with her gardening and culinary experimentation; and there were two sons: Evan, aged sixteen, and Owen, aged fourteen, both in boarding school. It seemed that neither boy was particularly outstanding in ability or appearance. Most informants were hard-pressed to describe the two youths. Even Angelica had been a faint vague shadow in people's minds, a quiet solitary girl not known for striking handsomeness or wit, but just the good doctor's daughter. Recounting the glowing and undamaging reports, Angus Dunbar had even owned up to a great feeling of unease about the whole annoying matter, especially Lady Isabella Bonny's part in it.

Taran rode with his eyes pinned on Simon's nodding head, which he could see through the carriage window. A disquieting conversation he had had with Angus Dunbar played in his mind.

"What do you know of Lord Carringdon?" the Scot had asked him. He had been hard put to place a face to the name, but he conjured up a disturbing image of an aging popinjay who preyed upon very rich, very ancient women. He confessed he knew very little first-hand and had never had the dubious pleasure of meeting the man in question. Angus recounted an intriguing incident when a serving wench had descended on Tremayne House insisting she had a job with Lord Taran.

"She was driven away in Lord Carringdon's coach. For there isna way a mon could miss that great gaudy crest." Angus's Scottish brogue rolled in his head.

"So what?" Taran had barked impatiently, not seeing rhyme or reason in the Scot's tale.

"So what? Carringdon is engaged to marry Lady Melisande, the Carmichael chit's grandmother!"

"*Was*—I thought you said the woman died of mortification less than an hour after Isabella's solo performance?" he had added sarcastically.

"I dinna think Lady Isabella's performance was a solo," had answered the dour Scotsman cryptically. The conversation still repeating in his brain, Taran kneed his horse until he trotted beside the carriage.

"What do you know of Lord Carringdon?" he shouted to Simon over the rumble of the wheels.

"Carringdon?" mouthed Simon, mulling over the faintly familiar name for a moment or two before slowly shaking his head. Taran sneered triumphantly before kicking his horse into a wild gallop, now firmly convinced he had been trapped by a conspiracy that included the saintly doctor. What man didn't know the name of his soon-to-be father-in-law?

Simon frowned, not comprehending Taran's savage reaction. There was a distinct foreboding in the pit of his stomach, and he stared out blindly at the passing scenery, not noticing when the emerging soft green of spring gave way to hard grey cobblestones and clustered drab houses.

The sun was setting, streaking the Thames with red ribbing, when the carriage drew up in front of number ten Moreby Gardens. Simon allowed the coachman to assist him as he stepped stiffly down.

"Will you be staying here, sir?"

"I beg your pardon?" answered Simon demusedly, searching the sun-glazed windows for sight of his child.

"Should I take your trunk down?" asked the coachman as Taran dismounted.

"Thank you. Yes, maybe you'd better," said the doctor distractedly, reasoning that he could always hail a hackney and go to the most convenient hotel if there was a need. "Thank you for the use of the carriage," acknowledged Simon. "I think it best that I see my daughter alone," he added as Taran handed his horse to a hovering stableboy.

"Regardless of what you think best, I do as I see fit," was the curt answer. Taran strode up the wide stone steps, and the door was opened by a liveried manservant.

Iris squatted and peered through the banisters, straining her ears to hear the identity of the two men. To her frustration they were ushered into the library, where Lord Carringdon was loudly entertaining. Fleetly she scampered up to Angelica's rooms on the third floor and knocked softly.

"Miss Angel, it's me, Iris," she whispered. There was the sound of a bolt being drawn back and the door was opened a crack. "Good girl," approved the little maid as her mistress stood brandishing a poker. "Old Carringdon ain't wasted no time 'avin' a party. There 'as ter be about ten men 'ere . . . another two just come in. A fat man and one 'oo's so bloomin' 'andsome me 'eart nearly stopped at the sight of 'im."

"What are they doing down there?" asked Angel, wrapping the dressing gown tighter about herself.

"Gamblin', and from what I could 'ear, Lord Carrin'don ain't much of an 'and at that neither," answered Iris, staring out at the blood-red sky. "Crikey, did you 'ear that? That was me belly grumblin'! Aint you 'ungry? I'm bloody starvin'."

"You couldn't get to the kitchen?"

"I got there all right, but that rotten cook 'as orders from 'is lordship not ter let us 'ave nothin' 'til we show 'im some respect. And we both know what 'e means by respect, don't we?" muttered Iris. Angel was not at all sure what his lordship meant by respect, but the furious little maid soon enlightened her. "Flat on our backs! I told 'er we'd rather die first! Trouble is I think we will."

"After the funeral we'll leave," stated Angel firmly.

"Yeah? And go where?"

"Home."

" 'ome? You ain't got an 'ope in 'ell of gettin' there! You can't even remember where the bloody 'ell it is! And what money 'ave yer got ter get there if yer knew where it was? I got a bit, but it ain't enough ter get us round the corner . . . and another thing, what the bloody 'ell are yer going ter wear? Yer ballgown? Right fine pair we're goin' ter look, sneakin' away tryin' ter 'ide, me in this purple frock and you in that pink cage wif a bird's nest on yer 'ead!"

"What are we going to do? I'd rather die than marry Lord Carringdon!" cried Angelica. "Oh, why couldn't Grandmaman have married him before she passed away?" she lamented.

"There ain't nothin' for it but ter steal," decided Iris.

"Steal!"

"Well, I ain't spreadin' my legs no more fer 'is lordship's few coppers so we'll just 'ave ter pinch some of yer granny's knickknacks and pawn 'em."

"But how can Lord Carringdon march in here and take over everything?" questioned Angelica angrily.

"I 'spose Lady Em left 'im everythink in 'er will or somethin'."

"Then why is he trying to force me to marry him?"

"Yer mean 'er ladyship might 'ave left everythink ter you?" gasped Iris. " 'ere 'ush up, someone's comin'!" she hissed, making a dive for the hand-irons as Angel shot home the two deadbolts. Both girls took up positions one each side of the door: the maid with the coal-thongs raised and the mistress with the poker. There was a sharp rapping, and Iris pursed her lips and shook her head warningly as an indication for silence.

"Miss Angelica?" whined Simms's nasally voice. "Miss Angelica? Yer wanted downstairs."

"Fer what? 'igh tea wif the bloomin' king?" spat Iris.

"Miss Angelica's father is 'ere."

"Tell us another," jeered Iris.

"My father?"

" 'ere, don't fall fer it. It's a trap," hissed the maid. "All them randy muckers . . . drinkin' and gamblin all day . . .

and you ain't even dressed decent. Yer don't know men . . .
they'll 'ave yer nightie over yer 'ead and be pokin' themselves inter you 'fore you can say cock robin! I ain't lettin'
you out of 'ere 'ceptin' over my dead body!''

''What'll we do?'' gulped Angel, blanching at the terrible
picture Iris painted of men's carnal appetites.

''Leave it ter me,'' directed Iris. '' 'ere Simms, you still
out there?''

''Yeah.''

''Tell Miss Angel's dad that 'is precious daughter is dyin'
of starvation cos 'is lordship ain't let 'er 'ave any think ter eat
fer days . . . and she can't come down ter see 'im cos she
ain't got no clothes neither . . . so 'e better come to 'er
alone!''

''I carn't do that! 'is lordship'll 'ave me guts fer garters,''
wailed Simms.

''If it's really Miss Angel's dad, there's gonna be a lotta
guts 'ad fer garters around 'ere the way you've bin treatin' me
mistress since Lady Em went and kicked the bucket!'' Ivy
pressed her ear against the door and listened intently. ''She's
gone. Stay 'ere just in case,'' she hissed as she scurried into
the dressing room and rummaged under the mattress of her
cot. ''Miss Angel, do yer know 'ow ter use these?'' she asked
reappearing with two cumbersome pistols.

''Where on earth did you find those?''

''I got 'em off the wall in the 'all. I was goin' ter get them
crossed swords in the library, but I couldn't reach. I said ter
meself, Iris Wilkins, I said, there ain't no such thing as bein'
too prepared if push come ter shove! 'ere take one.''

Simon frowned as he and Taran were shown into a dimly
lit library, which appeared more like a gambling den. There
was a thick haze of tobacco smoke, and from the stale smell
and loud slurred voices it was very apparent that a great
amount of spirits had been consumed. Several dishevelled
painted females in different stages of undress were draped
across various pieces of furniture.

''By Jove, Taran, you're the last person I expected to see
here!'' exclaimed a jovial voice. Benedict ignored the man

but kept his eyes pinned to Lord Carringdon, who looked up with alarm at the tall young peer.

"What is happening here?" cried Simon. Although he had no love for his newly deceased mother-in-law, he was appalled at such blatant disrespect. "Where is my daughter?" he roared, trying to be heard above the drunken squabbling voices. Lord Carringdon stood unsteadily, plastered a rather wavery ingratiating smile on his face, and, taking very careful steps, advanced towards Taran and Simon with his hand outstretched. Both men very pointedly ignored the gesture. "Where is my daughter?" repeated the doctor.

"You must be Sh . . . Shimon Car . . . michael," pronounced Lord Carringdon, wagging a finger at the irate doctor.

"Where is my daughter?"

"She . . . she . . . ish up . . . shtairs."

"Who are you?" demanded Simon. "What are you doing here?"

"This is Lord Carringdon," supplied Taran, his eyes narrowing as he assessed the doctor. Either the man was a consummate actor or he was genuinely shocked and disturbed. Taran found nothing reprehensible or shocking about gaming, wenching, and drinking. His years in London had inured him. He did, however, find this particular display decidedly in bad taste, especially as Lady Moreby-Wentworth-Fowler was scarcely cold and not even in her grave.

"Sh . . . ir Benedict," greeted Carringdon. "You, Shir, are in my debt!" he loudly proclaimed.

"Explain," challenged Taran curtly.

"I sh . . . all take the tall country filly . . . off your handsh," announced the drunken man, smirking and swaying. "An upsh . . . standing lord of the realm like yourshelf shh . . . ouldn't be shaddled with shuch a provincial . . . shkinny . . . female."

"Are you referring to my daughter?"

"Where is my wife?" demanded Taran, placing a warning hand on the irate doctor's arm. There was an audible gasp from the other men present at the word *wife*. "Am I to believe that not one of you read this morning's *London Gazette*?" he added idly, glancing carelessly about at the gaping faces which included Simon Carmichael.

"Gazette?" questioned the doctor numbly.

"News of my marriage to Angelica Carmichael . . ." enlightened Taran. He was interrupted by Carringdon, whose already florid face was suffused with impotent fury until it turned alarmingly purple.

"Thash not fair . . . she'sh mine! Your pocketsh are well-lined! You don't need more money! How did you hear she wassh a rish bish?"

"That's quite enough, Carringdon!" said Taran steelily.

"Where'sh your pride, Tremayne? Taking my leavingsh! She'sh a trollop . . . a shtrumpet! Hopped shtraight from your bed into mine!" goaded Carringdon. Simon bellowed with rage and lunged at the teetering man, knocking him easily to the floor as the door was flung open. Two most oddly attired females entered waving large unwieldy pistols. Simon's mouth sagged open in disbelief at recognizing his own gentle daughter dressed in purple knee-britches and a servant's tunic.

"All right yer rotten lot . . . up against the wall wif yer 'ands on yer 'ead and no funny stuff!" shouted the smaller of the two, who was garbed in a matching purple maid's frock and apron. "That means you, too, fatty," she added, poking Simon in the belly with her formidable weapon. The portly doctor numbly obeyed by lifting his hands and backing away. He uttered strangled sounds, positive he would awaken at any moment and find himself back in his mundane predictable existence. "Wotcha doin' lyin' on the floor, yer lordship?" asked Iris, kicking the prostrate man and pointing the gun at his head. She roared with delight as Carringdon quickly scrambled across the floor to cower next to his dazed cronies, who thought they might be suffering from the effects of too much alcohol. Taran lounged in the shadows by the door, unobserved by both girls. He watched the proceeding with a wry smile on his face.

Iris was thoroughly enjoying her power. She grinned broadly and chuckled as she twirled the cumbersome pistol. Terrified squeaks came from the grovelling men, who were twice her size and more than three times her weight. "Well, what 'ave we 'ere?" she asked airily, strutting over to the scantily dressed whores. She shook her head in sympathy. "I 'ope yer got well-paid fer openin' yer legs fer that load of vermin? Yer didn't! That's a bloomin' shame. I'll 'ave ter do somethink about that, won't I?'' she said expansively. " 'ere you, you, you and you,'' she selected, prodding four men and ushering them towards the painted females. "Empty yer pockets. Go on, girls, take it. You've earnt it!'' The men thrust money into the greedily outstretched hands. "Now, ducks, get yer togs and scarper!'' With cheeky grins and saucy waves the girls complied, unable to resist gloating at the men, who had shown them little respect. "All right Miss Aye, do yer see any of them what's about yer size?'' asked Iris as the door closed behind the last satisfied call girl. "You can't go traipsin' around town dressed like that.''

Angel hesitantly stepped out of the shadows and shyly looked down the line of men. She felt another presence and spun about. She froze, the blood pounding in her ears and stiffening her flaming cheeks as Taran leisurely stepped into the flickering lanternlight.

"Benedict!''

"Angel,'' he answered dryly, removing the gun from her trembling hand just before she spiralled to the floor in a dead faint.

"Angelica!'' exclaimed Simon, ignoring the gun in Iris's wildly wavering hand as she tried to keep all the men under her control, and rushing over to his inert daughter. Despite his intoxication, Carringdon took advantage of the opportunity by lunging forward and knocking the firearm from the little maid's grasp. He viciously struck her across the face.

"Enough, Carringdon!'' roared Taran as the drunken man drew back his fist to continue his beating of the stunned girl.

"But the filthy wench—''

"I said enough! Now get out, all of you!'' Taran didn't have to repeat his command. The men scrambled for their possessions and fell over each other trying to get out of the door. Iris sat on the floor nursing her throbbing cheek. As Carringdon rushed by, intent on exiting, she grabbed his foot, neatly tripping him, and then flattened him with a well-placed blow to the head with a small footstool.

"I 'ope that kilt yer, yer slimy bastard!'' she spat, giving his limp body a sharp kick. Keeping her eyes pinned to the two men who bent over her mistress, she carefully edged towards the pistol that lay on the carpet several feet away.

"Don't waste your time on any more heroics," clipped Taran coldly. "If that antiquated firearm were capable of firing, it would have done so when you were twirling it about like a fan."

Iris stared at him suspiciously without answering. If what he said was true, why had all the men obeyed her so readily? she mused. She gazed up at the dark man and back to the discarded gun with speculation. Casually she picked it up and aimed it at him. Taran snorted with impatience and turned back to the stout man who knelt beside Angelica.

"If either of you 'arm one 'air on my mistress's 'ead, you'll 'ave me ter answer to," she threatened, brandishing a small dagger in her other hand. "If this don't fire," she added, aiming the gun, "this'll find it's mark."

"Don't be tiresome," dismissed Taran. "How is she, Carmichael?"

"It must be shock," fretted Simon, patting his daughter's hand ineffectually. "My medical bag is in your carriage."

"Girl, go out to my carriage. . . ."

"I ain't leavin' me mistress!" interrupted Iris stubbornly. "Anyways, there ain't nothin wrong with my Miss Angel that a bite of food wouldn't cure. She ain't eaten fer four days. I ain't neither," she added hopefully.

"Why not?" sputtered Simon.

" 'is lordship wouldn't let us . . . and she 'elped 'im," stated Iris, pointing an accusing finger at Simms, who trembled at the partly open door.

"It weren't my fault. I didn't wanta, but I 'ave an old mum and I didn't wanta get the sack like Mr. and Mrs. Smithers, and Lord Carringdon says 'as 'ow 'e'd sell me to an 'ore 'ouse if I didn't do what he says . . ." protested Simms in a long monotonous whine.

"Shut yer gob, yer grizzling bitch!" snarled Iris. "'Ere, 'ow do I know who the 'ell you two is?"

"He's Miss Angelica's dad and he's Lord Taran," sniffed Simms.

" 'ow do yer know?" challenged Iris, advancing towards the tall man. " 'andsome bugger, ain't you?" she said cheekily, covering the trepidation she felt. "So you say yer Lord Taran? And the fat man's my Miss Angel's dad?"

"I am Dr. Simon Carmichael, and it is much too draughty on this floor," he worried.

"I'll get some blankets right away, sir," gushed Simms, anxious to get into good graces. She darted out of the room and Iris muttered derisively. Taran picked up Angel easily in his arms and carried her across the room to a large couch. Iris nodded her approval of his strength.

"Put down those silly weapons and make yourself useful," barked Benedict, laying the unconscious girl against the soft cushions.

"I ain't leavin' my mistress, so save your breath," reiterated Iris. "You might be 'oo yer say you are and then again yer might not!" She snorted contemptuously as Cook bustled in with a loaded tea trolley, followed by Simms weighed down with eiderdowns and Sykes carrying Simon's medical bag. "You bunch of bloody 'ippercrits!" she sneered.

Angel awoke and stared into a round middle-aged face scarcely six inches from her nose. She quickly shut her eyes, unable to bear such close scrutiny from the strange man. Iris's lurid tales, colorfully describing the baser appetites of men, flared in her mind. Her nose wrinkled with distaste at the unmistakable odours of tobacco and spirits, two decidedly male aromas. She panicked, remembering Lord Carringdon and his cronies.

"Drink this," ordered a brusque voice. Strong hands gripped her, lifting her head, and brandy fumes burned her nostrils.

"No!" she screamed, kicking and flailing. The glass was knocked from Taran's hand and smashed noisely against a bookcase. "Let me alone!" she shrieked, determined that Carringdon and his base friends would not violate her in any way.

"My Angel," soothed her father.

"I'm not your Angel!" she roared, swinging a small clenched fist and punching the long-suffering doctor squarely in the nose. There was a brittle crack and then a torrent of blood.

"Good shot!" applauded Iris. "Now get yer 'and off of 'er!" she threatened, but Taran ignored her and successfully pinned Angel's arms and legs, frustrating her movements.

"Angel?" Taran stared down at her terrified face. Her eyes were tightly closed as though she was too frightened to see what was happening. Her small nostrils flared and her breathing was rapid. "Angel, look at me," he asked gently, bemused by her delicate features.

"Don't rape me," whispered Angel. "Oh, please don't rape me," she begged.

"Oh, my dear God, what has been happening to my child?" wept Simon, clutching a handkerchief to mop up the blood from his rapidly swelling nose. Iris frowned and edged closer, recognizing the love in the elderly man's voice.

" 'ere, are you really 'er dad?" she asked softly. Simon nodded, unable to say a word as tears poured down his cheeks. "Miss Angel?" called Iris after a contemplative pause, stowing her dagger under her frock in a garter and tucking the gun in her apron pocket. "Miss Angel, everythink's all right. I think it really is yer dad. Go on, lovey, open yer eyes and 'ave a look," she coaxed, leaning over the back of the couch and smoothing the thick chestnut hair from Angelica's brow.

Angel's eyes flickered open. Taran was again awed by the luminous unusual colour. She stared fearfully up at his harsh features, reading censure in his nearly black eyes. She longed to reach out and trace the cynical lines on his face, to soften the grim lean lips. But even if she had had the courage, her hands were securely held in one of his. Where their skin touched, her flesh burned.

"Well, my Lady Disdain?" he murmured mockingly, and Angel smiled tremulously not knowing what to answer. Her heart seemed to leap excitedly because of his close proximity. Every night since leaving the rustic retreat in the New Forest, she had dreamed of him, and now he was there touching her. His hard thighs pressed intimately against her, causing a tumult of newly awakened sensations. She felt light-headed, as though she was floating through a rosy sunset.

"Miss Angel, mind yer dad," hissed Iris, noting the dreamy vulnerability in her mistress's eyes that clearly mirrored her feelings for the enigmatic younger man. Iris frowned, unable to read any signs of love in the brooding swarthy features. "Don't feel bad, yer doctorship, but yer daughter can't remember nothin', not even 'er own face in the mirror . . . nor

you neither. 'ere, let's 'ave a look at that," she fussed,
pulling the handkerchief away and peering at his injured nose.
"Looks broke ter me . . . bit lopsided, too. Needs a pull or
it'll stick like that, unless it was like that before. Simms, get
a cold rag fer 'is doctorship's nose," she ordered imperiously.

"Get it yerself!" retorted Simms.

"I ain't leavin' me mistress."

"She ain't goin' ter need you no more," jeered Simms,
spitefully exchanging a gleeful smirk with the cook. Iris
sneered back, looking for reassurance from Angelica, but her
mistress was oblivious to everything except Lord Taran. Terror cut through her and she quietly backed away, her exhausted mind trying to plan her own survival. Everything
seemed bleak and hopeless.

Iris silently watched Simms and Sykes fussing about Angelica, tucking blankets around her long coltish limbs and
setting a tea-tray before her. The two-faced cook played
doting mother, urging her to eat the delicate little sandwiches
and petit fours. Fear cramped her guts and her mouth was dry
from terror. To be lonely and homeless again was more than
she could even bear to contemplate. She shuddered, remembering the many nights she had spent cowering in doorways,
the rain drumming on her head and running down her neck,
prey to any drunkard weaving his way home from the local
pub. She would sit on the cold doorstep with her knees drawn
up against her chest and her arms wrapped about her legs.
She had been unable to fall asleep for fear the very few
possessions she had would be stolen from her. Once she had
lost her shawl and her shoes. The nights seemed endless, the
darkness impenetrable. A sudden noise, the scream of a raped
cat, would set her heart leaping and her aching eyes would
desperately try to pierce the blackness. But her desperate
existence was better than an early death in a brothel, she
would remind herself.

Taran poured himself a drink and surveyed the room,
raising an eyebrow at the dubious pink decor. He noted the
six identical alabaster busts and shook his dark head with
disbelief.

"There's more'n a 'undred . . . all the same . . . they're
of Lady Em," informed Iris eagerly, deciding to try and curry

favour with the most powerful person present. In her estimation, Lord Taran was the one who was going to decide what was what. "One of 'er dead 'usbands 'ad about two 'undred made. There's some more in 'er 'ouse in Wimbledon and every bloomin' one of them's the same," she chattered when he made no sign he had even heard her.

"Iris, did you eat anything?" asked Angel.

"I ain't 'ungry." And she wasn't, the fear that clawed in her belly successfully covered any hunger pangs.

"But you haven't eaten for days!" protested Angel.

"I'm used ter it!" replied Iris. "I don't eat much . . . don't need much of anything, and I'm an 'ard worker, too, ain't I Miss Angel?"

"In a pig's eye," snorted Sykes.

"She's nothin' but a little 'ore, yer Lordship," stated Cook maliciously.

"She was Lord Carringdon's tart!" informed Simms.

"Stoppit! And get out!" screamed Angel hysterically, covering her ears.

"Out!" snapped Taran curtly, inclining his head towards the door. Cook, Simms, and Sykes hurriedly obeyed. "You, too," he added, glaring coldly at Iris.

"But . . . no . . . no," sobbed Angelica.

"It's all right, my Angel, everything is going to be all right now, my poor child," crooned Simon.

"Out!" repeated Taran holding the door open for the white-faced girl, who stared towards her mistress hoping for help. But Angelica was enfolded in her father's arms, mumbling incoherently into his jacket. Iris glared up at the tall autocratic lord. She masked her hollow despair with defiance and bobbed an insolent curtsey. She left the room, and the library door was firmly closed behind her. She stared at it, feeling shut out and infinitely lonely.

"Well, well, well, look 'oo's bin put in 'er place at larst," jeered a spiteful voice and Iris froze. Slowly she turned, her hand in her apron pocket grasping the pistol.

"Fergot yerself, didn't yer?" chimed Sykes.

"Thought you was better than the rest of us, didn't yer?" joined in Cook. "Well, ducky, I thought you was 'ungry? Come in ter me kitchen cos we 'ave a bone ter pick with you, me girl," she invited malevolently as she, Simms, and Sykes formed a line and advanced on Iris, who pulled the pistol from her pocket and aimed it at them. Sykes and Cook recoiled but Simms just laughed.

"I 'eard what 'is lordship said. It don't work!"

Iris fought and tried to scream for help, but she was no match for the three women who clamped hard hands across her mouth and dragged her into the kitchen, pulling her hair and spitefully twisting her flesh in the process. She was slammed into a chair. Her poor face, already discoloured by Carringdon's fist, was soon fiery red from vicious hands. Iris sucked at the salty blood from her split lip and glowered belligerently at the bullying woman who towered above her, sharpening a large carving knife.

"Are you goin' ter cut 'er throat and throw 'er in the river?" giggled Sykes.

"Cut 'er tongue out so she can't tell any ugly lies about us," suggested Simms gleefully.

"Yer know there ain't no way that posh Lord Taran's going ter want you around 'is Angel, don't yer? 'specially now he knows 'ow you've bin whoring about with Carrington. It's back on the streets or in ter the brothel with you, me girl, ain't it?" gloated the cook. Iris grinned, refusing to wince at the knife being waved under her nose. "I'm talkin' ter yer, yer know?" the cook spat, irritated by the girl's cocky attitude. She slapped her hard across the face.

"Cook, what are you doing?" cried Mrs. Smithers, standing at the open back door. "No! That's enough! Stop it at once!" The cook hit Iris again, this time with such force the girl spun off the chair and went crashing to the floor.

"It ain't none of yer business, Mrs. Ess, you don't work 'ere no more. You got the sack, remember? I'm in charge now, so go do yer bossing some place else," stated the cook with one hand on an ample hip and the other pointing the knife threateningly at Mrs. Smithers.

"What is happening here?" boomed a deep aristocratic voice.

"Get up, yer lazy trollop," hissed the cook, prodding Iris with her foot. She smiled ingratiatingly at Lord Taran. "The filthy whore come at me with this," she lied, brandishing the carving knife. "She was in a temper on account that I told you about 'er being Lord Carringdon's whore. She should never 'ave bin allowed near the likes of Miss Angelica or any other decent woman for that matter," ranted the nervous cook.

"How's the girl?" asked Taran, ignoring the woman and gazing down at the small groggy maid, who lay with her head pillowed on Mrs. Smithers' lap.

"The girl's as fit as a bloomin' fiddle," answered Iris, sitting up and attempting a pert grin, but her face was too stiff and throbbing. "Ooh, you bloody bitch, you've made me tooth loose!" she exclaimed, furiously wiggling the offending member with her tongue. She struggled to her feet, intent on doing similar damage to the cook. Taran steadied her as she wobbled uncertainly. He studied her stubborn little face and sighed.

"Between you and your mistress, I have yet to see two more battered females."

"Me mistress?" whispered Ivy fearfully, not daring to believe the hopeful words.

"She is making herself ill asking for you, but . . ." Before Taran could finish his thought that the girl should improve her bloodied appearance first, Iris had charged out of the kitchen.

"Iris Wilkins is really a good loyal person," defended Mrs. Smithers stoutly.

"And who might you be?"

"I am Mrs. Maude Louise Smithers," stated the elderly woman after she had silently assessed the strange young man. "My husband and I ran Lady Melisande's establishments before her demise."

"I am Benedict Tremayne."

"Lord Taran?" questioned Mrs. Smithers, and the tall dark man curtly inclined his head. "I thought you might be."

"And you are *the* Mrs. Smithers I have been hearing about in a somewhat hysterical manner." Taran ushered the little woman out of the kitchen and out of earshot of the cook, who still stood holding the large carving knife.

Peace finally arrived later that evening. Simon Carmichael was ensconced in a comfortable though cluttered pink bedchamber. Benedict Tremayne, after giving explicit instructions to the Smitherses as to Angelica's activities for the following day, had retired to his exclusive, all-male club. And Angelica sat before her mirror slowly and dreamily brushing her thick chestnut hair. Iris watched her, silently noting her mistress's euphoric mood and feeling uneasy.

" 'appy, ain't yer?'' and Angelica humming softly, nodded and smiled tenderly. Iris sat on the floor hugging her knees and looking up at the radiant young woman. She had never seen her appear so beautiful. "Wotcha thinkin'?'' she demanded after a long pause as she scrutinized the change in her mistress. It was as though Angelica was lit from within.

"I'm not sure. There are so many feelings. I have no memory of my father, but in just the few hours since he arrived I have such warm feelings for him.''

"And 'is lordship?'' probed Iris sharply. Angelica turned and gazed at her maid's battered little face, puzzled by the bitterness she heard. "Well, 'ave you got such warm feelin's fer 'im too?'' she challenged. Angelica frowned at her without answering. "You 'ave, 'aven't you? It's writ all over yer face!''

Angelica looked back at her reflection. "Is it?'' she said softly.

"Yer a babe in arms and yer 'eadin' fer a fall unless yer careful,'' warned Iris. " 'e don't love you, yer know?'' Angelica looked at her maid's image in the glass. "Well, if he does, 'e sure got a funny way of showin' it,'' she tempered her tone, uncomfortable at the hurt she read in the sea-green eyes. "I mean ter say 'e took 'is own bloody time gettin' 'ere, didn't 'e? And what about that bitch Lady Isabella Bonny? Aye? 'is fiancée?''

Angelica's dreamy euphoria promptly faded at the horrible thought of the tall, elegant older woman. "What about her?'' she said dully.

"I see'd yer face when you first saw 'er . . . even before she said nothin' and you looked like yer'd seen a ghost!''

"That's ridiculous! How could you have seen my face behind that monstrous feathered mask?''

"Yer 'ole body went funny like this,'' demonstrated Iris, pretending to elegantly fan herself and then going rigid with shock, her mouth gaping open. "You remembered 'er from somewhere, I know yer did," accused the maid. Angelica slowly nodded, her brow creased. "Well?" asked Iris impatiently.

"I don't know. Everything is vague and fuzzy . . . not quite real. I remember her voice . . . angry and strident . . . I recall thinking that she should have been wearing red . . . bright red with dark fur about the wrists . . . her hands in shiny black leather . . ."

"And in them 'ands I bet she 'ad an 'orsewhip!" interrupted Iris savagely, recalling the Smitherses' conversation she had overheard and the malicious gossip that had circulated amongst the kitchen staff.

"A whip!" gasped Angelica, her hands dropping her hairbrush and instinctively covering her breasts where faint scars still remained.

"Cor!" exclaimed Iris, just putting the pieces together herself. "It was 'er! 'is bloody lordship's bloody 'ore what whipped you! Well, don't that take the cake?" stated the outraged maid loudly. Then she fell silent when she saw her mistress's bleak expression. The beauty that had radiated a scant few minutes before had been extinguished. "It's still goin' ter be a fine life, Miss Angel. Tomorrer, 'is lordship's goin' ter buy you clothes posh enough fer the queen 'erself. Then after yer granny's funeral it's off ter 'is lordship's estate in Cornwall, and yer'll feel right at 'ome cos I'll be there wif yer . . . and Mr. and Mrs. Smithers, seein' as 'ow they're ter be 'is lordship's new 'ousekeepers . . . and yer'll be near yer own mum and dad so you can pop in and 'ave a visit anytime yer want. Ain't it somethin' you 'avin' two little brothers? Ain't you lookin' forwards ter meetin' them?" she chattered, feeling guilty at Angelica's sudden dejection.

"How can I be married to him now?" whispered Angelica.

"Don't talk daft! Course yer goin' ter marry 'im! All men are like that! It's true. Cross me 'eart! 'e ain't no different from all the rest," stated Iris, terrified as she saw her hopes of a comfortable life dashed. "I didn't mean ter put such a damper on yer. I just didn't want ter see you gettin' 'urt expectin' 'im ter love you back when 'e don't," explained the battered little maid miserably. "Oh, come on, Miss Angel, give us a smile?'' she wheedled. ''Everythink's goin' ter be loverly. We're all goin' ter live 'appily ever after like in the storybooks. You and me and the Smitherses . . . no more sluts like Simms, Sykes, and Cook . . . no dirty old lechers like Lord Carrin'don. It'll be sunshine and flowers and lots of little nippers runnin' around. Pretty little babies and I'll take care of them real good cos I love babies. I 'ad one once, but it died—you'll 'ave lots of 'ealthy babies . . .''

''You had a baby, Iris?''

''Years and years ago . . . it don't matter no more.''

''But you're only fifteen now!''

''So I was twelve or thirteen. I cried when it died, but it was all fer the best. 'ow could I 'ave taken care of the little blighter? Now wotcha gettin' me all morbid for? We 'ave ter look on the bright side, and there's always a bright side. Fer instance, Lord Taran is an 'ell of a lot better lookin' than Carringdon! Think of 'avin' ter kiss 'im wif 'is 'orrible stinkin' black teeth, let alone ter 'ave 'is cock pokin' inter yer! It ain't no treat, I can tell yer. So thank yer lucky stars it's Lord Taran who'll 'ave yer!'' Angelica shuddered with revulsion at the mere thought of suffering such intimacies with Lord Carringdon. ''Inter bed with you quick sharp, Miss Angel, before you catch cold and Mrs. Ess 'as me 'ead. We 'ave ter get our beauty sleep now yer goin' ter be a real lady.''

Angelica listlessly climbed into bed. Iris fussed about, smoothing the covers and tucking the blanket beneath the mattress as she avoiding looking at her mistress's blank face. ''Good night,'' dismissed Angel dully.

'' 'night, miss,'' whispered Iris, backing towards the adjoining dressing room. ''It's goin' ter be roses, really it is.''

Angel heard the door close softly and then a muffled rustling as the girl climbed into her bed. Everything was quiet except for the settling of the old house and the faint moan of the night breeze wafting across the river Thames. She gazed at the handpainted ceiling, feeling an emptiness. Though her head was spinning from all the events of the long day, there was a hollow ache in the rest of her. She had awakened that morning to a grim despair, defending her honour from Lord Carringdon's lecherous assaults. Had it only been that morning? she mused, her eyes following a stream of dusty moon-

light that dissected the dark room. Now she was retiring for
the night with the same grim despair, after finding a loving
father and a handsome prospective bridegroom. Taran was the
husband of her dreams, she admitted bitterly to herself . . . of
her girlish, naïve, foolishly romantic dreams. Whatever had
caused her to delude herself into thinking that she, a gawky,
untitled old maid, could possibly be loved by such a rich,
sophisticated, handsome man who had his choice of beautiful
women from the whole of European society? Angelica was in
awe of her own effrontery. She closed her eyes and envisioned
his chiseled face, desperately searching for some soft hopeful
glimmer, but the saturnine features remained harsh and mocking. He was marrying her only because he had been trapped
into an untenable position by the antics of his jealous mistress; her aching sadness increased. Absently she stroked her
thigh, remembering the sensations that had smoldered at his
innocent touch and wondering what it would be like to be
totally possessed by him. The mere thought was exhilarating,
yet terrifying and blushingly shameful. Angelica was aware
of what occurred between a man and a woman, but she had
never before allowed herself to dwell on the rather embarrass-
ing act. At least, she was reasonably sure she hadn't, she
thought ruefully, remembering the guilt her naked body caused
her. She also dared to wonder what his body would look like
unclad. She remembered the sight of his bared chest, and she
flexed her hands as though tracing the firm muscles. Lady
Isabella Bonny had lain naked with him. At the thought of the
couple intimately entwined, Angelica felt excruciating pain,
as though a knife had been twisted deep into her belly. How
could she marry Taran, loving him as she did?

PART TWO

DEVIL AND ANGEL

*Every man hath a good and bad angel attending him in particular,
all his life long.*

Robert Burton

CHAPTER 9

TORR PENDARVES limped along the wide portrait gallery that overlooked the formal banquetting hall at High Tor. A thick film of dust muted the intricate parquetry of the floor, puffing up with each laborious step, captured in the bright bars of sunlight that rippled across the vaulted ceiling—reflections from the vast sea outside. Sweat glistened on his grimacing, features and agony streaked through his tall lean body.

"Jago Pengelly, don't just stand there, stop him 'fore he hurt hisself," hissed Mrs. Goodie to the leathery man who stood beside her in the shadows.

"Nay, thet lad has to do what he has to do. He has lain idle full of pity long enough and near withered thet fine young limb. Remember what Simon Carmichael said afore he went off to London?"

"Where's your fine doctor now? Said he'd be gone no more than a fortnight!" she ranted, wincing with each step her young master took. "It breaks my heart to watch him. All that pain. He's just punishing hisself for Master Ajax running off to fight the French! Blaming hisself for the old lord up and dying like that! Just like that he went," she demonstrated with a click of her fingers.

Torr Pendarves was so engrossed he was unaware of the whispers. Nothing existed but his hammering heart and the searing agony of his disgusting, dragging limb. He sneered up at the ancestors who seemed to gaze down pityingly at him. He attempted a derisive bow, but his legs buckled, pitching him onto the filthy floor where he lay, laughing, cursing, and sobbing. Mrs. Goodie cried out and would've scurried to him, but Jago Pengelly put out a weathered hand, detaining her.

"Leave him be," he said curtly. "Allow him his pride!"

"I will not! I know the young master better than you! 'Tis been me being nurse and mother to him for the last six years," she protested, struggling to be free.

"That lad is hurting in more ways than one. He's punishing hisself, so let him! He'll have no thanks for you if you meddle. He'll just vent his anger and frustration at you and feel worser fer doing so. Come along. I aim to make a country woman of you, Betsy," he soothed. "We've thet vegetable garden to see to!"

"My name isn't Betsy," sniffed Mrs. Goodie, allowing herself to be propelled toward the kitchen but looking anxiously over her shoulder. "And where on earth is Master Felix? Gone all day from dawn to dusk with that fleabitten mongrel you give him . . . and it's all wild and uncivilized out there," she wailed, wishing she was back in London's familiar bustle. "Everywhere I look there's just nothing! Miles and miles of nothing!"

Torr clutched the panelled wall for support and hauled himself upright. He slapped angrily at himself, trying to brush off the irritating dust. He slowly and painfully resumed his way down the long gallery, perusing his forefathers.

"We are a legion!" he declared cynically. "Eight Sir Torrances of High Tor . . . all mighty, invincible heroes! All noble warriors who gave their lives for king and country . . . and in your case, heaven knows how many great grandfathers ago, laid down your life for queen and country," he said, gazing up at an Elizabethan knight, resplendent in doublet and hose. Carefully he backed away and sat gratefully on a carved wooden bench. He scanned the more than thirty paintings, dolefully shaking his head at the array of impressive uniforms and armours that changed with the ages. Those gaudy military costumes had fascinated him, spawning his childhood dreams. Each arrogant male forebear preened proudly with weapon and shield in hand, exhibiting the Pendarves coat of arms. A noble charger, obedient hound, and an occasional hawk completed each portrait.

Felix, his face flushed from the wind and sun, raced into

the gallery followed by a gangly, large-footed puppy. Both skidded to an abrupt halt at seeing Torr. Felix promptly lost his glowing happiness and became awkward, shuffling his feet in the dust and staring at the floor.

"Where have you been?" asked Torr, piqued by the quelling effect he had on the exuberant youth. The young dog collapsed limply, seeming boneless and stared mournfully up at Felix, his large head resting on his big paws.

"Out," shrugged the boy, edging backwards, wanting to be away from the gloom of his censoring older brother.

"Out where?" barked Torr, regretting the harsh tone as soon as it escaped his mouth.

"Just out . . . there . . . on the moors."

"Make the most of it, for soon you'll be returning to school," snapped Torr, pushing himself to his feet so he towered over the fourteen-year-old.

"You're not my father!" The words just burst out of Felix's mouth and he glared sullenly. The tension crackled in the long ensuing silence. Torr clenched and unclenched his hand, suppressing his rising violence, fighting the desire to strike the boy's insolent face. He took a deep breath, turned his back, and limped away, carefully placing his weight, determined not to debase himself by falling to his knees on the grimy floor in front of the surly youth.

Felix watched Torr's halting progress down the long gallery, feeling an agony of conflicting emotions. He hoped his fury burnt holes in his arrogant brother's straight back, and yet he was enraged and hurt by each limping step. Each step made him feel lonely and very vulnerable. The door at the end slammed shut and the noise echoed down the long expanse. Felix slumped to the floor and buried his face in the pup's soft coat, taking comfort from the musky warm smell.

"I'll not leave you, Lucan," he vowed. "Torr cannot make me. He's not my father! We shall run away to France and find Ajax." Felix turned on his back and stared at the high vaulted ceiling with his head pillowed on the squirming young hound, who nipped his morose master's ears and pulled his long blond hair in an effort to get him to play. Lucan whined his concern and lapped at the tears that trickled down the boy's smooth cheeks. "You are all I have now, Lucan," sniffed Felix, wrapping his arms about the rambunctious animal. Soon they were both happily wrestling. "Pax!" giggled the boy, rolling onto his stomach and burying his head to avoid the irrepressible boisterousness. "No more! Pax, Lucan. I'm hungry!" He jumped to his feet and with the puppy leaping and nipping at his sleeves, they raced the length of the dusty gallery. Nearly reaching the door, Felix stopped and stared almost fearfully at a portrait of an ethereal young woman. Lucan growled and pulled at the boy's clothing, not understanding the abrupt end of the chase.

"Felicity Armstrong Pendarves." Felix read the brass placque solemnly. "That's my mother, Lucan. I'm named for her. I am Felix Armstrong Pendarves." He had been eight years old when she died. He suddenly realized that she had been dead for nearly half of his life and that awful fact horrified him. One day she would be dead for most of his life . . . just a faint shadow . . . just a flat painting. He remembered sliding quietly into her bed chamber every day to have a story read to him. Each day she had appeared frailer, her gentle lilting voice becoming fainter until it was a whisper barely audible above the constant roar of the sea, above the constant whine of the wind on the moor. One morning there had been no sound at all. She had been white and still, like marble . . . like the cold statues on the tombs in the family vault.

Now Felix gazed up at the likeness imprisoned within the ornate frame that was too cumbersome for her delicate feyness, and she seemed to smile reproachfully, wistfully.

"I am sorry I couldn't kiss you, Mama," he said, remembering how Torr and Ajax had dutifully kissed the white frozen face. His father had screamed, his pain-filled voice sounding terrifyingly inhuman. His father had shaken him until Torr had made him stop. "Father didn't speak to me for a very long time. I know I was disrespectful and disobedient, but I couldn't kiss you when you weren't there—only when you were warm and loving me," he tried to explain, tears flowing down his already streaked cheeks.

Torr stood just outside the gallery, his hand on the opened door, eavesdropping on his young brother. He had been on his way to search out Felix and offer to play a game of chess to atone for his harshness and self-absorption. He had recalled the loneliness when his father had shrouded himself away, unavailable for comfort, and realized that he was guilty of the same. Now he was loathe to trespass upon the boy's privacy. He stood in the shadows as the noisy pair burst through the door and raced past toward the kitchens, their exuberant young voices somehow mocking the sadness of a mere minute before. The clatter and skitter of feet, barks, and giggles receded into the depths of the large house. Feeling oddly rejected and useless, Torr limped into the gallery to commune with the portrait of his mother. She was, as his father had constantly bemoaned, too delicate a blossom to survive the brutal Cornish storms . . . the harsh Cornish life. Torr stared up at the painting, remembering her gentle touch and her sweetness, which now seemed incongruous amidst the severe Cornish granite. Yet she had forged a flower garden out of the unyielding rock and filled it with forget-me-knots, baby's breath, and honesty. His father had never forgiven himself for his young wife's death. More than thirty years had separated their ages, and Torr recalled snide remarks about that fact, yet the love between his parents had been very evident, glowing like a beacon for all to see. That love had also been his father's downfall, leaching his manhood so that when his wife died, his father had been left incomplete.

Torr gazed at his mother, not allowing himself to feel emotion as he vowed never to be so vulnerable. He would not ever be responsible for curtailing such a life, nor would he put his own manhood in such frail hands.

Felix with Lucan at his heels charged into the kitchen and barrelled into Mrs. Goodie's solid girth, rocking her.

"Good thing I have a bit of meat on my bones or you could've knocked me to Kingdom Come! Now, what's your big hurry!"

"Sorry, Goodie, but Lucan and I are hungry and we're going into Penzance with Jago," panted the youth.

"Going into Penzance, is he?"

"Jonty Pengelly is going, too, and he's Jago's brother and lives in Pendarves Castle over the moor," chattered Felix, excitedly.

"That old goat, Jago Pengelly, is going to town where there'll be real people instead of seals and gillymops and he doesn't say word to me about it! 'Specially when he knows how all these quiet miles of nothing fair gives me the wind-up!'' she muttered, savagely sawing through a loaf of bread.

"Don't you like it here, Goodie?'' asked Felix anxiously, seating himself on the kitchen table and wishing she would hurry up.

"Gives me the willies, it does! But anywheres you are, my pretty lad, is where I want to be. But I have to confess, all this clean air and nature curls my toenails! Now, get your buttocks off my table!''

"Have you met Jonty Pengelly yet?'' asked the boy, obediently sitting on a chair and tipping it back dangerously.

"Who needs to meet such a paragon! All I hear is Jonty Pengelly this and Jonty Pengelly that! I need the vegetable garden dug and planted and am told that Jonty Pengelly will see to it! I need extra hands to get this monster of a house in order and am told that Jonty Pengelly will see to it. So far the house is under several feet of dust and the vegetable garden under several feet of weeds, and I have yet to see Jago Pengelly's brother, Jonty!'' ranted Mrs. Goodie, spreading freshly baked bread with strawberry jam and generously covering the whole with dollups of thick clotted cream. "How's that?'' She chuckled happily as the boy crammed the whole into his mouth and held out the empty plate for seconds. "Chew it slowly or you'll choke yourself,'' she admonished, liberally spreading several more large hunks of bread for the ravenous child. "Wash it down with this,'' she directed, pouring a tall glass of milk.

"Where's Jago? I don't want him to leave without me!'' worried Felix after a large gulp of milk which left a thick white moustache on his hairless top lip.

"For heaven's sake, sit down and eat peaceful or you'll make yourself sick! And don't tip on the chair or you'll come down on that poor animal's paw,'' scolded Mrs. Goodie, refilling the boy's glass. "Jago isn't going anywhere without his lunch . . . and speaking of lunch, look who's joining us?'' she exclaimed as Torr limped into the kitchen. Felix took one look at his brother, hastily grabbed his uneaten food in both hands, and bolted out of the door, followed by the bounding puppy.

"Felix?" shouted Torr, but the kitchen door slammed shut. "Felix, come back here at once!"

"He couldn't have heard you," defended Mrs. Goodie. "Now, how about some freshly baked bread? There's clotted cream and strawberry jam, too," she chattered nervously, trying to ignore the tension that crackled from the brooding young man. "There's cheddar and ale if it'll suit you better." She waited for Torr to answer, uncomfortable in the silence. "There's also fresh fish. Jago Pengelly took Master Felix out in his boat first thing, and they brung home a dozen mackerel, I was thinking of frying them up for supper, but if that'll suit your fancy now . . . ?" She busied herself, brushing the crumbs from the table as she waited for an answer. "Jago Pengelly's going into town this afternoon and I'll give him a list. Is there anything in particular you'd like?" she coaxed.

"A clean house!" he stated, brushing angrily at the dust that liberally soiled his clothes.

" 'Tisn't my fault! 'Tis well nigh impossible to run this great ruin of a house in the middle of nowhere with no help but a silly lout who calls everything and everybody Betsy!" she exploded. "Not a shop! Not a barrow! Not another living soul for miles and miles! Not a civilized noise! Dozens of locked doors and no keys to fit!" she ranted furiously.

"Hire whom you see fit," sighed Torr wearily, unable to cope with the hysterical woman. He turned away and Mrs. Goodie's bad temper abruptly evaporated.

"You've gotta eat something! You've gotta keep your strength up!" But he curtly left the room. "Shall I bring something up to you?" she called after him, but there was no answer, just the sound of his dragging step. " 'Tisn't healthy to miss meals," she muttered despondently.

" 'Tedn't healthy to get so het up," remarked Jago dryly, standing in the doorway to the pantry with a jug of bitter ale in his hands.

" 'Tain't healthy for a man to sneak up on a woman and listen to what don't concern him!" snapped Mrs. Goodie. "So you thought to go off to town without a bye-your-leave, did you Jago Pengelly? Well, I have a long list and permission from his lordship to hire who *I* see fit!"

"Tes taken care of," he sighed, seating himself at the table and cutting some bread. "Look out there," he directed, waving the bread knife toward the back door. "Towards the gardens," he added, leaning back and chewing methodically.

Mrs. Goodie's button eyes widened considerably at the sight of more than a dozen black-garbed figures working industriously.

"Oh, my," she gasped, gaping at the eerie uniformity. "They look like giant crows!"

"They'll have the gardens in tiptop shape in no time flat."

"Who are they? Why are they all dressed the same?"

"They're the staff you've been craaking about not having," returned Jago evasively, pouring himself a mug of ale.

"Craaking?" she questioned incredulously, unable to believe her eyes at the sight of the black clothes that flapped spectrally in the stiff sea breeze.

"Craaking means nagging, carping, complaining," he informed her.

"But so many! How am I going to feed so many mouths? There's not enough food in the house," worried Goodie. "Where will they sleep? The servants' quarters are filthy . . . haven't been used for six years or more!"

"Tedn't healthy to fret," chided Jago. "They just need a sip of water or a cup of tea . . . maybe a spot of bread and jam before they go home."

"Go home," repeated Goodie with relief. The thought of such ghostly people drifting through the shadows of the house would have haunted her, causing sleepless nights.

"I must go or I'll not be back before nightfall," said Jago.

"Wait a minute. My list!" she hissed, rummaging through her apron pocket. "Can you read?"

"Aye, but tes your spelling that is peculiar," he chortled.

"There's nothing wrong with my spelling!"

"Must be English spelling then," he laughed, striding out into the spring sunlight.

"Wait a minute," she exclaimed, trotting after him, all the talk of spelling bringing to mind a more ominous meaning. "You cannot leave me alone with them unearthly shades," she hissed, conscious of how voices could carry with no city bustle to cover.

"Master Felix is all snug in the wagon and raring to go.

We'll see you 'fore night, God willing,'' he sang out before vanishing around the corner of the house.

A chill wind blew and Mrs. Goodie hugged herself before turning about and looking fearfully at the bent workers. She reached behind the kitchen door for her shawl and wrapped it about her shoulders.

"Well, I suppose it's nice to have a bit of company in this lonely end of the earth," she muttered to reassure herself, walking bravely through the courtyard and down the steep path to the walled gardens. "Hallo, there," she called but there was no acknowledgement. The black shrouded heads remained lowered and they systematically toiled. "I am Mrs. Goodie, the housekeeper here!" she shouted down the long furrows, but there was no response. No wavering of the rhythm of the busy hands, no pause in the steady sound of tools rasping into the wind-burnt soil, no change in the ring and clank of metal. She watched them intently, bobbing her head this way and that, trying to catch sight of a cheek, a nose; trying to ascertain the age or sex of any of the eerie workers. They were all dressed in shapeless black robes like some strange religious sect; shapeless robes that flapped about emaciated bent bodies. Mrs. Goodie was afraid yet fascinated and she edged closer. They were very old, she realized with a sickening jolt, noting the gnarled hands that clenched the hoe handles. Very old fingers, almost skeletal, nimbly weeded and busily scrambled. She looked ruefully at her own plump, pink hands and then back to the only part of the workers that was not covered by the flimsy black fabric—their blue-veined hands and their corded wrists. She gasped with horror at the sight of the iron manacles that rhythmically chafed the skin with their unceasing movements. Feeling shakey and ill, Mrs. Goodie scurried back to the warm safety of her kitchen and fortified herself with a generous portion of cooking sherry.

"I don't hold with spirits but there are times. Ooh, wait till that Jago Pengelly returns; he'll be getting more than a piece of my mind," she muttered savagely, gutting the glistening mackerel from gills to tail and wrenching the entrails out. "How dare he hire convicts and go off leaving me alone with them!" she raged, chopping off the fish heads with a cleaver. A chill breeze ruffled her heated cheeks, and still mumbling angrily to herself, she looked up from her butchering to see the black-clad troupe clustered at the opened kitchen door.

"Oh, my! What do you want?" she squealed, backing away with the dripping cleaver still in her hand. Keeping their shrouded heads lowered, they slowly shuffled in, silently seating themselves at the table, where they sat with their hands clasped docilely in their laps. Their convicts chains were hidden in their laps, thought the housekeeper suspiciously, realizing that they had assembled for food. She placed her cleaver in a prominent place.

"I am sorry, I lost all track of time," she chattered, hurriedly soaping and rinsing her hands. She bustled about putting bread and jam, cups and saucers, spoons and knives on the table. She had second thoughts about the knives but reasoned that blunt butter spreaders could do little harm if she used the carving knife to cut the loaves and keep them at bay.

The people sat patiently, making no sound or movement until the very last cup of tea was poured, and then at some unheard and unseen signal, there was a sudden flurry of activity. An anticipatory rattling of manacles before a great whoosh as gnarled hands swooped and snatched, jaws opened and closed, lips sucked and slurped until not a crumb of bread, lick of butter, smear of jam, or drop of tea remained. Then all was still and very quiet again. Mrs. Goodie gaped with amazement as the eerie people silently filed back to the walled gardens. Dumbfounded, she stood at the open kitchen door, allowing the yard cats to slink in, following their twitching noses to the gutted mackerel that lay forgotten.

"Like a great swarm of locusts from the Good Book," she muttered to some strutting pigeons. "All quiet . . . could hear a pin drop and then this great humming and munching till not a speck was left!" The blood-curdling shrieks of two tom cats battling for the remaining fish snapped her back to reality. She chased them out before locking herself in the kitchen.

For the rest of the day Mrs. Goodie kept her anxious eyes on the window, pinned to the spectral shades in the walled gardens, wishing Jago Pengelly would hurry up. The sun was setting into the sea, streaking the sky with vivid red gashes, lengthening and darkening the ominous shadows which further increased her terror. The cats screamed in the stables and barns, shivering her spine, when to her horror the blackclad workers silently filed into the yard like an army of grim reapers, their tools over their bent shoulders.

"Now what do I feed them?" she wailed, expecting them to pick at her very bones and wishing Torr Pendarves wasn't shut away in his suite of rooms on the second floor of the vast mansion. There was no way she would leave the cosy sanctuary of the kitchen and brave the maze of dark corridors. She hid behind the curtains, watching the solemn procession approach, but to her relief they trod past the locked door. Grabbing the meat cleaver and carving knife, she furtively edged out of the house, feeling safer with the workers in her sight. They stood motionless by the barn in the darkness, staring intently at a movement on the bleak moor, so motionless it was difficult to distinguish their flapping robes from the shifting shadows. The movement on the moor joined with the rumble of wheels and soon Jago drove up in a laden wagon.

"I've some choice words for you, Mr. Pengelly!" she shouted.

"Hello, Goodie," hailed Felix cheerfully, leaping down, followed by his puppy. "What's for supper?"

"Now, which Mr. Pengelly would you be wishing to have those choice words weth?" teased Jago. "This is my older brother, Jonty. Jonty Pengelly, allow me to introduce you to this fine figure of a woman," he flattered, chuckling to the shrinking shadowy man beside him in the wagon.

"I thought ez how she wuz eating out of the palm of thy hand?" whispered Jonty, keeping himself hidden. "Seems to me she wants to give thee the back of et."

"Tedn't nothing but bluff and bluster," hissed Jago out of the side of his mouth. Mrs. Goodie stood with the meat cleaver and the carving knife brandished across her heaving bosom, absolute fury hardening her usually good-natured features, staring fixedly at the huddled mass of black flapping robes. "Yeo, unload the sacks and barrels," Jago called out after a long sigh. The bent, shrouded shapes moved silently in a group toward the wagon. "Tedn't no use getting hurried up about the Betsy," he comforted his brother. "Underneath she's as soft as a pussycat."

Jonty gave his brother a skeptical look. "Et would help if thee could get her back into the kitchen so we can fetch a few kegs from the cellars," he said tersely before climbing down from the driver's bench. He shivered as the crisp breeze cut through his flimsy robes, and he hurried across the courtyard to become one with the industrious shades.

Mrs. Goodie stood silhouetted against the moonlit moor, seeming like a Valkyrie. All she lacked was a horned hat, mused Jago. She was oblivious to the chill sea winds and the thick dew that beaded on her hair and clothes, and she was deaf to the pointed suggestions that she make herself useful in the pantry putting away the foodstuff. Luckily for the Pengelly brothers, she was also blind to the barrels that appeared out of the night to be furtively tucked under tarpaulins on the now empty wagon. The only thing she was aware of was the moment she had been waiting for; the moment when the eerie shapes detached themselves from the shadows of High Tor and clustered into a moving mass to be driven away across the dark moor. She didn't move until the rumbling of the iron wheels had faded into the distance and was lost within the rhythmic swelling of the incoming tide that surged against the foot of the steep cliff.

"Goodie, I'm starving!" complained Felix when she finally entered the kitchen.

"There's not a crumb of bread unless you want to go through the pig buckets. Ten loaves I baked this morning, but the locusts devoured them!"

"Where's the fish I caught?"

"The cats enjoyed it," she snapped. "And don't give me the evil eye . . . save it for him!" she accused, pointing at Jago, who entered with a sack of flour. "If I hadn't been left with those . . . those . . . those black-robed witches . . . those locusts . . . there would be a mouth-watering supper. I would have baked a pie, too, but how could I when I had to watch those creepy people all day? Creepy old people with chains on their wrists!"

"Chains on their wrists?" Felix's mouth sagged open.

"They come in my kitchen and sit without a word . . .

don't make a sound. It was enough to frightened a God-fearing person to death. They slid into the house like smoke. I put food on the table and *swooosh*—they swoop and gobble it up like a great wind . . . not even a please or a thank-you,'' she ranted.

"Did they do a fitty job in the gardens?'' asked Jago sharply, standing at the open door to the yard and brushing the flour from his shoulders.

"I said, 'Good day, I am Mrs. Goodie the housekeeper,' and did they have the common decency to answer? Oh, no . . . acted like I wasn't there,'' she continued.

"Did they work hard and long?'' he probed.

"Master Felix, it was enough to chill your blood. They hid their faces and if I took my eyes off them for a minute they would disappear. They moved that silently . . . like shadows,'' recounted the woman, ignoring the leathery man who stared speculatively at her.

"That's enough of your tonguing!'' he said sternly, causing her to bridle with indignation. "At sunrise you'll see how well and hard they worked. They'll not be a weed or stone, and the earth will be aired to a good two feet down, and what is more they will be back tomorrow and the next day and the next until all the jobs at High Tor are completed!''

"We shall see about that!''

"What did they do to you?'' challenged Jago, his usually twinkling eyes hard and piercing.

"Just a bit of bread and water, you said. Hah! I swear if there had been a whole cow on the table . . . they'd have sucked it up!''

"You begrudge them bread and water after working for hours?''

"It's not that,'' said Goodie defensively.

"What is it, then?'' asked Jago, tempering his tone. "You're afraid of them?'' he added when she didn't answer.

"And why shouldn't I be? They had chains about their wrists! Manacles like convicts wear!''

"Manacles?'' breathed Felix, leaning forward, entranced.

"So what?'' questioned Jago. "They are just old harmless people who do an honest day's work.''

"But, Jago, why do they wear manacles?'' asked Felix.

''Because they are used to them,'' answered the Cornishman sadly.

''Are they really convicts?'' queried Felix, his eyes bright with excitement.

''They paid for their crimes,'' answered the man shortly.

''Your brother Jonty Pengelly too?'' asked the boy.

''Enough of your questions!''

Felix looked from Jago to Goodie and frowned. The two people he could usually count on to be cheerful and patient were now as terse and censuring as his brother Torr. He sidled out of the kitchen followed by the rambunctious puppy.

''Keep that dog away from the new batch of chickens or he'll have to be tied up,'' snapped Jago. The door slammed noisily behind the boy and a gloomy silence shrouded. ''Them poor miserable old people is more afraid of you than you of them.''

''They make my flesh crawl. They're like wraiths . . . ghosts,'' she admitted.

''That's what they are . . . ghosts . . . shadows of people. The Living-Dead. They'll be back at sunrise.'' he informed her wearily before taking himself to his bed.

The next morning the sun rose over the moor, erasing the darkness, and Mrs. Goodie shuddered at the sound of iron wheels rumbling into the yard to dispatch the long silent line of shadowy people. She stood at her bedroom window watching Jago speak to his brother. They looked up and she stepped out of sight, sensing that they were talking about her and curious to see what they were doing. There seemed to be a heated discussion with Jago trying to convince Jonty of something, because the older man kept shaking his head. The contention was resolved when Felix bounded out of the house followed by his puppy. Jonty whipped his drays into a steady plod and drove out onto the moor.

''I hope you're not thinking of leaving me with them again?'' she said curtly as she slammed down a platter of eggs and bacon before Jago. ''Felix, take this tray up to your brother,'' she ordered. The youth, whose stomach was rumbling with hunger, groaned. ''Your legs are younger than mine!'' she snapped.

''But I'm not a servant,'' the boy complained.

"Until I get decent help you'll have to play maid, young-feller-me-lad," she answered acidly, giving Jago a pointed glare. But he was concentrating on his meal and ignored her. Felix gracelessly picked up the tray, and Mrs. Goodie held the puppy's collar so he wouldn't follow his master and leap up and spill the food. "Oh, my heavens, what do they want? It isn't tea time!" she hissed out of the corner of her mouth, staring with alarm at the four black-garbed people who silently huddled at the outside door.

"Come in," welcomed Jago, ushering the shrouded bent shadows into the kitchen. "Now, don't be afraid. This is Mrs. Goodie and she'll tell you what needs doing in the house. Mrs. Goodie, these are the Three-Marys, who'll have everything spic and span if you'll just give them buckets and brooms and—"

"They probably fly over the moon," muttered the house-keeper under her breath, staring at the witchlike women. "Who did you say they were?"

"The Three-Marys."

"But there's four of them?"

Jago shrugged, unable to explain as Felix entered the room to be greeted by the ecstatic puppy. He stopped and grinned nervously at the huddled people.

"How do you do? I'm Felix." He introduced himself, offering his hand, hoping for sight of the manacles, but the black-garbed foursome shrank back against Jago.

"Mr. Pengelly, I would appreciate it if you . . . er, dealt with those four Three Marys," said Mrs. Goodie, pushing Felix into a chair and plunking his breakfast down in front of him. "Eat," she ordered before turning back to Jago. "There's the smaller formal rooms to clean first. The library, Sir Torr's study, the small dining room, the breakfast room, and the parlour what overlooks the terrace. You can show them where the mops and dusters are."

The following weeks passed without too much incident. Felix played outside with Lucan. Torr kept to himself, pushing his injured body to the limit, determined to be whole again. Mrs. Goodie tried to relax with the ever-present 'Living-Dead,' who silently and efficiently returned High Tor to its former glory. April passed into May. By day the moor lost its inhospitable bleakness and blazed with purple and pinks, yellows and golds. Every afternoon at four 'they' flowed into the kitchen, dousing Mrs. Goodie's cheerfulness. One minute she would be merrily humming, the air redolent with fragrances of freshly baked cakes, pastries, and breads, the sunlight pouring through the latticed windows, but then 'they' would ooze in, dampening her lightheartedness with their dark silence. God was her witness that she had tried. She had effusively praised their diligent work, cooked all manner of treats, but never a sound did she receive in return. Except for one afternoon. Just thinking about the incident caused her skin to goosebump.

It was a teatime like any other and the last cup of tea was about to be poured. That day she had baked two large currant cakes, and generous bowls of jam and clotted cream were set along the table, ready to be spread on the cottage loaves she had taken from the oven that morning. She always made sure that everything was in readiness before she poured that last cup, knowing that the very second it filled to the brim was the signal for them to descend and devour. She had tipped the teapot and the steaming amber brew arced gracefully from the spout, watched over by the black shrouded eyes . . . breathless moment that made her feel almost powerful.

" 'Tis the Devil-Child!" was hissed, and she looked up in fear, her hand still pouring the tea, to see a dark face at the window. "Devil-Child, Devil-Child, Devil-Child" was chanted happily down the long row, only to be suddenly silenced by an ear-splitting scream of agony.

Mrs. Goodie gaped in terror and confusion at the shrieking person who shrank away from the boiling liquid, the black clothes wet and steaming. She dropped the teapot, and it crashed into pieces on the hard stone floor. "Oh, my! Oh, my! I'm sorry! So sorry!" she wept, dabbing at the scalded person who backed fearfully against the wall, moaning softly.

Jago was working in the barn with Felix when the piercing scream shattered the tranquil afternoon air. He dropped his rake and rushed to the house, followed by the boy. But the puppy, Lucan, was diverted by the sight of two fleetly moving dark shapes disappearing over the sweep of the moor and gave chase.

"There's too many unnatural goings-on," declared Mrs. Goodie later that evening, trotting back and forth across the kitchen floor. "Strange thumps and bumps in the night . . . ghostly convicts—the 'Living-Dead' as you yourself call them— and now a devil. I tell you, Jago Pengelly, they said 'Devil-Child' as plain as the nose on my face. I heard it with my two ears. 'Devil-Child, Devil-Child,' they said, and there at the window was a demon! I saw it with my own two eyes. Over there, peering in that there window as large as life. . . ."

"Did it have horns?"

"No doubt it did," snapped Mrs. Goodie. "And it is no laughing matter! Where is that boy? 'Tis not like him to miss his tea and now his supper," she worried, peeking fearfully out of the door at the moonlit courtyard.

"Master Felix can take care of hisself," soothed Jago, pouring himself some ale.

"Something's not right about here," fretted Goodie. "I don't think I've had a good night's sleep since 'they' started work about the place."

"They're not here at night, woman. What you need is a pair of strong arms to hold you tight, loving you into a dreamless slumber," he remarked.

"And whose arms would you be thinking of to fill the job?" was her acid answer. "Oh, those pretty words slide off your oiled tongue like honey. Well, you'll not pull the wool over my eyes, Jago Pengelly, something's going on here and it is not my imagination nor is it the sea and the wind moaning in the caves."

"What is it, then?" he challenged.

"I don't know, but I aim to find out," she promised. Several times she had taken her courage and her meat cleaver in both hands and tiptoed down the stairs, her ears straining to hear the voices that hummed with the wind. Furtive mutters and rumbles issued from deep within the earth. She had stood shaking, her heart leaping painfully in the darkness, peering down the cellar steps at the locked doors, which according to Jago had no keys and had not been opened since the sea flooded the lower wine cellars more than twenty years before. "Where is that child?" she cried. "If I had known what aggravation I was to suffer buried in the wilds of this . . . this

. . . godforsaken place, with a boy who runs wild till all hours of the night and a young master who locks himself away, spending every minute of the day trying to get that poor leg to be whole, I'd never have left London. And where is that doctor? It has been nearly six weeks and where is he?''

"Sit down, sip this," directed Jago, pouring a generous portion of rum, "and I'll go and find the boy."

"And if you don't come back?!" cried Goodie without thinking.

"Well, don't you fret none, my good Betsy, I'd always come back to you," he chuckled, kissing her heated cheek and dodging back out of range of her quick hands. "You have a good smell, my Betsy, cloves and vanilly," he sighed, striding out of the door.

"My name isn't Betsy and I don't hold with spirits," she whispered, cupping her burning cheek in her hand. She sat herself at the table and took a long sip of the rum, expecting it to be sherry. She gasped and then grinned with appreciation as the warmth curled into her cold corners. She sighed and relaxed, hearing Jago's strong voice and piercing whistle echoing over the rolling moors as he tried to locate the errant Felix.

"A woman could do worse than Jago Pengelly," she decided, seduced by the inviting picture he had painted of holding her in his strong arms. "But I'm not had cheaply, my cheeky fellow, 'tis a ring on my finger before there's any loving of this lonely body," she added, drinking deeply.

CHAPTER 10

DEVIL TREMAYNE wound numb fingers in the Bucca's shaggy coat and trod on leaden legs into the yawning recesses of the shadowy kitchen to face Miss Peller's wrath.

"How dare you disobey me! How dare you show yourself at High Tor!" she spat, trembling with suppressed rage. The eyes of the Living-Dead gazed sorrowfully at the small valiant figure. "What do you have to say for yourself, you ungrateful devil?" she screeched. The enormous hound tensed to spring, his hackles bristling. "Control that foul creature or I'll poison his feed . . . poison all feed and no one shall dare eat tonight . . . nor sleep!"

"Oh, Devil-Child," lamented the three Marys.

"Should have stayed hid, Devil-Child," cackled Mad-Biddy.

"Thou art a dreadful secret," chided Curate Pomfrey.

"But a natural curious youngster being forced to live a dark unnatural life," hissed Jonty.

" 'Tis true, 'tis true, 'tis true," was rhythmically intoned.

"What are you trying to do, Pengelly?" screamed Miss Peller, unnerved by the long lines of Living-Dead who sat each side of the long bare table, nodding and chanting their agreement of Jonty's words. "Isn't it enough with another accursed Pendarves back in High Tor to interfere with our livelihood? Isn't it enough with your brother, Jago Pengelly, threatening our very existence?" she ranted, and the old people covered their heads and rocked in terror.

"Would et be better thet Jago hire strangers to poke their noses into the lower cellars of the Tor and remark on the busy doings in the coves of a night?" challenged Jonty.

177

"Take care, Pengelly, don't cross me! I hold the bonding deed for your life, too!" she snarled. Devil turned wide, horror-filled eyes to the small wiry old man.

"You, too, Jonty Pengelly?" whispered Granny-Griggs with a wry chuckle.

"But you said that all would be free! You said all living things would be free! Why wasn't the bonding deed burned with the rest?" protested Devil.

"I am supposing thet none was burnt. Am I right, Repeller?" hissed Granny-Griggs.

"None burnt . . . none burnt . . . none burnt," was chanted down the long rows of rocking people.

"Hush now, hush," soothed Jonty, trying to calm the rising agitation and temper the rage that pounded through his taut body. "Miss Peller, et has been a grievous day but no harm ez done," he stated stiffly, bowing his head in deference to the woman when he recognized the mad danger signs in her hooded gaze.

"No harm?! A scalded arm is no harm? Show your cooked flesh, Minnie Pinny!" ordered the housekeeper, determined to retain control.

"It doesn't hurt, Devil-Child. Granny-Griggs potioned it," whimpered Minnie, seeing the tears that flooded the fathomless, dark eyes.

"You, Devil, you caused that pain!" accused Miss Peller triumphantly, seeing the telltale glistening on the young cheeks. *"You!* You caused pain because you disobeyed me!"

"You said all would be free. You said you burned the bonding deeds," whispered Devil brokenly.

"That's enough from you! You've caused pain just like your grandfather, you bastard child. You have no responsibility but to do my bidding because I know better."

"You are no better than my grandfather . . . keeping everyone afraid . . ." bravely stated Devil.

"How dare you speak to me like that! Is it you, Pengelly, filling this Devil spawn with lies that could mean death and destruction?" screeched Miss Peller, and the black-garbed people rocked and moaned louder. "Who has kept you safe all these long cruel years? Me! Who has kept you clothed, housed, and fed? Me! Who protected you when Godolphus

Pendarves died? Me! You should be down on your knees to me!''

"Why didn't you burn the papers?''

"I don't have to explain myself to a mere child, but what I chose to do or not do is for your protection . . . for our protection . . . for everyone's protection. I know best and if I'm obeyed no one will be hurt and we shall live in peace. Do you want to see the Living-Dead chained to the stocks in the town square? Lashed to the whipping blocks? Rotting in rat-infested gaols? Publicly hanged? Transported? Well, do you?''

"No,'' was huskily whispered and a glossy head was shaken.

"*You* can cause all that to them. *You* can mean agony, debasement, and death to these wretched shadows of people. *You*! Do you understand?'' And the glossy ebony head nodded. "Good . . . now we shall eat,'' and the rocking and sobbing abruptly ceased. The Living-Dead sat quietly, their heads lowered, but their eyes fixed hungrily to the cooking pot.

"Sit yourself down for the meal, skilliwiddens,'' sighed Jonty, seating himself on the bench, with his manacled wrists tucked in the opposite sleeve like a monk, but the Devil-Child backed out of the room.

The sad dark child stood high in the north tower, staring out of the slit window over the moonlit countryside thinking of the fair-headed boy and his puppy who were trapped in the tin mine on the moor. The boy had seemed familiar, and Devil looked down at the healed teeth marks, remembering the tall naked man with the terrible wound who had left the claiming scars. It had been an exciting chase, Devil and the Bucca easily eluding and out-running the loppy dog and his master, dodging around and over rocks, allowing a quick, teasing glimpse now and then so the blond boy's flagging energy and hopes were piqued. Devil had been disappointed to discover that the thick corn-coloured hair had belonged to a stranger instead of to the wounded soldier from France. Nevertheless it had been a merry chase. At dusk Devil had headed for home, instinctively taking the route across the stretch of the moor called Demon's Rise, assuming the boy would know better than to follow. Too late came the realization that he was a stranger and ignorant of the treacherous tract of land in the shifting light. The sickening crack of splintering boards covering a hidden mine shaft had shattered the still air. The high-pitched whine and barking of the frantic young dog as he scratched at the ground about the abyss; the spine-chilling howl as more boards had given way, sending the pup hurtling after his master into the dark depths of the disused mine, continued to reverberate in Devil's brain. There had been no sound or sign of life from the hapless pair. A faint mewing circling up through the dank, salty darkness had not been repeated. Devil had lain in the heather in a daze with jeering gulls screaming and circling above.

Devil stood at the window of the north tower listening to the night sounds, ignoring the twittering bats and cumbersome ravens. What if the boy and his pup were not dead but lying hurt and confused in the darkness of the mine?

"Bucca-Dhu, we cannot leave them there. I must know if I have caused a death . . . caused another terrible hurt like the blisters on Minnie-Pinny's arm," keened Devil, hanging a coil of rope over a thin shoulder and strapping a knife about a slim waist.

"Where are thee off to, Devil-Child? To ride through the fairy rings left by the tide?" asked Granny-Griggs, prancing out of the shadows as the child led the black stallion, Carrack, out of the central stables and through the barbican.

"Do you feel or hear anything with your special sight, Granny-Griggs?" probed Devil earnestly. "Anything different?"

"A body's pain? Besides Minnie Pinny's boiled flesh?" demanded the crone and the child nodded. The old woman concentrated, her wrinkled face upturned to the sea breeze, frowning into the moonlight. She cocked her head to the four cardinal points of the earth, her long hooked nose twitching as she sniffed the air. "I don't hear nothing but the wind whining through dark closeness and I smell a damp moldy hole, black and stale . . . not a cellar but deep under the ground. Is et a grave?"

"A grave?" echoed Devil miserably.

"No, not quite a grave . . . not yet a grave," sighed the hag.

"Oh, Granny, you smell death?"

"Not quite. I feel pain and fear within the bowels of the earth. What ez happening, Devil-child? Ez someone being buried alive?"

"The blond boy from High Tor fell through the earth at Demon's Rise," confessed Devil, leading the impatient horse out of the shadow of Pendarves Castle and agilely clambering upon the high bare back.

"Could mean more trouble from the Repeller. Thee're too soft-hearted, Devil Tremayne," softly chided the crone.

"It was my fault."

"Was et at the peak or ebb of Demon's Rise?" she asked, recognizing the grim determination on the poignant face.

"The ebb."

"Toward the cliffs or inland?"

"Toward the sea."

"Then tes fortunate for the boy. There's a tunnel leading from a cave in the bluffs above the Hellspoint Cove. Get the Carrack back to the mounting block," she directed.

"You're going to ride bare-ridged with me?" giggled Devil as the witchlike crone threw a sinewy old leg across the stallion and wrapped thin arms about the child's lithe body.

"I'd prefer a broomstick and the full moon," chuckled Granny. "I den't like to think of my good healing going all to waste at the bottom of Awd Tarkeel Mine. How's his leg? Does he move with much of a limp?"

" 'Tis not the same. The boy's much younger but with the same golden hair," sighed Devil, kicking the Carrack to a thundering pace.

Jonty Pengelly sincerely believed that there was nothing left on earth that could possibly surprise him. But his rheumy eyes widened considerably at the vision of the ancient crone and the vibrant child atop the black stallion, racing across the shadowy moor followed by the huge hound, a cloud of flickering bats and several spectral ravens. The old woman's hair streamed in silvery tendrils, her black robes flattening against her skeletal body and between her arms the beautiful child

whose thick shining hair caught the stark purity of the moon
and the iridescence of the raven's wing. There was something
frighteningly prophetic in the sight of vital youth clutched in
the boney arms of decay. He shuddered as he made his way
to the stables intent on following.

Jonty blessed the three-quarter moon as his sure-footed
pony picked her way across the treacherous moor. He strained
his eyes, searching the shifting shadows for the elusive
Devil-child.

"Well, brother of mine, what brings you out tonight?"
hailed Jago.

"I might be asking the same of you," returned Jonty,
evasively.

"Young Felix Pendarves is missing and a mysterious dark
lad was seen poking an inquisitive nose at the kitchen window
of High Tor shortly before the boy and his hound disappeared," informed Jago, shrewdly noting his older sibling's
unease. "Maybe I'm finally within sniffing distance of
Godolphus Pendarves's heir? Tragic Catherine's son?"

"I'm sworn to secrecy," answered Jonty quietly.

"A lad is missing and he doesn't know these perilous
moors like your will-o'-the-wisp. Et would seem both boys
were lonely. Mine mourning his father, rattling about in a
draughty house with none to comfort him but a surly older
brother and a half-grown pup . . . and yours incarcerated in a
cold fortress full of frightened old people whipped into a
cowering mass by thet evil Peller female," ranted Jago,
furious with his only living relative, who'd not confide in
him.

"What are you saying?"

"Thet maybe, just maybe two lonely lads have found each
other!" stated Jago. "What's thet?" he spun about, hearing
steady hoofbeats. "Oh, my sainted aunt! What in heaven's
name?" he gasped as an enormous black horse walked majes-
tically over the rise and stopped, silhouetted against the moonlit clouds. "Bats and ravens!" he exclaimed hoarsely, hastily
crossing himself as he made out two figures. A lithe child and
a bent hag. "Tes no wonder thet no God-fearing person will
set a foot in these parts! So thet's your young master! I see
there's some credence to the ghost stories thet abound in the

drinking parlours from here to the River Tamar! Bless my soul, ent thet Awd Granny-Griggs thet Godolphus Pendarves sentenced to death at the Assizes fer delivering a deformed baby on the Sabbath and selling it to Satan?''

''And folks from here to the River Tamar know thet babe was unnatural 'fore Granny-Griggs rid the tinker's lass of et's poor dead body. And what would you expect from thet wicked man's twisted seed? Sir Godolphus hisself sired thet deformed babe and the tinker's lass no more than ten years old!'' spat Jonty.

''Sir Godolphus? Our revered magistrate? Sir Godolphus Pendarves? That most religious man?'' said Jago wonderingly.

The two brothers fell silent as the small lithe figure leapt off the stallion and very carefully examined the ground. The wild-haired hag struggled to dismount but couldn't.

''Giddy-up, dobbin,'' she urged, trying to get the huge animal to move to an outcropping of rock, but the giant horse obeyed none but his master. ''Devil-Child?'' she called plaintively, drumming her boney heels against the firm girth. ''I cannot get down and this wretched creature's too far up off the ground for me to jump.''

''Why do they call the little lad Devil-Child?'' whispered Jago. Jonty tersely handed him the reins of his pony and briskly strode through the dewy heather to the stranded old woman.

''Jonty Pengelly,'' cackled the crone. ''Just in time to catch me, darling man.'' Between the two of them, the old man and the Devil-Child managed to haul Granny-Griggs off the motionless horse.

''Where's the Pendarves boy?'' demanded Jonty hoarsely. ''The fair-haired lad from the Tor?'' he explained when the unlikely pair stared at him in surprise.

''How do you know?'' whispered Devil.

''You getting the 'sight' in yer awd age, Pengelly?'' cackled the crone. The Bucca's hackles rose and he growled menacingly. ''Some one's there!'' she gasped.

'' 'Tes my brother out searching for the Pendarves boy,'' said Jonty. Jago stepped cautiously from the shadows. ''Do you know where he's at?'' The large, haunted eyes stared miserably toward the darkness in the heather. ''In a mine shaft?'' exclaimed the old man, and the Devil-Child nodded miserably. ''Is he alive?''

''He's snagged hisself on a shelf not too far down,'' informed the old woman, evasively. ''We went through the caves into the tunnels, but he was lodged far above us in the main shaft of Awd Tarkeel.''

''Is he living?'' hoarsely demanded Jago and the small dark figure looked up at him. He stepped back involuntarily at the sight of the beautiful, anguished face and terror stabbed through him at the message he read in the fathomless eyes.

''If you tie a rope about me and the Carrack, Jonty, I shall go down to the boy.''

''No, Devil-Child! Your life ez ahead of you . . . the rest of us are awd,'' argued the old woman.

''The shaft is too narrow for any but me and 'twas my fault that the boy fell.''

''Why do you call the little lad Devil-Child?'' hissed Jago angrily. The name sounding jarringly sacrilegious when applied to such an exquisite young being.

''Because 'tes his name,'' cackled the witch, watching the small figure walk carefully about the yawning dark hole in the heather. ''There's no way thet Devil-Child will risk his precious life for any Pendarves spawn!'' she muttered furiously.

''Isn't he also Pendarves spawn? Catherine Pendarves's spawn?'' returned Jago, keeping his eyes pinned to the child, fascinated by the natural grace. ''And Tremayne of Taran's whelp, too, I'll be bound,'' he added, noting the glossy ebony hair.

''You're sworn to silence!'' spat Granny-Griggs, fear streaking through her old body. Jago stepped back and silently watched Jonty tie a rope about the slim child.

''Neither lad is full grown, so we can manage their weight with help from my sturdy pony,'' decided Jonty. ''Now, my skilliwiddens, are thee set?'' he asked gruffly when the rope was looped about a stunted tree and the end secured to the pommel of his saddle. The two brothers held the middle length, prepared to feed it into the shaft as the lithe child descended.

''Bucca, stay,'' ordered Devil, and Jago raised a quizzical eyebrow at the clear sweet ring of the voice. The enormous hound slumped, his huge head resting on immense paws as he stared dolefully at his young master, who slowly disappeared into the earth.

Devil's keen eyes took several moments to adjust to the dense blackness in the shaft. Dirt and stones were dislodged, rattling against the sides and landing far below after a horrifying breathless pause. Sobs of terror caused Devil great relief. The blond boy wasn't dead, but any thought of resting on the ledge and transferring the rope were dashed at the sight of the rotting wooden shelf which obviously couldn't hold both their weights.

"I'm going to get just below you so you can wrap your legs about my shoulders before letting go and grabbing the rope," explained Devil. "Straddle . . . one leg each side of my head."

Felix's much greater weight caused pain to shoot through the smaller child's slim back and the coarse rope cut painfully into tender armpits as the youth launched himself at his young saviour with such desperate violence that the wooden ledge ripped out of the shaft wall, battering the Devil-Child. The rope dropped several feet with the added burden and both of them screamed in sudden panic, but the Pengelly brothers dug in their heels, bringing them to an abrupt halt. Excruciating pain gripped Devil's whole body as very slowly, inch by agonizing inch, they were hauled to the surface.

"He's alive," rejoiced Granny-Griggs when Felix's blond head appeared. "Where's the Devil-Child?" she fretted when the youth collapsed in the heather unable to help himself and scramble away from the unsafe perimeter. The Bucca howled his concern and padded back and forth. Devil was nearly screaming from the crushing weight of the inert youth and panicked as large chunks of rocks and gravel tore loose all around.

"I can bear the weight of the dark lad. Pull Felix clear," instructed Jago, through clenched teeth. Jonty crawled tentatively toward the sprawled youngster, terrified that the earth would cave, in burying the Devil-child, who hung suspended in the yawning abyss.

Finally the dark child lay fighting for breath on firm ground. The Bucca whined and lovingly nudged the lithe little body as aching muscles were thankfully stretched in the cool dew-laden heather. Jago and Jonty checked Felix for injury, but except for scratches and bruises, the youth was miraculously unharmed.

Felix sat up and stared at the boy who had saved him, amazed at his diminutive size.

"Tell the Pendarves whelp 'tes a secret! Make him swear in blood upon his mother's grave," hissed Granny-Griggs, and Felix gasped and recoiled from the macabre sight of the witchlike crone. He stood on very shaky legs and held out his hand to his rescuer but an enormous dog snarled menacingly. Felix hurriedly backed away, sprawling over a rock hidden in the brush. The hag straddled his prone body. "Boy, ef 'ee tell any of this night . . . ef 'ee so much as mention the Devil-Child and the Bucca-Dhu, 'ee will die a horrible death . . . worse than being buried alive in Awd Tarkeel!" she threatened, her spit pitting his terrified face.

"That's enough, awd woman!" snapped Jago, and the crone scrambled away. "Felix, 'tes important that thee keep a closed mouth about the happenings tonight," he said gently to the petrified youth, sensing Jonty's agitation. "The Devil-Child is a secret," he stressed, noting a fleeting sadness and disappointment in Devil's profound, dark eyes. Poor young lad with none but strange wild things for companions. No friends but the outcasts of the day and the outcasts of society, the Living-Dead, he mused sorrowfully as the lithe figure swung up onto the Carrack's high back and galloped across the moor followed by his companions of the night.

Felix lay in a daze. Everything seemed unreal. He gazed about the shadowy moor trying to locate the boy and his eerie pets. He avoided looking at the long-haired witch, whose scrawny bare legs gripped the rounded girth of a chubby dartmoor pony. He closed his eyes, his heart pounding fearfully with the steaming mist that rose from the shadows in the silvery moonlight, wishing he were curled in a warm bed, safely within the secure walls of High Tor. He must have fallen asleep, because suddenly Jago was shaking him awake.

"Come along, young feller-me-lad."

"Where's your brother?" asked Felix, looking about for Jonty and the frightening old woman. "Where have they gone?'' he cried out with alarm, certain that they had magically disappeared.

"Home to their beds, where we should be,'' answered Jago, pulling the boy to his feet.

"But they were just here. Were they ghosts?'' he sobbed, spinning round and round, expecting them to pounce out at him. Mist swirled about the ground and he recoiled.

"Tedn't healthy to get all bothered up about et. 'Tes just the moor of a night and her moods thet bends the mind to unearthly things, 'specially when the sea frets slither in. Nights such as these make full-grown men imagine they hear the mermaids luring them to watery graves, but tes just the whine of the wind in the caves of the bluffs.''

"He was such a little fellow,'' said Felix, breaking a long silence as they trudged wearily over the misty moorland toward High Tor. "Frail and yet he held my whole weight on his shoulders. How old is he? Who is he? Is he really a devil? Those bats and birds and that enormous dog . . . Oh, Jago, we must go back! Lucan! We must get Lucan!'' he screamed, turning and running back across the moor.

"You fool child,'' swore Jago, chasing after him. "Do you want to end up at the bottom of Awd Tarkeel? This stretch is called Demon Rise, and it is riddled with air shafts like the one you fell into. Now, stop!''

"What about Lucan?'' demanded the boy.

"Your pup must be dead, lad,'' stated the leathery man, wrapping a lean arm about the grieving youth.

"No!''

"Did you hear him?'' asked Jago gently. "You were down there several hours. A hurt young dog kicks up quite a rumpus. Did you hear him?''

"The noise of the sea was so loud down there. But I think I heard him below me . . . crying. Jago, we have to go back and see. We have to . . . we can't leave him there.''

"We have no choice. There's no way we could find our way through those mine passages. The tide is up cutting off all entrance.''

"That means he'll drown!''

"Ef he's not already,'' muttered Jago. "Pull yourself together and act the man!'' he stated firmly when it seemed the boy was losing control. ''Face the fact that there is nothing we can do until morning, when the tide has gone out and we have light to see by! I think tes best to hope the poor beast died with the fall and feels no pain!''

Felix fell silent and walked beside Jago, stifling his sobs. Not another word passed between them all the way to High Tor. The welcoming lights of the kitchen streamed through the swirling mist as they stumbled across the slick cobblestones of the yard.

''I've been worried sick. And what in heaven's name happened to you, Master Felix!'' exclaimed Goodie, shocked at the sight of the filthy scraped boy. Tears still streaked down his muddy face. ''Oh, my poor lovey, what is it? Tell your Goodie, what it is, my lambie?'' she crooned, enfolding the unhappy child in her arms. The kind words were too much for Felix, who had been trying desperately to obey Jago and act like a man. He turned his face into Goodie's ample bosom and wept. ''What is it? What's happened?'' she asked sharply of Jago when it was obvious the boy was too distraught to explain.

''Master Felix tumbled down an open mine shaft and the dog was killed,'' he answered succinctly, pouring himself a generous mug of rum.

''Tumbled down a what? Dog killed?'' she shrieked, sitting heavily and pulling the wildly sobbing youth into her lap so his long legs dangled incongruously.

''The moor is riddled with abandoned mine shafts,'' explained Jago, seating himself and sadly watching the grieving boy rocking in Goodie's arms. He idly wondered if the tiny dark child of the moors ever had a comforting lap to curl into. According to Granny-Griggs, the huge hound only allowed Jonty to touch the child; his brother, though a kindly soul, was not given to outward displays of affection, mused Jago. And from the few unpleasant encounters he had had with Rebecca Peller, he doubted if her acid mouth gave the boy many loving words.

''He fell down a mine!'' gasped Goodie. ''Oh, you poor motherless mite,'' she crooned, kissing the top of his blond head.

''What the hell is going on in here?'' thundered a harsh

voice. Torr Pendarves loomed at the kitchen door, glaring at his overwrought young brother. "It's after midnight!"

Jago hid his head in his hands and groaned inwardly when the hysterical boy tried to explain the night's happenings. Most of the long involved explanation was unintelligible, though punctuated with incriminating words such as *Bucca-Dhu . . . Devil . . . witch . . . ravens* and *bats*. Jago shrewdly noted the tall young man's eyes narrowing speculatively.

"A Devil-Child?" questioned Torr sharply, and Felix suddenly remembered that he was sworn to secrecy. To reveal more information would mean death, according to the wild-haired witch. His sobs abruptly stopped and he roughly pushed himself away from Goodie's cradling arms and fought to control himself.

"Devil-Child? Why that is what 'they' called the dark gypsy brat who was peeking in the window at teatime today," said Goodie.

"Young Master Felix has suffered a shock, sir. He fell down the main air-shaft of the Old Tarkeel Mine on Demon's Rise," informed Jago servilely. " 'Twas lucky he landed on a cattle shelf 'bout fifteen feet down, so my brother Jonty Pengelly and me was able to haul him up, but his poor pup weren't so blessed," he recounted, broadening his rural accent and staring with wide innocent eyes at the young lord, much to the housekeeper's puzzlement.

"What's this about witches and the Bucca-Dhu?" snapped Torr.

"Why, that's what you was ranting about when you came home from France and were out of your head with sickness," remembered Mrs. Goodie.

"The lad ez probably out of his head, too, with grief for his poor dead dog," suggested Jago. "Nasty spill he had . . . could have addled his brains a bit."

"Felix, what do you know of a Devil-child and the Bucca-Dhu?" probed Torr sharply.

"Nothing," lied the boy. "I was stuck down the mine for hours and hours . . . and it's misty and scary out there. I thought I heard ghosts and spriggans . . . and Lucan is still at the bottom of the shaft," he wailed rushing out of the room.

"The poor orphan child. I'll see he gets all tucked cosy in

his nice warm bed," said Mrs. Goodie, bustling after Felix, anxious to be away from the humourless young lord who stared pointedly at Jago Pengelly.

"Well?" Torr Pendarves snapped the long tense silence, his eyes still pinned to the seemingly relaxed older man.

"Oh ah, I'm right sorry about the missment to the young master, sir, but 'tedn't my place to play nursemaid or the like to the lad," drawled Jago, deliberately misunderstanding and playing the bumbling yokel. "I have these two hands full with the gardens and the livestock, sir." Torr paced the kitchen keeping his steely blue eyes fixed to the leathery Cornishman. "Thee's walking much better, sir. I doubt thee'll have much of a limp by summer, sir," observed Jago, wishing all the barrels of French brandy were out of the cellars at High Tor. Now that was a secret Jago understood, knowing smuggling was illegal and having had firsthand experience with excise men, but why was the dark child a secret? he pondered.

"Don't play me for an idiot, Pengelly!" hissed Torr.

"Never would I do that, sir," protested Jago indignantly.

"What do you know of the dark child?"

"What dark child?"

"I'm warning you, Pengelly," threatened the irate young man.

"Oh, the gypsy brat that peeked into the kitchen this afternoon?"

"Pengelly," stated Torr, pouring himself a stiff drink. "Before my father died, he told me that you had arranged for my escape from France," he said after a long punishing swallow.

"I sent word to . . . er . . . acquaintances," hedged Jago, puzzled by the seeming change of subject.

"Acquaintances? I understood from my father it was your own brother who arranged transportation," probed Torr.

"My brother? No, no, sir, not my brother, sir. Excuse me for saying, I don't mean no imperance sir, but I think thy father was mistaken. Et were acquaintances of mine what shipped thee back to these shores, sir, but not my brother," denied Jago. "And glad am I to be of help, sir. Does my heart good to see thee home safe and sound."

"What's that?" hissed Torr, clutching at Jago's sinewy arm.

"I don't hear nothing, sir," lied Jago, hearing the muffled hoofbeats. His heart sank, fearing that Jonty had panicked and thought to remove all the barrels that night instead of sticking to their original plan—taking one or two each day when he came to drop off and pick up the black-garbed workers.

"Open the outside door, Pengelly," ordered Torr.

"Tedn't nothing but barn cats on the prowl," stated Jago loudly, slowly getting to his feet. "Or maybe some cheeky moor ponies thinking to steal a sweet munch of Pendarves hay," he added, hoping whoever it was had sense enough to quickly hide. He fumbled clumsily with the door latch.

Devil cradled the limp heavy body of Lucan and rode the stallion Carrack into the stable-yard at High Tor. Jago's gruff voice shattered the silence and then the door was flung open and warm lantern light streamed through the cool wisps of moon-touched mist. Jago's mouth sagged open at the sight of the small wet child atop the huge horse. There were several moments of silence broken by a husky soft voice.

"The boy's pup is dead."

Jago sadly nodded and strode toward the child, intent on taking the limp body of the young dog, but there was a menacing growl. The Bucca appeared from out of the shadows.

"Stay, Bucca," ordered Devil. "He'll not harm you."

"You're sure about that, are you?" said Jago, slowly approaching and keeping a wary eye on the enormous animal. "Where on this earth did you find such a loyal pet?" he asked, covering his nervousness.

"He came swimming to me from Wolf Rock in a fierce storm. The Carrack was with him. Jonty said they must have been on the Spanish vessel that was wrecked that night," answered the child, and Jago prayed that Torr Pendarves was out of earshot. He gazed up into the sorrowful little face, mesmerized by the perfection of the features and the large expressive eyes.

"Et seems you have been swimming, too, lad?" he said gruffly.

"The tide is in and that's the only way I could reach the poor young beast," mourned the child, stroking a velvet ear. "Tell the boy he did not suffer." Jago nodded and reached up to take the dead puppy. "And tell the boy . . . I'm sorry," sobbed the tiny figure. Small bare feet drummed against the enormous horse who galloped into the thick sea-fog that swirled across the rolling moor.

Jago was very conscious of Torr Pendarves's eyes, but he didn't turn towards the house. He just stood for several long moments cradling the dead animal, listening to the Carrack's hooves recede into the night. Torr limped across the yard leaning heavily on a cane and looked enquiringly into Jago's lined brown face, quietly noting the brimming eyes that glinted in the moonlight.

"I'll help you bury the poor creature," he said awkwardly.

"Tes not for us to do, your lordship," replied Jago, his voice laced with bitterness. "Excuse my imperance, sir, but et is for young Master Felix to bury his own pet so he lays his grief to rest," he added, striding to the stables where he wrapped his sad burden in several burlap bags. Torr Pendarves watched, then the two men walked silently back to the kitchen and sat at the table.

"I've met this so-called Devil-Child and his formidable Bucca-Dhu before," Torr stated, hoping to cause some flicker of surprise to cross Jago's set features. But the older man just sighed deeply and reached for his mug of rum.

"Just one small lad and his pet," he muttered harshly.

"Rather awesome names for such a mundane pair, don't you think, Pengelly?" Jago shrugged and drank. "Who is he?" probed Torr.

"A tinker's lad who had the good fortune to luck upon a handsome black hound and steed from a Spanish vessel wrecked on Wolf Rock," answered Jago airily. "Now, ef you'll excuse me, sir, morning will be here any moment and I need my sleep." Torr nodded, knowing that there was no more to be learned from the tight-lipped man. Jago quietly quit the room leaving him alone with his brooding thoughts.

He had not been near enough to see the well-remembered poignant face, but the large dog had been unmistakable and the name 'Jonty' had not escaped his keen ears. His agile mind carefully assembled all the fragments of knowledge at his disposal. Jonty Pengelly was Jago's older brother—the very brother, according to his father, who had arranged his escape from France aboard the smuggling vessel where he first laid eyes on the mysterious dark child. Jonty Pengelly had been Godolphus Pendarves's manservant for many years until the day he died. Jonty Pengelly probably still lived in the hulking cold pile of granite atop the sheer cruel scarp facing the treacherous reef called Wolf Rock, where the Devil-Child had claimed his dark companions.

Torr stood up and flexed his leg. His thigh nearly felt strong enough to ride the five or six miles across the moor to Pendarves Castle, he decided. It was time he paid his respects to his obscure relative, Godolphus's heir . . . Catherine's son.

CHAPTER 11

"WHERE THE bloody 'ell is this Cornwall? Feels like it's at the end of the bloomin' earth!'' moaned Iris, echoing Simon's presentiments exactly. "Crikey! Is that the sea?'' she asked excitedly, staring with stupefaction at the vast expanse of rolling waves out of the coach window. Simon nodded wearily, wishing the pert little maid would stop her constant stream of chatter. They had been travelling for seven days and in all that time he doubted that the girl had stopped once except to take a breath. He looked at his daughter, but she remained remote, wrapped in the same aloof silence that had cushioned her throughout the last hectic month in London. She had docilely submitted to numerous fittings at a most exclusive couturiere, presided over autocratically by Lord Taran; sat elegantly draped and fashionably mute at her grandmother's well-attended (by the curious) society funeral, seeming oblivious to the veiled references about her behaviour with the arrogant lord; and attended the reading of her grandmother's will, which left the entire estate (except for the alabaster busts) to a home for cats, an animal Lady Melisande abhorred. (The busts were willed to Lord Carringdon, much to his fury.)

"Is it really salty?'' continued Iris. Simon looked at her in bewilderment. "The sea? Is it really salty like blood?''

"It is really salty,'' he replied. "Like tears,'' he added, gazing at his detached daughter. Iris followed his eyes.

"Don't she look lovely? At Lady Em's funeral, 'er and 'is lordship standin' there so tall and elegant. They fair took me breath away. Like statues in the museum,'' she chattered.

194

Simon nodded in agreement. Angelica and Benedict had looked like statues, cold and emotionless, tall, elegant chiseled people.

"Like I never thought of Miss Angel as a looker. Then seein' 'er in them fancy clothes 'is lordship ordered, took me breath away—I was speechless!" Simon nodded again even though he doubted the little maid was ever speechless. He had never seen his daughter look more beautiful or more sad. Several times he had tried to subtly probe her feelings for the arrogant young lord, but she had regarded him as a well-meaning stranger, not the loving father that he was.

" 'ere, 'ere, don't get yourself down in the dumps. Miss Angel'll get 'er memory back as soon as she sees 'er mum," sang out Iris, seeing how sadly the doctor watched his daughter. " 'cept she didn't remember nothin' seein' you, did she? Maybe we'll 'ave ter 'it 'er on the 'ead!"

"Hit her on the head?" repeated Simon in amazement.

"Yeah. Once I 'eard about this gentry-mort what got bonked on the 'ead, and fer years he couldn't remember nothin'. Then one day 'e got bonked again and 'e got 'is memory back. Cheer up, yer doctorship. Everythinks goin' yet be all right. Our Miss Angel's gettin' married to an 'andsome lord and we'll all live 'appily ever after."

"I am going to sleep," stated Simon, giving a loud yawn and very pointedly closing his eyes.

"Crikey, I think me bottom's broke," lamented Iris, stretching her aching body. "All this bouncin' around! It's a wonder our innards ain't all muddled up," she muttered, uneasy in the silence. Angelica's strange quiet behaviour frightened her, and she felt responsible, knowing it had started the night she had attempted to open her mistress's eyes to the real world. "I thought Miss Angel would come out of her funny mood when 'is lordship left last week ter get everythink ready, didn't you?" she asked of the supposedly sleeping man.

Simon kept his eyes tightly shut and nodded. He also had expected his daughter's icy detachment to thaw when free of Taran's autocratic shadow, but if anything the distance increased, making her even more unapproachable.

Angelica was uncaring of her maid's constant chatter and her father's concern. The countryside was a blur out of the corner of her eye. She was comfortably cushioned. Some-

where in the recesses of her mind she was aware of all that
was happening, yet nothing seemed to matter very much.

Angelica strolled across the manicured lawn smiling absently at the thick profusion of flowers as though she were
perusing a picture book.

"Emily?" called Simon, craning his neck for sight of his
wife. Maizie Skinner leaped up and down on the rockery
pointing a finger. "Emily?" Simon directed his voice in the
indicated direction. "Our daughter is home."

"That's your mum?" gasped Iris, gaping at the skinny old
lady who pranced on the pile of stones. She squealed with
surprise when a wild-haired, muddy-faced woman popped out
of a patch of pretty pink flowers.

"Hello, darling," sang Emily, scrambling to her feet and
smiling expectantly at her daughter. "Oh, deary, deary me,
the virginalis is blighted," she muttered, uncomfortable with
her daughter's blank stare and charging past her with her
pruning knife in hand, unwilling to deal with any unpleasantness. "Did you have a lovely visit?" she trilled over her
shoulder before plunging into a sprawling mock orange bush
and proceeding to hack away busily.

"That's your mum?" repeated Iris.

"Miss Angel, tes good to see thee," sniffed Maizie, leaping off the rockery. "Caleb and me wuz fair worritting ourselves into a tizzy 'bout thee, we wuz." Angel politely
nodded. "Come on, thee pretty childer, and give thy awd
nurse a hug." Angel moved away.

"She don't remember you, so you 'ave ter say 'oo you are.
She don't mean ter be rude or nothin'," explained Iris,
standing up to the scowling old woman.

"And who might thee be?" snapped Maizie.

"Wilkins, personal maid ter Lady Angel," stated Iris,
pulling herself up to her full height of five feet. "And 'oo are
you?"

"Maizie Skinner, personal maid and nurse to Miss Angelica before thee wuz even a lusty gleam in thy father's eye,"
growled Maizie jealously. "How long as she been like thet?"
she asked, shaking her head with worry at the sight of Angel-

ica staring blankly over the herbaceous border to the twinkling sea.

Iris looked at her detached young mistress and shrugged.

"Angel, you must be tired after that long journey," said
Simon, giving up all attempts to extricate his wife from her
arbor of mock orange blossom. "Maizie, take her up to her
room and have Caleb heat water for some baths."

"That's just the ticket!" cried Iris. "I betcha that Miss
Angel takes one gander at 'er own bedroom and remembers
everythink!"

"This way, my pet," directed Maizie. "Thou'll see thy
own sweet dolly Caroline and thy'll remember everything."

Simon, Iris, Maizie, and Caleb clustered at Angelica's
bedroom door, hoping to witness the miracle, but she just
glanced dispassionately about the sunny room full of girlhood
treasures.

The following morning Simon and Angelica sat at breakfast. Emily bustled in, took one look at her daughter's blank
expression and her husband's worried frown, and took herself
into the depths of her flower bed.

"I am riding out to High Tor this morning to see how
Torrance Pendarves is healing," informed Simon. "You and
young Torr were friends as children. Maybe seeing the house
and the moors will help you remember." Angel nodded and
continued eating her breakfast of toast and tea.

"Excuse me, Doctor, but Lord Taran ez just riding up,"
said Caleb, popping his grizzled head through the serving
hatch from the kitchen.

"Show him into the dining room and set another place,"
sighed Simon, wishing he could have a few uninterrupted
days to get back into the rhythm of his life.

Taran's thick black eyebrows met in a forbidding line at
seeing Angelica's cool detachment. He was dressed for riding
and had brought with him a chestnut mare whose glossy coat
reminded him of Angel's lustrous hair.

"If you have finished your meal, I suggest you change into
one of your riding habits," he stated dictatorially. Angel
nodded and automatically stood to obey. "I see there is no

change," he said harshly when the door had closed softly behind her.

"I was going to take her out to High Tor with me this morning. She and Torrance were childhood friends. I was hoping to spark her memory," said Simon, his irritation at the young man's cool manner evident in his tone.

"If her own home hasn't sparked her memory, why do you think Pendarves will? Were they old lovers?" questioned Taran acidly.

"My child has led a sheltered life," returned Simon. "She knows nothing of lovers and mistresses or other worldly pastimes practiced by city society," he added angrily.

"Sheltered life or not, in my experience such worldliness is an inborn trait of most females," answered Taran bitterly.

"Catherine Pendarves," pronounced Simon against his better judgment. He was goaded by the ruthless set of the chiseled face.

"What about Catherine Pendarves?"

"She bore a child before she died," continued the doctor, hoping to shatter the man's composure.

"The child could have been sired by any man. It was a mercy the poor bastard died with her," snapped Taran.

"The child didn't die."

Benedict turned his piercing dark eyes to the doctor and silently stared. Simon fiddled with his teacup wishing he had not introduced the subject. "So the wretched child didn't die?" cued Taran. "What are you implying?"

"I am not implying anything, Tremayne," sighed Simon. "Maybe I was wrong for bringing it up, but I feel uneasy about your marriage to my daughter."

"What has that to do with Catherine Pendarves's bastard?" asked Taran.

"Sir Godolphus called him Devil Tremayne before he died. Devil Tremayne, child of shame," recounted Simon.

"Godolphus Pendarves was an insane religious fanatic, as most of Cornwall can attest. He had reason to hate me when I threw his whoring daughter out of my house," hissed Benedict. "I can name at least six men who could have sired the child."

"Talk has it that you married the girl."

"I did. Are you going to hold the impetuous act of a callow youth forever against him?"

"I hold nothing against you, Tremayne. All I want is the happiness of my child, my only daughter, and I'm not sure she will find it with you," stated Simon.

"I do not make it a habit to beat women. Unless she behaves in a similar fashion to Catherine, I don't think she'll have much cause for complaint," answered Taran.

"Whoever sired the child is of no consequence, but if you were married to Catherine at the time of his birth, then you are the boy's legal father," sighed Simon, leaning back in his chair and lacing his fingers across his portly belly.

Benedict gave a long searching look and then stared out of the window at the bright array of colourful blossoms. "Have you seen the child?" he asked after a long pause.

"Yes."

"And his looks?"

"The light was dim. The lad's hair is also black, but Miss Peller adamantly denied the child was yours. She called him Devlyn Pendarves. He is small for his age."

"His features?" demanded Taran.

"I didn't note them. As I said, it was dim . . . all I was really aware of was the pain etched on the youngster's face. I have never seen such depth of suffering in one so young . . . except once before on his mother just before she died. Godolphus Pendarves made sure she paid for her mistakes," said the doctor sadly.

"In what way?"

"He sounded much like you in his opinion of women. He called them all whores even on his deathbed. He exacted vengeance by tying his daughter to the bed and letting her scream and bleed to death. By the time I was summoned, it was too late to help her. I was told the child had been born dead, and I had no reason to believe otherwise. . . ." Simon's voice trailed away.

"I would not wish such an end for Catherine," said Taran harshly, appalled by what he was hearing.

"I remember your terrible fury, Benedict Tremayne, and whether or not you wish it now . . . I doubt that you can truthfully say that about your feelings back then."

"You're right," admitted Taran, remembering the painful rage that pounded through him at the blatant sight of Catherine's betrayal. "But if your daughter is as pure and unworldly as you say, she'll have nothing to fear."

In the kitchen, Caleb's old face was creased with concern as he pressed his ear to the closed serving hatch listening to the conversation between the two men. Maizie watched him with her boney knuckles digging into each hip.

"What ez thee up to, awd man?" she hissed, and he frantically waved his hands, demanding her silence. Maizie pressed her ear to the hatch just as Angelica entered the dining room. "What wuz et?" she asked when he groaned and moved away.

"I have to go see Pengelly at the castle," he grumbled.

"Why?"

"Dr. Simon was speakin' of the Devil-Child of the moors," whispered Caleb.

"So?"

"Last thing we needs ez that hoity-toit Tremayne causing a confloption," he muttered.

"Thou'rt not talking sense, awd man. Tes good when there's talk of the Devil-Child. Et stops nosey parkers and excise men," answered his wife.

"Not when the doctor just about told Tremayne the lad wuz his own son!" hissed Caleb, hurrying out of the door.

Angelica's entrance caused the conversation between the two men to abruptly cease. She stood looking extremely elegant in the superbly cut black riding habit with the grey lace jabot around her long neck.

"I have a present for you," said Taran, ushering her out of the house to where a young groom stood holding the spirited chestnut mare. "I trust you ride?" Angelica smiled distantly and shrugged.

"My daughter rides very well, although she has never been so well mounted before," replied Simon, aware of the double-meaning as soon as it was out of his mouth. He flushed with embarrassment at the thought of his daughter being bedded by the formidable young man. Time passed so quickly, he lamented. It seemed only yesterday that she had been a tiny girl.

Angelica silently accepted Taran's help and swung herself onto the sidesaddle just as Caleb came riding out of the stables mounted on an ancient swaybacked cob.

"Morning, zurs, and Miss Angelica," he hailed, servilely touching his cap.

"Where are you off to?" shouted Simon.

"Flower business for Miss Emily," came the answer. The doctor sighed and accepted his medical bag from Maizie, who stared anxiously up at Lord Taran.

"Where ez 'ee all going to be?" she asked. "If'n Miss Emily wants to know or there's patients needing something or other?"

"I'm going out to High Tor," replied Simon, climbing in to his plain black carriage.

"Miss Angel going with you?" probed the old woman. Simon looked up enquiringly at Taran.

"Are you both accompanying me?"

"I'm curious to see how young Pendarves is faring," answered Benedict. He was also curious to know what young Pendarves knew of his cousin Catherine's child.

Angelica rode the high-strung little mare along the winding path down to the sandy beach, ignoring the calls from her father, whose cumbersome carriage churned the dust on the high moor.

"We'll meet you there," said Taran, wheeling his mount and following the girl. Simon watched them go with conflicting emotions. He was glad to see his daughter finally behaving in an independent way, yet he was loathe to allow Tremayne to be alone with her. The arrogant peer's high-handed manner could squelch any emerging spirit, he worried.

Taran rode beside Angelica watching her face slowly awaken. Her well-shaped little nose quivered, smelling the fresh salt spray. Her eyes lost their blank stare and sparkled, mirroring the grey green of the surging sea. Her curving lips opened and smiled, and she tasted the salt tang of the breeze. She rode the chestnut mare through the shallows, hearing the rhythmic splash, feeling her hair lose the restraining pins and stream behind her. She was home, she realized.

"Home." She rejoiced aloud, her face opening into a radiant smile. Taran caught his breath at her sparkling beauty.

Their eyes caught and held. Shock slashed through her, stiffening her body, and she struggled to shroud herself again
with the safe cushion of greyness, but everything was pointed
and bright . . . too bright . . . too much feeling. His dark
eyes bored into her and she felt their censure. She winced at
the tightening of his harsh face. For a split second it had
seemed he was carefree and joyful. His head had been tossed
back, his glossy black hair tumbling in the wind . . . his
mouth curving upward in a soft smile . . . his eyes glowing
with warm lights. But then everything changed. . . .

Taran reached out and tore the reins from her hands,
slowing their mad pace until both horses stopped. Angelica
looked out to sea, conscious of his gaze.

"Do you remember?" he asked, and she shook her head.
"You remembered something," he accused angrily. He recalled the battered little face sniffing the sea smell of the salt
marshes and rejoicing at being home before cracking her head
on the heel of his boot. Why did she have such an effect on
him? he seethed. Just a few moments before he had felt such
joy, only to have it cruelly doused by the look of pure terror
that froze her features when she recognized him.

"I remember the smell of the sea and the scent of spring
flowers," she whispered, unable to look at him. "Please
don't be angry with me," she begged, conscious of the rage
that crackled from him.

"What reason have I to be angry with you?"

"I think that possibly just by being myself I provoke your
rage," she answered honestly.

"Are you sure your father hasn't warned you of me?"

"Warned me of you?" she repeated, turning to him with
surprise.

"We shouldn't keep your father waiting," he returned, and
she frowned unhappily at the sarcasm that laced his deep
voice.

They rode across the moors, Taran pointing out various
landmarks, all of which seemed to have some ominous or
tragic reference.

"Nineteen maidens turned to stone for dancing upon the
Sabbath," she echoed sadly.

*   *   *

"Well, I would say it is about time you showed your face, Doctor," scolded Mrs. Goodie. "Nigh on a month and a half you were gone," she added, watching the chubby man clamber from his carriage. "And who might them there people be?" she asked when Angelica and Taran clattered into the stable-yard on their sleek horses.

"Sir Benedict Tremayne of Taran was here before, Mrs. Goodie," reminded Simon. "The young woman is my daughter, Angelica. How is young Pendarves?"

"The leg's mending but his disposition is poorly," was the acid answer. "He's not fit to be around man or beast."

"He's still abed?" questioned Simon.

"I wish he was," snapped Mrs. Goodie. "Overdoing it, he is. Pushing himself something awful."

"You have Pendarves Castle people working here?" exclaimed Simon when several black-garbed people shuffled up to tend the horses.

"They give me the willies, I can tell you," confided Mrs. Goodie.

"They are just helping out till we can hire some permanent servants," volunteered Jago, striding out of the barn. "Good to see you back home in these parts, Sir Benedict," he added to the tall dark man who leaned over the wall watching the rows of black-robed people working in the fields and gardens.

"It's making my day just having real-life visitors," rejoiced the housekeeper, ushering them into the small salon and ordering the four Three-Marys about as if they were ordinary uniformed maids instead of terrified shrouded hags. Angelica stared with amazement at the cowering figures who held trays of refreshments in trembling hands. "His lordship will be with you shortly," Goodie informed happily, plonking herself down in an overstuffed chair as though she were the lady of the house. "Dont mind 'them,' " she reassured, seeing the direction of Angelica's wide gaze. "They won't hurt you. Jago says that they're scareder of us than we are of them. If you can believe that! 'They' are convicts, you know?" she chattered conversationally, and Jago, just about to enter, groaned inwardly and remained outside, determined to hear what other information the talkative woman would volunteer.

"Convicts?" repeated Simon with astonishment.

"Convicts," giggled Goodie. "Take a gander at their wrists," she invited, delighted at all the attention after the long months of loneliness. The Three-Marys shrank back against the wall, the trays rattling in their trembling hands as Taran approached.

"They are wearing manacles. The connecting chains are removed but they've iron bands on each wrist. Who are these unfortunate people?" he demanded harshly, appalled at the weight of the bands on the skeletal arms.

"All I know of them is their strange black garb," replied Simon. "Of the manacles, I know nothing. They were Godolphus Pendarves's servants at the castle."

"Do I hear the Pendarves name?" asked Torr, limping into the room. "Dr. Carmichael, I thought you had forgotten all about me," he greeted, shaking Simon's hand. "Taran, you are most solicitous," he bowed slightly. "And is this most elegant creature, Angelica?" he added. "It may be very ungallant of me to say, but the long skinny plain Jane I used to know bore not the slightest resemblance to this stunning creature," he flattered effusively, taking her gloved hand and drawing it to his lips. Angelica looked into his handsome young face, noting the scar that marred one cheek, giving him a profligate expression. "I would like to renew our childhood friendship, Miss Carmichael."

"Lady Taran," corrected Benedict curtly. "Angelica is my wife," he stated.

"So congratulations are in order," said Torr, his eyes narrowing at the flush that stained the girl's set cheeks. It was obviously not a marriage made in heaven, he mused, staring from her stiff discomfort to Tremayne's smoldering dark eyes.

"You certainly have made a miraculous recovery," remarked Taran. "Soon I hope that those idle Pendarves mines will be producing again." Both men spun about with surprise at the strange mournful laments that burst from the Three-Marys.

"Don't mind them, your lordships," chuckled Goodie. "They come out with all sorts of unearthly noises. They are enough to turn your hair white sometimes."

"The Pendarves mines do not belong to me," replied Torr, absently staring with amazement at the four shrouded people.

"Maybe not, but after the child don't you stand next in line to inherit?" probed Taran. "Are you not guardian to the boy?" he added impatiently when Torr seemed not to hear.

"I am guardian to Ajax and Felix, my two younger brothers and I find that imposition enough!"

"Who is guardian, then?" demanded Taran.

"Biddles and Penrose were solicitors to Sir Godolphus," offered Simon. "Maybe they know," he added when both young men looked at him. "Biddles and Penrose, in Falmouth?"

"Biddles, *Biddles*, and Penrose," corrected Mrs. Goodie.

"You have no idea who is guardian to your own relative?" postulated Taran.

"He's a rather distant connection . . . a third or fourth cousin several times removed," answered Torr, pouring himself a stiff drink. "Will you join me?" he asked, holding up the brandy decanter to Simon and Taran, who both shook their heads. "When this cursed leg permitted, I had planned to ride out to Pendarves Castle to pay my respects. Maybe you'd care to accompany me?" he invited, taking a long swallow and turning to stare again with utter amazement at the trembling black-garbed foursome. "Mrs. Goodie, I do so hate to disturb you," he said sarcastically. "But would you bestir yourself and ask Felix to come down to meet our guests?"

"He's not here," replied the housekeeper, munching contentedly on a biscuit. "He took off across the moors first thing. Didn't even eat a proper breakfast, and that's not good for a growing boy of fourteen. Shouldn't miss meals, you know. I'm right aren't I, Doctor? But since his poor puppy was killed down the mine, he's been looking everywhere for that Devil-Child," she chattered, and the Three-Marys gave high-pitched shrieks and promptly dropped their trays with a resounding crash.

"So you do know Catherine's unfortunate offspring!" exclaimed Benedict.

"Catherine's unfortunate offspring?" repeated Torr, keeping his questioning eyes on the black-shrouded Marys, who clutched one another and rocked backward and forward emitting weird sounds of distress. "Cousin Catherine's unfortunate offspring? Of course! The Devil-Child is Godolphus's heir!" he muttered, slapping his tousled blond head. "How the hell could I have been so addle-pated? So dim-witted? It is all so obvious," he ranted, limping to the door and flinging it open. "JAGO!" he roared. "By the way, Mrs. Goodie, who on earth are these inept people?" he added, staring with distaste at the mess of crockery and food that splattered their black robes. "JAGO?" he called again as the housekeeper wiggled her copulent body out of the soft cushions of the overstuffed chair.

"Convicts," she replied after a very long pause. "I was positive that you knew . . . and had given Jago Pengelly permission. How can you not have noticed? They've been here for over a month."

"Convicts?" echoed Torr.

"Convicts," repeated Goodie dismally. "They're everywhere. In the stables, kitchens, fields, gardens, house . . . everywhere. How could you have missed them?" she queried unhappily, trotting over to the wide French windows. "Just look out there . . . they're everywhere, like crows. Well, they were everywhere! Where have they gone? It can't be teatime; we haven't had luncheon yet," she worried.

"Where did they come from?" asked Torr, shaking his head at the sight of the ancient crones, who quaked with fear.

"Jago Pengelly. His brother Jonty brings them each morning and picks them up each evening. Glad I am that they don't sleep here . . . I wouldn't get one wink of rest. . . ."

"JAGO!" roared Torr.

"Jago said as how nobody wanted to work out here on moors, and I don't blame them . . . and that they was the only help he could get. Living-Dead, he calls them."

"JAGO PENGELLY!" roared Torr.

"Please don't shout, you're terrifying them," protested Angelica, feeling sorry for the frantic old people who clawed at one another for comfort. "It's all right. There's no need to be afraid. No one is going to harm you," she soothed, slowly approaching. But the ancient Marys backed away. With a show of surprising agility, they ducked under Torr's arm and scurried out of the room, melting silently into the shadows.

*   *   *

"Human beings cannot just disappear into thin air!" stated Torr nearly an hour later when their combined efforts had failed to locate the four old crones.

"*If* 'they' was regular human beings," added Goodie, pointedly.

"You will stay for lunch?" Torr asked his visitors.

"No, thank you. Angelica and I will be on our way," said Taran tersely, ushering Angelica out of the dim house into the blinding sunlight.

Simon watched his daughter mount and trot the spirited mare out of the stable-yard, followed by Benedict Tremayne. From a distance they appeared an attractively matched couple, he mused sadly.

"When was the marriage, Carmichael?" asked Torr sharply.

"A few months back," replied the doctor awkwardly, uncomfortable with the lie.

"Rather a hasty match," stated Torr callously, refusing to be intimidated by Simon's indignation. "I heard some ludicrous rumours in London. The thought of the shy Angelica Carmichael of Penzance romping in Stephen Bellinger's bachelor retreat in the New Forest with Benedict Tremayne seemed totally absurd, but now to find them married . . . and neither party seeming overjoyed at the union . . ."

"I'm here to examine your leg, Sir Torrance," replied Simon stiffly, turning away from the lounging young man and fiddling with his medical bag.

"Angelica is not Taran's usual style, you must admit," probed Torr.

"I have no knowledge or interest in Sir Benedict Tremayne's usual style," spat Simon furiously.

"Surely you knew my notorious cousin Catherine?" continued Torr ruthlessly.

"I knew Catherine," answered Simon quietly, examining the young man's injured thigh. "The wound has healed well," he remarked, gently feeling along the angry cicatrix, noting how it dissected the muscle. "Flex your leg," he ordered tersely.

"Then you are very aware that Angelica is hopelessly out of her depth?" stated Torr, his aquiline nose flaring at the pain when the muscle was stretched. "If one quarter of the stories about my scandalous kinswoman and that rakehell Tremayne are true, she is most definitely out of her league,'' he added cruelly.

"I would hope Tremayne's manner and manners have improved with maturity,'' answered Simon coldly. "As will yours.''

"Touched a sore nerve, have I?'' remarked Torr dryly. "Obviously Tremayne of Taran is looking to sire himself heirs with a docile, fertile woman who'll turn a blind eye to his dalliances. But I wonder if your daughter will be so conforming,'' he mused.

"Why do you say that?'' asked Simon sharply.

"Your daughter is not what she appears. Well, she certainly wasn't as a child. Oh, for the most part she was quiet, modest, unassuming, but let any of us be guilty of an injustice or cruelty, and she became a regular virago.''

"Walk towards me,'' directed Simon.

"It was always such a surprise when Angelica showed her claws,'' Torr reminisced, limping across the room. Simon watched the play of muscles across the injured thigh. "She has a strength . . . a reserve deep inside, but I doubt that it is enough to cope with Taran. He can be a ruthless bastard.''

"I am well aware,'' returned the doctor. "You seem to have a somewhat ruthless streak yourself, young man.''

Similar thoughts rushed into Angelica's mind as she gave the chestnut mare her head and galloped across the heathered moor high above the rolling sea. She had felt most uncomfortable in the wood-panelled parlour at High Tor. She had not found the faintest glimmer of familiarity about Torrance Pendarves. She had openly assessed his handsome young face, sadly noting the scar and the cynicism that marred the finely sculpted features. What was it about the rugged Cornish country-side that made two men so harsh, she wondered. They were so different in appearance, like night and day. Torr Pendarves with hair the colour of ripe corn and eyes of clearest blue, and Benedict Tremayne as dark and brooding as a raven's wing, his eyes black and forbidding beneath thick brows. As she thought of Taran, she glanced across at the rider beside her.

"Tell me of the child," she said, loathe to call him 'Devil.'

"There is nothing to tell," he replied curtly. He had been thinking of the small dark rider he had encountered on Christmas Day. The rider who had looked like his twelve-year-old brother, Michael.

"Why would educated people call a child by such a name?" she asked, determined to have some answers.

"We are going to Taran," he informed, ignoring her question. He was equally determined to have no discussion of Catherine's elusive offspring until he had satisfied himself of the child's parentage. Angelica flashed a look of absolute fury at him and he laughed, surprised at her sudden spirit.

"Not on a witch hunt for a small child and some ancient convicts?" she spat sarcastically, goaded by his obvious enjoyment of her anger.

"There is no need to be afraid of your new home," he said patronizingly. "Mrs. and Mrs. Smithers will be there and that irrepressible maid of yours."

"I said nothing about being afraid," replied Angel, her green eyes narrowing suspiciously. "You have a very adroit way of changing the subject, Lord Taran."

"Thank you, Lady Taran," he laughed, accepting the backhanded compliment. Angelica felt a delicious shiver ripple through her at his deep voice and the warm smile he directed at her. She looked away in confusion.

"I am not Lady Taran," she said, urging her mare into a brisk canter.

"Tomorrow that will be remedied," he answered, easily keeping abreast of her.

"Tomorrow?" she mouthed, turning to him with such a look of abject dismay that his enjoyment of the sunshine and her company was jarringly destroyed. He knew of at least twenty young women of infinitely better bloodlines, appearance, and disposition who would have eagerly exchanged places with the green-eyed chit. He seethed, not understanding why he felt so hurt by her evident dislike of him.

"Tomorrow," he confirmed. Angelica looked away, confused by his sudden change. How could his deep voice be so warm and thrilling one moment, and the next be so coldly lacerating?

"I would prefer to return to my own home until that time," she announced stiffly, keeping her eyes trained straight ahead of her. He made no indication that he had heard. "I said I would prefer—"

"Regardless of your preference, arrangements have been made to the contrary," he interrupted.

"Without consulting me?" protested Angelica hotly, her green eyes flashing stormily.

"You have been extremely detached, not caring about anything for several weeks . . . content to allow the reins of your life to be taken over by anyone on hand," he stated harshly.

"Anyone on hand?" echoed Angel, feeling a terror snake through at what seemed to be implied.

"Carringdon," hissed Benedict, jealousy knifing at the thought.

"Carringdon?" repeated Angel, her face losing its glow. "He didn't . . . I didn't," she stammered. "Please, I don't know what you're talking about, and your anger is frightening me."

"Did you expect the world to grind to a halt until you were ready and willing to face it?" he asked roughly, touched by her honesty. He felt guilty for the tears that flooded her eyes. Angelica accepted the truth of his censure and flushed. He was right. She had wrapped herself against the world, refusing to be part of anything . . . content to have every decision made for her.

"I'm sorry," she whispered helplessly.

"Spare me your apologies!" he snapped. Angelica silently nodded her understanding and willed her brimming eyes to dry up. "And your tears," he groaned, seeing the heavy drops roll down her cheeks. He wanted to gather her into his arms to kiss away the hurt and sadness. But he savagely forced himself to recall the abject dismay that had clouded her features at the mere mention of their impending nuptials and resisted the temptation.

Angelica didn't know it was possible to feel more miserable. She prayed that the numbing shroud which had cushioned her emotions until that very morning would return. Everything about her stabbed painfully. Spring was blatantly evident on the moor, with lusty shoots thrusting through the earth and strutting males proudly wooing the playfully coy females of their species. On the land. in the sky, and in the sea the age-old ritual of renewal and recreation was being celebrated. The air positively quivered with joyous virility, increasing Angel's aching sorrow. Her mare trotted docilely in the shadow of Benedict's tall stallion, and Angelica clutched the reins and the pommel, trying to stifle the sobs that burst through her clenched teeth. She breathed deeply trying to control herself, her head averted and her eyes pinned blindly to the bright sea that winked in the golden sunshine. If only she could remember, she thought, maybe then she would feel more complete and able to cope with her life. What difference would it make, remembering or not? She would still be in the untenable position of hopeless love for a dark, harsh man who was marrying her to exact revenge on his spiteful mistress. At that sobering thought, her tears stopped and her back stiffened with fury.

"There is Taran," announced Benedict, reining his horse on the crest of a high hill that sloped down towards the ocean. Angel gasped with delight at the sight.

"Taran," she intoned, gazing at the large graceful manor cradled in a dip of the cliffs overlooking the sea. Despite her anger, she was entranced by the beauty of the majestic granite structure and its environment. The cold grey of the local stone was softened by the profusion of flowers in the surrounding formal gardens and the fertile green of the gently sloping fields where cattle and horses peacefully grazed.

"Our home, Lady Taran," he said. Angelica looked up into his face expecting to see cruel cynicism, but instead caught a fleeting hollow sadness.

CHAPTER 12

"WAKE UP, Miss Angel! It's mornin'," sang out Iris, placing
a tray with hot chocolate and biscuits on a table beside the
large bed where her mistress lay. She drew back the heavy
velvet curtains, and bright sunlight flooded across the attractive room. "It's yer weddin' day. Yer second weddin' day,
that is," she added loudly, in case there were any nosey
people about. She was especially concerned about a certain
pinched-face downstairs maid called Peg Hatch. "Aint it a
loverly day? Little dickie-birds singin' their little 'earts out.
Roses bloomin' all over the flippin' place and pretty butterflies doin' whatever they do in the flowers; so I ain't 'avin'
any grumpy mugs spoilin' it," she chided, cheerfully plump-
ing up the pillows.

"Well, you are certainly very happy," observed Angelica
dryly.

"I really, really like it 'ere! Funny, ain't it? I thought I was
goin' ter be buried alive stuck out in the middle of nowheres,
but it's ever so nice. It ain't just cos it's as big and grand as a
bloomin' palace nor cos Mister and Misses Ess is 'ere, it's
somethin' else."

"What?" asked Angel, sipping the fragrant chocolate.

"It's like there's nice warm feelin's comin' out of the
woodwork. Daft, ain't I? All I know is we're goin' ter be
ever so 'appy 'ere," she stated emphatically. "They 'ave
everythink 'ere, yer know. Real fruit trees what 'ave blossoms now, but the flowers are goin' ter turn into apples and
pears . . . even plums! It's the truth, honest. This old man in

the stables called Silas told me. Chestnuts, too . . . and these big glass 'ouses with grapes in 'em . . . and . . .''

"Iris, come and sit down," interrupted Angel, patting the bed. "Have you heard any strange talk?"

"What sort of strange talk?" replied Iris, helping herself to a biscuit.

"About a . . . Devil-Child?"

"A Devil-what?" choked the maid, crumbs flying in all directions.

"A Devil-Child," whispered Angel. "Drink some of this," she offered when the girl's coughing continued. Iris drank the chocolate thirstily, and she stared at her mistress over the rim of the cup. "Well, have you?" she coaxed.

"I ain't 'eard nothin' about any such thing," declared Iris. "Do you mean ter tell me that this place is 'aunted?"

"Oh, no, I'm not saying that," Angel comforted hastily when the girl lost her cheerful glow and her eyes flickered about uneasily. "Iris, listen carefully to me and please don't interrupt until I've finished," she said, handing the platter of biscuits to the maid and proceeding to inform her about all that had happened at High Tor the previous day. "That is why I want you to keep your eyes and ears open," she concluded quietly.

"Convicts and devils," gasped Iris. "Oh, Miss Angel, what the 'ell are we goin' ter do?"

"I may be forced to marry Benedict Tremayne, but I am . . . er . . . damned. . . ." swore Angel.

"You said a word!" exclaimed Iris.

"And I'll say it again . . . I'll be bloody-well damned if I'll be some simpering, docile, complacent . . ." pronounced Angel vehemently as Iris giggled with delight.

"Go on, miss," urged the maid, not understanding her mistress's sudden silence. She followed the startled gaze. "Whoops," she said at the sight of Sir Benedict Tremayne lounging at the open door of the connecting bedchamber. He was dressed for riding in high gleaming boots and tight pantaloons, and he held a crop in his strong brown hands.

"Good morning," he greeted, languidly strolling into the room. "Please don't let me interrupt," he added, smiling indulgently down at the two gaping females on the large bed.

"You were saying, my dear?" he prompted. "That you'll be bloody-well damned if you'd be some simpering, docile, complacent . . . what? I am most interested in the missing noun. Come now, my Angel, or are you a coward?" he taunted, softly sending delicious shivers up and down her spine.

"Simpering . . . docile . . . complacent . . . *wife*," pronounced Angel bravely. Iris held her breath and flinched, expecting the tall dark man to react violently.

"I am most relieved to learn that you'll not simper. I have a positive aversion to simpering females," he laughed. Iris looked at him as if he were mad.

"Ain't you goin' to 'it 'er for sayin' them things?" she asked.

"I'm not in the habit of striking women."

"Well, Miss Angel, you lucked out all right with 'is lordship," congratulated Iris.

"You have an aversion to simpering, but you made no mention of docility or complacency," challenged Angel, enjoying the excitement of the banter between them.

"It depends entirely how both conditions are obtained," he answered gruffly, cupping her chin in his large hand and raising her expressive face. He slowly bent and kissed her parted lips, meaning only to impart a cursory peck, but the feel of the soft warmth against his mouth seduced him.

Angelica could not believe the ecstasy that streaked through her. Her hands automatically crept up his broad shoulders and encircled his neck as she was drawn against his chest. Her senses whirled.

"You seem admirably docile and pleasingly complacent, my pet," he murmured huskily, staring into her glowing face, noting her misty passion-filled eyes and softly bruised mouth. "I shall not see you until the chapel this evening," he announced, abruptly releasing her so she sank back against the bank of pillows with an audible sigh of regret.

"Until this evening?" she echoed.

"I have some urgent business which will keep me away from Taran until that time." Before she could comment, he had left.

"Well, I'll be a monkey's uncle!" chuckled Iris, sitting cross-legged on the bed and gaping at her bemused mistress.

"Urgent business that will no doubt take him to Pendarves Castle to find a Devil-Child," she reasoned aloud.

"Hush yerself!" hissed Iris rudely, leaping off the high bed and tiptoeing across the room to the connecting doors, which were partly opened.

"What is it?"

"The bitch is gone! It was that bitch Peg 'atch. I see'd 'er pokin' her nose out of the master's bedroom. She's spyin' on us," replied Iris.

"In the master's bedroom?" repeated Angel, feeling as though she had just been doused with a pail of cold water. "What was she doing in there?"

"Men might 'ave their appetites, but you can bet the master wouldn't dirty 'imself with the likes of 'er, at least not on 'is weddin' day," comforted Iris. "She's just a nosey-parker!"

"That's probably why he kissed me," sighed Angel sadly, softly tracing her still-tingling lips with the tip of her tongue. "So we looked married to whoever was spying on us."

"Hah, 'e's goin' to 'ave to do a lot more'n that," chuckled the maid.

"What's it like, Iris?" asked Angel shyly after a long pause.

"Ain't you and 'is lordship done it?"

"Of course not! Why ever would you think that?" gasped Angelica, blushing crimson at the mere thought.

"But what about all that talk about you and 'is lordship in the woods?" whispered Iris.

"What talk?"

"About you stark naked in bed with 'im and some others?" hissed the maid.

"And some others?" repeated Angelica. "And some others? What do you mean 'and some others'?!"

"I knew it was all lies. Even told that rotten cook and them scullery sluts that my Miss Angel wouldn't do such things," said Iris smugly. " 'Ere, wait a tick, yer mean ter say you was in bed with 'is lordship stark naked, but you weren't with no others?"

"All I remember was waking up in bed with him. That's all."

"So you don't remember if you and 'e 'ad a go at it?"

"I don't remember anything. Wouldn't I know if something like that had happened?"

"I know I would, but maybe it's different for society people."

"How could it be?" giggled Angelica. "Everybody is made the same way regardless of class.

" 'ceptin' society ladies pretend they don't have nothin' between their legs . . . cos it's all too common," snorted Iris.

"Well, it isn't really polite conversation," returned Angelica. "What is it like?" she asked again after a long pause.

"I don't care for it much meself, but we 'ave ter do what we 'ave ter do so the best thing is to lie there and think of somethin' else and 'ope they bloody-well 'urry up," sighed Iris philosophically.

"Then why do you do it?"

"I don't 'ave much choice now, do I? If I 'ad my way I wouldn't open me legs for no man."

"How could you have . . . lain with Carringdon?" shuddered Angel.

"Men are stronger and they're goin' to 'ave their way with you anyways, so it's better to call the shots than get raped," stated the maid baldly. " 'Ere, ere, this ain't no proper kinda talk fer yer weddin' day, is it? What are yer goin' ter wear?" she asked, opening the door of a large dressing room.

"When?" replied Angel, getting off the bed and crossing to the door that connected her bedroom with Benedict's. "Now or for the ceremony?"

"Both."

"I want to go riding now, and I'll think of the wedding later," she answered, knocking at the door and then peeking in, curious to see his intimate surroundings. The large room was identical to hers in size and shape, the double oriel windows facing the sea, but there the similarity ended. Hers was tastefully and conventionally furnished, burgundy coloured carpeting and velvet draperies predominating with subtle traces of grey and blue in the embossed silk that covered the walls. His room was virtually bare, the only furniture being an

enormous bed and an immense hearth. No carpeting covered
the wide planked mahogany floor except for a lush animal
hide before the fireplace. A window seat with fur-covered
cushions overlooked the sea.

Angelica padded barefoot across the room and curled up on
the wide window seat. "What a wonderful room," she whispered, gazing out at the white-tipped waves.

"What a funny bedroom. Cor, all that's 'ere is a bloomin'
great bed and a couple of dead animals. There ain't even no
pictures on the walls!" exclaimed Iris.

"It is a lovely room," mused Angelica dreamily.

"Ain't my idea of cosy. Come on, get dressed or Mrs.
Ess'll 'ave me 'ead. She's 'ad the cook, Mrs. 'itchins make a
fancy breakfast for you, and so you won't be all flustered
she's 'avin' it served in the little dinin' room," chattered Iris,
leading Angelica back into her own bedchamber. "Wait 'til
you meet the rum old bugger in the stables, Silas Quickbody.
'e says as 'ow the name used to fit 'im to a tee but nowadays
'e's slowed upa mite cos 'e's more'n seventy. Oh, and just
you wait 'til you see the puppies! Loverly little fat fluffy
creatures. The bitch, that aint a rude word but what a lady
dog's called, let me touch them and Silas Quickbody says I
must 'ave the way cos a mother dog don't let no one touch 'er
babies unless a person 'as the way, yer know. Oh, and Silas
Quickbody says if you wants to go ridin', 'e'll get a groom to
go with you cos 'is lordship don't want you to ride about 'ere
alone." Angelica allowed Iris's excited chatter to wash over
her while she planned what she was going to do with her last
day of freedom. She assessed herself critically in the mirror.
It was hard to believe that the elegant woman who stared back
was the same self-conscious pink-clad wallflower of a scant
two months before. She had felt resentful of Benedict's arrogant attitude in selecting her entire wardrobe, but now she
grudgingly admitted that he knew exactly what became her,
what enhanced her long slenderness so her gawkiness appeared graceful. How had he become so adroit at selecting
female apparel? she wondered. Jealousy churned her stomach.

"You look a treat and that's the truth," admired Iris.
"Who'd 'ave thought it!" she added irreverently. " 'is lordship must 'ave 'ad a lotta practice."

"I'm sure he has," was Angelica's dry answer.

"Yer know Silas says everythin's grown 'ere. Yer don't 'ave to go to the shops or the barrows for nothin'. Really, it's the truth! And not just fruit and vegetables, neither, but everythin'! Chickens, ducks, gooses, porks, beefs, muttons . . . even crabs and oysters," she informed proudly as they made their way through the wide hallway to the stairs. "Do you want to see all the pictures of 'is lordship's dead relations?" she asked.

"When did you have time to do all this exploring?" laughed Angelica, allowing herself to be tugged into the portrait gallery that overlooked the ballroom.

"Yesterday, when you was off gallivantin' with 'is lordship, I was stuck 'ere with nothin' to do cos Mrs. Ess 'ad already seen to yer clothes and everythin' . . . so Silas Quickbody showed me about. 'ere, look at that! Weren't 'is lordship a pretty little boy?" she giggled. "The littler boy is 'is brother Michael what drowned."

Angelica gazed up at the formal family grouping. A petite dark woman was seated with a small sloe-eyed boy leaning against her lap. Behind her stood a tall broad-shouldered man and to one side slightly apart was a grinning youth of about sixteen. Mischief and joy sparkled from his dancing dark eyes.

"That is Benedict?" she whispered unable to take her eyes from the vibrantly jubilant youth whose handsome face was free of cynical lines.

" 'ard to believe, ain't it?" chuckled Iris.

"Yes," she whispered. The incredible contrast between the carefree, devilish boy and the dark brooding man stunned Angelica, and with the two vastly different faces flashing in her mind, she blindly walked through the majestic gallery. What had happened to the beautiful, joyous youth to cause such a change? she wondered. Iris's constant chatter abruptly ceased, and she stared with surprise at the wide-eyed girl who fearfully clutched her arm.

"What is it?" she asked, but Iris just swallowed painfully and looked at her feet.

"Good morning," greeted a deep Scottish voice. "I am Angus Dunbar, Lord Taran's secretary and estate manager."

"Good morning," answered Angelica automatically, torn between the young man who politely held the dining room door open for her and the white-faced maid who backed away and then fled back along the corridor as fast as her legs could carry her. "Thank you," she acknowledged, entering the room.

"Good morning, your ladyship," said Mrs. Smithers deferentially. Angelica laughed and impulsively hugged the round old woman, delighted to see a loving familiar face. Angus Dunbar remained standing and watched the exchange with a strange smile on his rugged face. "Did you sleep well?" asked the flustered housekeeper. She wished she could tell the girl she was forgetting her place, that it didn't behoove the new Lady Taran to be hugging the help like a long-lost relative.

"I slept very well. I didn't expect to but I did."

"This old house has soothing feelings," whispered Mrs. Smithers, patting Angelica's hand. "Now, would you like me to send in some servants or would you prefer to serve yourselves?" she asked.

"We shall serve ourselves, Mrs. Smithers," dismissed Angus Dunbar. Angelica watched Mrs. Smithers leave and wished she could follow and eat her breakfast in the cosy comfort of the kitchen.

"May I serve you?" offered the Scot. "There are ham and veal collops, eggs coddled and scrambled, smoked haddock and herring, sausages, kidneys, various pies, toast and scones," he announced, lifting the covers off the chafing dishes that lined the sideboard.

"For goodness' sake, how many people are eating breakfast?" exclaimed Angelica, looking from the abundant supply of food to the two set places, one each end of the very long table.

"Just ourselves. What might I get for you?"

"I shall serve myself, thank you, Mr. Dunbar," said Angelica, pouring herself a cup of strong black coffee and taking it to the large French windows that opened on to a wide terrace. Enormous urns overflowed with exotically coloured flowering plants and an ornate fountain complete with a leaping unicorn sprayed graceful arcs of water into a cloverleaf-shaped pond full of lilies.

Angus helped himself to a generous breakfast and sat at the table watching the elegant young woman. The morning sun shone on her rich chestnut hair and delineated her fine high cheekbones. She was rather like a young doe, poised and shy, long-legged and gracefully awkward, he mused. Not at all Taran's type. "The grounds are very impressive, aren't they?" he remarked.

"They are very beautiful," she answered. "I was led to believe that the estate had been neglected for many years," she added, turning to look at him.

" 'Tis true that most of this great house has been shut up, but the grounds, farms, and mines have been most carefully tended," stated Angus sternly. "It is a sin to neglect the land," he added.

Angelica sensed she had somehow offended him. She silently helped herself to some ham and scrambled eggs and then hesitated, not knowing where to sit at the enormous table. "Do you mind if I sit here?" she asked, indicating the chair next to his. "It seems rather silly for me to sit all the way down there," she explained. Angus stood and helped to seat her.

"I think your Mrs. Smithers is adhering to strict protocol," he remarked dryly.

"I don't understand."

"You are, after all, Lady Taran and I am a mere servant so-to-speak," he answered, rolling his arrs in a very exaggerated way. Angelica looked at him sharply, sensing a strong undercurrent of disapproval, but the man's face showed nothing but politeness. She ate quietly, wondering why her usually fearless Iris had been so cowered just at the sight of Angus Dunbar. "I am at your disposal today, Lady Taran," informed the man, neatly placing his knife and fork together down the middle of his empty plate.

"Thank you, but that won't be necessary. I am sure you have other, more important duties to perform," she replied, stressing the word *duties* slightly. His rust-coloured eyebrows raised quizzically in surprise.

"Be assured that *you*, Lady Taran, head my list of priorities," he returned. She stared openly at him, hearing the double meaning implied in his crisply stated words.

"Nevertheless, I am quite capable of occupying myself," she said stiffly. "Now, if you will excuse me?" she said rhetorically, dabbing her mouth on her serviette and rising to her feet with as much dignity as she could muster. Angus Dunbar stood and made the gesture of holding the back of her chair.

Angelica strode across the terrace very conscious of being watched by the suspicious Scot who stood at the open French doors to the dining room sipping his coffee. She walked down the stone steps and into the fragrant rose garden, anxious to be free of his scrutiny.

"Miss Angelica?" greeted a wheezy voice, and she looked with surprise at the old wizened man who doffed his cap. "Or should I be calling thee Lady Taran?" he added. "Could et be thou has forgot thy awd friend Silas Quickbody?" he enquired when she gazed into his weatherbeaten face blankly.

"Silas Quickbody?" repeated Angel. "Oh, yes, Iris told me about you."

"That pert skinnamalink told thee about me? I've known thee since thou wuz knee-high to a bee, Angelica Carmichael. Your daddy set many a broke bone of mine throughout the years, and I remember when 'ee wuz small enough to ride on these bent shoulders."

Angelica looked at him sadly. "I'm sorry. I don't mean to offend your feelings, Mr. Quickbody."

"Miss Angel? Miss Angel?" hissed a furtive voice, and Iris popped out from behind a bush.

"There's the skinnamalink now. What are thee doing, child?" he asked when she ducked out of sight again.

"Come over here," whispered Iris hoarsely. "I don't want that foreigner seein' me."

"What foreigner?" echoed Angelica and Silas together.

"That one over there spyin' on us," answered Iris, nodding towards the open French doors. "The one 'oo talks funny."

"Angus Dunbar?" laughed Angelica.

"That's the bloke."

"He's a good man," approved Silas.

"Why are you so afraid of him?" probed Angelica.

"I ain't afraid of no man!"

"Then thee are a fool, child," remarked the old man.

"I never said I weren't," replied Iris pertly. "Silas, show my Miss Angel the little puppies in the stables," she cajoled.

"Oh, t'es thy Miss Angel now, is et? Why I've known this fine Cornish lass since she wuz a babe in arms, but et seems she's gone and forgot her awd Silas now she's all growed up and bin to London Town," mourned the old man, a teasing ring covering his hurt.

"I wouldn't feel too bad about it if I was you. She's gone and lost 'er memory! She can't remember nothin', not even 'er own mum and dad nor 'er little brothers. She can't remember nothin'! I mean she didn't even know 'er own face in the mirror," Iris sang out airily as she skipped merrily ahead.

"That's a very lonely place to be," remarked Silas softly, looking shrewdly at the seemingly serene young woman who walked beside him.

"Iris is quite taken with you, Mr. Quickbody," remarked Angelica, wishing to be off the subject of her affliction.

"And me to her. She's a spirited Welsh imp and no mistake," chuckled Silas. "Pretty little dark girl. She's going to be sad to find some of the pups are gone," he sighed as they approached the stables.

"Gone?" queried Angelica, nodding her appreciation of the clean wide building.

"What 'appened?" screeched Iris, popping out from behind a stall with straw sticking in her springy black curls. "There's only four 'ere and where's their mum?"

"The bitch is off getting a bit of peace and quiet. She's done her work, and them there doglets are weaned and ready for the wide world," stated Silas.

"You mean three of the puppies went off into the world all alone?" gasped Iris.

"Someone took them . . . ferreted them off in the night, and tes strange that the bitch made no sound."

"Someone stole them?" exclaimed Angelica. "Who would do such a thing?" she added, leaning over the half-wall of the box stall and watching Iris rolling about, wrestling with the squealing little animals.

"What's been stolen?" asked a deep brogue.

"Pups," replied Silas. "Morning, Angus. Have 'ee met Miss Angel?"

"Lady Taran and I breakfasted together," answered the dour young man, staring over the stall wall at the dishevelled little maid who sat trying to cuddle four rambunctious dogs.

"And Iris?" added the old man.

"Iris is it?" I was under the impression it was a different flower all together," he muttered darkly. "Now, about this theft, Silas?" probed Angus, deciding to privately confront the girl who had called herself Daisy.

"Three of Sheba's litter wuz stolen in the night, and neither of the two lads sleeping in the loft heard a thing. Whoever stole them must've been known to the bitch or she'd have set up a rare confloption," informed the old groom.

"Are there any predators about who could have preyed upon the young dogs?" suggested Angelica.

"There are no predators left large enough except man," stated Angus, and adding "and woman" under his breath, unable to take his eyes off the flushed girl who sat on the floor playing happily with the puppies.

"I should like my mare saddled, please."

"Right 'ee are, my lady. She be right down here," said Silas, leading Angelica through the spacious stables and leaving Angus Dunbar still leaning over the stall watching Iris having her saucy little face thoroughly washed by four eager tongues.

"I think I prefer the name Daisy for you, you cheeky lass," he remarked after a long silence where the girl pointedly pretended not to notice him. "An Iris is much too graceful and elegant a blossom."

"Are there irises 'ere at Taran?" asked the maid, covering her trepidation.

"You walked by beds of them to get here. Come, I'll show you," offered Angus, deciding to try to put the girl at ease before prying information from her. Iris's eyes narrowed with suspicion, yet she scrambled to her feet and brushed the hay from her black uniform.

"I could be graceful and ever so elegant if I wanted to," she said truculently. "Miss Angel?" she called out, suddenly realising she was alone with the man.

"I'm going riding, Iris. See if Mrs. Smithers has anything for you to do." Angelica's voice came spiralling from the dark warmth of the stables where she watched Silas and a young groom swiftly saddle two horses.

"I shall accompany thee, my lady," stated Silas firmly, and she smiled, genuinely liking the leathery old man.

Iris filled with panic as she watched her mistress canter out of the stable followed by Silas Quickbody, who was perched like a tiny wizened jockey on the high back of a rawboned dapple-grey. She was all too conscious of the oppressive presence of the sturdy Scot beside her. She took a deep breath, summoning her ebbing courage, and turned to face him with both small knuckles digging into her skinny hips.

"All right, then, where's them irises?" she asked, trying to stop the tremble of apprehension in her voice at the sight of his forbidding expression. Silently she followed him across the cobbled stable-yard through the topiary garden. "Yer right, I ain't no fancy iris," she remarked bitterly after a long quiet assessment of the tall exotic flowers that proudly moved with the gentle sea breeze that swept over the cliff. "So call me Daisy if you want."

"What is your business with Lord Carringdon?" he asked roughly, and she gasped and turned very pale.

"It ain't none of your bloody business," she spat.

"You'll not swear at me," he said in a low dangerous tone. "I run things about here for Lord Taran, so if you value your position with her ladyship, I suggest you cooperate."

Iris gritted her teeth together and stared up at him, wishing she could brace herself against a wall or tree. "Yes, sir," she whispered.

"I repeat, what business do you have with Lord Carringdon?" Angus felt like a bully, towering over the little maid, who had lost her usual cocky bravado and stared up at him with her eyes round and dark with terror.

"Lord 'oo?" She made a lame attempt to recover her rebellious stance. She forced herself to meet his steely gaze as her agile mind desperately tried to fabricate an acceptable answer. How much did the man know? How did he know? All these questions and more flooded into her head. A sudden slight movement behind a hedge caused her to stiffen, and she caught a brief glimpse of Peg Hatch's carrot-coloured hair. She closed her mouth firmly, determined to say nothing, especially within earshot of the downstairs maid.

"I'm waiting for your answer," snapped Angus impatiently.

"Like I told you before, I ain't that sorta girl. I ain't no common slut, yer know. Now if you need an 'ore what'll spread 'er legs for you, it seems ter me there's one in the scullery by the name of Peg 'atch," announced Iris loudly. Angus frowned. At hearing an outraged gasp and rustle, he turned and saw the telltale red hair glinting in the sun behind a privet hedge; despite his anger he chuckled. Iris took the opportunity to take to her heels.

Angelica cantered along the high cliff path above the tranquil sea that gently rippled across the golden sand on the secluded beach below.

"That be Taran Cove," informed Silas, and a shadow crossed his good-natured face.

"Is that where Michael Tremayne drowned?" asked Angelica, sensitive to the old man's sorrow.

"Thee remember?" he exclaimed, and she sadly shook her head. "Why I's hurried in mind like Pomeroy's cat! How could thee remember when thou weren't more'n two or three? Aye, that's where the poor lad drownded and put the cloud over Taran. We's all hoping that thee and the young master will bring sunshine and childern back into the handsome awd place."

Angelica was unable to face the old man's hopefulness. She kept her eyes pinned to the sea. "Silas, please tell me what happened to change Benedict from the engaging joyful youth of his portrait into the cynical, harsh man he is now," she asked quietly after a long silence. They rode slowly along the high cliff path that skirted the edenic cove as the old groom told her about the young boy's death on that far-off early summer day. "And that's when Benedict shut up Taran and went to live in London?" she probed when he'd finished.

"His parents wuz still living. It wuz they thet shut up most of the rooms. Her ladyship took to her bedchamber. She stayed locked away for nigh on nine years except for her strange turns when she'd stand up here and scream for her youngest son.''

Angelica shivered despite the warmth of the sunshine at the thought of the grieving woman made mad by her loss, standing high on the steep cliff screaming to the sea to return her child. ''Poor woman,'' she whispered.

''And that's how it wuz, each locked in their own pain. Each blaming. His lordship tried to work hisself to death. Worked night and day in the mines . . . never coming home. Living down in the mine cottages. He was killed in a missment in the pits.''

The old man's voice trailed away and silence fell between them. Angelica debated mentioning the Devil-Child to him, but Silas appeared to be entrenched in the past. Tears poured shamelessly down his lean lined cheeks as he gazed down on to the tranquil cove where twelve-year-old Michael had died.

''That's why he wuz deaf to all the talk about Miss Catherine. He reached for her like she wuz a sunbeam . . . warm and golden to give him comfort and love,'' continued the old man, his voice cracking with emotion.

''Miss Catherine?'' repeated Angelica.

''Miss Catherine Pendarves wuz so beautiful, there wuz many a jealous woman who called her siren and witch, but she wuz just a poor unloved lass . . . and she hurt young Benedict in every place a tender young man was vulnerable. Poor, poor lad . . .''

''Pendarves Castle,'' interrupted Angel, and the old man recollected himself.

''Excuse me, your ladyship. I forgot my place,'' he apologized.

''Where is Catherine Pendarves now?'' she asked after a while.

''Dead,'' was the terse answer.

''And Benedict loved her?'' she probed stubbornly.

''Tedn't my business to tell.''

''I want to go to Pendarves Castle,'' she announced, sensing it was Benedict's destination that morning in his quest to find the mysterious child.

"Tes time we turned back to Taran. Looks like there's a storm abrewing," he muttered. Angelica frowned as she stared about at the cloudless blue sky and the calm sea where gulls bobbed contentedly.

"I might have lost my memory, Mr. Quickbody," she retorted. "But I have not lost my reason. There's no sign of a storm. But if you would prefer not to accompany me, I would appreciate your pointing me in the right direction."

"And what's at Pendarves Castle that has thy interest?"

"I could say 'Tedn't any of your business,' Mr. Quickbody," said Angelica wickedly. "But I won't because you told me that we have been friends for a long time and as a friend I'm imploring you for help."

"What kind of help?" he asked guardedly.

"I should like nothing better than to bring sunshine and happiness back to Taran, but it is very difficult when I'm totally in the dark. Not only have I no memories of myself but I'm also expected to accept on blind faith everything that is happening to me and be deaf to all I hear."

"All thee hear?"

"About a Devil-Child and convicts and Pendarves Castle," stated Angelica strongly, staring challengingly at the weather-beaten groom, who nodded knowingly before bursting into choking chuckles.

"I recall thy vinegar temper when thou were crossed as a child. Hang on to et, Angelica Carmichael, thou'rt going to need et in the days ahead, I'll be bound," he chortled.

"You'll help me?"

"Where I can," was the enigmatic answer.

"Then you'll take me to the castle?"

"Nay, tedn't my plaace."

"And you'll not explain to me about the Devil-Child?"

"What's to explain about superstition? The snortleywiggans do all come out of a night, and there's piskies, spriggans, and knockers guarding the mines on the moors, and witches fly across the face of the new moon. So we nail a horseshoe to the lintel to keep safe the hearth and home; leave fish on the shore at harvest time to feed the Bucca; bleed a white hen on the mill stone every seven years to keep the grist mill free from missments . . ."

"Mr. Quickbody, you know exactly what I mean," she interrupted furiously.

"Do thee know the tale of the knockers of the Ballowal Mine? Tes the oldest mine of near anywhere, wuz worked for tin e'en before Noah's flood, so tes haunted by millions of lost spirits not just knockers and spriggans but by the anguished souls of unfortunate miners . . ."

"I am well aware of the tale of Tom Trevorrow of Trencrom."

"Thee remembers?" he said quietly.

"Tom Trevorrow! Tom Trevorrow! Leave some of thy fuggan for Bucca or bad luck to thee tomorrow," recited Angelica bemusedly. "It is strange how I can remember such trivial oddments but not people."

"Tedn't so strange. Tes people thet do the hurting."

"So you won't take me to Pendarves Castle?"

"Tes just a cold pile of grey stones on the moor. Empty and sad, haunted perhaps by the cruel ghost of Godolphus Pendarves. Why would thee want to go to such a forlorn place on such a fine spring day as this?"

"Because that's where Benedict is," replied Angelica simply.

"Why would the young master go to Pendarves Castle?"

"To find Catherine's child. The one they call Devil?" offered Angelica tentatively. Silas looked long and searchingly at her before silently turning his horse's head so they plodded back the way they had come.

"Maybe tes all for the best. Tes time awd clothies wuz washed up and put away," sighed Silas after they had gone nearly a mile, each wrapped in their brooding thoughts.

"Time for what?" whispered Angelica fearfully.

"Thou shalt see but tes going to take all thy strength because tes sure to be a painful stormy time before the sunshine warms Taran again," he mourned, and she felt a grim foreboding shiver through her at the bleakness in the old man's rheumy eyes. She looked toward the estate. Although the sun reflected brightly off the sea, it seemed the graceful mansion and its extensive grounds were shrouded, as though a heavy shadowy cloud muted any vibrant warmth. "Well, spring be as good a time as any to put a house in order," he sighed resignedly.

"You won't tell me anything?" she tried one last time, and the old man shook his head.

"I would if I could but tedn't my secrets nor my plaace," he said sadly. "But I have wisdom for thee. Et may be hard. Et may seem well-nigh impossible, but have patience with your bridegroom. The tide do never go out so far but et do come in again, and I know that the fine, caring boy es still in the man neath his muggety darkness. Do thee love him?" Angelica couldn't answer for fear the admission would leave her totally without protection. "Thou does, I can read et in thy eyes," stated the old man. "And thou art wishing thy didn't and thou'rt probably right," he added cryptically. "Here comes the master now and from the way he be riding I guess et wuz a wild-goose chase."

Angelica reined her horse and watched Benedict galloping towards them, the dust churning by his stallion's iron-clad hooves.

"Peck of dust in May is worth a king's ransom," quoted Silas.

Benedict was indeed in a foul humour. He had hammered at the castle door to no avail, and the fortress was locked so tight there was no way to get in. The hulking building had appeared empty and desolate, the ominous ravens roosting in the slit windows regarding him with malevolent beady eyes. This time there had been no eerie howling reverberating from the heart of the granite structure and the ground outside the barbican was devoid of tracks, which was to be expected as no rain had fallen for several days.

"What, no devils and demons?" teased Angelica when Taran drew abreast of them.

"I think I shall be on my way, now thee has the master here," said Silas hastily, noting Benedict's thunderous expression and shaking his head in direful anticipation at the girl's taunting words.

"Obviously your witch hunt was not a success," mourned the girl sarcastically, her own anger sparked. Silas kicked his dapple-grey into a lumbering gait and rode swiftly away from the incipient altercation.

Angelica glared challengingly at the furious man, refusing to be intimidated. To her consternation, his thin lips curled into an engaging grin and his nearly black eyes lost their piercing hardness and twinkled with amusement.

"Jade," he laughed huskily, and she blushed with confusion, trying to hold on to her anger as a protection. She was totally unaware of the magnificent picture she made mounted on the chestnut mare, whose coat mirrored the same glorious rich colour of her thick tumbled hair. The sea breeze and her shyness caused her cheeks to flush and the green of her eyes to intensify. She sat poised and graceful on the high side-saddle, unable to wrench her gaze from him as he slowly reached out and cupped her chin in his large tanned hand.

"We shall be married immediately," he murmured. She was mesmerized by the lips that moved closer and closer until his breath blew softly on her hot cheeks.

"Why?" she whispered, but his mouth covered hers and she closed her eyes, forgetting all her nagging questions as once again the thrilling promise of ecstasy rippled through her.

Taran channelled his anger and frustration into his teasing kiss, turning it from tantalizing seduction into bruising urgency as passion flared. Angelica struggled and pushed away, frightened by the sudden intensity which caused her high-strung mare to prance sideways, mirroring her panic. Taran laughed harshly seeing her wide shocked eyes and trembling red mouth. He was furious with himself for losing control and her reaction just fueled his wrath.

"God save me from outraged virgins," he hissed cruelly.

"Then we didn't? You mean I still am?" she gasped with astonishment, forgetting her fear.

"You still are what?" uttered Taran, stunned by her sudden turnabout. One moment a terrified female and the next an inquisitive one.

"A virgin?"

"A virgin?" he echoed, totally bewildered.

"Yes," she answered patiently. "Am I still a virgin?"

"I should bloody-well hope so," he swore roughly. "What is this about, Angel?" he asked softly after a long searching look into her open, curious face.

"Well, I wasn't sure if we had . . . well, if you and I had . . . er . . ." she stammered, not quite knowing how to phrase it.

"Had what?"

"Had coupled," she stated crisply, lifting her chin high and trying to appear haughty, knowing her face was scarlet with embarrassment.

"I assure you that when we have "coupled," as you so delicately put it, you shall have no doubts at all as to what has occurred between us."

"And I assure you that I do not mean to insult your prowess in that department," retorted Angelica, goaded by his obvious amusement at her discomfort. "But I recollect nothing before awaking in your bed at the house by the salt marshes."

"And so you assumed I had taken advantage of your weakened state to ravish you?" replied Taran, his voice low and harsh with barely suppressed anger. "Despite what you might have heard to the contrary, I find nothing appealing about delirious females and have no need nor wish to satisfy my baser urges with unconscious girls who throw themselves out of public conveyances. . . ."

"I threw myself out of a public conveyance?" interrupted Angel, her green eyes round with awe. Taran shook his dark head, confounded by her ever-changing conversation, which served to circumvent his rage.

"I would prefer to continue this circumambulating conversation at another time," he sighed wearily.

"I really threw myself out of a public conveyance?" repeated Angelica, amazed that she had the courage and audacity to do such a reckless act. "I didn't know I was that sort of person," she added with a tinge of pride.

"What sort of person do you think you are?" he asked as they trotted towards Taran at a sedate pace.

"I thought I was modest . . . retiring . . . usual . . . ordinary. The governess-type of person," she mused frankly. "That's how I appeared to myself in the mirror, but nowadays I don't look the same. It's most probably the very generous wardrobe you planned and had made for me. It makes me look like someone else."

"Who?"

"Maybe the person you wish me to be."

"And who would that be?" he probed roughly, intrigued and yet threatened.

"I don't know," she evaded, hearing the warning roughness in his tone and not wishing for more anger. Their conversation stopped and they rode in silence, each wrapped in their own thoughts. Angelica admitted to herself that she was afraid she could never be the composed, elegant, worldly woman he was reputed to prefer as a consort. The consuming love she felt for him could become the means for her total destruction, she realized, unable to look at his chiseled profile.

Benedict didn't know what he felt. Angelica entranced and intrigued him. One moment she was a serene graceful angel and the next a spitting virago. He couldn't anticipate her reactions, and he found them a refreshing change from the usual mundanities exchanged with the opposite sex.

"It would appear that your father's visiting us," he remarked, espying Simon's rather dilapidated and outmoded carriage in the stable-yard.

"Miss Angel?" hissed a furtive voice, and Iris popped an untidy head stuck with straw out of the hayloft.

"Iris, what's the matter?" asked Angelica, noting the tear-tracks down the girl's muddy face.

"Oh, Miss Angel," wailed the waif, not knowing how to get down as the ladder had been removed. "Don't let that foreigner find me."

"Foreigner?" questioned Taran.

"That's what she calls Angus Dunbar. For some strange reason she is absolutely terrified of him," informed Angelica.

"I didn't think Wilkins was afraid of anything or anybody," remarked Benedict dryly, remembering the small maid being severely beaten by Lady Melisande's cook and maintaining her irrepressible humour.

"Neither did I."

"So that's where the wee lass got to," chuckled Silas, taking the reins of the two horses. "Everybody has been searching high and low for thee, Skilliwiddens," he called.

Benedict stared thoughtfully up at Iris, recalling the tale

Angus Dunbar had told him. "Maybe it is good for the chit to be afraid of someone," he said.

"Why?" asked Angel. "Maybe Mr. Dunbar is guilty of some cruelty to Iris."

"Never," denied Taran sharply. "Angus Dunbar, unlike myself, is neither cruel nor judgmental. He's a fine, honest man, a most loyal friend, and we shall trust him to handle and deal with young Wilkins, who incidentally is about the most inept, untrained servant I have ever met."

"Just as Mr. Dunbar is your loyal friend, so is Iris Wilkins mine," retorted Angelica heatedly.

"There is no need to get into a pet, my dear," said Taran, firmly taking her arm and leading her away from the stable.

"Miss Angel? Miss Angel, don't leave me," wailed Iris.

"I can't leave her up there," protested Angel.

"We are about to get married, which is infinitely more important than an insolent little snippet stuck in a hayloft. I'm sure Silas and Angus can manage to extricate her."

"Miss Angel?" screeched Iris, deciding to jump just as Angus Dunbar strode around. He looked up and gasped at the undignified sight of the little maid backing out of the loft on her hands and knees. He gazed up with amazement as two thin legs encased in black stockings flailed into space. Then the girl hung suspended, ready to drop the twelve feet or so to the cobblestoned yard.

"Iris, what are you doing?" screamed Angel, terrified for the girl. "Benedict, do something! She's going to break her neck!" she implored.

"Angus Dunbar seems to have the situation well in hand," soothed Taran, amusement crinkling his suntanned face. He wrapped a comforting arm about her, pulling her close. "When you've finished there, Angus, I need you to ride into Falmouth," he called.

"Falmouth?" queried Angel, remembering that had been where a certain firm of lawyers to do with the Devil-Child were purported to be.

"I had meant to go there myself, but preferred to spend the day with you," he confessed, idly keeping his dark eyes pinned to the dangling maid.

"Let go, lassie. I shall catch you," directed Angus, standing beneath her and opening his arms. At the sound of his gruff Scottish brogue, Iris froze and hung stiffly for a few minutes before wildly kicking her legs and trying to scramble back into the hayloft.

"Thou cannot get back in, Skilliwiddens, so thy best let go," observed Silas sagely. Iris felt her arms were being wrenched from their sockets but she stubbornly refused to let go. She rested her hot face against the cold granite of the stable and wept. If she could not stay with Angelica and her newfound friends at Taran, she didn't want to live. She couldn't bear the thought of returning to the streets or the workhouse now that she had experienced a more bearable way to exist.

"Come on, my sweet skinnamalink, your awd Silas'll let none harm thee, especially not the foreigner," soothed the old groom, instinctively knowing why the girl was so afraid. "Thee must come down from there so we can find those missing pups," he coaxed.

"Missing pups?" queried Benedict.

"Three pups were stolen in the night," informed Angelica.

"What is happening here?" exclaimed Simon, stepping out of the house and staring about with amazement at the drama in the stableyard. "Angelica, what is your maid doing hanging out of the window?"

"Let Angus catch thee, he has strong young arms," cajolled Silas.

"No! He'll tell on me," howled Iris. "And then Miss Angel won't like me no more and she'll send me packin' and . . . and . . . I wish I was dead!" she wailed, and with that her numb fingers lost hold and she dropped. Angus caught her and fell back with the force, awkwardly jarring his elbow. He lay flat on his back on the cobblestones, the sobbing girl held tightly in his arms despite the pain that flooded through him.

Iris was too distraught to wonder if she was alive or injured. She buried her face in the strong male chest and, feeling infinitely safe for the first time in her wretched young life, gave into the indulgence of hysteria.

Angelica, Benedict, Silas, and Simon moved towards the fallen pair when they made no motion to rise. They formed a ring and stared down, listening to Iris's nearly incoherent confession. Angelica made a move to bend to the girl, but Taran stopped her, wanting to hear all that the maid had to say, especially as certain names piqued his curiosity.

"I didn't mean no 'arm, 'onest I didn't," Iris hiccoughed when her long discourse about 'is lordship this and 'is lordship that, liberally peppered with references to Lord Carrin'don and Isabella Bonny, was ended. "Oh, Miss Angel, I'm ever so sorry . . . I didn't want 'im to spoil yer loverly ball, but 'e 'urt me somethin' awful and was goin' ter send me to some poxy 'ore'ouse if I didn't tell 'im what I was doin' at Lord Taran's town 'ouse," she wailed, tears pouring down her grubby cheeks and muddying Angus's shirt. The Scot tightened his arms about the sobbing girl, ignoring his own pain which seemed trivial compared to the hopeless misery that shook her slight frame. She was little more than a child, he realized, feeling very protective.

" 'Tis alright Daisy-Lass," he crooned, and Silas and Benedict exchanged wry grimaces and quizzically raised eyebrows. This was a side of the solemn young Scot that neither of them had seen before.

"I didn't mean fer Miss Angel to 'ave ter marry Lord Taran if she didn't wanta. I just wanted to 'ave a look at 'im and see if 'e was any better than Carrin'don," declared Iris, pushing herself into a sitting position. Angus Dunbar suddenly gasped, turned very pale, and fainted. "I've killed 'im!" she shrieked.

"Just a broken arm," said Simon after examining the unconscious man.

"Which means I shall have to ride into Falmouth after all," sighed Benedict, signalling several manservants to carry Angus into the house.

"Before or after our wedding?" asked Angelica dryly.

"I was under the impression that the idea of marriage to me was abhorrent to you," remarked Taran softly. "Maybe I should give you a little time to consider if I am a better catch than Carringdon," he added teasingly, remembering Iris's hysterical words.

"The Reverend Helston sends his regrets and will not be able to perform a ceremony today or tomorrow, for that matter," informed Simon a trifle smugly. "Most probably not until next week," he added happily.

"It was arranged for this evening," snapped Taran tersely.

"Death of a relative in Plymouth. A certain Gillian Helston, who used to live in these parts," chattered Simon, his eyes twinkling with suppressed humour. "I dropped by to bring you the message and to see if my daughter would like to accompany me home to become reacquainted with her brothers, who are home from school for the holidays. They arrived this morning."

"I should like that, father," answered Angelica after a side-long look at Taran's stern expression. She was filled with great relief at not having to rush into marriage. Perhaps she could talk her young brothers into taking her to Pendarves Castle.

"Luncheon is served in the small dining room," announced Mrs. Smithers, standing to one side and holding the door open for her husband and the servants, who carried Angus into the house.

"Have your luncheon, Angel, while I bind and splint young Dunbar's broken wing. Then we'll return home," directed Simon cheerfully, conscious of Taran's dark scowl. The portly doctor followed Mr. Smithers, trying to temper the jaunty spring in his step, rejoicing triumphantly at the postponement of his daughter's nuptials.

"Now, I'm sure ter get the sack," bawled Iris, allowing Silas to lead her into the stable. " 'e's dead! I know 'e's dead! I've killed 'im!" she wailed.

"Et'd take more'n a little skinnamalink like you to kill thet hefty Scotsman," laughed the old man, sitting her on a bale of hay and placing a squealing puppy in her lap.

Angelica watched Iris disappear into the stable, knowing the old groom would comfort her. She took a deep breath, gathering her courage, and then stared challengingly up at Benedict. He returned her glare silently. She grinned trying to coax a softening of his thin-lipped scowl, but it served to intensify his grimness.

"Am I that repugnant to you?" he asked sharply, and she shook her head.

"On the contrary," she replied, refusing to meet his eyes

for fear he would guess her secret. "Will you at least have luncheon with me, your lordship?" she added mischievously, covering her feelings of vulnerability.

"There are other men of the cloth who could marry us, you know," he said slowly, looking at her with speculation, puzzled by her heightened colour.

"I am sure there are, but I would appreciate a little more time to get to know you and rediscover myself," she answered frankly. His expression grew gentle and he nodded before indicating she should precede him into the house.

"I should be honoured to lunch with you, Miss Angel," he accepted with a gallant bow. "Then I shall be on my way to Falmouth," he added. She bit her lip, wishing he would confide in her but knowing it would be futile to ask. It would be more advisable to keep the easy camaraderie between them and find out the answers for herself, she decided as they strolled arm in arm to the small dining room.

"Would you like me to woo you?" he asked softly. Her pulses raced, but she pretended not to hear, as she did not know how to answer. "Well, Angel?" he persisted.

"I don't know," she replied.

CHAPTER 13

DEVIL TREMAYNE rode the Carrack across the moors to High Tor. Leaving him to graze behind the barn out of sight of the main house, Devil quietly stole into the shadowy building, clutching an awkward sack of wriggling puppies, wondering where to put them so they'd be safe from harm and unable to get into mischief before Felix Pendarves found them. The young animals were confused and hungry. Their muffled yelps and squeals caused the roosting chickens to cluck warningly and then frantically flutter, squawking loudly.

"Baistly varmints!" Jago's deep voice just outside the barn made Devil freeze. "Weasels and foxes after the eggs," he hissed. The Bucca growled warningly as the wide barn door was flung open, allowing the silvery moonlight to stream in which captured the floating feathers. Jago, with gun in hand, was silhouetted against the stable-yard. Devil made no effort to hide but just stood motionless, cradling the squirming bundle, surrounded by cackling birds. "Well, my dear life and days if et tesn't my brother's young master," declared Jago as his eyes acclimatized to the dimness and he recognised the poised slight figure. The Bucca continued to growl deep in his throat. Behind the barn a horse snorted and whinnied in answer.

"This is for the boy," explained Devil, stiltedly. "A dog and two bitches. They've not eaten since this morning."

"Then let's take them to the kitchen and feed them," softly suggested Jago, sensing the tension. He knew that any sudden movement or sharp sound would cause the huge hound to attack, driving away the dark child of the moors.

"The kitchen?" repeated Devil, fighting waves of dizziness. The awkward, wriggling bundle was becoming unbearably heavy.

"We cannot leave young dogs in here to chase the fowl or I'll hev addled eggs. Thee look a mite pinched and hungry thyself," he observed, noting the smudges that circled the unnaturally sparking eyes and the perspiration that beaded on the flushed cheeks.

"Here," said Devil, shoving the sack at the shrewd man who stared too intently. "Tell the boy . . . I am sorry. Tell him, I know these young strangers cannot take his friend's place but . . . maybe they'll give some comfort."

Jago reached for the bundle and frowned with concern at the heat that emanated from the thin arms. Instinctively he grasped the trembling limbs.

"You're ill, child!" he exclaimed, ignoring the Bucca who snarled possessively and tensed to spring. Devil abruptly pulled away and silently darted into the shadows. Within moments Jago heard the Carrack's hooves pounding away from High Tor. He sighed deeply and strode toward the warm light that streamed from the kitchen.

"Who was that, Pengelly?" Torr called out from the open door. "And what have you there?"

" 'Tes a present for Master Felix from the dark child of the moor," replied Jago, loathe to use the macabre name. "Aye, tes a present for you," he repeated pensively as he entered the house. Felix just continued to toy morosely with his food.

Mrs. Goodie bustled into the kitchen just as Jago untied the sack, spilling out the three plump puppies who skittered and tumbled over each other in a race to reach Felix's uneaten supper.

"Get those filthy animals off there!" she scolded, whipping the platter of food out of reach. She clucked indignantly when the excited puppies puddled the scrubbed wood of the table. "And right where I roll out my pastry, too," she lamented, trying to remain disapproving despite the fat little dog who leaped on wobbly legs to lick her face. Encountering her ample bosom, he lost his balance, rolling over and over with adorable grunts of exertion. "Oh, the little lovies," she succumbed, tickling a round milky tummy.

"Fine healthy golden retrievers. About two months old," remarked Torr, running a practised hand over the young male while the smaller of the three tugged and worried Felix's sleeve, trying to growl ferociously. "Purebred, too. Now, where would that Devil brat steal such pedigreed animals?" he added, staring speculatively at Jago for several moments before limping out of the kitchen door. The older man watched him leave, listening to the uneven boot-steps cross the cobblestones, hearing the labourious creak of the heavy stable door being opened.

"The dark lad said he knew thet they'd not make up for Lucan, Master Felix, but he hoped thet they'd be of some comfort to thee," sighed Jago, turning his gaze to the sullen youth who resisted the antics of the comical puppies. "They've not fed since morning," he added. Mrs. Goodie poured a large shallow pan full of milk and the three little dogs promptly fell in, finally eliciting a rueful grin and then infectious giggles from Felix. Three little tails wagged wildly and wetly and three pink tongues lapped noisily until every drop of milk was consumed. The bowl was filled three more times until the three were sated and sleepy, nestling together, hiccoughing contentedly.

"Does my heart good to see Master Felix getting back to his happy self again," sniffed Mrs. Goodie, gazing fondly at the boy, who was sprawled on the hearth rug with the sleeping puppies cuddled on his chest. "Wish there was something that could melt through Master Torr's grim dolor."

Jago nodded his agreement, although his thoughts were amid the cold stones of Pendarves Castle with another dolorous young being. Hearing the clatter of hoofs on the cobbled yard, he looked out just in time to see Torr disappear over the rise of the dark moor.

"No whispering behind my back!" snarled Miss Peller. "I know you all hate me. No whispering!" she hissed, even though the Living-Dead were silent. She spun about, sensing that the dark shadows were alive with malicious spirits. "Not a sound or you'll be like that foul witch, Granny-Griggs!" The old people bowed their shrouded heads nearer to their bowls, furtively scanning their long rows for a sign of Granny-

Griggs. A low mournful moan drifted from them. "Silence or you'll never eat again." They fearfully devoured their frugal fare before it could be snatched from them.

Devil slowly stepped into the quiet kitchen. There was a smattering of brittle clatters, of spoons being dropped into tin bowls, as one by one the Living-Dead became aware of the small dark figure who swayed in the arched doorway. Devil clung to the massive head of the Bucca because the vast underground room seemed distorted, the granite floor and walls constantly shifting. Miss Peller's angular face seemed grotesquely contorted, swooping in and out of focus.

"So you finally decided to come home, did you?" said the gaunt housekeeper scathingly. Devil pointedly ignored her and trod unsteadily toward the Bucca's feeding bowl, knowing the hound was ravenous. "I hope you don't expect to be fed, too?" The woman said softly, her voice chillingly sweet. Devil silently shook an aching head and watched the dog eat. "And where have you been? Nearly two nights and a day you've been gone! Up to more wickedness that could mean the death of all of us, no doubt," she continued, her voice rising, goaded by the stoic silence. Devil kept burning eyes fixed to the Bucca, who drank thirstily, wishing Miss Peller would temper her strident tone. "You are a liar, Devil Tremayne, child of shame! A liar! You say you care for all of us but you lie! You say you love Jonty Pengelly, yet because of your wickedness he has been out risking his neck, searching high and low for you! Because of your wicked selfishness, Tremayne of Taran was here trying to break down the door . . . frightening those miserable creatures witless," she ranted, stabbing her long fingers to indicate the ancient people who rocked, moaning with terror. "Because of your wicked disobedience we are doomed! Forty barrels of brandy are still in the cellars of High Torr and, thanks to you, they'll stay there! What do we tell our customers? How do we pay the smugglers? There's a boat due any night now. We could have our throats cut! What are we supposed to do?" She watched the hound cunningly, throughout her tirade, stepping closer and closer to the small swaying figure. "Answer me! What are we supposed to do?" she demanded, tentatively raising her hand as though to smite Devil. The Living-Dead gasped. The hound tried to growl menacingly but staggered, seeming as dazed as the dark child.

The room spun alarmingly and Miss Peller's discordant voice ripped into Devil's pounding head; the woman's contorted face grimaced through the misty veils that covered burning eyes.

"What are you going to do, Devil-Child?" chorused the old people.

"Answer us, you demon!" hissed the housekeeper triumphantly, feeling in total control.

"Answer us, Devil-Child," pleaded the Living-Dead.

"Answer us!" shouted Miss Peller, raising her hand again and this time savagely striking the feverish face. The old people recoiled with a gasp. The hound tensed to attack but instead staggered from side to side, unable to coordinate his movements. Miss Peller laughed victoriously and struck again. The huge animal tottered and slowly sank to the stone floor with a long low lament.

"Answer us!" repeated the insane woman, trying to control her choking mirth. "Answer us!" she gurgled as the dog rolled heavily on its side, its breath laboured. The Living-Dead clustered together, shrinking into the protective shadows, their eyes fixed to the dying animal.

"Answer us!" screeched Miss Peller, grabbing Devil by the hair when the child bent to tend the suffering creature. "I said answer us!" she repeated, shaking the dark head brutally from side to side.

"No! No! You mustn't harm the Devil-Child," muttered the black-garbed people, clutching each other and hesitantly approaching the crazed woman. "You mustn't harm our Devil-Child or the Bucca-Dhu shall harm you," they mumbled, moving closer to the enraged housekeeper, who slapped and shook the unresisting child, infuriated by the silent passivity.

"There is no Bucca-Dhu, I've poisoned the beast!" she claimed triumphantly, her heavy ring of keys swinging on a long silk cord and wrapping and rewrapping about her gaunt body. "There is no one now who'll disobey me . . . no one now who'll dare to defy my authority!"

"Granny-Griggs?" chorussed the Three-Marys, and soon the cry was picked up by the whole mass of Living-Dead.

"Granny-Griggs?" they called desperately, summoning the only one of their number beside Jonty who might possibly stand up to Miss Peller.

"Call all you want! Call her from the grave! Call her down from the gibbet in the stables!" laughed the woman. "She's dead! Call her until you're all as mute as Yeoman!"

"We'll help you, Devil-Child," whispered Minny-Pinny bravely.

"We'll help you," agreed the Three-Marys.

"We'll help you," chorused all the Living-Dead.

"Get away! Go to your cells!" barked the woman, her bloodcurdling laughter coming to an abrupt halt. She backed away from the shrouded forms, but they shuffled closer. "I said go to your cells or you'll die like that cur!" she snarled.

"No one must harm our Devil-Child," they intoned, circling the terrified woman.

"Get away, I say! Get away, you miserable creatures," she screamed, releasing the limp youngster who fell across the inert body of the Bucca. Miss Peller flailed the air to ward off the tightening band of the Living-Dead. "You owe me your very existences! You cannot survive without me!" she screeched, whirling her heavy ring of keys to keep them at bay. But the old people moved inexorably closer, unflinching even when they received vicious blows across their lined faces, which caused bloody gashes. They shuffled closer, their manacled hands joined and raised until they were within striking distance. Then they rained blow upon blow, their iron bracelets making sickening thuds. Miss Peller bent double to protect herself, whimpering and shielding her face and head, but they rhythmically struck, not uttering a word. They made grunts of exertion, that quickened, escalating into a low buzzing roar, and then there was a final spine-chilling scream from Miss Peller.

Jonty was relieved to find the Carrack grazing patiently on the few weeds that managed to sprout between the stones of the sunless central courtyard. It meant that his young charge had returned. He frowned, noting the horse had not been tended. It was most unlike Devil to leave the stallion sweating and obviously unwatered. Knowing better than to touch the feral animal, he clicked his tongue, hoping the Carrack would follow him and his old pony into the stables. He was gratified to hear the steady clap of hooves behind him. He swung open the door and gasped at the ominous spectacle of a noose dangling from the rafters.

"What's been happening here?" he worried aloud, noting the Carrack's sudden agitation. "Oh, my dear heart and soul, what's been happening," he muttered, leading his pony into a stall and filling a trough with water for the stallion who blew through dry lips and whinnied shrilly with concern. A blood-curdling scream shattered the uneasy calm and Jonty froze, dread gnawing into the core of his old bones. He strained his ears, but the chilling cry was not repeated. Hastily closing the stable door, he raced through the central courtyard, his worn boots slipping on the dew-slick cobblestones.

He entered the basement kitchen, and in the dim lantern glow everything seemed tranquil. The Living-Dead sat quietly on the long benches that lined each side of the table.

"I heard a scream," he stated after a long pause, and the old people stared silently at a crumpled shape on the floor. Jonty turned the wick up on a lantern. Dread pounding in his heart, he walked slowly to the body of Rebecca Peller. Blood was splattered across the cold grey stones of the floor and walls. "What has happened here?" he uttered when he could speak. To his horror the emaciated wrists of the Living-Dead were silently held up for his inspection, blood still dripping from the iron manacles that ringed each shrivelled limb. "What have you done?" he whispered, appalled by the gory evidence. Immediately there was a wild wailing.

"No one shall harm our Devil-Child!"

"Where is our child?" demanded Jonty fearfully. The mass of shrouded people turned and stared silently into the deep shadows. The four Three-Marys squatted on the floor in a protective circle about a small limp figure who lay with arms about the Bucca. "Oh, my dear life!" he breathed, almost too afraid to approach, but a sobbing sigh shuddering through the slight figure caused him to quicken his step. The Three-Marys silently shifted aside, and Jonty knelt on the cold stone floor.

"He's dead," whispered Devil. "Dead just like the

Pendarves's hound, Lucan. My Bucca-Dhu is dead. Grandfather said 'twas written 'an eye for an eye, tooth for tooth, hand for hand, foot for foot.' ''

"The Bucca can't be dead," huskily protested Jonty, feeling behind the shaggy ears, expecting to find a pulse. There was nothing; the huge black beast was still and cold. Jonty had no words of comfort. He mutely stroked Devil's ebony head and frowned, feeling the fever.

"The Bucca's dead because of me . . . an eye for an eye," muttered the Devil-Child.

"Thee are making thyself sick with grief, my pisky. Don't blame thyself. The Bucca knows thee loved him. Et wuz thet evil female, Rebecca Peller, who killed thy pet and I should hev known. If any's at fault tes me," sobbed the old man. "I knew her twisted ways, greedy, dangerous controlling ways," he lamented, wrapping his wiry arms about the dark child, needing comfort for himself. Devil fought free, wildly battling and pushing until Jonty staggered to his feet and moved away.

"Leave me be! All of you! Go and leave me be!"

"Go," said Jonty quietly to the rest of the Living-Dead. "Let the Devil-Child grieve alone." The black-garbed people obediently shuffled out of the cavernous room, staring back sorrowfully at the dark pair.

"You, too, Jonty Pengelly," spat Devil harshly and the old man nodded. He strode away without a backward look and sat outside on the stone staircase, waiting.

The silence was long and heavy. It painfully weighed Jonty's spirit. Then sharp agony stabbed him at the terrible sound of human grief that burst out of the Devil-Child. It was echoed in every cold, inhospitable corner of the grim fortress by the Living-Dead, who clustered in clumps, trying to find comfort.

Torr Pendarves reined his horse at hearing a macabre lamentation moan with the wind across the treeless moor. He looked toward the hollow-eyed castle unable to believe what he heard. Was it a capricious sea breeze playing through the caves, causing the eerie keening? If so it certainly gave some credence to the superstitious tales of mermaids and drowned souls haunting the lonely coves of Pendarves Point. Again the terrible sound of raw pain wailed in ululating waves across the moonlit-tipped grasses of the wasteland. It touched a deep sorrow within him. Torr's eyes filled with tears and he yearned to add his own voice to the chorus of grief, to howl his own unbearable loneliness. He kneed his horse to a walk and approached the grim castle, sensing he was not hearing just a trick of the wind. Suddenly a wild-haired hag leaped out from behind a boulder; his mount reared and whinnied in panic.

"Help me!" babbled the unkempt creature hoarsely. Torr dashed the tears from his eyes and gazed with amazement at the witch from his delirious dreams. It was the very crone who had bound his thigh with mud and herbs while the Devil-Child and the Bucca Dhu watched.

"You," he gasped, blinking at her distinct features, which appeared spectral in the shimmering moonlight. He expected her to magically disappear.

"Help me," she hissed, clawing at his leg. He saw dark shining rivulets of blood that poured down her wrinkled face from underneath her snakey white hair. "You must help before the Repeller kills us all." Torr dismounted stiffly and she grasped at his clothes.

"What is it?"

"Hush thyself," she spat, lifting taloned hands to the air in a bid for silence as she listened to the howl of grief that ebbed and flowed with the tide and the night breeze. "Et is too late! Too late! A coronach . . . a dirge . . . a knell," she mourned, falling heavily to her knees and covering her face with her bloody hand.

"What is too late? Tell me and I'll do what I can," urged Torr, filling with an inexplicable terror.

"Tes a knell . . . a wake," sobbed the crone.

"For whom?"

"The Devil-Child and the Bucca-Dhu," howled Granny-Griggs, before pitching forward and lying still in the heather. Torr lifted her up and stared with horror at the violent marks that ringed her scraggy neck where the imprint of a coarse rope was firmly etched. He shrugged out of his warm cape and wrapped it about the unconscious old woman and placed her out of the wind behind a looming granite boulder.

"I shall return," he muttered, remounting and proceeding towards Pendarves Castle. He was determined to understand the reason for the chilling lamentations that still skirled with the mist across the desolate heath. Torr rode backward and forward in front of the hulking building. He stared up at the dark slit windows, hearing the eerie keening, not knowing how to gain admittance. He peered through the entrance to the barbican at the patterns of light on the stone-flagging. It was caused by the moon filtering through the gridwork of the lowered portcullis which was locked firmly in place. At the huge main door he dismounted; grasping the heavy iron knocker in two hands, he dashed it against the metal plate, hearing the sharp report echo through the stone hallway inside.

At the discordant sound of the knocker reverberating off the granite floors and walls, the pained cries suddenly ceased. Devil sighed and relaxed, drained of all emotion and energy, still embracing the dead animal. The huddled black-garbed figures wearily sagged to the ground and collapsed in the hollow shadows. Only Jonty was curious. He stealthily made his way to the vast entry hall hung with every instrument of torture and peered out of the peephole at the moonlight shining on Torr Pendarves's bright blond head.

"Tes the true master of this sad, sad place," he said softly to himself. "A circle has ended for thee, my little pisky-child. Et is time thee had a natural life and younger arms to hold thee and teach thee warmth and loving, and younger voices to teach thee to laugh and sing," he whispered huskily, gazing down at the small dark figure pillowed on the still hound. "Do thee hear me, child?" he asked reaching to caress the ebony hair and once more feeling the heat. "Thou are sick with grief," he mourned, loosening the hot bare arms and lifting the slight figure. He stared down at the dusky flushed cheeks, at the thick, dark lashes still hung with tears.

"No! I don't want you nor your comfort! I don't want any comfort ever!" protested Devil, struggling free of Jonty's arms and turning back to the Bucca.

"Thee shall grow up! There shall be no more secrets to stunt and bind thee," fervently vowed the old man as once more a hot face was buried in the cool shaggy coat of the dead hound. Lithe legs curled up and a small body cuddled into the curve of the motionless creature. "No longer shall you be buried alive with the Living-Dead in this great tomb of hate," promised Jonty as the heavy knocker repeatedly crashed against the castle door, resounding through the corridors, making the throngs of black-garbed old people cower in the shadows.

Torr Pendarves was determined to gain access, but the Norman fortress was impregnable. His leaden arms ached from the futile pounding, and he wearily remounted cursing his stiff leg.

"I will be back!" he screamed impotently, waving a sore fist at the looming edifice and riding back to collect the battered old woman. He laughed cynically, expecting her to have melted magically into the mists, but she was there, her pale, bloodied face appearing ghastly in the moonlight.

The eastern sky was lightening when Torr's overladen horse trotted into the stable-yard at High Tor. Every inch of his body throbbed painfully with fatigue and the emaciated old woman, cradled across his thighs, weighed heavily against him.

"Jago Pengelly?" he bellowed impatiently, unable to dismount without assistance with his precarious burden. "Jago Pengelly?" and the Cornishman appeared out of the shadows by the barn. "I'm glad you're not still abed. Take this hag from me," he ordered tersely.

"Who have you there?" asked Jago, who had been prowling anxiously throughout the night waiting for the young peer to return. He reached up and lifted down the inert woman. "Tes awd Granny-Griggs!" he exclaimed as the bloodied face lolled against his broad chest.

"You know that miserable crone?"

"Everyone in these parts knows of Granny-Griggs," replied the Cornishman, tenderly carrying the old woman into the house. "She's healed most at some time or other," he added, angered by Torr's deprecating tone.

"What's a repeller?" Torr demanded, sliding painfully out of the saddle and staggering after his manservant, leaving his weary horse to take care of itself.

"A repeller be a dispeller of witchcraft or the opposite . . . a person to remove curses or to repel them thet would remove them," informed Jago. He placed the old woman on a settle, where she mumbled incoherently and thrashed about. "Who did thet violence to her?" he asked, appalled by the livid marks on the old face and wrinkled neck.

"She said the Repeller did it. She said that the Repeller has killed the Devil-Child and the Bucca-Dhu," answered Torr, keeping his eyes on Pengelly's weathered face.

"Rebecca Peller was housekeeper for Sir Godolphus Pendarves," said Jago. "Killed the dark child and his pet?" he repeated when the meaning of the awful words seeped into his head. "Why? Why would the female do such a terrible thing?" he cried.

"You are more likely to know the answer to that than I," snapped Torr roughly.

"Tes first things first," stated Jago, striding from the room to rouse Mrs. Goodie to tend to the injured old woman.

"Now, Pengelly, what do you know of all this?" demanded Torr when they were ensconced in the privacy of his study and Granny-Griggs was tucked into a comfortable bed within hearing distance of the grumbling housekeeper.

"Nothing," answered Jago dully, his brooding thoughts with the lonely dark child of the moors.

"I don't accept that! Jonty Pengelly is your own brother, so you must have knowledge of that Devil-brat!" Torr imagined the expressive, fathomless eyes clouded and lifeless, and he channelled a rush of choking grief into impatient fury.

"I've laid eyes on thet poor lad but twice. First at Awd Tarkeel when Master Felix lost his pet and again just last evening . . . before you went a'chasing after," sighed Jago wearily.

"You must know more!"

"Oh, I knew of ghosts and ghoulies and the Bucca-Dhu, but they were useful stories to keep nosey strangers and excise men away from Pendarves Point," he admitted sorrowfully. "But I dedn't think fer one moment there wuz truth to et."

"Smuggling?" probed Torr, and the older man nodded. "Wrecking?"

"Never! Not wrecking! Never! Thet I dent approve of!"

"But perhaps your brother and the other macabre occupants of Pendarves Castle do!''

"Never!" repeated the Cornishman adamantly. "I'll not believe thet!''

"All right, just smuggling," conceded Torr grimly. "But what do a small urchin and a large hound have to do with it?''

"Thet teases my mind, too," confessed Jago. "Smuggling's a way of life hereabouts, especially since your kinsman closed the pits and quarries. A man has to feed his family.''

"I counted more than forty barrels of remarkably fine cognac in the very cellars that you insisted were flooded and unsafe. Here, Pengelly, sample some of your wares," offered Torr, pouring two snifters of rich amber liquid. "But smuggling doesn't answer any questions about my cousin Catherine's little bastard or those ancient convicts, one of whom is lying in one of my bedrooms with her scrawny neck wrung!" hissed Torr savagely as the thought of his teethmarks in a small limp hand slashed into his head. "Who are those wretched black-habitted creatures?''

"The 'Living-Dead,' as Jonty calls them, wuz Sir Godolphus Pendarves's bonded servants. Slaves is more like et! Poor wretches who happened to be sentenced by him when he wuz magistrate of these here parts.''

"Couldn't he have availed himself of younger servants?" remarked Torr sardonically, swirling the cognac and appreciating the stinging aroma that teared his eyes.

"Weth enough sense of self to rebel and defy him?" retorted Jago scornfully. " 'Sides most of them cowering creatures were quite young when they wuz first sentenced and ent too old now. My brother wuz barely thirty when he wuz first bound to thet merciless man and thet wuz more'n thirty years ago.''

"Why did he stay? If he takes a ketch to France on smuggling runs, surely he could have freed himself? Started anew somewhere else?''

"I dedn't say my brother ded any such thing as smuggling!" stated Jago, glaring at the young peer as terror streaked through his lean body. What if Torrance Pendarves was as merciless as his kinsman? Torr returned the glower and there was a crackling tension between the two men.

"Jonty stayed for me," sighed Jago, breaking the long silence after he'd stared into the chiseled young face, searching for a shred of compassion in the steely blue eyes. He had found none but he had remembered the bitter man as a sweet boy. "The tide do never go out so far but what et do come in again," he muttered, in an attempt to reassure himself. "Sir Godolphus convicted my brother for a crime thet I committed. I kilt a man when I wuz but sixteen. Et wuz a fair fight in thet we wuz both drunk and he wuz armed. If'n he'd been a common lout like me all would've been forgotten, but he wuz English gentry so someone had to pay. 'Fore I could sober up, I wuz signed on a vessel on its way to China and Jonty had taken my plaace," he confessed bluntly. "Thinking back, Godolphus Pendarves must've known the truth of et. So my brother stayed in chains to save my wretched neck, but then I am supposing thet he stayed when Miss Catherine's poor babe wuz born weth none to love et." Jago took a punishing swallow of cognac and stared blindly out of the window at the morose nearly morning sky.

"Catherine's poor babe," repeated Torr wonderingly. " 'Tis so strange that none knew of his existence until old Godolphus died. Why keep such a secret?" Jago shrugged helplessly. "Yet, talk of a Devil-Child riding a phantom horse with a ghostly hound has been rife for years?"

"Nay, just the past four or five . . . since the pits were closed and the smuggling increased."

"Why would Godolphus lie about having a grandson? It makes no sense," puzzled Torr. "He even went out of his way to lie, telling Simon Carmichael that the child was stillborn," he stated, trying to unravel the mystery. "Why? A grandson would seem something to boast about!"

"Aye," agreed Jago. "Tes thet part of a man thet goes on living after he's in his grave. Maybe him being so religious and Miss Catherine being . . . er, free weth herself so to speak . . . well, could be Sir Godolphus wuz ashamed of the bastard?"

"Maybe. But why would anyone else want to hurt the wretched bastard?"

"Maybe et wuz just the mad ravings of a sick awd woman," dismissed Jago, loathe to even contemplate the death of the vibrant young spirit of the moors.

"If you had heard that awesome keening," muttered Torr distractedly. "You'd know there was no maybe about it."

"I've heard many a ghostly lament on the moors of a night. Tedn't but the sea wind in the caverns or thet child's big beast baying at the moon."

"No animal bayed at the moon last night. It was pure, unadulterated human grief . . . deep, deep sorrow," stressed the young man. "How can we get into that dismal pile of rocks?"

"We can't lest we're let in," sighed Jago. "I'll send word to my brother. We hev our secret ways to get messages back and forth," he comforted. An iciness suddenly clutched at his gut. "Jonty Pengelly would not let any harm one hair on thet elfin child's dark head . . . and weth thet great stallion, Carrack, and the Bucca-Dhu to protect . . . who'd dare try?" He forced a laugh, knowing that if he was wrong his brother was also dead.

A morose silence blanketed the two men, who sat gazing despondently into the dying fire. A radiant dawn brightened the sky but not their inner gloom.

"How can a day be so fresh and innocent when such pain and misery wuz wrought in the night?" wondered Jago as crisp sunlight dappled the carpet and birds chirped merrily outside. "I'll not be long," he said shortly.

"I'm riding with you," insisted Torr, unable to remain waiting. The memory of the poignant face with the dark luminous eyes haunted him.

"Thet imp cannot be dead," stated Jago gruffly, striding into the cobbled yard.

"No, he cannot be dead," repeated the younger man, gazing about at the glorious sunny day. There were no shadows, no clouds. Nothing could be wrong on such a perfect day. His poor horse, still fully saddled, stood dejectedly, dew beading on the leather trappings and matted hide.

"You'd be put to better use tending to the poor dumb beast there," snapped Jago shortly. "I'm not riding anywheres and you'll not miss but a smokey fire in the damp heather," he

added, briskly jogging out of sight, leaving Torr to lead the
shivering horse into the dry stable.

Angelica awoke in her girlhood bedroom and lay watching
the sun dapple the flower-sprigged wallpaper. Outside birds
sweetly trilled and busily fluttered, and rambling roses climbed
the trellis until they nodded at the open latticed window
filling the airy room with delicate perfume.

"Home," she sighed contentedly, feeling warm and comfortable, her body light and suspended in a half-dreaming
state. "Home," she said again, picking up a well-worn doll
and balancing it on her stomach. "And what did I call you?"
she asked, smiling at the handpainted porcelain features and
sparse blond hair that looked depleted from too much brushing. "Home," she whispered again, swinging her long legs
out of the bed and gazing about the pretty room. Tenderly she
touched each book, ornament, and picture, trying to evoke
memories. Even though she felt an affectionate nostalgia,
there was no specific recall and she found herself staring out
of the window at the tall budding hollyhocks thinking of
Benedict's dark eyes and broad hands.

"Angel?" called a husky adolescent voice accompanied by
a robust rapping.

"Just a moment," she answered, slipping her arms into a
robe and tying it about her slim waist. "Come in," she
invited, and two gangly youths peered around the room.
"Owen and Evan," she greeted smilingly.

"You remember us?" they asked shyly.

"Only from yesterday," she admitted ruefully.

"I thought we were riding over the moors to Pendarves
Point first thing this morning so we can help you find your
memory," proclaimed Owen anxiously.

"And so we are," comforted Angelica. "But I can scarcely
go cantering about the countryside in my night attire, can I?"
she laughed.

"You can but it'll cause quite a confloption with the
locals," giggled Owen. "Hurry up and get dressed because
it's a beautiful day and after riding with you, father says he'll
take me out to High Tor to meet Felix Pendarves, who is my

age . . . and then maybe I'll go out fishing . . ." chattered
the long lanky youth.

"And what is your age?" interrupted his sister gently.

"Fourteen," stated Owen proudly. "Only fourteen and I'm
as tall as Evan, and he's nearly seventeen." His older brother
silently and firmly propelled him out of the door, smiling
apologetically at his sister.

"I'll see you at breakfast," laughed Angelica.

There was a loud clatter as the boys raced down the stairs,
nearly knocking over Maizie and Caleb.

"Well, well, looks like peaceful times ez over weth these
two holler-pots home!" chortled Caleb.

"We're going riding up on the moors to chase ghosts and
ghoulies through the old Pendarves graveyard by the haunted
chapel near the logan-stone where shipwrecked sailors play
the organ on a starless night and where mermaids sit on the
weedy rocks combing their beautiful hair," sang Owen happily, all in one breath.

"I dunno 'bout childers riding 'bout up near Pendarves
Point. There's bin strange happenings lately," growled Caleb.

"What strange happenings? Tell us, Caleb," said Owen
excitedly.

"I don't want thee to have nightmares, Master Owen, so I
shan't tell thee," evaded Caleb.

Angelica smiled happily at the adolescent banter between
her siblings as they cantered across the verdant countryside.
She enjoyed their refreshing company as they vied for her
attention like rambunctious puppies, each wanting to be the
one to spark her memory. The warm spring air was sweet and
redolent with a multitude of blossoms in the dense hedgerows that rose to each side of them. The tender green of the
many different shrubs—hazel, sloe, elder, and hawthorn—
reached and curled across the winding lane until branch-tips
touched and entwined, weaving a leafy ceiling. Hundreds of
years of weather and wagon wheels, working boots and hooves
had deeply carved the country byways between the sown
fields until the banks were steep, carpeted with primroses,
cowslips, and violets in spring, and foxgloves, poppies, and
wild orchids in the sultry months. Angelica closed her eyes,

recalling the soft patter of a gentle summer rain that released the achingly tender scent of wet wild roses and honeysuckle.

"Are you all right?" asked Evan anxiously, and she smiled and nodded.

"When we were caught in a summer storm, we'd ride down this lane and not a drop of rain would fall on us," she said softly, opening her eyes and gazing up at the mottled effect of the new growth against the bright sky. "I can see the dark shiny mature leaves with beads of water sliding down. I can hear the drumming of the rain and the wondrous damp smell. . . . Even on the hottest day it always was refreshingly cool in this green tunnel. I can remember sounds and scents but no people," she sighed. Once more she thought of Benedict, seeing his large brown hands loosely holding the reins and yet masterfully controlling his large stallion. "Did I know Benedict Tremayne of Taran before?" she asked.

"We knew of him but we didn't know him," answered Evan.

"That's because he's been living in London for absolutely years and years because of his brother drowning and a tragic love affair which broke his heart and his father was killed in an explosion in one of his mines. . . ." chattered Owen, stopping to take a noisy breath.

The horses broke free of the winding lane and trotted onto the cliff path on the edge of the rolling moor, where the almond-scented gorse was budding. "More than a thousand . . . probably more like a million ships have been dashed to pieces out there," informed the irrepressible boy, pointing a finger to the jagged teeth of Wolf Rock that rose out of the deceptively calm sea. "When the tide is in, you cannot see the reef. Caleb says it is lethal . . . razor-sharp and could cut a man's head off like that." He demonstrated, slicing his flattened hand across his neck. "Just like that," he repeated with relish and grinning proudly when his sister shuddered.

"What is all this I've been hearing about a Devil-Child?" ventured Angelica.

"The Devil-Child and the Bucca haunt the moors on moon-lit nights before a wrecking storm . . . protecting the mines for the spriggans and knockers, says Caleb and Maizie," chanted the fourteen-year-old.

"Have you ever seen him?" she asked.

"Now he's going to lie and say he's seen all manner of outrageous things just to impress you," laughed Evan. "Well, go on, Owen Carmichael, tell us of all the ghosts and ghoulies you've seen."

The boy looked away, furious with his brother's teasing, and his eyes widened with disbelief. He gasped, trying to speak but was unable to make any sense, just strangled sounds as he wildly gesticulated towards the eerie spectre of a long line of faceless bent figures all garbed in loose black robes that streamed in the sea breeze.

"Look," gulped the boy, and his older brother fell silent and stared with frightened intensity at the ghostly procession that wended its way in a single file across the stark wasteland carrying what appeared to be two coffins.

"Hide," Evan hissed hoarsely. They quickly rode behind a large rock and dismounted.

"What is that stone ruin they are entering?" whispered Angel. Evan fearfully peered out, expecting the shrouded people to be a figment of his imagination after Owen's spooky talk, but there they were, moving slowly into the old graveyard.

"That's Pendarves's Chapel. It belongs to the castle," he answered. "Oh, my Lor'!" he exclaimed when over the treeless heath was heard the macabre notes of a church organ. The eerie sound wheezed and squeaked, agonizingly gathering momentum before bursting into beautiful harmony. "Whoever that particular lost spirit is, he certainly is a fine musician," he proclaimed admiringly. Angelica nodded in agreement, but Owen shuddered violently, his usually ruddy face pale with terror.

"Where's Pendarves Castle?" asked Angelica.

"Over there on that headland. You can just see it through the mist," whispered Evan impatiently, not wanting to miss one note of the music wafted over the countryside.

"How quickly these frets come in from the sea. One minute the day is sunny without a cloud in the sky. Then within a blink of an eye the fog swirls in, veiling everything," remarked the girl, just managing to make out the grey turrets.

"I thought ghosts only came out at night after sundown,

but it's like they've made the sun set in the middle of the day. Let's go home," Owen urged tearfully.

"Don't be such a baby," chided his older brother. "Listen to that . . . it's Bach . . . the ghost is playing a Bach piece I've never heard before. It's wonderful," he breathed, so enchanted he wasn't afraid in the slightest. His long sensitive fingers played against the cold granite, picking out the notes.

"That's how the mermaids get their victims," sobbed the younger boy. "They sing so sweetly that the sailors are entrapped and die." Angelica wrapped a comforting arm about her little brother.

"I promise you we shall not be seduced. We shall stay here quietly until they have finished and then steal quietly away," she soothed, the word seduce reminding her of Benedict. "Shall I woo you?" he had said, and she sighed deeply, admitting to herself that she would dearly love to be wooed by the dark handsome man.

"They're digging in the graveyard!" cried Owen, hearing the sharp rhythmic sound of shovels cutting into the gravelly, dry soil and mingling with the Bach requiem that skirled with the tendrils of sea fret. After nearly an hour the music plaintively came to a stop and the single file of twenty or more black-garbed people slowly left the graveyard, wending their way back across the barren land, disappearing into the mist.

"And now the sun comes out and the fret is dispelled and the birds begin to sing and you say there is no such thing as ghosts and Buccas and the like," said Owen hotly, regaining his truculence.

"Those poor old people weren't ghosts," said Angelica softly.

"How do you know that they're old?" exclaimed Evan.

"Because I've met some of them," she replied.

"Where?" chorussed both youths.

"At High Tor. They were working there when father and I visited. They used to be Godolphus Pendarves's servants, I believe. They're just poor old people who've had a very hard life," she explained, not wanting to mention the manacles about the thin brittle wrists to her talkative youngest brother.

"Who were they burying?" asked Owen fearfully.

"Let's go on to the castle," she said evasively when they were all remounted.

"No! I want to go home. Father said I could go with him to see Felix and Torr after lunch, and I don't want to miss that," returned Owen stubbornly.

"Then of course we'll return home."

"But what about your memory, Angel?" protested Evan. "What if you never remember?"

"I shall have to make lots of lovely new memories," she whispered, trying to comfort herself as much as him. Again she thought of Benedict Tremayne's striking dark looks and found she was as eager as Owen to return to her parents' quaint rose-covered cottage in the hopes he would be there waiting for her. Her heart raced and she urged her chestnut mare into a smarter pace, realizing how much she had missed Taran's strong presence in the last twenty-four hours.

Benedict Tremayne returned from Falmouth shaking his ebony head in disbelief. How three supposedly educated men could spout such pagan, superstitious rubbish was beyond him. The doddering Mr. Biddles had the excuse of senility, but for the son and Mr. Penrose, two learned members of the bar, to rant and rave about Black Magic, bats, and demons was utterly unforgivable. Not bothering to stop at Taran, Benedict had ridden straight to Dr. Carmichael's house in the village, feeling unaccountably bereft of Angelica's presence. On finding her away from home, he paced backward and forward to Simon's low-ceilinged parlour. He told the doctor about the long frustrating interview he had had with Messrs. Biddles, Biddles, and Penrose the previous evening. His height and the broad width of his virile shoulders were incongruous in the small cottage. He dwarfed everything. For the first time since their acquaintanceship, Simon felt comfortable and relaxed in the agitated young peer's company. Benedict was merely a perplexed man. In his own abrupt way, he was attempting to resolve his life after more than sixteen years of avoidance.

"Did you see a will?" probed Simon, pouring the dusty, harassed young lord a thirst-quenching mug of home-brewed ale.

"I saw a strange bundle of papers naming a certain Devil Tremayne as heir. Who on this green earth would name a poor brat such a way?"

"Godolphus Pendarves was a vicious, ruthless man," hissed Simon. "You are sure the will read Devil Tremayne?"

"On the first two pages it read Devlyn Pendarves, but as I pointed out to those three incompetents, it had obviously and none too adeptly been altered."

"In all other places it was Devil Tremayne?" asked the doctor.

"That's right," confirmed Taran, ceasing his pacing and looking piercingly at the stout man. "What do you make of that?"

"When he was dying Godolphus Pendarves called the boy Devil Tremayne, child of shame," he said softly. "But the housekeeper Miss Peller adamantly denied the child was yours. It was she who used the name Devlyn Pendarves."

"Penrose needs a few lessons in diplomacy, amongst other things. After spending the better part of an hour describing this Devil child as some sort of diabolical creature complete with horns and cloven feet, he had the audacity to remark on the Tremayne family resemblance. It's a wonder that a bifurcated phallus wasn't ascribed to us," remarked Benedict, and Simon put back his head and roared with laughter. "I was also treated to an exceedingly detailed account of Godolphus Pendarves's funeral, which took place in the old family graveyard on the moors. The poor lad apparently recited the Lord's prayer backwards in Latin accompanied by a chorus of bats and an enormous black wolf called the Bucca-Dhu," he laughingly added. Simon's mirth abruptly stopped, but he thought it prudent not to mention that the story wasn't so farfetched. He wondered when Tremayne was going to get to the point.

"Do you think he's my son?" asked Taran sharply, as though reading the doctor's mind.

"As I've told you before, if you were legally married to Catherine at the time of his birth then legally you are the father."

"Forget legality. Do you think the child is from my seed?" Simon gazed into Benedict's beseeching eyes, and the poi-

gnant face of the child flashed into his mind. Silently he
nodded as he superimposed the boy's thick ebony hair and
profound black eyes onto the more mature features of the
earnest young man. Before, Tremayne's face had been harsh
and forbidding, very unlike the sensitive countenance of the
lonely child, but now the man's guard seemed down and his
usual arrogance thrust aside. "I was not sure until this moment," he admitted huskily, wondering what had happened to
soften the commanding lord. At that moment the door was
opened and the younger man's eyes lit up joyously at the
sight of Angelica's flushed, wind-blushed face and tousled
chestnut hair.

"Angel," he whispered hoarsely, striding across the room
to greet her. He meant only to take her hand, but some primal
springtime madness caused her to offer inviting lips and he
crushed her to him, availing himself of her sweet mouth.
Then Owen burst in babbling incoherently about a funeral
procession at Pendarves Chapel.

Angelica shamelessly wrapped her arms about Benedict's
neck and pressed against him, delighting in the male aroma.
The salty scent of sea and sweat mingled with all the perfumes of the dusty Cornish lanes and the heathered moor, to
create a heady, intoxicating fragrance.

Recollecting his surroundings, Benedict reluctantly released
her lips and buried his nose in her sweet-scented hair, trying
to regain his swirling equilibrium as the fourteen-year-old
boy's high-pitched voice dug into his consciousness.

". . . two coffins and organ music that caused the sun to
disappear from the sky and a heavy fret to whirl in from the
sea to shroud everything . . . even the birds stopped singing
and the gulls were silent as they buried their dead and Evan
was seduced by the ghostly music like the mermaids seduce
the sailors with a song," ranted the overwrought youth.

"It was Bach, father. A Bach etude or requiem that I've
never heard before. Truly exquisite. I wish you could have
heard it," described Evan, walking to the piano and trying to
play some remembered notes.

Angelica felt Benedict stiffen. She gazed up at him questioningly and frowned at the intensity of his expression.

"It's nothing to be anxious about. It was just those poor

unfortunate people we met at High Tor,'' she said softly.
Simon and Benedict exchanged solemn looks, causing Angelica to glance suspiciously from one to the other. ''I told Evan
and Owen that they were not apparitions, just poor old
people, so don't you two start any nonsense of ghosts and
spriggans,'' she added feistily, unhappy at the sudden change
in mood. Taran's strong arm that held her so masterfully a
bare few seconds before now dropped away from her, she
stared up into the remote face of a stranger. ''No, no more!''
she decided spiritedly. ''Excuse me, father and brothers,''
she said, hinting that she wished them to leave the room.
Simon nodded knowingly at her and herded the two protesting
youths out, shutting the door.

Taran stared absently out of the window at the glorious
garden where Emily Carmichael happily hoed. His mind was
seething with the thought of his child isolated within the grey
stone walls of Pendarves Castle. Fear had stabbed through
him at hearing of a second macabre funeral on the moors.

''Benedict?'' Angelica broke a long heavy silence after
watching his brooding features. He turned and frowned. ''Share
with me,'' she begged softly. ''Don't shut me out. I have no
memory of a past, but I have promise of a future with you
. . . share with me,'' she pleaded. Benedict silently opened
his arms and she walked into them. She was enfolded so
tightly she could feel his heart pounding. He breathed deeply
and once more buried his face in her sweet-smelling hair,
wondering how to go about explaining Catherine to this precious person who had miraculously come to mean so much to
him.

''I have a son,'' he said huskily, recalling the small figure
on the dark horse who had galloped out of the thick mist on
Christmas Day. ''I saw him once, and he looked so much like
my brother, Michael, I thought I was seeing a ghost.''

''He's the one they call the Devil-Child?'' she asked softly,
and she felt his affirmative nod.

''I must claim him. Somehow make up for all the years.''

''May I help do that?'' The strength of his arms holding
her tighter was the most eloquent answer. ''Why was he kept
from you?''

''That is something I mean to discover, but first things

first. When will you marry me?'' he demanded hoarsely. ''I need you,'' he confessed. ''In every way possible,'' he added, roguishly covering his immense feeling of vulnerability.

''You have me whether we marry or not,'' she said simply, her sea-green eyes filling with tears at recognizing the love-lights that flickered in his. ''But I think the child should be claimed first. May I ride with you to the castle to get him?''

Taran felt so full of emotion he was unable to say a word. He gazed lovingly into her upturned face and then tenderly kissed her. Both of them ignored the persistent rapping and the creak of the door being opened.

''Luncheon is ready,'' snarled Maizie after a disgusted snort of disapproval at such a wanton display of affection.

''For heaven's sake, Maizie, can't you see that they are most pleasantly occupied,'' trilled a chiding voice. They all gaped in stupefaction at Emily Carmichael leaning comfortably on the sill of the open window. ''Carry on, Angelica,'' she encouraged.

Angelica peered over Benedict's broad shoulder at the beaming woman whose cheeks were liberally daubed with mud and whose wild hair sported unconventional adornments—mulching straw and drooping weeds.

''One must honour one's mother,'' Benedict declared, obediently offering his lips to his lady love.

CHAPTER 14

ANGELICA STARED at her shadowy reflection, lit by the warm glow of a flickering lantern as she pensively brushed her hair. In the adjoining bedroom she could hear Benedict pacing back and forth, his riding boots ringing sharply on the bare floor. It had been nearly a week since she had admitted her love by unconditionally offering herself to him in her parents' small parlour, yet there had been no marriage or any kind of intimacy.

It seemed much longer than a week since they had left the cottage hand in hand. They had joyously galloped over the blossoming moor to the dreary grey castle to fetch Catherine's child, but the granite fortress had been impregnable and the return to Taran shrouded by an icy mist that dampened the golden glow that had blazed earlier.

In fact, it seemed a lifetime since Angelica's father had met them on their return at the gates of Taran Park with the terrible tidings of the child's death at the hands of the insane housekeeper, Rebecca Peller. Unable to believe such tragic news, Benedict had wheeled his horse and ridden like a madman out to High Tor, determined to speak with Granny-Griggs. Angelica had sorrowfully followed with Simon. They had silently stood in the dark bedchamber listening to the frail old woman and Torr Pendarves huskily recounting the chilling lamentations that had skirled across the moor on the night he had discovered the crone half-strangled with blood pouring from her brutal head-wounds.

"The Devil-Child and the Bucca are dead," the ancient

hag had weakly concluded, her boney chest wracked by painful sobs.

"And you've had not a word or sign from your brother, Pengelly?" Benedict had demanded.

"None. Jonty must be dead. He'd not allow any to harm thet dark lad 'cept over his dead body," croaked Jago, his throat constricted with grief.

Angelica's eyes flooded with tears, remembering how Benedict's face, gentle and loving for so short a time, had hardened back into the old forbidding lines until he was once again unreachable, armoured in cynical arrogance. She could only guess at the agony that ate into the very core of him. His eyes became hooded, shielding his soul from her sympathetic gaze. Jago Pengelly on the other hand shed tears unashamedly, looking no less a man. Silently they had trooped out of High Tor into the blinding sunshine, and the boyish giggles of Felix and Owen had seemed blasphemous and jarring. She had watched Benedict cock his dark head to one side, listening intently to the youth's boisterous play as though imagining he was hearing his own son's laughter. He had almost run to where the two boys tumbled in the hay with three golden puppies.

"Where the hell did you get those animals?" he had demanded. Angelica, noting his clenched fists, had been alarmed by the violence about to explode.

"The dark child of the moor give them to Master Felix to replace one thet wuz kilt," informed Jago, placing himself protectively between the two boys and the enraged man.

"My son gave those retrievers to Felix Pendarves?" echoed Benedict. His face contracted as though he had been punched sharply in the gut. "My son was at Taran? My son was within reach, stealing my dogs from my very stable?" he muttered brokenly. Without another word he mounted his horse and rode swiftly away from High Tor.

The rest of them had silently followed to the crumbling chapel on an isolated rise of the gale-swept moor.

"My seed lies in that dirt," he had stated, staring at two mounds of newly turned earth in the neglected graveyard. His voice had been flat and emotionless, his eyes hard and dry.

Jago Pengelly had stood beside him, his tears dropping on the unmarked plots.

Leaving the two men to the privacy of their grief, Angelica had moved to join her father, who gazed sadly at a weathered tombstone. She had gasped with outrage at the bitter words that were so deeply gouged in the cold granite, the years of moss and lichen illuminating rather than concealing the hateful inscription. She had been so very sickened that she had been unaware of Benedict's approach until his tall frame had blocked the sun and she had shivered in his shadow.

"Catherine Pendarves. Born 1759. Died 1776.
Beneath this moor, forsaken, wild
Lies a whore and her bastard child.
Pendarves curse the house of Taran
May all Tremayne wombs be barren."

He had read the epitaph out loud and Angelica had felt an aching cramp and had wrapped protective arms about her flat belly. "Seventeen seventy six? More than sixteen years?" he had puzzled, his thick brows knitting as he recalled the chance Christmas meeting with the dark child. "More than sixteen years?"

"More than sixteen years," sighed Simon. "December thirty-first, seventeen seventy-six." The cold stormy night was forever etched in his mind, not because of a birth but because of Catherine's death.

"It cannot be. He was not that old . . . not nearly a man. He was not a strapping youth like Felix and Owen who are two years younger. He was a little boy like Michael . . . slight and narrow," Benedict ranted. "It was misty and I had just a vague glimpse." Angelica had reached to comfort him only to be pushed roughly aside. "Carmichael, take your daughter home to the safety of her mother," he had ordered harshly before striding out of the desolate graveyard. Sadly she had watched him swing into the saddle and gallop wildly over the lonely moor toward the endless grey sea.

Torr Pendarves had shrewdly interpreted her stricken expression as she kept her brimming eyes pinned to the spurts of dust kicked up by the hooves of the swiftly vanishing horse.

"Why, Angelica, you silly chit. I do believe you are smitten with that rakehell," he had chided teasingly, putting a comforting arm about her trembling shoulders.

"You are most definitely wanting in tact," snapped Simon. "Come along home, Angel," he had said.

"My home is at Taran with Benedict," she had stated, stubbornly refusing to accompany her father, hoping that when the initial shock had softened, Benedict would reach for her. But it had been nearly a week and each night she went to bed in the adjoining chamber only to lie sleeplessly, listening to him pace the floor. Each morning she had awakened heavy-eyed to find he had already risen and departed on some business venture. On the rare occasions he was in the house, he locked himself up with Angus Dunbar in the study or sat silently at the end of the long dining table, oblivious to Angelica's presence.

For the last days Angelica had resolutely thrust self-pity aside and concentrated on teaching Iris and several of the cottage children the rudiments of reading, trying to assuage the ache of loneliness.

"Are you alright, Miss Angel?" asked Iris anxiously, watching a tear slowly slide down the girl's smooth cheek. Angelica nodded. "Are you sure?" Angelica nodded. " 'Ere let me draw the curtains so it's more snuggy in 'ere," she decided.

"No, leave them as they are and run along," ordered Angel, blowing her nose and forcing a watery smile. "How's Mr. Dunbar?" she asked mischievously.

"Yer know, I ain't never felt this way about no one before," confessed Iris, following the direction of her mistress's eyes to the connecting door. "So I know 'ow yer feel about 'is lordship, cos I feel the same way. Why don't yer go to 'im? Go on, march in there as bold as brass," she challenged. "Well, what's the worstest thing 'e could do, aye?"

"Tell me to get out," whispered Angelica.

"So what? Yer already out so it'd be the same! Can't lose what yer never 'ad, can yer?" rallied the girl cheerfully, eager to visit Angus Dunbar.

"Oh, yes, you can," replied Angel softly, thinking of the child Benedict had never touched. Iris gave her a strange look, but she waved her away. "Run along, Iris." The maid hesitated for a second and then blew a kiss and darted from the room.

Angelica stood and examined herself critically in the mirror before sighing with discouragement, wishing she were alluringly voluptuous, exuding an attraction that Benedict could hardly refuse. She turned down the wick of the lamp and walked to the wide oriel windows that bowed out towards the moonlit sea. The surf rhythmically surged and there was the occasional haunting cry of a hunting owl that touched a desolation deep inside of her. She looked at the closed connecting door. Benedict's pacing had ceased and she wondered what he was doing in his clean spartan bedchamber. Should she go to him as Iris had suggested? she wondered. Was she strong enough to survive his rejection? she questioned, slipping out of her dressing robe and sitting on the edge of her bed, stroking the soft sheerness of the nightgown he had chosen for her. She kept her eye pinned to the connecting doors, summoning up her courage, hearing the minutes tick by with the pounding of the sea and her own heart.

Resolutely Angelica stood and placing one bare foot in front of the other slowly walked to the door. Once there she didn't know what to do. Should she knock or just turn the handle and march in? What if it was locked? What if it wasn't? What if it wasn't and she walked in to find him undressing, or with another woman? Many, many *what ifs* tortured her mind; she wavered with her hand raised to knock. Adamantly she rapped on the shining wood, stinging her tense knuckles. She gasped when the door was abruptly opened, as though he had been standing just the other side, waiting. She froze, not knowing whether to whirl away or to obey her instincts and fling her arms around his powerful body. She did neither. She just stood poised and vulnerable, her pulses hammering and shaking her trembling frame, gaping at the handsome man who stood in britches and boots, stripped to the waist, his suntanned torso gleaming in the flickering light.

Benedict took an involuntary step backwards and surveyed the vision of the girl who looked ethereal, the rippling moonlight causing an aura about her lustrous chestnut hair. Her long lithe body was silhouetted through the sheer fabric of her flowing nightgown.

"I ordered you to return to your father's house," he clipped harshly, trying to quell the aching tenderness that rose in him at the glorious sight of her.

"And I refused to go," she whispered, thankful that her voice didn't reflect her quivering limbs.

"Why?" he barked coldly, and she swallowed hard, fighting to remain steadfast and not be deterred by his icy stoniness.

"I want to lie in your arms. I want your seed in my womb," she stated bravely, her voice low with a slight tremor.

"Why?" he snarled. "I thought marriage to me was abhorrent to you?"

Angelica opened her mouth, wanting to admit her love for him, but no words came out. He took a step forward, but she raised her hands to ward him away.

"Oh, am I too ugly for you, Lord Taran? Too tall and gawky? All elbows and knees?" she spat furiously, successfully masking her pain with derision. "Of course I am not beautiful enough to grace your bed," she challenged. Taran watched her silently, enchanted by her fiery spirit and the exquisite features that sparked and flared with pain and rage.

"You are very, very beautiful," he whispered softly. He put his head back and laughed delightedly at her sudden confusion. Full of fury and sneering indignation, Angelica had felt cushioned and in control, but with a gentle phrase he had adroitly disarmed her. Once again she stood precariously balanced on the edge of a precipice. She was poised gracefully like a quivering deer, and he could see the rapid pulse in her long swan neck and the frantic swell of her uptilted breasts thrusting against the fluttering nightdress.

"You are very, very beautiful, too," she answered after a long tense pause in which she had ached unbearably, watching the reflected moonlight ripple from the surging sea and seductively limn the strong planes of his chiseled face and muscular arms. "And . . ." Her low musical voice trailed away.

"And?" he prompted huskily, as mesmerized as she, conscious of the sparks that flowed between them, igniting a fire in his loins. "And?" she said again, keeping his dark fathomless gaze pinned to her wide luminous eyes.

"And . . . I love you," she bravely confessed.

"Come here, my Angel," he ordered hoarsely, opening his arms, and without a second's hesitation she ran into them. With an audible cry of ecstatic delight she buried her face into the warm strength of his bare chest, feeling she had finally come home to rest. His arms encircled her, holding her close. She breathed deeply of the male fragrance of him, and he felt her tears trickle down and trickle his taut belly. "How is it you're obedient now?" he asked tenderly, cupping her chin and lifting her face so he could look into her overflowing eyes.

"I shall always obey you when you order me to do things I agree with," she sniffed. Taran laughed and kissed the salty stream that ran freely down her smiling cheeks before capturing her eager mouth.

Angelica murmured appreciatively and returned his kisses, opening her mouth hungrily to the domineering pressure of his tongue. She pressed against him, needing to be as close as possible after the long days and nights of cold loneliness. She revelled in the sinuous heat that throbbed through her sheer garment from his bare skin.

Benedict reined his rising passion, not wanting to frighten her, remembering how she had recoiled from his ardor once before. He tempered the thrusts of his tongue, letting her set the tempo as he teased her pliant lips, but refused to enter the soft recesses of her inviting mouth. Angelica moaned with frustration and writhed against him. He grinned broadly, stilling his movements, eager to see if her newly aroused sexuality could surmount her puritanical upbringing. He breathed deeply to control himself, allowing Angelica's smooth graceful hands to glide over his back and head as she naturally and rhythmically moved against him, her body intuitively knowing the age-old ritual that was mirrored in the ebb and flow of the tides and in their mounting heartbeats. Firmly Benedict put her from him. When her eyes flew open with alarm and he saw the stark fear of abandonment reflected in the sea-green depths that were misty with passion, he groaned and picked her up in his arms. He carried her to the window seat and gently placed her on the fur pillows.

"You are beautiful . . . an enchantment," he admitted

gruffly, trying to soothe away the panic he saw on her bewildered face.

"I did something wrong? I'm sorry," she said, wrapping her cold arms about her bereft body.

"You've done nothing wrong," he reassured.

"But you don't . . . want me?"

"Angel, look at me," he laughed, opening his arms wide and standing before her. She frowned up at his open, smiling face not understanding. Then she followed his pointed gaze down the length of his firm torso. Angelica blushed and looked hurriedly away from his obvious arousal, which distorted the excellent cut of his tight britches, "Oh, my Angel, I forget what an innocent maiden you are," he chuckled, sitting beside her and chastely kissing her forehead.

"I apologize for not being worldly," she remarked stiffly. "But surely that is something a man of your infamous reputation can easily remedy?" she added wickedly, and he gave a loud shout of laughter.

"If you will help me off with these accursed riding boots I shall attempt to live up to my awesome reputation," he bantered. "Or would you prefer I summon Mr. Smithers to help me disrobe?" he added when she looked silently and solemnly at him. "What are you thinking about?"

"I am thinking that I am scared. Oh, not of being hurt this first time, but . . . well, that I have a lot to compete with, being such an innocent maiden and quite out of your usual . . . er, league," she confessed with a tearful giggle. "It's an awesome responsibility. What if I'm a dismal failure?"

"You couldn't possibly be a dismal failure," he comforted. "But I on the other hand could very well be. I am after all the one with the awesome reputation to uphold," he admitted dryly, pulling her into his arms so she cuddled into his lap, feeling the coolness of the night air on his smooth skin. They stared over the beautiful vista of the serene sea in companionable silence.

Benedict rested his cheek on the top of her head and buried his nose in her sweet-smelling hair, feeling that he finally held the promise of happiness within the circle of his arms. He panicked at the thought, his eyes raking the dark cliffs, searching out the arc of moonlit sand at Taran Cove, where his brother, Michael, had drowned. Catherine's execrable epitaph chanted in his mind.

"What is it?" asked Angelica. He sighed deeply and tightened his embrace.

"Are you a witch that you can be so sensitive to each change of mood or thought?" he murmured.

"Please tell me?" she urged, smoothing back a lock of jet-black hair from his furrowed brow.

"Pendarves curse the House of Taran. May all Tremayne wombs be barren," he recited roughly, and Angelica picked up his hands and placed them palms down across her belly.

"It's not a Tremayne womb yet," she said lightly. She shivered at the sensuous waves that radiated out from the warm strength of his intimate touch, which turned her limbs to liquid fire. "We shall prove that odious man wrong," she stated huskily, seductively nuzzling his mouth, trying to coax the grim line of his lips to soften. Benedict resisted for a few seconds and then his hands urgently caressed the soft curves of her breasts, causing her nipples to tingle and harden. He kissed her passionately. Angelica gloried in his arousal, excited at her power. She matched his ardent kisses and roving hands, impatient with the garments that prevented her from connecting with every inch of his hot silky skin.

"Whoa," he hissed hoarsely, remembering her virginal state and trying once more to temper the frantic pace. But she clung to him tenaciously, shamelessly thrusting and rubbing against the core of him. "My boots," he added lifting her in his arms and holding her cradled against his rapidly pounding heart. He carried her across the room and set her gently on her feet. "Now, woman, pull!" he ordered officiously, sitting on the edge of the large bed and extending his foot.

"Yes, sir," saluted Angelica with a chuckle.

"What on earth are you about, you saucy minx," he laughed when she turned her back, hauled up her nightie in a very wanton way, and intimately straddled his lifted leg, presenting a very inviting view of her pert derriere. "Thank you, very much," he murmured roguishly when both tall boots were limply lying on the floor and Angelica panted for breath, flushed and very aroused, still feeling where his broad hands had erotically explored. "Into bed, my love," he said huskily. Suddenly she felt unaccountably shy and quickly scrambled under the covers.

Angelica lay with the sheet drawn up to her small quivering nose, her eyes pinned apprehensively to the ceiling where the evermoving sea was reflected in wavering patterns, hearing the rustle of Benedict swiftly stripping off his britches. The mattress sagged under his weight.

"Regretting your unladylike impetuousness?" he teased, gazing down at her wide eyes, which peered above the sheet. Silently she shook her head, wishing he would take her in his arms, but he seemed content to loom above her, smiling fondly. "Why are you hiding?" he asked, his deep voice warm with barely suppressed mirth.

"I am not!" and with that she threw back the sheet, but kept her eyes diplomatically averted from his lounging naked body.

"You don't need this silly bit of frippery, my pet," he said, sitting her up as though she was a rag doll and expertly divesting her of her nightgown. Angelica modestly crossed her hands over her exposed breasts. "You forget that I am intimately familiar with every inch of you," he proclaimed wickedly, possessing himself of her hands and kissing each of the quivering nipples.

"You are . . . intimately . . . familiar . . . with . . . everything?" she stammered breathlessly, thinking maybe she should display some maidenly outrage at such a titillating revelation.

"I am."

"But . . . you said . . . you didn't," she protestingly panted, arching to connect with him.

"I didn't then . . . but I will now," he stated thickly, and she put all coherent thoughts aside as she was drawn under the hot length of him and his manhood rose throbbingly to claim her.

Much later, Angelica snuggled into the hollow of his shoulder gloriously happy and complete. She tingled and glowed all over. There had been the briefest tearing pain, but it had been inconsequential next to the soaring ecstasy of being totally possessed. She giggled, remembering Iris's sage advice.

"What is that wicked chuckle?" asked Benedict gruffly,

thinking her melodic laughter quite the most beautiful sound
he had ever heard.

"Iris told me that . . . er . . . coupling was most horrid
and that the best thing to do was just lie there and think of
something else and ' 'ope they bloody-well 'urry up,' '' she
imitated. "Maybe I should try that," she added pensively.
"But I am not at all sure it would be possible." She sighed
contentedly as his hand idly ran down the length of her silky
back.

"And what sound is that?"

"A purr," she whispered, stretching her long graceful
limbs like a cat and leaning on his broad chest to gaze
lovingly down at his relaxed handsome face.

"You look exceedingly pleased with yourself," he observed.

"You certainly live up to your awesome reputation," she
remarked mischievously, wiggling her slim hips against his
muscular thigh. Benedict grinned at her, appreciating the
devilry that sparked her green eyes and the seductive curl of
her top lip.

"I think my awesome reputation is rising again," he sighed
roguishly, turning her on her back and pinning her down. She
crowed with delight and moved against him. "Take Iris's
wise advice. Don't move. Think of the weather and pray that
I hurry up," he directed, parting her willing legs and posi-
tioning himself.

Angelica giggled with excited anticipation and froze as he
cruelly teased her, doing lots of tantalizing things without
entering her. Finally she gave a frustrated squawk and bucked
against him, unable to remain passive. He laughed triumphantly and slowly sheathed himself in the pulsating heat of
her, and they both lay still, consumed by the incredible
sensations that built. A furtive rapping at the door caused
them both to start. Intimately joined they stared with amazement at the door to the hall, not sure if they were imagining
the sound. The furtive rapping was repeated and Silas
Quickbody's gruff voice hissed urgently.

"Yer lordship? Yer lordship?"

"It's Silas!" exclaimed Angelica, mewing regretfully when
Benedict broke their loving connection by rolling off her and
leaping from the bed. "What could he possibly want with you

at this time of night?'' she worried, scrambling about for her nightdress and hastily pulling it over her tousled head.

''Whatever it is must be of supreme importance,'' Benedict replied tersely, shrugging into a dressing gown and opening the door. ''What is it, Silas?''

''Sorry to disturb thee but . . . tis thy child,'' whispered the old man gasping for breath.

''My child?''

''Aye. Yours and Miss Catherine's . . . the Devil-Child from the high moors,'' panted the agitated groom. Angelica thrust decorum aside and padded on bare feet to Benedict's side, listening to the disturbed old man.

''What cruel joke is this? The child is dead and buried,'' spat Benedict harshly. ''Have you reached your dotage, Quickbody?''

''Hush thyself,'' chided Silas, frantically looking behind him. ''I don't mean no imperance, sir, but Jonty Pengelly said as how it wuz a secret and that nosey flink Peg Hatch is always fricking about in the shadows sniffing after what don't concern her.''

''Jonty Pengelly, too!'' repeated Benedict dazedly. ''What is this? The witching hour? Are we being haunted by ghosts and wraiths?''

''Come in, Silas,'' whispered Angelica, pulling the old man's sleeve and hauling him into the room, ignoring Taran's thunderous glare at her presumption. She quickly scanned the corridor to see they were unobserved before closing the door.

''None wuz to know save thee and me,'' worried Silas. ''But I'm sure Pengelly won't mind your ladyship knowing. The child is very ill . . . so very ill that Jonty Pengelly fears he will die. That is why he brung him to thee,'' babbled the old man.

''Where are they?'' asked Benedict, curtly climbing into his britches.

''The long meadow behind the farm stables.''

''It's a miracle,'' sniffed Angelica, smiling brightly through the tears that poured down her face. ''A wonderful miracle on a most magical night,'' she whispered softly, gently touching his lean cheek and trying to ease the distrustful scowl. With a deep groan, Benedict pulled her into his arms and held her in a bone-crushing embrace, as fear clutched his heart and churned his guts.

"Get dressed, my love," he said, emotion restricting his throat. Angelica nodded, kissed him, and when his arms dropped away, whirled quickly into her own bedchamber. The two men cautiously made their way out of the dark sleeping house, their eyes flickering uneasily at each creak of the floorboards. Silently they strode through the formal gardens, past the stables to the farm buildings.

"There," breathed the ancient groom, pointing a gnarled finger to the proud stallion who stood like a statue in the long shadows of the meadow. On his high back hunched a wiry old man cradling a still figure whose lean legs dangled down. "Jonty Pengelly, here's Tremayne of Taran," he introduced unnecessarily as Benedict strode towards the still tableau. The stallion snorted and bucked his noble head threateningly.

"Calm thyself, Carrack," crooned Jonty when the horse sidestepped away, his nostrils flaring and eyes rolling white in the moonlight. Benedict ignored the menacing whinny and bared teeth, staring up into Pengelly's lined face. Jonty stared back, scrutinizing the dark fathomless eyes and ebony hair before gazing lovingly into the small still face cradled in the crook of his elbow.

Benedict silently raised his hands, demanding his child. The old man nodded, kissed the glossy head, and released the motionless body so it limply slid into the tall man's offered arms. Benedict frowned and filled with terror at the lightness, thinking the boy dead, but then he felt the great heat that throbbed through the strange black garments. He looked down at the face that rested against his chest, achingly touched by the fine sensitive features.

"Ride for the doctor," he ordered, horror coursing through him at the child's brittle frailness. "He weighs near nothing! What have you done to my son? Have you poisoned and starved him? Has the hatred of Godolphus Pendarves been wrought upon an innocent child? Have you stunted my flesh and blood to fulfill that evil man's curse?" he hissed, fury distorting his face. Angelica stepped back into the shadows of the elms that surrounded the meadow. She was repelled by the venomous bitterness in her lover's voice, yet she noted how tenderly he cradled his child. She saw the tears that glistened in the moonlight trickling down the bent old man's face as he stiffly dismounted from the stallion's high back. The huge horse walked up to Benedict and nuzzled the slight still figure.

"I'll ride for the doctor," offered Silas.

"The doctor has been fetched. Simon Carmichael will be here shortly," informed Jonty gruffly.

Angelica slowly approached and smoothed the unruly black hair from the child's burning face. The delicate nostrils flared rapidly, and the large closed eyes flickered wildly beneath the lids that were heavily fringed with curling lashes. "Bring your son into the house, Benedict," she urged, feeling an overwhelming tenderness at the sight of his large hands holding the child who looked so much like him. Benedict looked at her as though just waking from a dream. He couldn't believe what was within his arms. He nodded silently and they walked across the dewy meadow, followed by the stallion who whickered with alarm.

"Quickbody, stable the animal."

"I ent touching that wild beast, yer lordship," growled the old groom, wiping his tears away on the back of his hands.

"Let the Carrack satisfy hisself that the child is in good hands," said Jonty. "And then I shall see to his needs."

"When my son is settled, you and I have need of a long talk. You owe me an explanation, Pengelly," commanded Benedict.

"Aye, I owe you an explanation," agreed the old man sadly, watching the horse gently nudge the child.

"Carrack," whimpered Devil, and the stallion blew through dry lips in answer before meekly obeying Jonty's whistle and trotting after the two old men towards the stables.

"Carrack," repeated Benedict carrying his precious bundle into the house and up to the back stairs to his chamber. "Strange name for a horse," he muttered, unable to take his eyes from the delicate features. He sat on the mussed bed, lovingly rumpled such a short time before when he had claimed the graceful woman who now knelt beside him stroking the hot, dry cheeks of his child. "He is so frail and small," he cried hoarsely. "What did that evil man do to him? Look at these pitiful wrists," he directed brokenly. He easily circled the slenderness with his finger and thumb and found room to spare. "He weighs nothing at all. What hell has he had to suffer all his life because of my youthful folly?" he sobbed, his tears falling heavily on the inert body.

"This isn't the time for bitter recriminations," Angel said, hardening her tone and hiding her pain at Benedict's agony. "Undress him and put him to bed while I fetch cooling cloths and water to tend his fever until my father arrives," she ordered, bustling into her room to get the pitcher and basin from her washstand.

"Angel?" Benedict's panicked cry caused her heart to leap. Thinking the child had died in his arms, she rushed to him. She stopped in horror, feeling her worst fears were realized, at the sight of him immobilized, staring down at the still child on the bed. His face plainly showed undisguised shock. Slowly she approached to comfort him, sobs bursting disjointedly at each step, furious at the absolute cruelty of life that could cause such unbearable pain—to have a son die twice was unsupportable. "Angel," he croaked hoarsely, and she stared blindly up at him. "Look, Angel," he begged, gesticulating wildly, but she was unable to look upon the dead child. She wrapped her arms about him and held him close, wishing she could ease his suffering while she prayed that his seed would grow in her womb so she could give him another child. "No, look!" he demanded, ripping her arms off him and spinning her about to face the bed. "Look!" he shouted, his voice breaking. "It's not a son . . . . not a boy!"

Angelica stepped forward and gazed down at the child whose shirt was open to the waist exposing newly budding breasts which rose and fell with the laboured breathing. Angelica laughed aloud with the relief of knowing the child wasn't dead.

"You have a very beautiful daughter, my love." She wept and giggled, sitting on the bed and carefully removing the rest of the severe black clothes. Then she covered the girl with a cool sheet.

"A daughter," echoed Benedict with confusion. "The Devil-Child of the moors is a female! Why?"

"Surely you don't think we have our choice of gender, do

you?'' said Angelica softly, gently sponging the hot little face.

"Catherine's daughter," he said bemusedly, searching the still features for some sign of her wayward young mother. "Doesn't bear any sign of her."

"She's your daughter. She looks like you, had you been born female," replied Angelica, ashamed of the jealousy she felt gnawing at her womb, knowing how intimately Catherine and Benedict had been entwined to bring into existence the tiny exquisite girl who lay ill and helpless in the large bed. "She even bears the same sign as you," she added drawing down the sheet to show a shield-shaped birth-mark on the child's shoulder. "Except yours isn't in such an accessible place," she added lightly, mischief curling her mouth as she remembered the distinguishing mark just below his left hip bone.

"My daughter," he repeated, as though trying to get used to the words. "My daughter."

There was a soft rapping at the door, but Benedict stood gazing at the unconscious girl with absolute amazement. Angelica opened the door to her father, who bustled in like a disgruntled bear.

"What's all the secrecy? I'm tugged from my cosy bed by a gesturing mute from Pendarves Castle who waves a badly written note. It's the middle of the night! Are you all right, Angel?''

"Shush," she soothed. "Thank you, Silas," she whispered to the old groom who had ushered Simon up the back servant's stairs like a thief in the night.

"Thet Peg Hatch is up, prowlin' the shadows like a she-cat in heat. So I says as how thee wuz right poorly, yer ladyship, and thet is why thy father es here at this witching hour," growled the old man. Angelica impulsively kissed his stubbly cheek before quietly closing the door.

"What is this intrigue?" fretted Simon as he was led to the bed. He gasped at seeing the poignant little face. "Devil Tremayne, child of shame," he whispered. "He's alive! Who then is buried in the graveyard on the moor?" he babbled, before his professional concern gained the upper hand and he noted the laboured breathing and dehydration of the fevered skin. He threw back the drenched covers and tottered back-ward in surprise. "Not a boy!" he said, amazed. Angelica giggled tearfully and wrapped an arm about Taran's waist. "A little maid! A very, very sick little maid," he added, realizing the scales of life and death were evenly balanced. "We'll have a long battle to bring her back," he hissed, rolling up his sleeves.

The sun rose and set several times before the dangerously high fever finally broke. The dark girl, so small and vulnera-ble in one of Angelica's nightgowns, lay in Angelica's bed, breathing more easily. Iris and Angus, both sworn to secrecy, had taken turns sitting each side of the bed to allow Simon, Benedict, and Angelica time for refreshment and rest. Mrs. Smithers had bustled in and out, Silas Quickbody had guarded the corridor against intrusion by nosy servants, and Mr. Smithers had transported Peg Hatch more than fifty miles to her new place of employment in Devonshire—a friend of Simon's who owed him a large favour, namely his life.

Benedict had to be urged to leave his daughter's bedside. He couldn't fill his eyes with the sight of her; neither, it seemed, could Simon Carmichael. Angelica was puzzled by her father's preoccupation. He gazed down at the petite girl.

"Catherine's daughter? Catherine's daughter?" he mut-tered over and over to himself.

"Benedict's daughter," Angelica corrected vehemently.

"Oh, but Catherine is imprinted there, too," he said dream-ily, recalling the vibrant figure galloping across the golden moors with the sun sparking her fiery auburn hair.

"Catherine is dead," hissed Angelica. Simon recollected himself when he saw the hurt in her eyes.

"Yes, my daughter, Catherine is dead, but she did exist and you mustn't deny that. Don't be jealous. She was a hurt, lonely child who never knew or trusted that she could be loved. You'll hear many sad stories about her wantonness but she was just searching for love and affection the only way she knew how," he explained. "And now her daughter is going to need you to show her how to love and trust, just as you seem to have shown that funny little maid of yours," he continued, nodding his head toward Iris's animated freckled face that gazed adoringly at the Scot.

"I'm frightened for Iris. She really is smitten," whispered Angelica.

"Dunbar is a good man," comforted Simon, patting her arm before crossing the room to confer with Benedict.

"But my Iris hasn't been a very good girl," murmured Angelica, looking thoughtfully at the dour young man, wondering if he would stand in judgment of all the things Iris had done to survive.

"The bedchamber across the hall is ready for the young lady," informed Mrs. Smithers.

"It would be a shame to wake her now that she's sleeping more naturally," whispered Angelica.

"What's the young lady's name?" asked the old housekeeper, looking fondly at the dark girl, noting the distinct Tremayne colouring yet diplomatically making no mention. Iris looked up expectantly, waiting for Angelica to answer, but her mistress just stared with confusion toward Benedict, who stood at the bay window, his eyes pinned to the shimmering sea.

"Well, Miss Angel, what's 'er name?" asked the maid. Angelica shook her head distractedly, unable to use the term. *Devil*. "I'm afraid I don't know."

"But we 'ave ter call 'er somefink," hissed Iris. "What's 'er name, yer lordship?" she whispered, following her mistress's gaze to the tall dark man. Angelica longed to feel Benedict's strong arms encircle her, erasing the hollow dread and aching fatigue. She made a tentative movement but was deterred by the forbidding set of his broad shoulders.

Conscious of the expectant silence and the questioning eyes pinned to him, Benedict suddenly turned, his handsome features harsh and unyielding. He did not know what to call his tiny, dark daughter and to use the name 'Devil' was profane, punishing her still further for his sins. He strode out of the room without uttering a word. The door slammed and the sleeping girl thrashed restlessly, muttering frantically and incoherently.

"It'll be a few days yet before the child is aware, so just call her soothing, loving names," suggested Simon hoarsely.

"It's all right, lovey-ducks," crooned Iris, tenderly dabbing a cooling rag over the anguished little face. "Yer 'ome all safe and sound and there ain't no one goin' ter 'urt yer no more.''

Angus Dunbar's dour expression softened. He sensed that the indomitable street waif was comforting the part of herself she saw in the sick girl.

Angelica allowed her father to usher her from the bedchamber, down the stairs, and into the sunlit fragrant gardens that surrounded the house. They sat in silence as Mrs. Hitchins and several uniformed maids bustled about setting out refreshments on the wide terrace.

"Tes proper peaked thee are, yer ladyship. Tes no wonder thet thy father come galloping here to set you ter rights. Proper leary, thy must be. Thee ent et enough ter feed a sparrow fer nigh on a week now," fussed the cook, believing the tale that it was Angelica who was the cause of all the concern at Taran.

Angelica was deaf to the good-natured, chiding words. She was deaf to the pastoral sounds of buzzing bees and merrily chirping birds.

"You're exhausted, daughter," observed Simon gruffly. "Eat and then sleep. Worries grow too big in a tired brain," he chided, feeling helpless at her deep sadness. "What is it, my Angel? Tell your daddy what ails you," he coaxed, and she turned to stare at him incredulously.

"Tell your daddy what ails you?" she whispered. "Tell daddy what ails you!" she rejoiced, tears flooding her green eyes. "Daddy, I remember! I remember!" she cried, burying her face in his rough tweedy jacket. How could anyone feel two such opposite emotions at the same time, she pondered. "I feel so happy and yet so very frightened and sad," she admitted. "I remember times just like this when I cried and you held me. I remember the smell of your pipe mingled with medicines and heather . . . and sometimes with a little rum. And I remember that you always made me feel better . . . but now you can't. It isn't your arms I need," she sobbed, and his hands fell away.

"You truly love Taran?" asked Simon, trying to quash a pang of jealousy of the tall dark man who had claimed two very precious females, first Catherine and now Angelica.

"Aye, you are all grown up, a woman, not my little girl anymore."

"I don't feel very grown up," she confessed tearily.

"People cannot change all at once no matter how much they want to," stated Simon. Angelica frowned, unsure whether he was talking about the conflicting mixture within her of child and woman, or of Benedict.

"You're speaking of Taran?" she asked softly, and her father nodded.

"You've a right to be frightened. You have a hard road ahead of you, my dear. It would seem that both Taran and his child have had to fend for themselves . . . alone, with no one to rely on, for a very long time. Loving them will not be easy. They'll hurt you, reject you, fight against you, most likely do everything in their power to prove that they do not need your love."

"But they do need my love and I need theirs," sobbed Angelica.

"Are you strong enough?"

Angelica watched Benedict stride toward them, his thick brows knitted together in a menacing black line, In his hollow cheeks was a tense ticking warning of impending violence.

"I am going to have to be strong enough," she sighed, hastily scrubbing the tears from her cheeks. "I have no other choice. I love that man with every fibre of my being."

PART THREE

𝕯𝖊𝖛𝖎𝖑

O woman, perfect woman! What distraction was meant to mankind when thou wast made a Devil!

John Fletcher

CHAPTER 15

DEVIL DREAMED that she was skipping through the cobwebs of foam where the tide lapped gently in the shallows of a secluded beach. Bubbling with joyous laughter, she played with the Carrack and Bucca, who splashed the crystal water into rainbow arcs through which she dived, her skin turning into each tingling colour she touched. It was a gloriously happy dream, brimming with all the pleasures in life. There were no people just plants, animals, butterflies, and fish; everything natural and free from bondage and fear. She was safe, protected in her haven by the towering cliffs that embraced the golden sand and tranquil pool. She was able to exist unafraid and unclothed, to soar with the larks, kittiwakes, and cormorants, to dive through the soft salt water and glide with the porpoise and grey seal. She was free to mount the Carrack's high back and feel his powerful rhythm pound with hers; the loyal Bucca bounding beside her, scattering the pied wagtails and curlews that foraged at the shoreline.

Devil rejoiced with the sunshine that radiated through her whole being, totally submerging herself in the ecstasy, only too aware of how fleeting were such joyous moments. Any second a storm could rend the sky and whip the serene water to an inhospitable frenzy, turning her sanctuary to a place of peril, of murder.

At the thought of death, the sun changed from gold to silver, stabbing javelinlike rays that reflected starkly off the iron-grey manacles that descended with sickening thuds into living flesh. Descended over and over until black rain thickly dripped from a cloud that blocked all warmth. And from behind that cloud sailed the horrendous Blood Moon of the Sixth Seal, casting an eerie glow. And her grandfather's stentorian voice pronounced from the Book of Revelations.

". . . and the sun became black as a sackcloth of hair, and the moon became as blood: And the stars of the heaven fell . . ." Devil winced as her naked shivering flesh was pelted with sharp rocks and the whole earth shuddered and reverberated with the leaden tread of approaching feet. Wrapping her thin arms about herself to hide her nudity, she searched desperately for the mandated black raiment but there was no sign of her clothes. She whistled urgently for the Bucca and the Carrack, but there was no sign of the dark pair. She shouted but her voice bounced off the sheer scarps, returning to mock her. She crouched in the darkness of a shallow cave in the cliff, hearing the ominous tread thunderously shake the soaring bluff above, dislodging shale and rocks that fell with the stars to pierce her cowering nakedness.

Suddenly the raging sea flattened to glass and lifted, reflecting the long line of the Living-Dead silhouetted against the blood-red moon on the perilous cliff path. The four Three-Marys led and Curate Pomfrey brought up the rear, prancing on comical skinny legs as he played a penny whistle. The music was sharp and macabre, the treble piping like the scream of a high wind over the desolate waste. In single file they marched to the very edge of the precipice where one by one without hesitation they stepped off into space to be dashed onto the jagged rocks below.

"No!" she cried, forgetting her nakedness and racing across the shifting sand to where the sea beat its fury against the cruel teeth. One by one the ancient people continued to step off the cliff, and she was splattered by the salty spray of blood. "No!" she screamed, splashing through the roiling water to the limply floating corpses, raising her arms to the sky, desperately trying to break the fatal falls. "No!" she howled to the long line of bent people high above her, but one by one they launched into space and zoomed towards her like enormous crows, their eyes bulging hideously and their gnarled fingers clawing like the talons of a stooping hawk reaching for her as though she were their prey.

''Shame, Devil-Child, hide thy shame! Thou art a secret!''
they screeched. ''Hide thy shame! Thou art a secret!'' they
cawed as one by one they dropped to their deaths.

''No!'' she lamented, trying frantically to hide her nakedness from their bulging eyes and yet stop the mass slaughter.
''I'll take care of you all! I promise!''

''Hush yerself, little lovey, it's just a rotten dream yer
'aving,'' crooned Iris, struggling with the delirious girl, who
battled against her restraining arms. ''Cor, she might look
like a little runt, but she's got an 'ell of a punch. Give us an
'and, Missus Ess,'' she asked ruefully when a small fist
cracked her cheek.

Devil's eyes flew open and she stared with abject terror at
the women who held her down. Her wild struggles ceased and
she froze, her slim body rigid and her delicate nose twitching
like an animal's, sensitive to the alien surroundings. She was
imprisoned by two strangers, and her heart raced painfully as
her eyes searched for a means of escape. Where was she?
Everything was frighteningly unfamiliar. The walls were
coloured and embossed like a fine woman's gown, as were
the floor and other furnishings. Being used to hard unrelent-
ing granite, to Devil the pretty room seemed nightmarishly
unsubstantial, like flower petals able to be dispersed by a
gentle breeze, like a dandelion clock blown away by a sneeze.
She closed her eyes tightly, expecting it all to disappear.

''That's right, little lamb, go to sleep,'' crooned Mrs.
Smithers, releasing her hold and nodding to Iris to do the
same. She smoothed the shining black curls back from the
girl's forehead and placed on it a cooling cloth. Devil kept
her eyes tightly closed but flexed her arms experimentally.
She was free. She fought to calm her frantic breathing, and
she licked her dry lips. Then she pursed them, emitting a
piercing whistle to summon her hound.

''Crikey, she cracked me ear'oles,'' complained Iris, banging the flat of her hand against her head to stop the ringing
noise. Devil lay tensed, waiting for the sound of the Bucca's
large soft paws or a scratching at the door. There was nothing. She whistled again, refusing to believe her dog wasn't
within calling distance. Since the age of seven when she had

first seen the handsome hound and the black stallion swim out of the swirling mist from the Spanish vessel wrecked upon the Wolf Rock, the Bucca had remained by her side protecting her from both loving and hurtful hands. She strained her ears for one sound, but there was nothing, just the furtive whispers of the two strangers.

Mrs. Smithers gazed with compassion at the petite girl, who lay with her eyes tightly closed, a panicky pulse throbbing in her slender neck. The well-shaped little mouth pursed again, and the shrill sound rent her eardrums and the still afternoon air. Again and again she whistled and Iris and the old housekeeper didn't know what to do.

"What is it you want, lovey-ducks?"

Devil opened her eyes. She was still in the delicate fragile room. With one swift movement she thrust the bedclothes aside and leaped out of the bed onto the soft floral carpet. The room whirled as dizziness overcame her. She staggered and leaned against the brocaded wall, her hands splayed in front, warning Mrs. Smithers and Iris away.

"It's all right, little lamb, no one's going to hurt you," soothed the old woman. "Iris, go get his lordship." she whispered.

"Jonty? Where's Jonty?" demanded Devil.

"You wanta see Jonty Pengelly?" questioned Iris. Devil nodded. Despite her fear, she stared curiously at the girl who appeared to be the same age and size as herself, but who spoke so strangely. "Shall I get 'im, too, Missus Ess?" asked the maid, winking mischievously at the wild-haired girl who crouched like a feral creature.

"Best leave all that to his lordship," replied Mrs. Smithers. Devil watched the uniformed maid leave the room. She pressed her thin back against the wall and watched the old woman warily. "Now, why don't you pop back into that cosy bed," coaxed the housekeeper, but the tousled ebony head was adamantly shaken. "Well, then, at least put this on so you don't get a chill. You've been ever so ill," she explained gently, holding up a dressing gown of delicate pink. Devil frowned with confusion at the feminine soft colour. Then her dark eyes widened with panic; still staring at the stranger, she ran her hands frantically down her body, feeling the unfamiliar fabric. She then gazed down with horror at the pretty pink nightdress edged with French lace.

"No!" she howled, doubling up on the floor, trying to hide the revealing garment. "No!" she screamed. As in her dream, she heard the thunder of approaching footsteps. She wrapped her arms about her legs, feeling the ominous vibration shudder through her. What could she do? she panicked. Someone knew the secret and terrible things were about to happen. More terrible than had ever happened before. Nobody else must see, she decided, and quickly crawled under the bed. She curled into a ball to wait for the awful nightmare to end. "Wake up, Devil, wake up," she begged herself.

Benedict heard his child's howl of fear and he increased his pace, unaware that the sound of his racing feet increased the girl's terror. His riding boots jarred through her shivering body.

"Benedict, what is it?" asked Angelica from the door of her room. He didn't answer and burst into his daughter's chamber, staring at the empty bed with amazement.

"Where is she?" he demanded harshly of Mrs. Smithers.

"Oh, my goodness, she's gone," breathed Angelica, following him into the pretty pink room. Mrs. Smithers put a finger to her lips in a plea for silence and then pointed under the bed. Benedict frowned and strode in the indicated direction. Mrs. Smithers shook her head trying to deter him.

"She's terrified, your lordship. Maybe we should fetch Jonty Pangelly," she suggested. "She's been asking for him."

"She's my daughter," replied Benedict tersely. Devil backed far away as she heard the boots approach. She tried to make her petite body even smaller in the darkness as she saw a scowling man regarding her. Benedict's eyes accustomed to the gloom under the bed and he regarded the wide-spaced, terror-filled eyes of his child for a long time, unable to believe that he gazed upon his own creation. Full of aching tenderness he reached his hands towards her, but she shrank away, baring her small pearly teeth like a feral animal. "Out you come, my pet," he ordered softly, but she snarled, covering her fear with savage aggression. He lay flat and wiggled under the bed towards her, and she spat at him like a cornered wildcat.

Devil knew she was no match for the large swarthy man, but she had to fight. As the huge hand reached to grab her, she sank her teeth into his flesh, but he neither cried out or recoiled. He simply curled his long fingers about her bottom jaw forcing her mouth apart as he inexorably dragged her toward him.

"No! You mustn't see! No, 'tis a secret!" she howled, trying to double up and hide her feminine gown and soft curves from his piercing eyes. "No! You mustn't see!"

"Mustn't see what?" whispered Angelica, wishing Benedict would be gentler with the hysterical child, whom he dumped roughly onto the bed, pinning her down when she tried to leap off. Benedict was amazed at the petite girl's strength and tenacity. He gazed down at her, mesmerized by her exquisite perfection as she kicked and spat, refusing to admit defeat.

"There are no more secrets, my child. Jonty Pengelly told me all!" he shouted trying to be heard above her squeaks and grunts as she continued to battle against his strong grip. "There are no more secrets! Do you hear?" he repeated loudly, giving her a sharp slap, which effectively stopped her wild struggles and caused a gasp of outrage from the two women who watched.

"Benedict!" chided Angelica in shock.

"Either leave or shut up!" he hissed harshly. Mrs. Smithers took Angelica's hand in hers comfortingly, and they both observed silently, not daring to interfere or protest Taran's savage intensity again. They kept their worried eyes pinned to the tall dark man and the tiny dark girl, who were locked in a battle of wills. Despite the child's obvious weakness from illness and her much smaller stature, they both had to admit there was an even match of willful Tremayne spirit. Angelica sighed and shook her head, prophetically envisioning a tempestuous future.

"Did you hear what I said?" enquired Benedict again. The poignant little face snarled, acknowledging nothing except the fact that she regarded him as the enemy. "I am your father.

This is now your home," he informed her, tempering his tone even as his fury mounted at her rejection of him. "You are my daughter!" he stated claimingly, wanting to undo the hurt and loneliness she had suffered all her life.

"No!" she screamed, renewing her battle. The pain in her voice caused tears to well in all who listened.

"Yes! You are my daughter!" he repeated firmly.

"No! Hush yourself! No one must know! I'm a secret! It must be a secret," she begged frantically, impotently thrashing her head from side to side in an effort to smother his awful words.

"There are no more secrets. It is all right for you to be a female." Angelica and Mrs. Smithers exchanged mystified looks.

"No! Seal your lips! Grandfather will hear, and if he finds out he'll kill me while I sleep so I don't grow to be a whore like the mother you killed," she wept, chilling everybody's blood. "He doesn't know. He mustn't know. He'll kill everyone for lying to him to save my life."

"He's dead. Your grandfather, Godolphus Pendarves, is dead. He cannot hurt you anymore," comforted Benedict, trying to still her panicky movements for fear she would injure herself.

"Miss Peller said he could reach from the grave to destroy us all!"

"Miss Peller is also dead," he soothed, and at the words the girl lay still, her dark eyes full of terror as she remembered the gaunt woman's brutal death at the hands of the Living-Dead.

"And my Bucca-Dhu is also dead," she mourned. "And all because of me."

"No, no, my little daughter, you've done nothing wrong. None of this was your fault," he crooned huskily.

"Not a daughter! All daughters are whores! All wives are whores! All women are whores! Unto woman God spake thus, 'I shall greatly multiply thy sins. . . . Ye shall eat off the tares and the thistles of the land. . . . A woman's lot shall be one of pain and suffering.' It's in grandfather's Bible. I'm not a daughter . . . Not a female!" she howled.

"Beggin' yer pardon, yer lordship," ventured Jonty Pengelly's subservient voice from the open chamber door. He stood with Iris, whose belly gnawed with guilt and fear hearing the girl's impassioned quotes from the Old Testament. They were brutal words from her own beginnings, words thrown at her mother by a drunken father and then at her by all manner of pious, groping men.

"Jonty? Help me?" cried Devil piteously, reaching out to the only familiar voice and face. Taran turned his thunderous gaze on the wizened old man, jealous of his child's trust and affection.

"Why are you still on my property, Pengelly," he demanded roughly. "We had an agreement!"

"I meant no imperance, yer lordship, but I had to stay 'case the Devil-Child needed me," stammered the black-clad man, deliberately using the unfortunate appellation wanting to see the young man's reaction.

"Don't call my daughter by that abominable name!" he hissed savagely, turning furiously on the old man, who flinched, expecting a blow. Yet Jonty was unable to hide the jubilation in his rheumy eyes, knowing Tremayne of Taran would not only protect his child, but would have the strength to guide her.

"That is my name. I am Devil Tremayne, child of shame," stated the girl hotly, taking swift advantage of her father's loosened grip by twisting out from under his strong arms. She leapt from the bed to race to Jonty Pengelly, who backed away from her, silently shaking his head. "Take me home now . . . please take me home," she begged, but he continued to shake his head in silent refusal even though she beat him with her small fists. "You said we all must be free, yet you'd imprison me with this bastard father who killed my mother!" she spat angrily.

"This is your home now,. my skilliwiddens. No more secrets. No more unnatural life with the Living-Dead," he said softly, his deep voice cracking with emotion. "I was only waiting 'til thee wuz healed 'fore taking my leave, and now I must be off."

"No!" she protested, fury flashing in her dark eyes. "You

may not!'' she added, dictatorially reminding Angelica so much of Benedict.

"The Carrack is fretting hisself something fierce so thee best hurry and get strong 'fore he pines hisself to skin and bone,'' advised the old man, ignoring her tyrannical stance.

"You cannot just go away and leave me with strangers, Jonty,'' she said softly, fear widening her fathomless eyes. "There has never been a time that you weren't near. First my Bucca and now you,'' she intoned hollowly, appalled at the terrible prospect of losing both loyal friends.

"I cannot leave the Living-Dead to fend for themselves. Thy father has generously promised cottages and stipends, but they need me to lead them or they'll just run about in circles, the poor lost souls,'' croaked the old man, tears trickling down his lined face.

"You will not leave me!'' shouted Devil, entwining both small hands in Jonty's black robes. Benedict made a move to wrest her from him, but Jonty raised his hands in a silent gesture.

"Dedn't I teach thee better?'' he scolded. "Dedn't I teach thee to be unselfish? To look to the rights of those weaker than thee? Thee now has a loving family to guide thee to womanhood . . .''

"No!'' howled Devil, covering her ears.

"Aye, womanhood . . . hear it, my little piskey. 'Tis all right to grow to be a beautiful woman. Thee have a father and a new mother, and those pitiful Living-Dead have none but me.''

"I want to be with them, too. I'll help you with them,'' begged the girl, tears finally spurting and spilling down her flushed cheeks.

"Thee have never been a coward. Mop up that weak wetness and bid me good-bye. Glad am I to be rid of such an untamed brat,'' snapped the old man cruelly, belying the softness of his own brimming eyes. Devil's face hardened and her hands dropped away from Jonty. She stepped back and stoically watched her oldest friend turn his back and walk out of her life.

Angelica felt wrenching at her heart, and she longed to

gather the forlorn waif into her arms. As if reading the sympathetic thoughts, Devil snarled, and Angelica shook her head sadly at seeing the familiar menacing glower that marred the delicate features. She turned to Benedict, wondering as she noted his similar stormy expression, if he recognized himself in the frightened feral being who was backed against the wall keeping them all at bay. Had he bartered for his child? she mused, shrewdly sensing he had given Jonty Pengelly an ultimatum. Had he made the old man promise never to contact the girl again in return for food and shelter for the pitiful black-garbed people?

" 'ere, yer silly old thing, pop back inter yer bed, yer as white as a flippin' ghost," cajoled Iris.

"Get to the kitchen!" snapped Benedict, and Iris looked beseechingly at Angelica for confirmation. She nodded silently and the confused maid scurried from the room, her eyes clouded with tears. Devil watched her go and pressed her thin back harder against the brocaded wall, trying to gain courage to face her father's fury. Angelica stared from the girl to Benedict, wishing she didn't have to witness any more painful strife. She was equally disgusted with herself. She felt impotent, not knowing how to break through the crackling intensity that encased them both. She longed to order the sick girl into bed and summarily demand Benedict's presence so she could be informed of all he'd learned from Jonty Pengelly, but she knew this would be futile. She'd most likely be dismissed to the scullery, as Iris had been, for her presumption.

Angelica looked from father to daughter and admitted to feeling very lonely, isolated from them both. Was there any future for her at Taran with the two tempestuous Tremaynes? she pondered sorrowfully. The glorious love, the consuming passion, that had been fired between herself and Benedict was nothing more than a lukewarm memory that had served to torture more than comfort her in the cold nights since. He didn't even know that she had regained her memory. Was he even interested? Would she ever be married? Would she ever lie in his arms again, she wondered, and then she angrily berated herself for her selfishness.

Devil covered her pounding terror with a challenging sneer, wishing everyone would stop staring and go away, giving her privacy to sort through the nightmarish muddle that churned her mind. Her limbs ached and she felt light-headed. She dug her bare toes into the soft carpet where stippled sunlight caused dizzying patterns amid the floral design. Her father's strong arms caught her as she limply sagged and slid down the wall; too weary to fight anymore. She closed her eyes, erasing his forbidding features, and strained to hear the familiar rhythm of the tides, hoping it would lull her into dreamless slumber.

Benedict tucked his daughter into bed and sat gazing silently at her. Angelica hesitated before crossing to him, afraid that he would resent her presence. She sat with his child between them, and quietly they watched the ragged breathing calm until the girl slept soundly. Benedict held one small brown hand in his, examining the perfection of the slender fingers and well-shaped nails. He turned it over and looked at the palm, his eye-brows raising with consternation at seeing the elliptical scar that was deeply etched in the heel of her right hand.

"What is it?" whispered Angelica softly.

"A cicatrix. It looks like a human bite. See the individual tooth marks?" he answered, and she watched his finger trace the two arcs that curved and met at the base of the child's small thumb. Angelica shivered at Benedict's close proximity, smelling his beloved fragrance and aching to be touched by his strong hands.

"Let the poor little lamb rest now," chided Mrs. Smithers, and to Angelica's complete surprise Benedict docilely nodded his agreement. "Mrs. Hitchins has a cold collation set out on the terrace," she added, ushering them into the corridor and firmly closing the door after them.

Without a word Angelica and Benedict walked side by side down the graceful sweeping staircase and through the elegant house to the flower-filled terrace that overlooked the beautiful formal gardens. Angelica stared about, a cynical smile touching her sad face.

"What are you thinking?" asked Benedict warmly, about

to tell her how much her serene presence had meant to him throughout the preceding turbulent days where he hadn't known if his newly found child would live or die.

"I was thinking about all this tranquility. This seeming serene facade," she said bitterly, her graceful hand gesticulating derisively at the house and grounds. Benedict frowned, seeing her green eyes deepen with unshed tears.

"Continue," he ordered harshly, but she shook her head unable to go on. Luckily the appearance of several servants saved her. She took the opportunity to compose herself.

"All these years Godolphus Pendarves believed her a boy?" she asked, thankful that her voice was low and steady when the servants had discreetly retired. Benedict didn't reply for several minutes. He chewed steadily and watched her intently.

"Yes."

"Why? Please explain it to me," she begged.

"Only if you explain your cynical reference to 'a seeming serene facade,' " he replied sternly.

"I think we've had quite enough wrangling for one day. I would prefer a tranquil repast," she said lightly.

"What is it, Angel?" he asked tenderly, and she fought the tears that welled at his concerned voice.

"Damn you!" she hissed, bounding to her feet to storm to the parapet and stare blindly over the rose garden. Benedict leaned back in his chair and stretched his long legs, watching her with narrow-eyed scepticism, somehow knowing she would either sedately compose herself or whirl about and attack with a vengeance. He idly wondered which choice she would make. He acknowledged the odds were even, a trait he found very appealing. "I feel like a lap dog!" she attacked, her eyes sparkling a deep green with the angry tears. "How can you suddenly decide to notice me? Be kind to me? Pat me on the head and strew a few crumbs of attention?"

"I admit to being preoccupied with my sick child," he returned coldly, and she sagged defeatedly.

"I'm sorry. I am being very petty and self-centered," she admitted wearily. "It's just that I wish you would share with me. I feel so alone sometimes."

"At night?" he asked huskily, and she nodded, her tears spilling over and wetting her cheeks.

"Especially at night," she admitted. "And especially in the day."

"Then why didn't you come to me?"

"Why didn't you ever come to me?" she returned after a long pause.

"Maybe because my need wasn't as great as yours," he answered frankly. Angelica turned away so he wouldn't see how much he had wounded her. "I didn't mean that the way it sounds," he amended, sensing her hurt.

"It doesn't matter," stated Angelica resignedly. "You are right. Whatever you meant, you are right and I really don't wish to discuss it further." She busily helped herself to an enormous platter of trout, salmon, veal and ham pie, and other choice victuals, not wanting to meet his eyes.

"Do you propose to consume all of that?" he asked idly, and she was startled to observe the great mound of food before her. He took the plate from her trembling hands, desperately wanting to heal the rift between them. "Angel?"

"Please, don't pity me, it makes me quite uncomfortable. It has always made me quite uncomfortable. Even when I was a little girl, if I ever was a little girl, it made me uncomfortable. I was the tallest plainest girl in the village, and I hated the well-meaning people who—"

"You grew into a beautiful woman," he murmured, hoping to confuse her so he could draw her into his arms.

"Stop it!" she shouted. "Don't addle my brain. Tell me about your child. I don't want your seduction . . . I don't want—"

"You remember!" he rejoiced. "You have your memory back!"

"I have my memory back."

"When?"

"Several days."

"And you didn't tell me?" he reproached. Angelica shrugged unhappily, feeling it more prudent to apologize than defensively remark on his unavailability.

"It seemed relatively unimportant, almost anticlimatic, compared to your daughter. Now, please tell me all about it?" she begged.

"Rebecca Peller lied to Godolphus about the sex of Catherine's child," he stated, after a long appraisal of her. "He died believing that he was denying me a son."

"Why?" Angelica struggled to make sense of it.

"He hated me. You read his words on Catherine's tombstone. 'Pendarves curse the house of Taran. May all Tremayne wombs be barren,' " he recited bitterly.

"But why would Rebecca Peller lie about your child's gender?"

"Godolphus Pendarves hated all females. He needed them, lusted after them, but hated the unholy emotions they raised in him," hissed Benedict brokenly. He turned away, unable to go on.

"I don't understand," whispered Angelica.

"Godolphus Pendarves . . . raped his own daughter! Not just once but repeatedly! Was it any wonder she was as she was? What choice did she have? She could have been cowed and submissive like one of those pitiful Living-Dead creatures or brazenly become the very thing he had called her since she was a tiny little girl . . . whore! Whore! A golden whore to shame him and show him for the foul hypocrite he was!"

"So the Peller woman lied to protect your child?" whispered Angelica, sickened by what she had heard. "To protect her from her grandfather's perversion?" she added when he didn't answer but stared blindly over the gardens, his lean cheek ticking with tension.

" 'Twas not mere altruism! There was an ulterior motive for such a lie! Survival! Those pitiful dregs of humanity knew that if Sir Godolphus died without a male heir, the castle and mines would revert to Pendarves of High Tor, making them not only homeless but bringing to an end a very lucrative smuggling business. With a male heir their futures were secure!" he stated savagely.

"Jonty Pengelly and those pitiful old people didn't appear to be so mercenary or contriving," Angelica ventured to argue.

"Survival can make monsters of us all! It was the Peller woman, mad with power at the helm," sighed Taran, taking a long drink before succinctly and unemotionally informing her of all that he had learned of his daughter's birth and life in the bleak fortress, ending with the brutal deaths and the burial Angelica and her two brothers had witnessed on the moor.

Benedict thrust his plate of food away. All that Pengelly had told him still shocked and disgusted him. If only he had known. He groaned, remembering how he had nearly killed Catherine and her youthful lover with his bare hands. He had come to his senses just in time. Leaving the battered boy of no more than fifteen unconscious in the stable, he had dragged Catherine to the gates of Taran and thrown her out onto the dusty road. It had been the very height of summer, a blazing day in August. The sun had glared off her auburn hair as she posed rebelliously on the shimmering earth, her hands on rounded hips, laughing jeeringly. Her bodice had been open to the waist and her bared breasts were thrust brazenly at him, showing where another's hands had recently fondled. At the time he had hated her with every fibre of his eighteen-year-old being, wanting to grind her brutally into the hot gravel, destroying her tantalizing beauty. But now, after learning the truth about her brief tragic life, he was painfully aware of the terrible agony that her jeering laughter and rebellious stance disguised. "Oh, Catherine, if only I had known," he sighed hoarsely, unaware he had spoken aloud. He refilled his glass and gazed blankly into the effervescent wine.

Angelica watched him, wondering if she should quietly leave him to his reflections. But if she did, would he notice her absence? she mused sadly. "If you had only known what?" she asked courageously.

"I threw her out. I opened the gates and flung her in the dirt. She didn't cry . . . didn't beg to stay . . . didn't beg for forgiveness. She just laughed. Stood up, posed like a whore, and laughed. That was the last time I saw her. Standing outside the gates laughing with the imprint of my hand raised on her cheek," he recounted, his voice deep with self-loathing.

"You were just a boy."

"And she was just a child. A seventeen-year-old girl. A seventeen-year-old pregnant girl. My young pregnant wife. She must have truly hated me to crawl back to her father, begging that monster to take her in after what he had done to her."

"I think she truly hated herself, not you," said Angelica softly.

"Why do you say that?" he asked sharply, thrusting the ghost of Catherine aside and giving her his full attention.

"My mother had a miserable childhood. My grandmother was always eternally youthful. The belle of the ball. She was ashamed of her only child, belittling her with constant criticism and hiding her away. Consequently my mother still hides herself away weaving happy fantasies in the middle of her flower beds, and in winter she concocts rosewater comfits and crystallized violets to comfort herself until spring," explained Angelica shyly. She sighed, remembering her own humiliations at her grandmother's hands.

"Go on," urged Benedict, and she looked at him with confusion. "What has your mother to do with Catherine?" he coached.

"Catherine was raised by a monstrous man who did abominable things to her and yet called her a whore. She must have felt she was to blame. That she caused him to behave so despicably."

"She was a little child of no more than four or five when he started his heinous practices!" shouted Benedict, his rage rekindling just at the thought.

"I used to think the reason my mother wouldn't comfort me when I was hurt was that I didn't deserve it. She would only talk to me when I was happy . . . when I didn't need comfort. I felt it was my fault even though I was a small child. I knew she didn't like unpleasantness, so I assumed I was unpleasant," struggled Angelica.

"Why?"

"I didn't think a parent could be wrong. It was too frightening to even contemplate," she explained. "If I hadn't had Simon for a father to teach me how to love . . ." Her voice trailed away.

"No one to rely on. Having to stand alone," added Benedict softly, remembering how the ground had seemed to slip from under his feet when his brother, Michael, had drowned, how his mother had silently but so eloquently blamed him for the death. Without question he had accepted that blame and the subsequent responsibility for his parent's estrangement.

"So you see, Catherine didn't hate you. She loved you very, very much. Maybe that is why she did what she did. Perhaps she believed the name her father called her and didn't think she was deserving of your love," stated Angelica earnestly, sensing it was of supreme importance that he believe so he could let Catherine rest in peace. "Benedict, I know she loved you. I don't know how I know or why I am so positive, but I do. Maybe I can see the proof in the beautiful child you created together . . . and maybe it's because I love you so very much that there's a part of Catherine inside of me now."

Benedict cupped her passionate little face between his broad hands and gazed into her fervent green eyes for several moments, too full of emotion to say a word. "Will you be my wife?" he managed, and she nodded mistily. "When will you marry me?" he asked huskily.

"When will you make love to me?" she answered, offering trembling lips.

Iris had been hiding in the cool shade beneath a pollarded pear tree furtively watching Angelica and Benedict lunch on the wide stone terrace. Her hot flushed cheeks bore the evidence of angry tears and her mouth was clenched in a mutinous line. Several times her eyes had lit up hopefully when it seemed an argument had been brewing. She was too far away to hear any of the conversation, but she shrewdly read her mistress's agitated gestures. She fervently prayed that Angelica would hurry up and storm away so she could speak with her privately.

In the beginning Taran had seemed the most wonderful place on earth to be, an enchanted refuge where she could live happily ever after, never to be hungry or abused again. But now everything about the estate seemed to mock her. The colourful profusion of beautiful flowers, the rainbow butterflies, and the graceful swans that elegantly floated upon Taran Lake all served to symbolize her awkward unworthiness, all made her feel soiled and ugly. Angus Dunbar was right. She was a common Daisy and not a regal Iris. She was a lonely stranger imprisoned in a beautiful Eden. Even the village with the pretty thatched white-washed cottages made her feel alienated, grubby. The local people looking at her askance, distrust oozing from their pores as they referred to her as a "furriner."

Iris was oblivious to the sturdy Scot who stood several yards away watching her dig her nails into the manicured lawn, furiously wrenching up the short lush stems. A low cry of frustrated rage burst from her mouth when it was apparent that Angelica and Benedict had resolved their differences.

"Talk about decorum! That ain't very proper ter do in front of the 'elp," she snarled, watching them join mouths in a passionate kiss. "Bloody disgustin', if you ask me!" she added derisively when Benedict swung Angelica into his arms and swiftly carried her through the French doors and into the house.

"Nobody did ask you, lass," murmured Angus Dunbar, and Iris was startled, her freckles standing out on her wan little face.

"It ain't nice ter spy on a person," she spat fiestily.

"I was about to remark on that fact myself," he chided, and Iris scrambled to her feet intent on escaping from his presence. His gentle strength confused her, even his scoldings seemed like caresses tingling her blood, yet he made no motion to touch her. The time he had broken her fall, and consequently his arm, was etched hotly in her memory. The firm feel of his embrace, the steady beat of his heart, and the safe clean smell of him had given her a moment of security that she had never experienced before and longed to experience again. Feeling very shy and vulnerable under his gently chastising gaze, she struck an impudent pose.

"So now you've remarked on it," she challenged. "You ain't my boss," she added, disconcerted by his fond warm look. It was as if he could see right through her to the cowering little street sparrow beneath her cockiness.

"Mrs. Smithers is asking for you, lass. She's wie the wee mistress."

"I don't think 'is lordship wants this dirty 'ore around 'is little daughter," she spat, turning away so he wouldn't see the tears in her eyes. But he reached out easily with his uninjured arm and drew her to him.

"What happened?"

"All I did was try to 'elp and 'e jumped down me throat like me bein' around 'er weren't right. 'Get to the kitchens!' he yells, and I 'adn't done a bloody thing except tell the little mistress ter pop back into bed. I ain't a scullery slut no more. I'm an upstairs maid," she wept, and buried her face into his chest.

"There, there, my lassie. The master's just worried about his child. Now she's healing, it seems everything will be back on an even keel," he comforted, stroking her unruly curls.

"Now she's 'ealing I bet I'm sent off like Peg 'atch so I ain't a bad influence around the little darlin'!" she shouted, pushing herself away from him. "There ain't no use in nothin'! I've listened to all the talk and it don't make sense. If it 'appens to one of us, it's all right but let it 'appen to gentry and it's a bloody great crime!"

"What are you talking of, lass?" he asked gently, leading her away from the house and into the orchards, where the young plums, apples, and pears were just taking shape, the petals curling on the grass under the spreading branches.

"You wouldn't understand, yer really like one of them, ain't you?" hiccoughed Iris, thrilled to be in his company, yet feeling hopeless about herself.

"Old Lord Taran, that is Sir Benedict's father, found me in a workhouse in Glasgow. My father was a miner in the Ayrshire coalfields, and that is about all I know of my beginnings."

"But you can read and write and everything!" protested Iris, intrigued at the information.

"You can read," he confirmed.

"I ain't very good. Miss Angel don't 'ave much time these days."

"I have time," he offered.

"Really? You'd 'elp me learn things?" she asked incredulously, unable to believe her ears.

"Really," he laughed, flattered and touched by her genuine excitement. "Now, tell me what's all right for the likes of us yet is a crime for gentry."

"I can't," she whispered, afraid of his judgment when he heard.

"You were talking of rape, weren't you lass?" he said gently, and she nodded, tears spurting and coursing down her freckled face.

"Why is it all right ter rape a poor common thing like me, and it's ever so terrible for the likes of them?" she shouted, trying to control herself. "I don't know what's up with me. It's this place. Softens a person up."

"Rape is never all right." Iris looked suspiciously into his open face and for some reason wanted to drive him away.

"It weren't always rape. I 'ored for money. Well, a girl 'as to eat, yer know," she said flippantly, but she was unable to remain cocky under his steely gaze and once more burst into tears. "It got so that I was a coward. I was so afraid of bein' 'urt, I'd see what they wanted in their eyes and lie down and spread before they could 'it me," she confessed, waiting to see his face darken with disgust. To her horror his eyes filled with tears. "You ain't 'earing me, Mr. Dunbar!" she screamed, not knowing how to deal with the obviously caring man. "I ain't a nice girl, Mr. Dunbar. I'm an 'ore! You 'ear me?"

"I hear you, lass, I hear you," he soothed.

"And you ain't revolted? What's up with you, Scotty? You one of them warped gents who gets 'is jollies in twisted ways?" she attacked. She closed her eyes waiting to be hit, but instead was once more cradled on his chest, her hair tenderly stroked.

"Go wash your grubby wee face and see Mrs. Smithers," he ordered gently when he felt she was in control of her emotions. Iris looked up at him blearily. She sniffed and bit her lower lip thoughtfully, wondering what it would be like to be taken by him. Angus sensed the sudden change in her and followed the direction of her eyes. The air was charged and he stood quickly, brushing the apple petals from his clothes, but she kept her gazed pinned curiously to his groin. She reached out her hand—supposedly to help remove the blossoms—and boldly touched him, her fingers lightly tracing the root of him. He caught her wrist.

"Nay, lassie," he said.

"You don't want me cos now yer know I'm a common 'ore," she spat tearfully.

"Nay, because you're a wee child who needs a little more

childhood and a different kind of love,'' he explained gruffly. ''Now, run along to Mrs. Smithers,'' he added, spinning her around and sending her on her way with a loving pat on her small bottom. He fondly watched her merrily scamper away, blissfully unaware of what she muttered.

''I ain't no wee child, Mr. Angus Dunbar. I felt you rise to my touch. One of these nights yer bloody-well going ter find out what a child I am,'' she planned mischievously, feeling suddenly deliriously happy, delighted with everything she saw and smelled.

CHAPTER 16

DEVIL LAY in bed watching the rippling patterns of reflected moonlight flow across the white plaster ceiling. She listened intently, and hearing nothing but the rhythmic *whoosh* of the outgoing tide on the beach below the towering cliffs, she flung the bedclothes back and swung her lithe legs to the soft carpetted floor. Padding barefoot to the door, she strained her ears and smiled with satisfaction, hearing the noises of the sleeping house, so different from the nighttime scramblings and moans of Pendarves Castle. Many steady alien rhythms, from ticking clocks and musical chimes to gentle sighs and muttering snores, intermingled with the comforting sound of the sea. For the more than two weeks since her cure, Devil had been planning. Each night she explored a little more of the enormous mansion until she was familiar with each corner, knowing who slept where and with whom. She had located a nursery wing and spent many nights examining miniature houses and tiny armies, china dolls and wooden rocking horses, all fascinating and absorbing to a child who had never possessed a single toy. Best of all, she had discovered wardrobes and chests filled with masculine attire. Britches, doublets, capes, and boots in every size from toddling tot to robust youth. To her joy, she now had several changes of perfectly fitted attire that didn't embarrass her or hamper her movement, hidden in her armoire behind the frightening rows of limply hanging gossamer gowns. She had also located a small armoury and was the proud possessor of several small daggers, a large cutlass, and two flintlock pistols.

Each morning Devil had allowed herself to be dutifully

dressed in one of the pristine, fragile dresses that her father insisted she wear, steeling herself against the terror that pounded through her, refusing to look at her reflection in the mirror, deaf to the compliments that flattered her delicate femininity.

Each morning she sat obediently at the long shining table between her father and stepmother, silently eating breakfast, burningly aware of their scrutiny. She kept her gaze on her plate, the sharp clatter of the cutlery tearing into her ears until she ached to scream, shattering the tension.

Each day she visited the Carrack in the meadow. But never alone. She stood mutely between her father and the tall woman, the summer breeze blowing her gown against her body so her new curves were exposed to all eyes, causing terror to churn her stomach. But she kept her head high, eyes pinned to her stallion, wanting desperately to leap onto his shining back, yet afraid he would shy away from the unaccustomed flapping material.

Each day she silently obeyed the demands, and although she felt drawn to the ancient groom Silas Quickbody, and the pert little maid Iris, she kept her reserve, trusting nobody. Her keen eyes and ears took in everything until she knew the intricacies of all the relationships of the people at Taran. She felt a bittersweet sadness at the comical courtship of Iris to Angus Dunbar.

"Now I'm to ride my Carrack," she whispered excitedly to herself when she was dressed in the dark britches and shirt. The night was warm and her feet well-used to the sharpest rocks, so she left the riding boots hidden and slipped barefoot into the carpeted corridor. She stood outside her father's suite of rooms, but there were no sounds. She knew he slept with the tall woman in his arms like every other night. Several times she had crept right into his bedchamber to watch them sleep, feeling a strange mixture of emotions at seeing how intimately they were intwined. Raised to stand alone without cradling arms and never having witnessed human warmth except in the huddled rocking of the black-garbed living dead, she was fascinated by their closeness. She also felt a deep pain, remembering how she often slept pillowed on her giant hound.

Devil thrust aside all sorrowful thoughts, and keeping her

hand firmly on the dagger and the gun in her waistband, she fleetly ran through the sleeping house. Hearing a furtive creak she ducked into the shadows and smiled, seeing Iris tiptoe toward Angus Dunbar's room. When the girl had slipped inside the door, Devil quickly continued on her way, wondering what the dour Scot would do at finding the maid in his bed.

Iris's heart was beating triple time. She leaned back against the closed door, her eyes accustoming to the dimness, as she wondered whether to return to her own room. She chided herself for being a coward, remembering the several other times when she had shivered outside his door not daring to enter. Now she had entered, but could she cross the several yards and slip into his bed? What could he do to her? she fretted, and she grinned wryly in the darkness, remembering the advice she had so glibly given her mistress. What was the worst he could do? Throw her out? Then it would be the same, she answered herself, suddenly forgetting her apprehensions. Full of curiosity, she approached him, eager to see what he looked like asleep.

Iris knelt beside the bed gazing into Angus's sleeping face. His thick thatch of russet hair, usually tidily combed and tied back, was engagingly mussed, giving him a devil-may-care rakish look. Very carefully she drew aside the light sheet and blanket that covered him and slid into the bed. She lay motionless, firmly convinced her thundering heart would awaken him, but he peacefully slept without stirring. Very tentatively she moved closer and although she wasn't touching him, she felt the warmth from his body pulse through her thin night-shirt. She tried to temper her breathing as the small space between them seemed charged and her skin tingled with excitement. Iris edged closer until with a shock she rolled against his nakedness. She froze but he didn't stir, and for a moment she wondered if he was dead. His gentle breathing ruffled her hair, and she relaxed and curled into him, her arm across his chest. For a while she was content just to lie with him, hearing his heart beat comfortingly close to her ear, the soft swell of his chest a lullaby rocking her to sleep.

Iris sighed and closed her eyes, wishing his unbroken arm

would embrace her as her hand ran down his torso curiously. She delighted in the firm ridges of muscle. There was no soft flabbiness or fetid smell that she usually associated with male bodies. She rubbed her nose into the soft warmth of his neck and curled her leg about his sturdy thigh, and he muttered but didn't wake up and her confidence grew. She flattened her palm on the taut planes of his stomach, delighting in his virile leanness and her hand inched down until her fingertips were sensuously tickled by the curls that surrounded his nestled manhood.

Iris watched his peacefully sleeping face when she first touched the most intimate part of him. His nostrils flared and his breathing quickened as he grew pulsatingly in her hand. Rhythmically she stroked, wondering how she could give him the most pleasure. He groaned and arched, caught in a most erotic dream, and she increased the pressure, aroused by his surging excitement. She gazed at his parted lips and without a break in the tempo placed her mouth on his, her tongue fervently darting in and out rhythmically.

Angus's eyes flew open and he lay still, totally aroused but half-asleep, trying to sort through the confusion of wonderful sensations.

"I ain't a child," informed Iris breathlessly. "I'll show yer," she added, her mouth hungrily moving down his chest before circling towards her busily moving hand.

"Nay, lass," groaned Angus, intent on rolling away from her, but she grasped his manhood firmly. Amid the delicious whirling sensations, he feared for himself.

"Aye, man," she hissed savagely, more aroused than she had ever been before and somehow furious about it. "I'm takin' you! This time it ain't goin' ter be the other way around!" and with that declaration her mouth encircled him and streaks of unadulterated ecstasy shot through him.

"Gently, lass," he groaned, wishing he had the use of two hands as her saucy little tongue kept him painfully on the brink. He was trying mentally to control the situation.

"Move!" she ordered dictatorially, reaching between his legs and pushing him up to meet her. "Move," she repeated, but he lay rigidly.

"Let me enter you, lass," he begged.

"I'm raping you," she panted urgently, keeping firm hold of him, her lips desperately milking, her hands rhythmically kneading, her elbows thrusting his legs further and further apart until Angus surrendered to her and strained to meet her ravenous mouth, obeying the pace she set.

Later he lay limply, feeling absolutely drained yet trying to appear severe and censuring, but her pert little freckled face grinned proudly.

"You feel victorious, lass?" he laughed, drawing her down so she snuggled on his chest like a contented kitten.

Devil rode along the beach at Pendarves Point. It was low tide, and leaving the Carrack to roam across the sand, she entered the hidden caves in the sheer cliff below the castle. She whistled shrilly, and there was a sudden flurry of excited activity as several bats fluttered about her, one coming to land on her outstretched hand, where it hung twittering a welcome while she gently stroked its furry little body.

"It's so very quiet," she whispered, wading through the shallow water and pulling herself onto a ledge where she sat, her legs dangling, hearing the ghostly remembrances of the furtive smuggling activities of the past. No word would be spoken, the Living-Dead scurrying to and fro, from shadow to shadow, rolling the heavy barrels in a race against the incoming tide that would righten the beached vessel and take it back out to sea under the cloak of the night. She turned her eyes fearfully to the top of the stone steps expecting to see Miss Peller's gaunt, forbidding figure standing like a statue, holding a burning torch so high it flickered on the sharp angles of her bony face, making her appear demonic.

Devil stood and reached for a torch that was in a bracket on the wall and lit it with the tinderbox hidden nearby. The reflection of the warm flame caused snaking shadows to dance about her as she climbed the steep stone steps to the vast underground room. She sucked in her breath with surprise when something soft and warm pounced from the darkness and rubbed against her legs.

"Malkin!" she exclaimed stooping to stroke the arched back of the cat. "Is Granny near?" she asked excitedly, racing up the steps, but the hearth was cold and forlorn.

Granny-Griggs's medicine pot, incrusted and empty, hung on the hob. The cat mewed piteously, and Devil picked it up and leaned pensively against the healing table, the flat slab of rock where she had first seen a naked man; the golden-haired Sir Torr Pendarves, who now owned the castle and the mines. All but the Old Tarkeel Mine were in the process of being reopened, she knew from conversations she had absorbed. Several times her father had ridden out to High Tor at Pendarves's request to lend his expertise to the venture. Devil hadn't gone because once again her existence was a secret. It was said that the Devil-Child was dead, but she was hidden within pristine pastel frocks; imprisoned within a pretty floral room within the walls of Taran.

Devil put the cat away from her, intent on entering the castle to see what mark Torr Pendarves had put on her childhood home. She listened at the heavy turning-stone that was part of the kitchen wall, and not hearing a sound, she shifted the lever and with an agonized screech, the enormous block of granite rolled away.

Accompanied by the cat and bats, Devil groped her way through the deserted castle. Each stark comfortless room brought to mind the airy, gracious chambers of Taran, and she felt confused and traitorous. She climbed up to the north tower, which had been her domain ever since she could first remember, and there was a welcoming cawing. The ungainly ravens bobbed large heads, hopping heavily from their roosts in the slit windows to the rungs and backs of the uncomfortable furniture. Devil stared over the dark moor before sitting dismally on the hard bed and looking about the inhospitable chamber, the flaming torch bringing no warmth to the grey granite walls.

"This is where I belong," she told herself firmly, fleetly running down the winding steps from the tower. She hesitated outside her grandfather's room, remembering the day he died and how Miss Peller vowed he would reach from the grave if he ever found out she was female. "Can you reach from the grave, Grandfather?" she whispered, not daring to open the door. The cat howled loudly and raced down the dark hallway, its claws scraping eerily on the stone floor. Devil froze, hearing a shuffling step. She stood with the blazing torch held high, bravely facing the approaching wraith who appeared out of the shadows cradling the cat in thin boney arms.

Granny-Griggs shook her old head, her wild grey hair swinging from side to side, as she tried to rid her eyes of the glorious vision of the child. "Oh, Devil-Child, have you come from the grave to avenge?" Devil mutely shook her head, not knowing if the old crone were herself a ghost. "Is thee flesh and blood?" and Devil nodded, tears running down her face and sparkling in the warm torch light. "Can I touch thee?" and again Devil nodded, grinning through her tears when the old hag poked her sharply with a gnarled finger. "Thou are not dead!" rejoiced the woman, blubbering through her toothless mouth. "Thou are not dead, my Devil-Child! I want to hold thee close, but I'm afeared of thy great black pet. Where is the Bucca? Where is that shaggy creature? I don't relish being devoured by him after surviving the Repeller's worst!" chattered the crone, prancing about with delight and peering around for the enormous hound. "Oh, no, say et ent so," she mourned, seeing Devil's silent sadness. "No, no! I heard talk but gave et no credence, thinking nothing could kill that great spirit of the night. Say et ent so, Devil-Child. Tell me the Bucca lives and still protects thee," she begged.

"The Bucca-Dhu is dead!" stated Devil harshly. Granny-Griggs's shoulders slumped, and she stepped back from the girl, sensing any attempt at comfort would be repelled.

"Where has thee been?" she asked after a pause.

"I'm now a secret in my father's house," was the bitter answer.

"Your father? Tremayne of Taran?" gasped the crone.

"He claims that I am dead. He tells all 'the Devil-Child is dead.' "

"Thet is the truth. He does tell all thet thee are dead," confirmed the hag. "Several times a week he comes to High Tor with his new bride, Simon Carmichael's leggy daughter . . . and many's the time he has said that the Devil-Child is no more. Thet is why he's helping young Torr Pendarves open up the mines. All this belongs to him now."

"He claims I am dead, so I obey. All day I am dead . . . like one of our own living dead except instead of the black robes I wear coloured female gowns that cling to my rounded breasts and show the flatness at the cleft of my legs!'' she shouted fiercely, flinging open the door of her grandfather's chamber. "But at night I'll come alive and ride the Carrack across the moors,'' she sighed gently after a fearful pause when she waited for something terrible to happen, but all remained tranquil. "And at night I'll sail a ketch across the sea and come alive with the wind in my face.''

"And I shall help thee, Devil-Child,'' comforted the old crone. "Where are the Living-Dead? Et has been as quiet as a tomb here for more'n a fortnight.''

"Tremayne of Taran drove them away with promises of money and cottages, but I had a terrible dream. Their bodies were mixed with the dark weed at the shoreline, drifting in and out with the tide. Have you sight of it, Granny-Griggs?''

"No,'' the crone shook her head. "I've no sight nor feeling of such, but there is trouble. There's angry men grumbling for their brandy and tes locked in the cellar at High Tor.''

"There's none left here at all?''

"None and the Repeller took monies in advance. Each night I have come here looking for where the greedy bitch hoarded all thet wealth . . .''

"I know where it is,'' interrupted Devil. "You mean to pay back the money and not give the brandy?''

"How's a frail old witch like me and wee runt like you going to carry them heavy barrels out of High Tor from under the noses of Jago Pengelly and the young lord?''

"Jago Pengelly'll not help?''

"He's a changed man since his brother died.''

"Jonty died? But you said you had no sight or sensing of death!'' cried Devil.

"Supposedly he died thet same night as thee. The self-same time as the Bucca-Dhu and the Repeller. Thet awesome night when I was hanged by the neck,'' croaked the old woman, hoarsely rubbing her throat nervously at the memory.

"Jonty didn't die that night. It was he who took me to Taran. It's just another of the lies! My father paid him to take the Living-Dead far away, but I shall find them,'' she promised fervently.

"Thee knows where the Repeller hid the monies?"

A thunderous knocking from below echoed hollowly through the chill stone fortress, stopping Devil's answer.

"Thet must be young Pendarves, and he's seen thy light," hissed Granny-Griggs, looking shrewdly at the flickering torch. "He's been driving hisself mad trying to break into this great plaace," she chortled. "Jonty Pengelly must've taken the Living-Dead out through the caves, leaving this castle locked and barred as tight as a drum," she giggled as they made their way back through the secret passage in the kitchen.

"Are you and Malkin living here all alone?"

"Nay, I'm all comfy-cosy at High Tor. Oh, tes a fine place to spend my awd age now there's a housefull of decent servants running hither and thither to my bidding. Silly twits think I'm a magical witch. They're so afeared thet I'll put a hex on them, I just have to lift my little finger and they fall over theirselves," chuckled Granny. She leaned against her stone healing table and ran a gnarled hand over the cool surface. "Do 'ee remember thet fine figure of a man lying there as naked as the day he was born with a great gaping wound in his thigh?"

"I remember," whispered Devil, remembering the firelight gleam off the golden blond head and play along the muscular planes of the long lean body.

"Little did we know et was thet self-same man who'd rob thee of thy birthright, Devil-Child, Sir Torrance Tamar Pendarves, and t'es him hammering at the castle door as if he was trying to knock et down. Et is best thee should go back to Taran before he spies the Carrack roaming the sand by the caves. Be here by my healing table tomorrow at midnight, and I'll bring thee all the news I can glean," vowed the old woman. "Now, off with thee before the sky lightens, my Devil-Child."

Granny-Griggs watched the fleet dark figure leap onto the back of the Carrack and ride across the moon-touched beach, spraying the salt spume at the water's edge. "T'esn't the end, my awd Malkin," she cackled softly, scratching behind the ear of her one-eyed cat that arched its back and rubbed against her in ecstasy. "Tes a lusty new beginning," she sang, happiness flooding through her, easing some of the heavy old age from her stiff cold limbs. Her toothless mouth curled into a puckish grin as she recognized Torr Pendarves's shining head silhouetted against the starry sky where he sat his horse on the high cliff path transfixed by the dark racing rider on the silvery sand below. "Maybe I will play at a little magical witchcraft and bring those two beautiful young Pendarveses together," she planned gleefully.

CHAPTER 17

"WE'VE OPENED those mines none too soon, Pendarves. I've just received word from London that war with France has been declared," greeted Benedict, effortlessly swinging from his saddle and holding his strong brown arms out to Angelica, who was perched elegantly on her sidesaddle. She laughed joyously, delighting in his possessive grasp about her slim waist. She shamelessly slid down his hard body before he set her on her feet in the walled courtyard at High Tor. She blushed at meeting Torr Pendarves' intense blue gaze.

"War?" he echoed blankly, the dismal news seeming incongruous in the face of the perfect cloudless summer day and the infectious happiness of his two guests.

"Oh, come now, Pendarves, it cannot be a complete surprise. We've been unofficially at war with France, as you are most painfully aware, for more than two years now," chided Benedict, his dark eyes following Angelica as she went to greet her two younger brothers, who were visiting Felix. The three boys were rolling about in the newly cut hay with the retriever pups. Torr flexed his injured leg, his fingers absently kneading the long jagged scar in his lean thigh, remembering the French sabre.

"I was thinking of Ajax."

"Still no word from your brother?"

"I haven't expected one. We didn't exactly part on the best of terms," sighed Torr. The two men strode into the handsome house, and Mrs. Goodie bustled about, her round cheeks rosey from the kitchen where the delicious aroma of fresh baking spiked the air.

"Your housekeeper certainly looks content," remarked Benedict.

"And so do you," was Torr's mischievous reply as he threw his morose thoughts aside. "Marriage has mellowed you, Taran. I wouldn't have believed it unless I had witnessed it with my own eyes. By heavens, you look positively complacent and Angelica is ravishing," he continued, looking out of the library window at the glowing young woman who laughed and played with the rambunctious youth and dogs.

"Take care what adjectives you use to describe my wife, Pendarves," returned Benedict, standing beside him and gazing fondly at his bride. He and Angelica had been married in Taran Chapel, witnessed just by Simon and Angus. Later that same night they had exchanged vows in a more intimate ceremony, alone on the moonlit sand of Taran Cove.

"Which adjective don't you care for?" teased Torr. "Ravishing?"

"I am a most jealous husband and lover," admitted the older man ruefully. "I never thought to confess to such a thing. Be warned, I'll not have my most carefully wrought rakehell reputation besmirched by such sentiments, so keep a guard on your tongue," he joked, turning to the younger man, who stared moodily into space not sharing the light banter. "Is your leg bothering you?"

"No, it improves each day," he answered absently. "Taran, don't think me touched for asking this . . . but . . . do you believe in ghosts or the like?"

"No, I don't believe in ghosts or the like," laughed Benedict. "Neither do I believe in knockers and piskies. What is this about?" he asked seriously, seeing Torr was serious. "Are you having trouble with the miners and old Cornish superstitions?"

"No, 'tis nothing like that. The men are so eager to work that I have more servants here at High Tor than I have use for. The miners' wives and daughters are so grateful . . . 'tis like they pay homage . . . bowing and scraping. That is part of the reason for Mrs. Goodie's self-satisfied grin," recounted Torr dourly. "She now has a veritable army to boss about."

"And what's the other part?"

"She finally wrung a proposal of marriage from Jago

Pengelly. Poor old Jago, he's not been himself since his brother Jonty died," he explained morosely. Angelica, who was just entering the library, frowned at hearing the words.

"Since Jonty Pengelly died?" she whispered, gazing beseechingly at her husband, not wanting to believe him guilty of perpetrating such a ruthless lie. She waited for him to correct the statement, but he remained silent. Angelica was deliriously happy with her marriage in every aspect save one, and that was how he chose to deal with his newfound daughter, who graced their table and company, never conversing except with a slight nod of assent or a silent denial. Angelica had begged Benedict to supply his child with a riding habit, having seen the fervor in the dark eyes when she looked at her proud stallion, but that had been in the first few days after her recovery. Now Devlyn, as her father called her, stared dully, showing nothing of her thoughts and feelings. Angelica had pleaded but Benedict had adamantly refused, stating his daughter was too frail to ride such a lusty animal who had already serviced several of his fertile mares. This had somehow angered him, increasing his trepidation. Angelica had even ventured to enlist her father's professional opinion, but Benedict had furiously overridden the doctor's reassurance.

"Since Jonty Pengelly died?" she repeated, appalled at his cruelty. Even to protect his child there was no justification for such a painful falsehood.

"You are interrupting, my pet," scolded Benedict gently, possessing himself of her gloved hands and avoiding her accusing green eyes. "Continue, Torrance, you were speaking of ghosts?"

"Several times in the last month I've seen lights in the windows of Pendarves Castle, and on my oath, I tell you, I have seen the Devil-Child of the moors riding that great horse across the sand at the point," he stated.

"And the giant hound, the Bucca-Dhu, no doubt bounding beside the demonic pair spitting fire?" ridiculed Benedict, but his eyes were cold and hooded.

"No, there was no hound, just the dark horse and rider. But that is not all—"

"I think it's quite enough!" interrupted Benedict impatiently. "I think you're not fully recovered from your injury, and you've overtaxed yourself in the mines."

"That was not all?" questioned Angelica gently, daring to challenge her husband, who glared at her furiously, an angry tic working his lean, suntanned cheek.

"I did not ride all the way out here to waste my time hearing nonsensical prattle about goblins and ghosts!" ranted Benedict, his black eyes hard and piercing.

"Tell me, Torr?" begged Angel softly.

"Music. I heard the most exquisite music mingling with the sea-mist on the high moors," whispered Torr, his chiseled face mellowing at the memory. "Music, Angelica, that could melt the hardest heart. So incredibly wondrous that I actually cried and by the time I had recollected myself and raced into the tumbledown chapel . . . no one was there. There was one crashing discord and the wail of the air in the organ pipes . . . and the sound of hoofbeats galloping away."

"And yet you had seen no horse grazing in the grave-yard?" scoffed Benedict derisively. "And were there mer-maids combing long weedy tresses, luring you with haunting melodies?" Torr grinned ruefully at him.

"You are right, Taran. I'm insane. It is all this sea air and solitude," he laughed.

"I have heard the music from Pendarves Chapel. So have my brothers, Owen and Evan," offered Angelica, ignoring her husband's exasperated snort. "It was the day we wit-nessed the burials."

"On the very day the Devil-Child and Jonty Pengelly were interred. It was most probably one of those wretched convicts with a musical bent!" stated Benedict, a steely edge of finality in his tone, hoping once and for all, to close the subject.

"God, I am haunted by this Devil-Child," confessed Torr lightly, his short laugh belying the anguish in his blue eyes, unable to admit the horrifying attraction he felt for the dark lad of the moors. In his twenty-three years it had never occurred to him to question his sexual preference. He had a normal healthy appetite for winsome young females and often for winsome mature females but his lust had never deviated to include his own gender. Not even in adolescence, when many of his contemporaries at school had hero-worshipped older males. He had not quite understood their adulation but also hadn't the time nor inclination to ponder it. Now he was in turmoil. He was persecuted, his dreams tortured by a poignant little face, the dark fathomless eyes boring through him. So he rode over the moors at night seeking solace in the stark vista only to be pursued by the ghost of the dead child. Four times he had sat on his horse, hearing the organ music skirl with the sea-frets, wafting from the desolate ruined chapel. Sometimes the music was full of impotent but eloquent rage, building and gathering with the rolling thunderclouds, the chords clashing with the summer storm. Sometimes the pipes blew as sweetly as the falling dew, beads of plaintive melody seeping sadness until he wept for the lost Devil-Child. "The dark child of the moors saved my life. He was on the smuggling vessel that brought me home from France," he said huskily, staring out of the window unable to face Taran's sardonic sneer or Angelica's sympathetic smile.

"And we go on, Pendarves. People die and times change and we go on. We are at war and you have a responsibility to put childhood aside. You are a man, not a puling infant. You are guardian to your own young brothers and owner of several mines," he ranted. "When do you propose to take your seat in the House of Lords?" he asked, abruptly changing the subject.

"House of Lords? I hadn't given it a thought," replied Torr dazedly.

"Well, it's time you did. We are at war and you are in control of a sizable resource that could aid the country," snapped Benedict, knowing he was repeating himself. "Angelica, we should be on our way," he added. She looked at him with concern, having just removed her saucy plumed riding hat and gloves.

"But you were here to go over the books and give me counsel!" protested Torr. "Mrs. Goodie has been preparing a lavish luncheon. We'd agreed that today's visit be in part social."

"My counsel is for you to go to London to claim your seat in the House," he replied curtly, purposefully avoiding his wife's indignant expression. "Let some city life rid you of this country superstition!"

"But the mines?"

"With my man Dunbar and your manager they can run themselves for a while."

"And what of your seat in the House?"

"I leave for London by the end of the week. Maybe you should accompany me!" was the surprising answer, and Angelica smothered a shocked gasp. Benedict ignored her and strode out of the library, nearly colliding with Mrs. Goodie, who ushered in three smartly uniformed maids and two footmen, each balancing silver trays piled high with all manner of delicacies.

"Did you know Taran was off to London?" probed Torr, noting Angelica's sad confusion and impatiently waving the servants away. They obediently deposited their trays and left, but the housekeeper remained in the middle of the room with her dimpled hands placed firmly on her ample hips.

"How is Granny-Griggs?" asked Angelica cordially, not willing to discuss her husband or face Mrs. Goodie's speechless umbrage. She stood in front of a handsome mirror pinning her plumed hat back atop her elegant, upswept coiffure, trying to control her anger and confused hurt.

"Granny-Griggs! Huh!" snorted the housekeeper.

"That will be all, Goodie," snapped Torr firmly, and with another eloquent snort the buxom woman trotted out of the room, banging the door behind her. "Granny-Griggs seems to have found a new lease on life. You'd not recognize the pitiful, half-dead creature of barely a month ago."

"Mrs. Goodie doesn't seem too enthralled," observed Angelica wryly, standing back and surveying her appearance.

"Unfortunately Granny adopted a one-eyed feline with a nasty disposition who sits on the old witch's chest hissing and spitting like water in hot fat. Together they wage war on poor Goodie," he jokingly recounted, but his lean face was taut.

"Granny-Griggs is going to stay here?"

"Granny-Griggs is my link to the Devil-Child. They were together. It is that old witch I have to thank for saving my leg."

"Oh, please, don't mention that to Benedict," Angel burst out without thinking.

"What is it?" asked Torr, frowning at her apparent agitation.

"It's nothing . . . nothing. It's just that Benedict has such impatience with any talk of goblins and ghosts," she improvised.

"And Devil-children?"

"And Devil-children," she laughed dismissively as she pulled on her gloves and avoided his eyes. "Oh, dear, I am so sorry about this botched-up visit. I'm still not sure what happened," she giggled nervously.

"Maybe I'm the one who should apologize with all my silly prattle, but I'm still in a quandary as to why Taran got into quite such a snit," he puzzled, opening the library door and accompanying her through the house and into the bright sunlight, where Benedict waited impatiently astride a high-strung prancing horse.

"Hearing we are at war with France is disconcerting," she offered lamely, trying to excuse her husband's rudeness.

"To say the least," replied Torr dryly, cupping his hands and helping her to mount the chestnut mare.

"Please tender our apologies to Mrs. Goodie," begged Angel.

"I shall," he reassured, watching them ride away. His cerulean eyes were narrowed speculatively, recalling the infectious golden love that had bubbled from them at their arrival less than an hour before. Now there was a brittle coldness.

Angelica and Benedict rode for more than a mile in silence across the blossoming moor towards Taran. He kept his dark brooding gaze averted, and she stared pointedly at his grim profile.

"So you are bound for London!" she finally stated bitterly, not knowing how else to broach the subject of his hurtful behavior. Benedict slowed his pace and turned to face her. He gazed searchingly at her, his dark eyes troubled and confused.

"I have been summoned to court. I didn't mean to inform you in such a brutal fashion, but I was sorely put to test with Pendarves's childish ravings. It is time that young man grew up and stopped mooning about like a halfling. What is done is done, and it is best for all concerned," he hissed harshly, unnerved by the soft reproach he read in her eyes. "Angel, stand by me?" he pleaded, losing his hard arrogance. "I must do what I think is right."

"I shall always stand by you, my love," she whispered. He opened his arms to her and held her against his heart, their horses standing quietly, grazing on the sheep-cropped grass.

"I must have no ghosts and cobwebs holding my child to that abominable past," he muttered fervently against her shining hair, knocking her elegant hat sideways. Angelica kept her peace sadly, knowing no one could legislate memories. "In time I shall reach her, you'll see, and she'll lose that mute detachment and become the joyful child she should be. But she needs time. Time free from those pitiful black-garbed creatures and any other reminder of her suffering," he stated, and she knew he was desperately trying to convince himself.

"Like Jonty Pengelly?" she whispered, and felt him stiffen.

"Like Pendarves's self-indulgent ramblings," he snapped, putting her from him. She knew how much he was wounded by his daughter's rejection and frustrated by her protective silence and defiant docility. "Torr Pendarves didn't grieve as much for his own father's death," he blustered.

"Maybe it is all mixed together, one grief joining to another, releasing aching tears that should have been spent at an earlier time," she said softly, not thinking of Torr Pendarves but of the sorrows still locked within her formidable husband. She instinctively felt his approach to his silent daughter was wrong, but she had no alternative to offer. Every advance she made to Devlyn was silently repelled. All she could do was be a witness to the mute war between father and daughter and wonder if there could possibly be a winner. She continued talking to the girl, sharing pleasurable observances about paintings, and books, hoping to spark interest in the profound hollow eyes, but Benedict seemed to mock his child's rebellious silence, refusing to coax or make any attempt to draw her out of the quiet protection she hid behind.

"When my daughter desires something from me, she will ask," he had snapped after catching his wife's reproachful gaze. "If Devlyn Tremayne desires suitable riding attire, she only has to open her mouth and request them," he had stated challengingly, his black eyes pinned to his daughter. Angelica had observed the answering defiance and had known not to interfere between the two dark Tremaynes. Devlyn was very much her father's child, despite the lifetime apart. There was a strong, unbending spirit in the petite frame equal to Benedict's.

They resumed their ride home at a leisurely pace, and

Angelica wondered if her husband gave any credence to Torr's sightings of the dark child of the moors. She knew that Devlyn could no more be confined than Benedict. Suddenly she realized without a doubt who rode the giant stallion across the moonlit sand at Pendarves Point and who played the organ in the solitary chapel.

"When do you propose to make known the presence of your daughter?" struggled Angelica, not wanting to disturb the harmony between them. "I understand and appreciate your need to protect Devlyn, but isn't keeping her very existence a secret rather extreme?"

"When all the superstitious prattle of a Devil-Child has died down, I shall make it known. Fortunately now with all the talk of war, local people will have better things to gossip about," he sighed.

"And how will you explain the sudden acquisition of a nearly grown daughter?"

"Who will have the confounded impudence to question?" he snapped, and she giggled. "Did that sound very pompous?" he asked ruefully and she nodded. "Well, as you have so often pointed out, my daughter does resemble me . . . a delightful-looking creature, and so the least observant person will be aware of our relationship. Ergo, with my most disreputable past—long before I met you I hasten to add—it will be assumed that any number of shameless woman could have borne her," he quipped roguishly.

"But her age?" protested Angelica. "Even if people are too cowed by your arrogance or too well-bred to ask, even the least observant can add," she returned mischievously. But her green eyes were very serious. "They will know she is Catherine's daughter and Godolphus Pendarves's grandchild."

"Devlyn is a petite girl. She looks much younger than her sixteen years," he replied, and she frowned, uncomfortable with yet another lie. "Don't wrinkle that pretty nose at me, Lady Taran. Trust me?" he begged again, and she smiled tearfully at him. "We have just a few more days of peace together; let's not waste them with furrowed brows and recriminations?" he cajoled.

"Will you have to . . . fight . . . in France?" Angelica finally dared ask the question that had been eating into her, and an icy fear stabbed at his mute assent. She took a shuddering breath and closed her eyes, feeling the mare's plodding gait jar discordantly with her painfully hammering heart. "When?" she whispered.

"Not for a while, my pet," he reassured huskily, seeing the tears seep from under her tightly closed lashes, and reaching to enfold her hand that clenched the saddle pommel.

Devil stood at the attic window watching her father and stepmother ride through the wide gates into Taran Park and up the rhododendron-lined driveway. They rode hand in hand, immersed in each other, her father's booted calf intimately brushing against Angelica's prim knees as she sat facing him, perched on the side-saddle.

"How anyone can ride a horse in that ridiculous position!" she hissed scornfully, furious that they had returned home much earlier than expected.

" 'ow anyone can ride an 'orse in any position," chuckled Iris's cockney voice, and Devil spun about in alarm with a dagger in hand. The maid grinned cockily. "You ain't the only one 'oo 'as to live by 'er wits, yer know," she stated proudly, twirling an equally lethal-looking knife. " 'ere, it's all right, Miss Devlyn, I ain't no tattler. I won't tell on you, honest I won't," she assured, seeing the dark girl's eyes widen and flicker towards the piano that was shrouded with dust-covers in a corner of the attic.

"My name is Devil."

"I'll call you anything you want in private, but I ain't about to lose me job callin' you that around 'is lordship. Your dad'll 'ave me 'ead. I don't think 'e's too 'appy about me bein' around you no 'ow. If it weren't for Miss Angel, I bet I'd be back on the streets or sent off somewhere like Peg 'atch. 'Ere, can't we be friends?" asked Iris, stowing her knife in her garter and holding out her hand. "Really, I won't tell no one, honest, I won't, Miss Dev . . . il," she pleaded, but the dark girl glared at the earnest freckled face with distrust. "Yer right. 'ow can I be yer friend? I ain't nothin' but a common guttersnipe, and you're the daughter of a lord," sighed Iris, dropping her hand.

"I'm the daughter of a whore!"

"It ain't really nice to talk about yer mum like that . . . not when she's dead and all . . . when she ain't 'ere to tell 'er side of it. Sometimes a woman 'as ter do what she 'as ter do just to live, yer know." Iris stalked away.

Devil watched the maid thoughtfully. "What have you had to do," she asked softly, "just to live?" Iris stopped with her hand on the door handle.

"And what if I 'ad?" she snarled, whirling around and challenging the silent girl. Devil shrugged, not knowing what to answer, but her eyes were full of sympathy. "I could've told on you but I didn't! Oh, there's lots I know about you Miss 'igh and mighty Devil! I know you ain't in yer bed of a night!"

"And Angus Dunbar locks you out of his bedroom of a night," promptly retorted Devil, and she was unable to suppress a grin at Iris's look of surprise.

"And if you wants ter get all dressed up like a boy and go ridin' about on that big black 'orse, that's your business, ain't it?" replied the pert maid, recovering herself and chuckling, "'Ere, you and me's a pair all right, ain't we? Same age, same size . . . like we're different sides of the same penny," she giggled.

"Are you paid to spy on me?" Devil spat, pushing away from the genuine affection she felt. "Anything to survive?" she accused acidly. The freckled face hardened, but not before Devil had seen the startled flash of hurt.

"Better clean them smuts off yer face and frock," sighed Iris as she opened the attic door. "Or yer mum and dad'll catch on," she hissed over her shoulder before scampering down the steep narrow stairs.

Devil listened to the receding footsteps, sadly wishing she could trust the vivacious girl. There had been a few minutes when she very nearly had reached out to clasp the proffered hand. She was lonely, lonelier than she had ever been in her whole life, and she had thought she was inured to loneliness. Once more she was a shameful secret, this time in her father's house surrounded by loving couples. Her father and his new wife, Mr. and Mrs. Smithers, even the comical courtship of Iris and Angus Dunbar exuded a genuine caring which made her feel solitary and out of place.

"I am a prisoner," she whispered hoarsely, uncomfortable with her feelings of self-pity and preferring to be angry. She was a prisoner within the walls of Taran, not even able to seek solace with her own horse. She was only free from scrutiny when she furtively stole her freedom, slinking out under the cover of night when everyone slept or sneaking up to the attic on the fifth floor, comforting herself through music. It now seemed both respites could be endangered by her stepmother's little maid.

Devil sighed and gazed out of the window at the moors that blazed with golden gorse and purple-pink heather, towards Pendarves Castle. Why hadn't she felt such bleak loneliness before? she wondered. She frowned, realizing it had never occurred to her to feel lonely, because she had not known any other way of life except to be solitary. She had relied on no one but herself, her only company being the Carrack, the Bucca-Dhu, and any number of wild animals.

"I shall not trust anyone," she resolved, brushing the dust from her pale yellow gown. "I hate Tremayne of Taran," she pronounced, remembering how she had seen herself reflect in her father's dark eyes. "I've always been a shameful secret, but never before a prisoner!" Never before had she been so bound and harnessed. Not even Rebecca Peller with all her threats could control her to the extent her father was doing.

"Miss Devil! Miss Devil!" Iris's urgent whispers from the open door caused her to spin about with dagger in hand. "You was seen ridin' yer 'orse and yer dad is fit ter be tied!"

"You told!" accused Devil, her nostrils flaring with fear and rage.

"Cross me 'eart, I didn't. I ain't even talked ter them. I 'eard 'em through the door. So I pops inter yer dressin' room quick sharp and found where you 'ad 'id yer boy's togs. You ain't too nifty at 'idin' things, yer know. They was in the second place that I looked."

Devil surveyed the panting maid, who clutched an untidy bundle of clothes in her arms. "Why?" she asked.

"We all need a friend. Quick, 'ide them," gasped Iris, ignoring the dagger and heaving them into Devil's arms. "I 'ave to get back so they don't miss me. Don't 'ide them under the piano covers neither cos there was talk about you playing music, too," she added before scampering back down the stairs. She reappeared two seconds later and flung a boot across the room. " 'ere, I dropped this one and you'd better 'urry up cos 'e's 'ollering for you. 'e ain't 'alf angry," she wryly commented before once more disappearing.

Devil quietly descended to the second floor, conscious of her father's raised voice. She was afraid and her heart was hammering. She wished she had the Bucca's shaggy head to touch and give her courage, but she was alone. The Bucca was dead and could no longer walk beside her, protecting and giving comfort. She walked towards her rooms knowing her father was there, terrified that the maid had lied to her or that in her haste had dropped more incriminating articles of clothing. The thought of being a total prisoner unable to mount the Carrack and ride over the moors by the moonlit sea made her stomach churn and her breathing difficult.

Devil stood at the open doorway to her bedroom listening to her stepmother's low melodic voice tearfully remonstrating with her father. From the dressing room she could hear drawers being wrenched open and furniture scraped across the floor. She stood quietly waiting, expecting to hear a cry of triumph when he discovered a weapon or piece of male clothing, but all she heard from his mouth were muffled curses and grunts of exertion.

"Benedict, please stop. This is a violation," begged Angelica.

"This is my house, my daughter," he snapped tersely. Angelica's green eyes were tearful when she stumbled out of Devlyn's dressing room unable to witness any more. She came to an abrupt halt at seeing the small dark figure in the delicate cowslip dress. She read reproach in the black eyes and shook her head helplessly, not knowing how to excuse the rude intrusion.

"I am so very sorry," she whispered and Devil shrugged carelessly, covering her hurt and fear. On hearing Angelica's apology, Benedict stormed into the bedchamber and glared at his daughter, his dark brows scowling and his lips thin and bloodless. There was a long crackling moment and then he strode past her. Devil nearly sagged against the wall with relief but remembering Angelica's presence, she maintained her disdainful stance.

"I'll send Iris to set your dressing room to rights," said Angelica softly, shrewdly noting the faint tremor that ruffled the gauzy skirt of the girl's gown and realizing how truly shaken Devlyn was despite her seeming nonchalance. "There's no need to be afraid of your father. All he wants is to love you and make up for all the years . . ." Her voice trailed away in defeat. She did not know how to reach past the harsh uncompromising expression. The exquisite features were set and the enormous dark eyes hooded, seeming to stare contemptuously through her. "You are so much alike," she muttered sadly, wanting to pull the frightened girl into her arms and smooth back the lustrous ebony hair.

Devil tapped her foot impatiently, willing the tall woman to leave, as once again she felt her resolve weakening. She could trust no one, she told herself. Finally Angelica left, quietly closing the door behind her and Devil thankfully leaned against it as hot angry tears coursed down her face. Nobody had ever dared violate her privacy before. Her comfortless retreat in the tower at Pendarves Castle had been solely her domain, where no one had ever dared to trespass.

"Miss Devil? Miss Devil?" Iris's knuckles, rapped sharply, reverberating through Devil's spine, and she quickly dashed the tears from her cheeks. She walked to the window and stared out at the tranquil sea. "Miss Devil?" hissed the maid, looking about her fearfully, not wanting to be heard calling Devlyn by the forbidden name.

"Come in." Iris slithered into the room and hastily locked the door behind her.

"Cor, that was a close one and that's a fact," she gasped. "You all right?" she asked when there was no sound or movement from the slight girl who stood at the open window, the gentle sea breeze ruffling the dark hair.

"You are my friend?" challenged Devil sharply, suddenly wheeling around. Iris nodded blankly. "Then you must help me."

"I just did, didn't I?"

"Tonight you must be me."

"What! Ride that big black 'orse? Not on yer life!"

"Be me . . . here in this bed. In the darkness we'll appear the same," stated Devil.

"Shouldn't you give it a rest? Aye? Wait until the end of the week when is lordship goes off ter London?"

"He's going away?"

"Yeah, in a few days. Then you can ride yer 'orse to yer 'eart's content," cajoled Iris.

"It has to be tonight."

"Why?"

"I can't tell you."

"Then I can't 'elp you," returned Iris airily, sauntering into the dressing room and surveying the wreckage. "What a mess!"

"It's not my secret to tell." Devil was in a quandary. How could she even attempt to explain the intricacies of smuggling brandy and English soldiers out of France to the little cockney maid who couldn't even sit a horse. What if the maid wasn't to be trusted and it all had been an elaborate setup to gain her confidence?

"You still don't trust me, do you?" charged the maid, and Devil stared at her without answering. "You don't. It's writ all over your face."

"It's not my secret," repeated Devil, thinking of Granny-Griggs, Caleb Skinner, and the other local people who were risking their lives. She silently watched Iris methodically setting the room to rights. "I'm sorry," she added lamely.

"Don't be . . . it ain't no skin off my nose," chanted Iris, covering her hurt feelings.

"We're at war, you know?" ventured Devil, breaking a long brittle silence.

"I've got ears. I 'ear things, too," was the pert reply. The little maid efficiently continued tidying the dressing room while Devil stared moodily out at the sea, watching the gulls wheeling freely in the limitless sky. She wished she could launch herself into the air and fly away from the confines of Taran.

The rest of the day passed uneventfully. Devil sat silently at luncheon and dinner, her eyes pinned to her father's empty chair. Apparently he was locked in his study with sheafs of government papers, in a very bad mood. Angelica and Angus conversed, trying to draw out Devil but she pointedly ignored them, ate her fill, and waited until the interminable meals were over before escaping to the privacy of her own room.

After the evening meal Devil sat dejectedly on her bed as the sky darkened over the sea. She wondered how she was going to ride the Carrack to signal the smuggling vessel dressed in her elegant evening gown, or in any of the fresh virginal frocks in her dressing room. She jumped at a sharp knock and the door was abruptly opened by Iris, who quickly locked it behind her.

"What do you want?"

" 'ere, take yer togs," hissed the maid, thrusting a bundle of clothes into Devil's arms.

"Why?" asked Devil as she hastily wrenched off her grown and petticoats and clambered into the tight trews and jerkin.

"I dunno," shrugged Iris. "If we're caught I'm the one that'll be deported or 'anged," she lamented, pulling one of the delicately embroidered nighties over her tousled head. "Oh, it's ever so soft and pretty," she sighed, stroking the silky material and dancing in front of the mirror. "Yer ever so lucky. All them lovely clothes and this great big 'ouse. Can you read and write?" she asked suddenly, and Devil giggled and nodded. "So can I. Angus, Mr. Dunbar, that is, says I'm a very quick learner."

"Shush," warned Devil, her keen ears hearing approaching footsteps. "Hide," she ordered, recognizing her father's gait. Iris scampered into the dressing room as Devil pulled a nightie over her stableboy's clothes and leaped into the bed, pulling the covers to her chin. She tried to even her breathing, not responding to the soft rapping. She frowned in the darkness, hearing a strange scraping, and then she understood the sound of a hard object falling to the carpeted floor. Key was inserted in the lock, dislodging the other. The door was softly opened and she felt his presence. He stood for several moments staring down at her, and then he strode away, stopping to retrieve the other key before leaving and locking the door behind him. She listened to his footsteps recede before sitting up and staring with dismay at Iris, who padded dismally out of the dressing room. As the freckled girl's mouth opened to lament, Devil silently put a finger to her lips in a bid for silence. She swung her legs out of the bed and tiptoed to the window, staring thoughtfully at the ornate ledge that ran the

length of the house. If she could make her way to an unlocked window, she was free.

Iris's eyes were as round as saucers and both hands were
crammed into her mouth to stifle her nervous squeals as she
watched the lithe girl lower herself out of the window. She
remembered her own fall from the hayloft, but that had been
a mere stone's throw compared to the yawning precipice of
three stories plus the sheer cliff that dropped straight to the
sea.

"Get into bed and cover your face so just your dark hair
shows," directed Devil. Iris nodded numbly but kept her
frightened eyes pinned to the small figure who edged agilely
along the narrow ledge. Only when she saw Devil shimmy to
safety through a window did she relax and clamber into the
soft bed.

Even though Devil yearned to sit astride the Carrack and
gallop over the moors, she deliberately avoided the pasture
where he spent the hot summer nights, reasoning that her
father was most certain to check on the stallion's whereabouts. Remembering how he had callously invaded her privacy she slipped into the stables and helped herself to her
father's spirited stallion. Silas stood in the shadows watching
the girl, a smile creasing his weatherbeaten face. He was back
twenty years, privy to young Benedict's nightly rides. He
nodded his appreciation of the girl's expertise in handling the
enormous horse as she guided him silently along the grassy
border of the yard, then giving him his head when they
reached the high cliff path.

"I tedn't see a thing, did you, Sheba?" he chuckled softly,
patting the large retriever.

CHAPTER 18

THE WEEK before Benedict's departure for London sped by too rapidly for Angelica, who desperately tried to grasp each precious second of his presence, but those seven days positively dragged for Devil, who chafed against her confinement. Much to Iris's relief, the dark girl had curtailed her nighttime activities, and now they sat glumly playing whist or chess to while away the long evenings.

Devil shuddered, remembering her two narrow escapes on the night she had taken her father's stallion; she shivered, recalling the masculine scent of Torr Pendarves's strong body. At the onset everything had gone routinely. She and Granny-Griggs had signaled the vessel and guided it safely through the teeth of Wolf Rock and into Pendarves Cove, where Caleb Skinner and some local men had quickly unloaded the brandy. It had been later, up on the high moor, as they were rolling the barrels up wide planks into the wagons, that a furtive scuffling and the whirring wings of disturbed grouse had alerted them to the presence of approaching revenue men. Quickly they had cut the ponies loose and dispersed across the wasteland, hunkering in the wet heather or behind stark boulders. Devil had raced through the darkness, stopping short as a tall figure loomed before her. It had been Torr Pendarves, so close and yet not touching, the space between them quivering. She could smell the heat of him steaming from his night-damp clothes. The shouts of the revenue men boomed across the moor, and she had waited breathlessly, her dark eyes imprisoned by his. But he hadn't betrayed her, nor had tried to detain her when she had recollected herself, regretfully tearing her gaze from his and making her escape. She had felt bereft.

Luckily a sea-fret had blanketed everything, and the band of disgruntled customs men had dispersed without discovering the half-loaded wagons. It had taken several hours to round up the grazing ponies and finish the job. All the while, Devil had been haunted by thoughts of Torr Pendarves, wondering if he watched their illegal activity. The sky had been lightening when she wearily returned to Taran; lightening with a pale promise of the infinite blue of his eyes; lightening with a pale promise of the sun-gold of his thick hair. Dreamily she led the purloined stallion into the stable and was about to rub him down when she heard the distinctive sound of her father's stride. She hid under the prickly straw, listening to him autocratically bellow for his grooms.

"What the hell is going on here!" he had roared, seeing the lathered condition of his fatigued horse.

"I wuz about to give him a grooming, your lordship," wheezed Silas. "I just brung him in from the meadow where he was frollicking," lied the old man, and Devil was astounded. "He has spring in his blood. He has to show that Carrack who's the boss about here. He's jealous of his mares," he had improvised in the face of his master's obvious disbelief.

Devil was certain that her father could hear her rapidly beating heart in the ensuing silence. She had no need to look to know what was happening. For all his faults Benedict Tremayne was no fool and from the sounds, she knew he was checking his mount, examining the sandy hooves and feeling the stiff salt that had dried on the horse's coat.

"If that little devil has even dared to . . ." he hissed.

"Dared to what, sir?" pronounced Silas innocently.

"This horse has been ridden hard," he had accused.

"This horse has been covering some mares. Showing off his oats," insisted the old groom. Benedict had made no other comment but silently selected another steed. "You can come out now," hissed Silas when the furious hoof beats had died into the distance. Devil had stood up and frowned into the wrinkled weatherbeaten face, not understanding why the old man had protected her. "Quick, into thy bed, Skilliwiddens, and don't break thy neck falling from that high ledge," he had growled, and her eyes had filled with tears, remembering Jonty.

"Young wild things have to learn to trust slowlike," she had heard him mutter as he started to curry the exhausted stallion.

Devil now stood at an upstairs window watching her father's departure for London. His large brown hands cupped his wife's face and he kissed her long and lingeringly before mounting his impatient horse.

"I wonder what a kiss feels like," she mused, softly running her fingertips across her lips and thinking of Torr Pendarves's chiseled mouth.

"Depends 'oo yer kissing," remarked Iris sagely. "Well, 'e's off at last," she declared when Benedict finally galloped down the long driveway followed by two grooms and a carriage.

Angelica stood on the wide stone steps of Taran feeling her own gently bruised lips, which still tingled from the last possessive kiss, watching until Benedict was out of sight and the dust had settled. They had spent the night in each others arms, loving each other almost desperately as if they might never lie together again. A wonderful bittersweet night where she had reached new heights of ecstasy and consequently new depths of fear knowing that in the morning he'd be gone. At one point she had fallen asleep only to be awakened by a terrible dream in which she saw Benedict's body lying in a pool of blood. There had been a shadowy figure bent over it, seeming to be prostrate with grief, the shoulders shaking uncontrollably with weeping. When she had neared, Isabella Bonny had raised her painted face and tears of merriment streamed from her eyes, muddying her thick mascara and dropping onto Taran's lifeless body. Angelica had pressed against his warm nakedness, reassuring herself of his reality.

"Lady Isabella Bonny will never hurt you again," he had comforted after hearing the cause of her distress.

"Will you be seeing her when you're in London?" she had asked tremulously, hating her jealous insecurity and expecting to incur Benedict's impatience. Instead he had kissed away her fears and informed her that Isabella Bonny had fled in her fury to Florence, unable to face the ridicule of her friends at court. Any other questions she might have had were brushed aside as once more he showed her how much he would miss her in the proceeding months.

Angelica thrust her sadness aside and gazed up at the window, where Iris and Devlyn stood side by side. She smiled fondly at the two dark waifs. It was time to put her plan to work, she decided, marching purposefully into the house.

Devil dutifully listened to her stepmother, unable to believe what she was hearing, yet carefully keeping her expression blank.

"Well, what do you say, Devlyn?" prodded Angelica after a long silence. "I am sure you'd appreciate your freedom. All I ask from you is your mornings, and then the afternoons and evenings are yours to do with as you wish."

"And what does *he* say about it?" enquired Devil roughly, scrutinizing Angelica's face for signs of cunning and deceit, finding nothing but genuine caring.

"I am sure your father would approve of his daughter learning how to dance, how to paint pictures of the sea and the moors, to appreciate literature and fine art . . . and *music*." She stressed the last word pointedly and smiled frankly into Devlyn's stubborn little face. "It is truly wonderful that you have so many accomplishments, some of which I hope you'll teach me, but you are also a beautiful young woman with a long exciting life stretching before you . . ."

"Teach you what?" interrupted Devil. "What accomplishments?" she asked suspiciously.

"I understand you are an expert marksman with both pistols and throwing knives. In this time of war I think it is an admirable accomplishment especially with the men away from home," replied Angelica.

"I didn't tell on you, honest I didn't," protested Iris when Devil spun about and glared accusingly at her.

"Iris didn't tell me anything. Your reputation is widespread."

"My reputation?"

"The Devil-Child's abilities are legendary," said Angelica gently.

"Am I still a secret?"

"I am afraid so. It is something I very much regret, yet I cannot go against your father's wishes."

"Then how can I have my freedom?" challenged Devil.

"The same way that you've apparently always had it."

"Furtively hiding in the shadows? . . . disguising my sex?" the girl spat bitterly, and Angelica shrugged sadly.

"I'm so sorry but maybe in time things will change," she whispered, wishing she could hug the defiant little figure who glared out of the window at the brightly coloured flowers that bloomed in the hot August sun. "Do you realize that we are having a conversation for the first time?" she added with a rueful giggle.

Many conflicting emotions muddled Devil's mind. Part of her wanted to reach out and trust Angelica, yet she was afraid. "I don't want you to get into trouble because of me," she finally stated. "I seem to get lots of people into trouble without meaning to," confessed Devil remembering Minny-Pinny's burnt arm, Felix's dead hound, and Miss Peller's vitriolic fury.

"Your father wants what's best for you, and if you're . . . er . . . discreet with your freedom, he can only be pleased and proud of your other accomplishments," struggled Angelica, knowing she walked a perilous line between the wavering girl and her husband.

"Proud of Devil Tremayne, child of shame?" she derided. "Is that why he keeps me hidden like a guilty secret?" Angelica splayed her hands helplessly, unable to find appropriate words. "Proud of me? Why? Because inadvertently I was able to do what he wanted to do with his bare hands?"

"What he wanted to do with his bare hands?" echoed Angelica.

"Kill the whore who had disgraced his noble name!" spat Devil, and Angelica shook her head sadly. She hadn't expected to have an easy time with the wild solitary girl but she also hadn't expected to be posed such lacerating questions. "Is that why I am hidden? Because he is proud of me?"

"He's never been a father before. He's doing what he genuinely feels . . . is in your best interests," pronounced Angelica, choosing her words carefully.

"How does he know my best interests? He doesn't know

me! If I found a baby bat or baby mouse, I would have to understand what I had found before acting in its best interest or I might think it a fish . . ."

"And put it in the water and drown it," interrupted Iris, enthralled with the conversation.

"But Devlyn, you're not a bat or a mouse or a fish," reasoned Angelica gently. "You are a person."

"To him I am just the whore Catherine's child!"

"No! That's not true! You are *his* child!" defended the tall woman hotly, putting aside her gentle patience.

"Right! Just like a bat or a mouse or a fish! *His* child, not me! Labelled but not known!" shouted Devil in frustration, struggling to explain her feelings.

"Did you give him a chance to know you?" challenged Angelica. "Yes, he's autocratic and overbearing, but you were equally uncommunicative. Did you want him to know you?"

"No," answered Devil frankly. "I was afraid to."

"I know. I think you were both afraid," sighed Angelica. "So you agree to my plan?" she asked after a long searching pause. "I don't want to mold you into anything. I just want you to be able to choose. . . . I want to share with you and learn from you and maybe let you have a little more childhood," reassured Angelica, smiling tenderly at the defiant little face.

"That's what Angus Dunbar said to me," offered Iris eagerly.

"I haven't been a child for a long time," stated Devil.

"You had a lot of people to take care of." Angelica thought of the pitiful band of old frightened people.

"Where are they? Do you know?" demanded Devil. She had desperately searched through her father's desks and the sheaves of papers in his study for some clue to Jonty's whereabouts and found nothing. Angelica shook her head. "I think it only fair to tell you that in the afternoons and evening when you give me my freedom, I shall be looking for them. I shall find Jonty Pengelly and the rest of my family," she vowed.

"You don't need me to make bargains for your freedom especially with your father away," stated Angelica.

"I know," answered Devil defensively, unable to admit that she found something intriguing about her stepmother's proposal. Many nights she had crept into her father's study and examined his books. Poetry, prose, and drama filled the shelves instead of dreary legal tomes in Latin. Works by Homer, Seneca, Ovid, Montaigne, Shakespeare, and many other great authors were lined from floor to ceiling instead of the dusty religious theories of her grandfather's library. It had been like finding a treasure. "I will spend my mornings with you . . . but only if Iris is with me . . . not as a servant but an equal."

"What?" exclaimed the astounded girl.

"I agree," shouted Angelica with delight.

"Not just in the mornings but forever . . . for always. To sit at the table with us . . . to be dressed as we are . . . to have a pretty room next to mine and sleep in a sweet-smelling bed as we do. To be my sister," declared Devil, looking fearfully at the astonished girl. "If she wants to be. Iris, please be my sister?" Iris didn't say a word but burst into noisy tears, her thin chest shaking with grateful emotion. Devlyn hesitated a moment and then awkwardly patted her shoulders.

The following months raced by. Angelica missed Benedict terribly, although every fortnight or so a messenger arrived with an extravagant present and a tender love note. She wrote him amusing letters, carefully omitting facts she felt he might have difficulty understanding being so far away. She knew if he could witness the incredible change in his beautiful daughter, he would not condemn her for countermanding his orders and allowing Devlyn freedom to resume her old way of life. She trusted that given free rein, Devlyn would eventually balance the old with the new, selecting what suited her. Already Angelica, along with the rest of Taran, marvelled at the incredible change in the dark girl. The wary, silent defensiveness had dropped away and an enchanting elfin young woman had emerged, delighting all with her amazing musical ability, her quick intelligence, her compassion, and whimsical sense of humour. There was still a reserve but that just added to her charm.

Angelica had also omitted informing Benedict of her newly acquired skill with duelling pistols. She giggled nervously, wondering what his reaction would be if he could see the three of them high on the moors in one of the abandoned quarries practising their marksmanship; or helpless with laughter trying to teach Iris how to ride a horse. Iris had also flourished. At first she had been ill-at-ease and fidgety at mealtime, not knowing which utensil to use. She had nearly collapsed into her food as she bent over her plate, trying to hide her embarrassment from Angus Dunbar, knocking over water and wineglasses in her nervousness to impress.

It had been a wonderful two months, marred only by Benedict's absence, and there was a bittersweet realization that his very absence had helped both Devlyn and Iris. Now Angelica wished he would hurry home to see the miraculous emergence of two beautiful young women.

Summer passed in a blaze of glory as did autumn. Frost spiked the air, sparking the crisp colours of bracken and maple. Devil galloped over the moor, her lithe legs pressed into the Carrack's muscular girth, enjoying the stinging cold that ruddied her cheeks and teared her eyes. Her lustrous ebony hair streamed behind, longer than it had ever been before. Miss Peller had always insisted that it be hacked off to her shoulders and neatly tied in a masculine style but now it reached half way down her straight back. The past months had been more wonderful than she had ever dreamed. So wonderful it frightened her. She had never been acquainted with anyone her own age before and had never really had a strong friend. Jonty had been a benign parent and Miss Peller and her grandfather harsh dominating presences. The only human friends she had had were those older and weaker than she. She hadn't known that time could pass so happily and quickly. There had been no bleak loneliness gnawing at her. Often the mornings had stretched clear through until sunset, and she had felt free and relaxed in the company of Iris and Angelica.

Devil was so lost in thought she failed to hear Jago Pengelly's wagon trundling along the winding dirt road until it was nearly upon her. The Carrack snorted through dry lips and pranced sideways. There was a stunned moment as Jago reined sharply and his heavyset cobs halted their plodding gait. He shook his head in disbelief and sat unable to make a move, staring with stuperfaction. The Carrack reared, pawing the air before leaping over a stone wall and galloping away, with his small rider bent over the arched neck. Jago resumed his steady pace back to High Tor not knowing if the rider had been a figment of his imagination. The child appeared different, he realized. The exquisite little face was elated and vibrant, the hair flowing free and long. If he hadn't known better he would have sworn he had seen a beautiful young woman in boy's clothes. He angrily shook the notion from his head, deciding he had seen just what he wanted to see. If the Devil-Child was alive then there was hope that his brother also lived. But he had seen the two graves with his own eyes in the cemetery at Pendarves Chapel.

Devil's heart was racing with panic. Instead of leaving the Carrack to roam the sandy beach of the point, she carefully guided him through the shallow waters and into the cave beneath the castle cellars.

"What happened?" hissed Granny-Griggs, shrewdly noting the girl's heightened colour and furrowed brow.

"I was seen by Jago Pengelly," she confessed.

"Could've been worse," remarked the old woman. "Jago Pengelly I can deal weth. The poor chap's been dipping into the rum since his marriage to thet foreign cook at High Tor. Folks'll think he was tiddley. But I do wish thee'd give some thought to getting him to work weth us. 'T'would make everything a mite easier," she suggested. "Was just a thought," she snapped impatiently when Devil shook her head emphatically.

"It would cause trouble for Angelica. She's to have a child and I'll not have her in trouble with my father because of my indiscretion when she's been so good to me."

"We could swear Pengelly to secrecy and weth Torr Pendarves off in London . . . ?" wheedled Granny, thinking it would be so much more convenient having transportation to and from High Tor of a winter night.

"No!" shouted Devil. She wished she could confide in Jago, tell him his brother was alive, so together they could find him, but just the thought made her feel disloyal to Angelica.

"We need all the help we can get," grumbled Granny. "Caleb Skinner received word from Major Forester. We hev to hide several Englishmen and ferret them over to France."

"Hide Englishmen?"

"Spies, they be."

"When?"

"Caleb'll get word to Silas Quickbody," replied Granny.

"Silas?"

"And thet old man is near eighty if he's a day. We need Jago Pengelly, he's but a mere fifty."

Devil rode back to Taran, her mind humming with all that Granny had told her. That Silas Quickbody had been inducted into their small band surprised her. She thoughtfully entered the dark stable after leaving Carrack in the high meadow to graze in the moonlight. The bitch Sheba thumped a heavy tail in welcome, and Silas Quickbody hobbled out of the shadows.

"Granny told me that you'll have word for me," she whispered.

"We all hev to do our part now the younger men hev marched off to war. Makes me feel useful . . . puts youth back in these creaky bones," he chortled.

"Have you word for me?"

"Wont hev for days, maybe a week. So get thee to thy bed, Skilliwiddens, and catch up on thy beauty sleep."

"Do you know where Jonty Pengelly is?" she demanded suddenly, and the old man silently nodded. "And you won't tell me?" The grey head was regretfully shaken. "Jonty is happier than he's ever been, knowing thee is growing into such a fine young lady."

The following days passed with much excitement as Iris and Angelica pored over baby patterns eagerly planning the wardrobe for the expected child. Devil tried to get into the spirit but was distracted by the impending excursion to France. She was the only person fluent in French, and it would be the first time going without Jonty and the Bucca. She sat at the piano idly playing, not realizing how eloquently she was expressing her fear and excitement. She was so immersed she was unaware of Simon's entrance until she looked up in confusion to see him with an arm about Angelica and Iris, listening to her playing.

" 'Ere Dev, that ain't . . . I mean isn't very 'appy music," reproved Iris. " 'Ere, Doc, 'ave a look at what I made all by my self."

"Very nice, my dear," praised Simon, examining the tiny, lopsided dress that the girl proudly displayed.

"Are you sad?" asked Angelica, and Devil grinned, shrugged and proceeded to play a mischievous reel to reassure them.

Torr Pendarves rode through the ornate gates of Taran and up the long driveway, his warm breath misting the frosty air. He reined in his horse, hearing a melancholy melody wafting through the thick rhododendron bushes and over the manicured lawns of the enclosed park. A melancholy melody like the music of the moors that struck an aching chord, bringing to mind the elusive elfin spirit that continued to haunt him. His horse sidestepped impatiently, the hooves crunching the gravel, and Torr guided the animal to the grass, not wanting anything to mar the plaintive sound. Suddenly the music changed to a whimsical reel, and he urged his mount into a bracing gallop toward the imposing mansion, most eager to meet the musician who could conjure such magic.

Torr Pendarves paced the wide central hall as Mr. Smithers took his calling card up to Angelica in the small salon on the second floor. He was frustrated at hearing nothing but his sharp boot steps on the polished marble floor and unaware of the dark eyes that gazed down on his bright golden head. He looked up sharply, hearing a rustle on the stairs, but saw nothing.

Torr strode into the sunny salon and his eyes rested lingeringly on the open piano.

"Who was playing?" he rudely demanded without greeting either Angelica or Simon.

"And I'm delighted to meet you, too, Torrance," laughed Simon.

"I beg your pardon," replied the young man ruefully, shaking Simon's proffered hand and turning to survey the glowing Angelica. "When is the blessed event? Or is it a break of etiquette to ask?"

"Benedict got my letter? He knows?" squealed Angelica excitedly, not expecting it possible.

"I don't know if he knows, but it is certainly very obvious to me," laughed Torr.

"You mean I'm fat?" squawked Angel indignantly, turning this way and that, scrutinizing herself in a mirror.

"You are radiant . . . glowing . . . Madonna-like," explained Torr.

"You should have been a doctor, young man," chuckled Simon.

"Actually, it wasn't so hard to surmise," remarked Torr, indicating the patterns for baby clothes and the tiny garments strewn about. "However, Taran asked that I deliver these to you. Actually he told me to give them to Angus Dunbar," he informed, his eyes narrowing. He remembered how adamant the man had been about his not delivering the packages in person.

Angelica gazed with disappointment at the two parcels. One very large and the other tiny. "Just these?" she asked wistfully. Torr laughed and withdrew several letters from his pocket. "Well, aren't you going to open them?" he mourned mischievously when Angelica held the envelopes against her cheek. She breathed deeply as though to detect some essence of her absent lover. "Not the letters. Of course those should wait until you have absolute privacy, but could you not open the parcels? I haven't received a present for so long. I'm positively dying of curiosity."

Angelica laughed and tucked the precious letters down her bodice so they nestled close to her heart. "Which one shall I open first?" Torr indicated the tiny box, and she undid the wrappings to find an exquisite little heart studded with emeralds. Simon fastened the delicate gold chain about her swanlike neck so the jewelled heart dangled intimately in the valley between her breasts and her eyes mirrored the verdant green gems.

"I have never seen a man so happily entrapped. He was quite boring to be with. No longer is he the dashing man-about-town but quite literally a stick-in-the-mud. Work, work,

work . . . politics, politics, politics. Even the Prince of Wales is complaining,'' lamented Torr roguishly.

"Benedict's in trouble in court?'' fretted Angel, knowing how disastrous it was to incur royalty's displeasure.

"No, no, the Prince is too busy with his latest flirt, Lady Jersey. Poor Mrs. Fitzherbert has been cast aside yet again.''

"Lady Jersey!'' exclaimed Angel. "Isn't she the wife of the master of the horse?''

"The Prince is keeping everything under his own roof,'' quipped Torr.

"And to think that is the calibre of the man who'll one day rule this country,'' mourned Simon disgustedly.

"It's even worse. The Prince is in such debt that he tried to sell the palace library to the Czar of Russia. Fortunately he was caught before it was a fait accompli. The latest ondit is that Parliament promises to pay off his debts if he consents to marry his cousin, the Princess Caroline.''

"And how did you fare in London, Torr?'' asked Angelica mischievously.

"How I fared is not a polite subject for delicate feminine ears,'' he countered, thinking wryly of his round of rollicking parties.

"You do look rather lean,'' remarked Simon dryly.

"Debauched and dissipated, don't you mean, Doctor? But now I am back to the clean pastoral life to live like the proverbial monk,'' sighed Torr. "Open the large parcel, Angel,'' he directed, wishing to change the subject. He had spent three months in the pursuit of sybaritic pleasures, mostly in the company of the heir to the British throne. He had awakened each new day with a blinding headache in a strange bed with various beautiful, voluptuous females. But he had remained haunted by the poignant little face and the profoundly sad eyes of the Devil-Child.

"Oh, how lovely,'' whispered Angelica, lifting the lid from the box and gazing at a burgundy velvet riding habit. She smiled tenderly and stroked the soft fabric, knowing how well it would look on Devlyn.

"Granted it is exquisite, but it's really not suited to your colouring,'' remarked Torr, eyeing the deep red material and her chestnut hair. "Doesn't look your size, either," he observed, frowning at the narrow width of the shoulders.

"As you yourself stated, Benedict is very busy these days. Work, work, work . . . politics, politics, politics," laughed Angelica, hastily replacing the lid. "Tell me, when is he coming home?"

"He sincerely hopes he'll be home for Christmas. That's less than five weeks," he comforted, seeing the bleak look in her eyes. "I think that we should join our households for the festivities. Get the youngsters together—"

"What do you mean?" asked Angelica. "What youngsters?"

"Your brothers and Felix," replied Torr. "Is anything wrong?" he added, noting her agitation.

"Wrong? Why, what could possibly be wrong? I'm just tired," improvised Angelica, relieved that he knew nothing of Devlyn.

Torr Pendarves rode back to High Tor wondering at Simon and Angelica's strange almost inhospitable behaviour. He had not been invited to luncheon nor offered any refreshment, which was very unlike the Carmichaels. The more he thought about his brief visit, the stranger it seemed. Both Angelica and Simon had seemed very ill at ease and extremely evasive when he had asked who had been playing the piano. They both abruptly admitted to having been practising and at further urging both had blushed rosily with embarrassment and declined to play for him. Then there was the riddle of the burgundy riding habit. Why on earth would Benedict Tremayne, whose taste was universally known to be impeccable, purchase such an unflattering colour for his adored wife?

Lost in thought, Torr guided his horse out of the gates of Taran, nodding curtly to the keeper, who clanged it shut behind him. Suddenly he reined and stared back along the driveway towards the imposing house, sensing he was being watched. But he saw nothing and heard nothing except the gatekeeper's feet shuffling back to his cottage. He wheeled his steed about, urging him into a brisk canter up the sharp incline to the moors, his mind puzzling through the series of events since returning to Cornwall the previous day. He had arrived at High Tor very late to find Jago Pengelly sleeping fitfully at the kitchen table beside an empty rum jug. When he had shaken the man awake, Jago had started ranting wildly about the Devil-Child turning into a beautiful mermaid. He had attempted to help the hallucinating man to his bed, but the chamber had been barred from within. Goodie's voice had informed him in no uncertain terms what he could do with her brand-new but inebriated husband.

"Enough of fairy tales," Torr roared aloud above the whine of the winter wind on the desolate grey moor. He had more important things to occupy his mind than an uncivil reception and a drunken steward. Namely to coordinate a covert operation that would make use of local smuggling vessels in order to transport English spies into France. He had attempted to reenlist into his old regiment, hoping to serve his country and find his brother Ajax, but he had been informed by a Major Forester that he would be more useful aiding the very organization that had saved his life. "Caleb Skinner," he muttered wryly, wondering if Dr. Simon Carmichael knew how his ancient caretaker was occupied in his spare time.

Devil and Iris watched Torr Pendarves canter away from Taran.

" 'bout time 'e come home to take care of 'is own business so Angus'll 'ave more time for me," declared Iris. " 'ere, why 'ave you got that funny look on yer face?" she probed, noticing how Devil's eyes clung to the blond horseman.

"Here you both are," said Angelica, walking into the room. "It's lunchtime."

"Good, I'm starved! Ain't you coming, Dev?"

Devil silently shook her head. she had been so content, almost complacent, and Torr Pendarves's unexpected visit had shattered the illusion. Having to hide so her presence was not discovered had shaken her newly found composure. She realized she was caught in a sickly-sweet trap; a seductive haven that could eventually rob her of all her defences. She was like a wasp crawling into the honeypot. If she wasn't careful, soon she'd fall in and be unable to extricate herself.

Angelica and Iris watched the subtle play of emotion cross Devlyn's fine features, and they exchanged worried glances, recognizing the stony expression.

"Iris, run along to luncheon. Poor Father and Angus are patiently waiting, and I'm sure we can hear their stomachs growling from here." Iris gave Devil an impulsive hug and scampered off.

"If I wasn't a secret, Torr Pendarves would be sharing your luncheon," Devil baldly stated.

"That's right," was the soft answer. Angelica knew it was futile to prevaricate because Devlyn would know and be hurt and insulted. "But it is not your fault."

"I need to be away from here." Angelica nodded her understanding and ached for the pain and desolation she saw in the wide haunted eyes.

"Be patient with us?" she whispered, sensing the girl was slipping out of touch. "Look, that is for you," she exclaimed, spying the large dress box that had been placed on the bed. "It is from your father. Open it. See what he has sent," she begged. "Look, Devlyn, look, it's a riding habit. His way of giving you permission to ride," she chattered, shaking out the velvet garment and holding it up for inspection. There was no reaction except for a hardening of the stubborn little face. Angelica sighed and draped the habit across the bed. She longed to pull the stoic girl into her arms, but she knew Devlyn would just stand stiffly submitting to the embrace. "Please take care," she said softly.

Devil closed the door firmly after Angelica and stood staring into space for several minutes hearing the decisive click of the latch repeating in her head. It somehow symbolized the barrier that separated them. She realized she could never fit into the pattern of their lives without causing pain to them and herself. It was too late. She was grown. She was formed. She was a woman.

She stood in front of her mirror and slowly unbuttoned her gown, watching detachedly as it slid down her lithe body exposing the firm but gentle curves. She unlaced her chemise and it fluttered to the floor. She stepped out of the mound of frothy lace, keeping her eyes on her completely naked body. She was a woman, not a child. She was a woman and the knowledge did not frighten her; in fact it made her feel powerful. She grinned conspiratorially at her reflection as she pulled on the tight riding britches that hugged her lean hips and thighs and stamped into her high boots.

"I am a woman," she whispered, thrusting her bare breasts towards the mirror. How would a man react to her? she mused. How would Torr Pendarves see her if she stood before him like this? she wondered, remembering his naked body as it glistened in the leaping firelight. It had appeared so virile and yet vulnerable. "He is a man," she stated thoughtfully, slipping her brown arms into a boy's shirt and lacing a tight jerkin across her tingling breasts so the sensuous curves were concealed. She had witnessed the lusty mating of birds and animals in the wild, and had observed how her father and Angelica slept intimately curled in each other's arms. She felt the sexual tension that throbbed between Iris and Angus Dunbar. She tried to imagine what it would feel like to have Torr Pendarves's strong hands stroking her bare skin as they lay together. Lost in thought, she absently tied back her thick hair and crammed a woolen seaman's cap onto her head. She stepped back and was startled to see herself so transformed from the sultry siren of a few minutes before. She flung a dark cape about her shoulders and thrusting away all fanciful thoughts, she cautiously made her way to the stables.

"There's bin word from Caleb Skinner, and I hev unease in my bones about et," grumbled Silas, leading the Carrack out of his stall. "Thet Major Forester from the admiralty has sent an outsider to organize us. Organize us!" he repeated disgustedly. "For hundreds of years us Cornishmen hev been organizing ourselves very nicely."

Devil didn't pay much attention to Silas's furious mutterings; she was too absorbed in her own brooding thoughts. She agilely mounted her horse, and deaf to the old man's admonishments about avoiding the smuggler's cave at Pendarves Point until they all had time to assess the new man, she rode towards the cliff path.

Silas shook his head dolefully, wondering what had occurred to cause the girl to revert to her silent ways. Gone was the enchanting pixy who had brought sunshine to the dreariest day with her ready smile and lyrical laughter. Back was a dark, brooding stranger whose eloquent defiance warned all to stay away.

Devil gave the Carrack his head and they galloped across the sand, splashing through the shallows of the incoming tide towards the caverns beneath Pendarves Castle. The sky and sea mirrored her morose yet furious mood as the storm clouds gathered and darkened.

Torr Pendarves shook his blond head in stunned amazement as he stared about the enormous cave. Granny-Griggs cackled with glee, knowing he recognised the vast underground room.

"And thet's where thee lay in thy all-together," she chortled, placing her one-eyed cat on the cold stone slab. "There on my healing table weth thet great gaping hole in thy leg."

"And the hearth was ablaze . . . the flame shining on the wet rock walls," he intoned.

"Could do weth a hot hearth now. This damp chill aches my awd bones something dreadful," she complained, picking up her cat and cuddling it close for warmth.

"When do the others get here?" he demanded roughly, thrusting the memory of the dark youth and the enormous hound from his mind.

"Thee den't recall the Devil-Child and the Bucca-Dhu?" probed the old woman wickedly, shrewdly noting the tightening in his lean cheek. "Thee den't recall the claiming mark thet thee left on thet perfect little hand?" Torr glared at her without speaking. "Thee den't recall the sweet taste of thet young flesh?" she whispered, and he ran his tongue across the cutting edge of his teeth, tasting the tang of blood.

"When do the others get here, old hag?" he repeated harshly.

"When they gets here," chuckled Granny-Griggs. "Fact I hear someone now," she added. Torr strode to the head of the rough-hewn steps in the sheer rock that led down to the water just as Devil rode the Carrack through the fissure of the cliff. There was a still moment when their eyes locked; each was incapable of movement. "Night meets day. Sun meets moon," sighed the crone, delighted in how each young person complemented the other.

Devil couldn't believe her eyes. There on the top of the stone steps where Miss Peller's forbidding figure used to loom stood Torr Pendarves. The silence crackled between them, joining with the gathering thunderclouds. Lightning slashed over the churning sea, flashing off the waves, jolting her out of her stunned inertia. She wildly wheeled the Carrack about, knowing that she must escape before it was too late.

"No! No, Devil-Child! Don't go!" shouted Granny-Griggs. Devil's hands tightened on the reins, confusing the great stallion, who pranced around and around, panicked by the ferocious storm and his young rider's fear and indecision. Torr strode down the steep steps, keeping his intense blue gaze pinned to the wide dark eyes.

"Get back!" snarled Devil, pulling her ragged thoughts together and aiming a cocked pistol at him.

"Best obey the Devil-Child," chortled Granny. "I ent in the mood for healing, and if thee take a step closer there's apt to be blood spilled." Torr gazed at the gun pensively and leaned nonchalantly against the granite cliff.

"Why have you betrayed me?" demanded Devil savagely, trying to stop the trembling in her voice. There was something about the man's searching, steady eyes that jumbled her emotions and she blushed, remembering her sensuous fantasies.

"I hev never betrayed thee, Devil-Child," snapped Granny indignantly.

"Why is he here, then?" she cried brokenly.

"Would thee believe thet he's the man sent by the English admiralty now thet Jonty Pengelly . . . has . . . er, gone. Besides, my pisky-child, this is his land," wheedled the old hag.

"You are my cousin Catherine's child?"

"And what if I were the whore Catherine's spawn?" challenged Devil.

"Then this would be your land, and I would be guilty of appropriating your mines," replied Torr casually, intrigued by the slight figure on the nervous stallion. There was something about the lad that disturbed him. "How old are you?" he barked after doing a quick calculation. His cousin had died nearly seventeen years before, and this small boy could be no more than thirteen from the puny size and unbroken voice. His fifteen-year-old brother Felix was much taller and huskier.

"I am obviously not your cousin Catherine's spawn," lied

Devil, correctly surmising what was passing through his mind. "So be assured that you are neither trespassing nor misappropriating," she added.

Torr's eyes narrowed speculatively at the child's choice of words. The small gypsy was evidently educated.

"Do thee hev to talk so uncomfy-like? I'm getting a crick in the neck and I'm near frozen to the marrow. Let's go into the kitchens," complained Granny.

"You can get into the castle?" exclaimed Torr, turning to the old hag.

"Go where you please. Just give me word when I'm to set sail!" shouted Devil, wheeling the Carrack around and galloping out of the sheltering cave into the raging storm. She was confused and distraught. No place was safe from Torr Pendarves. Not Taran, where she was her father's shameful secret. Not the familiar home of her childhood. Not even within herself, she seethed as she sped over the moor.

Silas heaved an audible sigh of relief when the Carrack loomed out of the storming darkness. He shook his head sorrowfully when the bedraggled rider slipped numbly off the steaming back of the exhausted stallion. "I'll take care of the poor beast, thee see to thyself," he muttered, noting the bleakness in the dark eyes. "I hear t'es Torrance Pendarves thet has bin sent to organize us," he added. "Well, at least tes one of us and not zum Englishman." She stood silently staring into space. "Get to thy bed," he ordered roughly when he saw a shudder shake her small frame. He watched her trudge towards the house through the icy rain before signalling with his lantern to let Angelica know Devil was safely home. The poor mistress would not sleep until she knew the dark child of the moors was back; that was not good for the unborn babe, fretted Silas, briskly toweling the shivering horse.

Sleep eluded a lot of people that night. Angelica tossed and turned, wishing Benedict was home to help with his solitary daughter and to feel his unborn child kicking in her womb. Devil lay in the darkness, her thoughts painfully jumbled with Torr Pendarves's chiselled face caught in her mind.

Torr Pendarves stood at his bedroom window watching the spent storm shudder the night sky. The rain had lessened to a misty drizzle, and he wondered where the elusive dark child was. Granny-Griggs had led him into the inhospitable castle. He'd explored the vast comfortless interior, shuddering at the instruments of torture and cautionary pictures depicting horrendous methods of slow death that decorated the walls. Of the Devil-Child, Granny had proved to be singularly exasperating, refusing to divulge anything except loud elated cackles.

"Such a dangerous mission is no place for a child," he had firmly stated, eliciting another whoop of mirth.

"Then there's no mission," she had declared. "Except for Jonty Pengelly, none know the secrets but the Devil-Child."

"What secrets?"

"Tides, shoals, hidden French coves, and the like," she had merrily recounted. "What's gnawing into thy guts, my pretty?" she had wickedly probed. "Does the Devil-Child take thy fancy?" She had collapsed into hysterical laughter when he had curtly slammed out of the room. Now he gazed blindly out over the moor, haunted by the large dark eyes.

CHAPTER 19

THE WEEKS preceding Christmas passed in a whirl of activity as the whole Taran estate fervently prepared for the yuletide celebration. But there was a pall within the house caused by the morose weather, Benedict's absence, and Devlyn's quiet detachment. Each morning she abided by her agreement to Angelica and dutifully presented herself to teach Iris the rudiments of the piano and to play minuets, quadrilles, and waltzes so they all could practise their dance steps and carols. Even though Devlyn was note-perfect, there was no longer any magical lilt in her music, just an undertone of profound sadness that threaded through the liveliest of reels. There were times when her natural curiosity and sensitivity overcame the tight rein she kept on her emotions, but sadly something usually occurred to douse the elfin spirit—for example, the arrival of Torr Pendarves to discuss business of the mines with Angus Dunbar, or the unexpected visit of Angelica's two younger brothers home from school for the holidays. It was almost as if Devlyn's keen senses could detect such outside presences even before they reached the front door, and her delicate face would lose the animated sparkle before she swiftly whirled away to hide herself. Each time Angelica silently screamed.

On one such visit Torr rode over with Felix, Owen, and Evan. The young boys excitedly begged Angelica to invite them for Christmas Day, their boisterous, husky voices quite audible to Devil, as was the disappointed chorus when it was obvious they had been gently rebuffed.

"Secrets are such poison," Devil hissed, knowing it was

her very presence that robbed Angelica of a joyous family gathering. She wished she could ride away from Taran, never to return, but she owed Angelica and the unborn baby more consideration. She would leave, but only after she had confronted her father so there would be no blame directed at any except her. There was also the mission. How she wished she would receive word, as her nights were tortured with anxiety about the trip. She'd wake up sweating, her heart pounding, with Torr Pendarves's derisive laughter ringing in her ears. She wanted to wake up with the long dangerous trip accomplished. She had sailed to France innumerable times but always with the Bucca and Jonty.

The days were long and cold. Not wishing to meet Torr Pendarves, who now had access to the castle and the caves, Devil had no refuge. She either kept to her rooms or hid in the storage attic, where she occupied herself making Christmas presents for everyone at Taran. For the unborn child she had carved a unicorn, and for everyone else there was a bird, intricately whittled out of driftwood bleached and polished by the tides.

It was a few days before Christmas. She was sitting cross-legged on the dusty attic floor, busily putting the finishing touches to the graceful swan she was carving for Angelica, when she heard a furtive creaking on the steps. She quickly wrapped her work in a piece of cloth and watched Iris edge stealthily around the door.

"What is it?" asked Devil.

"It's this," declared Iris, holding up a twist of paper.

"And what's that?" asked Devil, returning to her work. Iris watched her for a few moments.

"You 'ave to 'ave magic in yer fingers to make them little statues, Dev," she said enviously, forgetting her errand as she stared entranced by what the girl was creating.

"What is that paper?"

"It's a note from someone to you, and I know it ain't from Silas, cos he can't cipher. He don't know I can neither, else he would'nt 'ave give it to me. It says 'Eve of Christmas Eve,' " read Iris victoriously, " 'ere!" she angrily protested when the slip of paper was snatched out of her hand. "What does it mean?" she asked, frowning at Devil's sudden pallor.

"I have to go away just for a few days and you must stop Angelica worrying," pronounced Devil after a long thoughtful pause.

"Going away? When?"

"Tomorrow."

"You going to miss Christmas?" exclaimed Iris. "Who sent that note?" she demanded.

"I can't tell you," she answered.

"And 'ow the 'ell can I stop Miss Angel from frettin' 'erself ter skin and bone?" whined Iris. "And what if 'is lordship comes 'ome and you ain't 'ere?"

"I have no choice!" stated Devil harshly. "I'll leave the Carrack so Angelica knows that I mean to return," she added softly. "On Christmas, if that's when they give each other presents, will you give these to them?" she asked wistfully, remembering Angel's wonderful description of the Christmas ritual and putting the tiny carvings in Iris's lap.

Devil worked swiftly, checking the rigging and readying the sturdy ketch for the channel crossing. She was conscious of Granny-Griggs and Caleb Skinner herding the strangers onto the listing boat, but she was too shy and fearful to raise her head. Their furtive footsteps reverberated sharply along the deck planking, jarring through her tense muscles. The harsh rustle of the nets and tarpaulins that cunningly concealed them scraped at her nerves. Devil was used to working in complete silence alongside of Jonty Pengelly with the Bucca guarding, poised to warn of impending danger, but now she was alone and vulnerable. Her fingers felt clumsy and numb. Her heart pounded, muffling her ears, which strained to hear the slightest suspicious sound.

The tide came in and the vessel righted itself, the waves gently slapping against the rocking craft. She heard the scrambling of feet on the rocks; the anchor was raised and they were off. Devil hunched down by the tiller, skillfully guiding the boat between the razor teeth of the hidden shoals as the wind bellied out the sails, and they skimmed out of the shelter of Pendarves Cove into the open, unprotected sea.

Torr marvelled at the expertise. "Bravo," he said softly, and he saw the small figure stiffen with shock.

"Where's Caleb?"

"Caleb preferred to spend Christmas with his wife . . . and as I had no such liability, I volunteered."

"There are just you and the three strangers aboard?" Her voice was tremulous and her throat dry. She gazed frantically about, unable to bear his searing scrutiny. "Where are they?"

"It is best you don't see their faces."

"So I can't identify them if I am a traitor?" she challenged acidly.

"We have a very long night ahead of us. Tell me about yourself?" he demanded, and she stubbornly pursed her lips and glared at him. He was entranced by the delicate but defiant features. Was it a trick of the moonlight that transformed the scruffy gypsy boy into a desirable woman? He snorted derisively, remembering Jago's drunken ravings about the dark-child of the moor's ability to change into a mermaid. "Are you truly the Devil-Child?" he whispered, trying to exorcise the fascination he felt for the valiant little figure.

Devil stiffened, sensing the difference in the way he gazed upon her. The air felt charged and her skin tingled, every pore burningly aware of him. She backed away, reaching for the dagger at her waist.

"Don't pull a weapon on me unless you truly mean to use it," he said in a low voice with a steely ring. There was a rhythmic creaking of oars accompanied by a tuneless singing. Torr waved casually to the old fisherman who laboriously hauled in his crab and lobster pots as they sailed past him across the moonlit sea towards the French coast. Devil took the opportunity to hunch down by the tiller. She pressed her back against the hard wood and pulled her dark cape about her ears, trying to be as unobtrusive as possible, hoping Sir Torrance Pendarves knew how to tend the sails.

The long night passed without incident. Of the three spies there was no sight or sound, and Devil surmised they were sleeping under the shadowy mound of canvas and nets. The only noise was the hum of the wind in the taut sails and the slap of the water against the sides of the boat, but Devil did not relax. She was tense and fearful, keeping her eyes glued to the tall disturbing presence of the man who painfully stirred her emotions.

The sky was barely lightening when to her relief she saw signs of approaching land. Shore birds screeched and wheeled, and the water roughened. She stretched her cramped, cold limbs and stood up, straining her eyes through the murky predawn. Deftly she guided the vessel through sharp reefs towards what appeared to be a sheer cliff that rose out of the churning sea. There was an audible intake of breath when it seemed a devastating collision was inevitable as the ketch skimmed directly at the impenetrable wall of rock. There was an even louder gasp when a narrow schism in the soaring cliff became apparent. One wrong move, the slightest miscalculation, and the small vessel would be dashed to pieces. Every eye was trained on the tiny figure. Every fibre was strained, each muscle rigid. Then there was another gasp, this time of stunned relief as the seeming small child adroitly steered the racing vessel through the narrow aperture with only a foot or two to spare on each side.

"My God, 'tis like the ends of the earth!" exclaimed one of the huddled men, staring about the uninhabited cove. It was a most desolate spot with a grim rocky shore and a stark grey cliff. There was not a tree or sign of living vegetation to soften the harsh landscape, and blackened sea-weed and rotting fish floated in the brackish foam.

Devil was drained and exhausted. For more than ten hours she had not relaxed her guard but had kept every sense alert. She leaned against the gunwale of the ketch watching Torr Pendarves row the three anonymous men to the pebbled beach. Her eyelids drooped but she attempted to stay awake, not wanting to miss the tide and be trapped in the dismal cove for twelve hours.

Torr rowed back to the sailing vessel. "Ahoy, sleepyhead," he hailed, and she looked up and was startled to see him towering above her. "You fell asleep," he answered, seeing the dazed confusion. Devil stared up at the stormy dawn sky, trying to orient herself as the ketch bucked wildly against the anchor in the choppy sea. The last thing she had remembered was watching him rowing towards the shore, but there he was looming over her with his piercing blue eyes. She abruptly turned away from him and reached over the side to splash cold water on her face, hoping to shock herself to alertness. Her confusion made her clumsy and her stocking cap fell off. Her ebony hair cascaded, obstructing her vision, just as a large wave crashed against the side of the boat. Torr reached out too late to stop the small figure from toppling overboard.

Devil gasped at the cruel shock of the freezing water. She felt the slimy weeds closing around her face. She kicked, trying to surface, but she was weighed down by her boots and sodden woolen cape. Torr reached over the side and wound his hand in the thick black hair, hauling her to the surface and into the boat. Devil was too numb to feel the pain of her abused scalp. She hung choking and dripping between his strong hands like a half-drowned urchin, the sea water stinging her skin and eyes.

"Get out of those wet clothes," he ordered tersely after thumping her inelegantly on the back and setting her on her wobbly feet.

"Nnno time . . . have ttto make the tide," she protested, her teeth chattering painfully. "Bllankets in the cccabin," she added, waving in that direction while squelching painfully towards the tiller. Torr frowned at the violent tremors that shook the small figure who tenaciously steered the vessel towards the narrow fissure in the looming rock wall that protected the entrance to the hidden dismal cove. He draped a blanket about the shaking shoulders and prayed that the tiny trembling hands would not send them to their deaths on the razor sharp rocks. He exhaled loudly with relief as once again the Devil-Child completed the seemingly impossible feat and the ketch sailed into the open sea.

"Now get out of those wet clothes," he sighed. Devil was unable to say a word; her teeth were painfully clenched. She made no motion to obey but just hunched over the tiller, her wet hair hiding her face. Her body shook violently from the cold and the tremendous concentration she had just exercised to steer through the dangerous reefs.

Torr pried her frozen hands from the tiller and locked it in position before carrying the trembling figure to the cabin. The very moment he held her against his chest he knew she was female. His feelings had nothing to do with her shape, because for all intents and purposes she was just a sodden shapeless mass of cape and blanket. He carried her into the cabin and set her on the narrow bunk.

Devil sat frozen in body and mind, watching him strip the cold wet clothes off her. It was someone else she watched, not herself. She was detached and numb.

Torr marvelled at the perfection of the female body he unwrapped. Though blue and goosebumped with cold and shivering violently, she had the most wonderful, most desirable woman's body he had ever seen. From this moment, she was his, he decided. He briskly rubbed her lithe well-shaped limbs until she glowed with a rosy hue and then he swaddled her in blankets, cradling her in his arms. He wanted to sing with delight. He wanted to rejoice. An enormous burden had been lifted from his heart and he was free. His fanatic fascination with this petite Devil-Child had been so right, so perfect, so true. He gazed down lovingly at the exquisite little face that rested on his broad chest, wishing she were awake so he could tell her of the torment she had caused him. Suddenly he understood all Granny-Griggs's wicked innuendos, and he put back his head and laughed aloud.

Devil felt Torr's deep laugh reverberate through her, and she stiffened, not knowing where she was. She was warm and her skin tingled. She was asleep but not in her bed. Her head was not resting on a pillow. She listened and heard the steady beat of a heart. Something held her like an iron bar. She couldn't move, and she panicked and started to fight.

"Hush, it's all right. You're safe," crooned Torr, supposing she was having a nightmare. "It's just a dream," he comforted, but she fought like a wildcat and it took all his energy to contain her. The blankets were kicked aside and Devil opened her eyes to see his strong arms surrounding her nakedness. She stopped struggling and fearfully looked up at his face expecting to see derision or anger. She was confused to see him grinning fondly. "Merry Christmas," he greeted huskily after a long pause in which blue eyes met puzzled dark brown ones. "You are without doubt the most wonderful Christmas present I have ever unwrapped," he growled tenderly, confounding her even more. "But it is December and there's more than a chill wind, so much to my regret, those sweet charms should be snugly hid."

Devil frowned, bewildered by her emotions and his words. She followed the direction of his eyes to where his strong brown hand rested below her white breast, his forearm lying intimately across her flat belly. She shivered, feeling his touch searing her skin, causing a strange hot ache in the core of her. Torr felt the tremor and solicitously wrapped her like an Egyptian mummy, hiding her tempting curves from his adoring eyes. He regretfully laid her on the narrow cot and covered her with his cape. She struggled to sit up, but he had pinned her arms under the tight covers.

"The tiller?" she cried, remembering where they were and hearing the rising whine of the wind. "Must drop some canvas," she muttered wildly, recognising the signs of a storm. "Drop the sails," she begged. "Or we'll blow over."

"Stop your worrying," he soothed, tucking her more firmly, but she defiantly kicked, trying to free her imprisoned limbs. "You are aptly named," he said, grinning into her stormy eyes.

Devil stopped her struggles, mesmerized by his clear blue gaze. Her mouth softened, losing the stubborn line. Her lips parted tremulously as his face neared and she felt his warm breath. She closed her eyes, unable to bear the suspense.

Torr gently kissed her and she lay quietly, making no movement to repel or encourage. She felt dazed, in awe of what was happening to her, and he knew it was the first time she had received a man's lips. The whine of the wind brought him to his senses, and he ruefully stood up.

Devil's eyes flew open, and she glared reproachfully up at him. Freeing her arms, she reached up to draw his mouth to hers again, eager to continue the new experience.

"First things first," he laughed hoarsely, capturing her little hands within his larger ones. He stared down at the crescent scars on the heel of her right hand and reverently kissed it. "The fates prophesied our union, my Devil-Woman, even to the point of setting my brand on your flesh two years ago," he rejoiced.

Devil watched him leave the small cabin and a happy warmth curled through her, lulling her into a deep slumber. She slept soundly, unaware of the violent storm that buffeted the small vessel like a cork in the raging water. The tiller snapped and they were blown off course. The tempest raged throughout the day, and Devil dreamlessly slept. She awakened to the rosy glow of the sun setting across the tranquil sea and lay happily, rocked in the warm suspension. At the sound of water softly lapping, she sat up and looked about. Remembering where she was and confused by the direction of the setting sun, she swung her lithe legs off the narrow bunk and stared down, dismayed by her nakedness. She wrapped a coarse blanket about herself and walked onto the cold wet deck, her breath misting the crystalline air.

"We're going the wrong way," she stated flatly after watching Torr Pendarves silently gaze across the rippling water. He turned and grinned wearily at her. Then he ruefully indicated the broken tiller and shattered mast. She smiled back shyly. " 'Tis a clean purged time," she said, appreciating the storm-washed evening, not knowing what else to say to the tall man who stared so intently at her.

"Come here," he ordered softly, opening his arms invitingly. Many feelings raced through Devil at the loving gesture. She stood poised, hesitating . . . tempted yet terrified. Then she slowly walked into his arms to be enfolded against his strength. She didn't remember having ever been held before. Everyone had been afraid to touch her for fear that the Bucca would attack. Devil stood within Torr's embrace, loving yet afraid of his strong arms. Her straight back was taut against his chest, and his cheek rested on the top of her head, weighing her down.

"If we're lucky we'll reach one of the Channel Isles," he murmured against her ebony hair.

"And hope there are no French," she answered huskily.

"As long as there is warm shelter and food," sighed Torr. "And a large comfortable bed," he added, his arms tightening possessively about her. Devil panicked, afraid that he'd never release her.

"You're hungry?" she enquired, desperately trying to wriggle free. Torr turned her about to face him and looked questioningly into her luminous eyes.

"I am hungry for you, my little Devil," he answered huskily before kissing her lingeringly. He laughed triumphantly when she responded with eager curiosity.

"Hungry for me?" puzzled Devil breathlessly. "I have food and a small flask of brandy," she offered, feeling shy and awkward, not knowing how to deal with the tumultuous emotions that surged through her. She felt fragmented, as if he were to remove his arms she would whirl away to merge with the sea-mist that steamed from the crests of the waves; and if he did not remove his arms she would never be free but would lose all form and merge with him. She gazed into his profound blue eyes, searching for an answer. She suddenly knew what a lark felt on a summer day when it soared high against the sun into the limitless sky. She also wanted to burst with an exultant song. She ached to express herself with music, allowing the incredible surging emotions to spill through her fingertips . . . yet beneath the exhilaration was a bass drone of fear.

"Food? Brandy?" Torr repeated. She nodded and fleetly twisted out of his arms to fetch the small bundle that Silas Quickbody had given her. "Our first Christmas dinner together," he declared as she unwrapped a beef and almond pie and an apple tart. Devil struggled with the cumbersome blanket, wishing that her clothes were dry or that she had thought to stow some extra garments in the cabin. She felt inhibited, too conscious of his bright eyes that clung to her every move. Her usual graceful movements were heavy and clumsy, her numb fingers fumbling, her frozen feet tripping over the edge of the blanket, which slipped off her shoulders. She shivered and he frowned, seeing her small blue toes. He picked her up and sat her across his hard thighs, pulling the blanket snugly about her.

"You should be in the cabin out of the wind," he said, but she adamantly shook her head. "Then be still and you shall be the banquetting table." Devil giggled as he solemnly placed the food and flask on her narrow lap. "No jiggling," he cautioned. "Keep your arms tucked in and I shall feed you." He held the brandy flask to her mouth and she sipped. She gasped and then grinned as the burning liqueur teared her eyes and then spread warmth through her belly. Torr placed his lips on hers, tasting the two intoxicating essences.

"Listen," she murmured against his caressing mouth. "Bells!" she cried excitedly, and he leaned back, entranced by her wonder-filled face.

"Christmas bells," he said.

Over the moonlit water pealed a joyous carillon, and Torr's arms tightened about his Devil-Woman, afraid that she might be just an elusive fantasy. It was a magical moment, adrift on the tranquil sea. Only he and his small demon existed in the pure crystal dusk. He had never felt so completely happy and at peace with himself and the elements.

"You, my Devil-love, are the navigator. What town do you suppose that is?" he asked, regretfully dispelling the mystical moment. He traced her delicate nose with his forefinger as she stared pensively up at the night sky, pinpointing their direction from the lodestar and remembering where the sun had set.

"Unless we sailed between the isles of Guernsey and Jersey while I slept, it must be one of the Channel Islands," she pronounced.

"And if we did pass through the islands?" he probed.

"It's the Manche Peninsula of France," she replied miserably, watching the lights of a small town reflect on the dark rippling waves. "Where are my clothes?" she demanded abruptly, trying to wriggle off his lap so the remains of their meals were strewn across the deck.

"You're not putting on those cold wet garments," he stated firmly. "Besides, my Devil-Woman, I prefer you as you are," he teased roguishly, before kissing her mutinous mouth. Wickedly she bit his lip and he nipped her back. "Now be still and quiet." Devil tried to slither off his lap, but he held her tightly, his strong arm like an immovable iron-band.

She was furious and afraid. Not only was she naked under the coarse blanket, but she was unarmed. Her knife and gun had been removed with her clothes. Savagely she jabbed her sharp elbows into his hard belly, trying to free herself, but he ignored her struggles. She glared up at his face silhouetted against the cold night sky and the lean scarred cheek appeared harsh and satanic, increasing her determination to fight free so she could protect herself. She had never relied on anyone before except the Carrack and the Bucca. She had been the protector of the Living-Dead, the strength among the fearful weak.

Torr felt the frantic breathing and the rapid pulse that shook her. He tried to contain her wild struggles as he strained to discern whether the low rumble of voices was French or English. He heard the drone of an organ and a Christmas carol lustily trolled.

"Stop!" he hissed as she tried to bite his chest but was unable to get a toothhold in the hard flat muscle. "I said stop!" he repeated. "Is that Latin, French, or English?" he muttered with exasperation. Devil lay helplessly pinned across his thighs as the ketch drifted closer to the rejoicing voices. "It's English! It must be one of the Channel Isles," sighed Torr with relief, kissing the top of her head and releasing her to fetch a lantern so he could signal for assistance. Devil took the opportunity to grope and rummage about the dark wet deck, desperately hoping to find her weapons.

"Where are they?" she demanded, rushing after him into the tiny cabin. Torr turned and surveyed her snarling face. The warm lantern light flickered across her wild eyes, and he saw the terror that she tried to conceal beneath her fury. "Give them to me!" she demanded when he didn't answer. Her eyes raked the floor of the cabin, and she pounced on the mound of sodden clothes, shaking them like a worrying animal but there were no weapons. "Where are they?" she repeated, looking frantically about as she stepped into the cold wet trews and with difficulty pulled them up her shrinking flesh. She cursed with frustration as the stiff material tangled and twisted but she at last managed to cover her slim hips.

Torr leaned against the wall watching her, and a smile of amusement curled his thin lips. He had never seen such an attractive sight, he mused. His Devil-Woman looked glorious with her wild hair and eyes, her bare breasts thrusting in fury, her lean lithe legs encased in the clinging wet fabric.

"Where did you hide them?" she snarled, reminding him of an angry kitten. He shrugged and held his hands up helplessly. "My knife? . . . the gun?" Realization flooded across Torr's chiselled features just as several gruff voices hailed from shore. Devil's dark eyes widened in terror. "Please, I'm unarmed," she cried. He longed to enfold her in his arms and tell her he would protect her, but he sensed she would bite and kick. He nodded and looked towards a small shelf before striding on deck to greet the Channel Islanders.

Devil hastily snatched up her weapons and tucked them into the waistband of her trousers. She wrapped a blanket about her like a cape and hunkered down in the shadows of the cabin, not wanting to be seen by the men on shore. Through the open doorway she watched Torr Pendarves signalling with the lantern.

"We're Cornish, our boat wuz caught in the storm," he bellowed in answer to their query, roughening his cultured tones to a regional accent to match his seaman's clothes.

"How many are you?"

"Just the wife and me," answered Torr, and Devil's eyes widened.

"What are you doing out in a storm on Christmas?" roared a suspicious voice.

" 'Tis my honeymoon and t'wuz the only way I could get away from my new mother-in-law . . . and what with one thing and t'other being busylike . . . time, tide, and the weather got away from me," he roguishly replied and was greeted by a chorus of lusty chuckles.

"Anchor the ketch and row yourself in," invited one of the men.

"The dinghy broke free in the storm," he confessed ruefully.

"Don't fret, sonny, we'll be out to fetch you and your bride."

"Well, my little Devil-bride," murmured Torr. "What's your name?"

"My name?" she repeated blankly, staring at his tall silhouette, which blocked the doorway. "My name is Devil."

"I cannot introduce you to those simple God-fearing people as Devil," he returned, and she shrugged, not knowing how to answer him. "If you won't tell me your name, you shall be Betsy," he decided with a chuckle.

"Betsy?" Devil was torn between his seductive banter and the ominous sound of approaching oars.

"Jago Pengelly calls every female a Betsy whether it is a boat or a woman."

"Jago Pengelly," echoed Devil numbly. Sadness surged through her at remembering Jonty.

"In fact we shall be Jago and Betsy Pengelly! Mister and missus," he laughed, swinging her into his arms and striding out on to the deck. Devil's heart pounded, hearing the laborious creak of oars and the gruff mutter of voices. As the dory loomed out of the darkness, she fumbled for her knife. Torr felt her tense. "Put it away," he ordered. "Trust me," he hissed, but she kept the lethal weapon drawn and concealed beneath the blanket.

"Is yer little woman hurt?" enquired one of the men when Torr stepped into the rowboat with Devil bundled so tightly. All she could do was kick her legs and make furious, grunting noises.

"She fell overboard in the storm. Lost all her clothes and is right embarrassed to have you see her. My little Betsy is a right modest woman, God-fearing and churchgoing but doesn't have her sea legs," informed Torr, hastily sitting in the frantically rocking craft. He pinned Devil across his lap and pulled the muffling blanket from her face. "I'm Jago Pengelly and this is my bride, Betsy." Devil glowered at the three curious men.

"Looks a mite imperant to me," observed one of the fishermen. "You've your hands full there, young feller-me-lad," he pronounced direly.

"She promised to obey me," mourned Torr, trying to keep his humour but anger tightening his jaws. Devil felt his mounting fury and lay still, her cold hand still clutching her dagger. Why was she so afraid? She forced herself to think rationally as she watched the men steadily rowing towards the neat stone harbour town. She had no control over what was happening, she decided, and that terrified her.

Torr stepped off on to dry land with Devil firmly cradled in his arms. Instantly they were surrounded by a crowd of people who clattered out of the small church. She longed to close her eyes and hide her face but fear kept her alert, her dark eyes scowling at all the clustering curious people.

"Young honeymooners from the mainland got caught in the Christmas storm," was whispered backwards and forwards.

Finally they were esconsed in a large airy bedroom where two bathtubs steamed in front of a blazing hearth.

"Only the best for young lovers at Christmas," fussed a

buxom woman bustling in with a laden tray. "Now if'n you need anything just ring, else you'll not be disturbed," she reassured, gazing fondly at the romantic picture of the tall handsome blond man who cradled his petite dark bride in his strong brown arms. She emitted a heartfelt sigh at the loving scene and then tiptoed out, discreetly closing the door after her.

"All right, Devil, give me the knife," he snapped tersely, relaxing his murderous grip. His arms ached from holding her so tightly for so long and his leg throbbed unbearably. Devil sullenly shimmied off his lap and the blanket fell to the floor. She defiantly tucked the dagger in her waistband and massaged her arms where he saw the red angry marks made by his hands. "Why?" he asked hoarsely. "Nobody wanted to hurt you. They are simple, kindly people," he continued when she didn't answer. He stared at her, sadly noting her truculent expression. Then he limped to the door and locked it not wanting any intrusion. "Devil, I'd not let anyone harm you," he tried one last time to break through her fury.

Devil did not know how to explain. She watched him silently, knowing he was hurt and angry as he turned his back on her and poured himself a glass of wine, which he drained at once. He then stripped off his clothes and stepped into the steaming water, hoping to ease his cold aching muscles. He pointedly ignored her, leaning back and closing his eyes. Devil saw the fatigue that lined his face and she thoughtfully approached him. She grinned despite herself at the comical picture he made, his long lanky body folded into the small bathtub. She knelt beside him and gently traced the jagged scar that bisected his lean thigh. She knew it was paining him, for she had seen him limp, his long fingers kneading the muscle. However, it had healed well, better than she had expected, and silently she thanked Granny-Griggs for her white-witch knowledge of folk medicine. She remembered the night that they had cut the bloodstained trousers from him and stared with horror at the terrible wound. It had seemed doubtful that the leg could be saved. Her eyes moved lower as she recalled how he had reached down to his manhood for reassurance, causing Granny to chuckle with delight.

Torr opened his heavy lids and was surprised to see her

regarding him so solemnly. He sensed she was struggling to articulate, and he quietly waited, marvelling at the various expressions that crossed her poignant features.

"Don't be angry," she finally whispered.

"I'm not. I'm tired and hungry."

"I am used to being alone," she confessed.

"Very self-reliant," he snapped sarcastically.

"It is hard to trust," she admitted, instinctively knowing why he was hurt. Torr groaned and pulled her to him.

"Could we have a Christmas truce? Would you consider disarming for just a little while?" he asked plaintively as her dagger and gun dug against him uncomfortably. Devil complied by carefully placing her little flintlock pistol and the knife under the pillows of the large bed. "Very romantic," he remarked dryly, but then he nodded appreciatively as she shimmied out of her tight trews and stepped into the other bathtub. He ran his blue gaze over her delectable body as she stood before the fire, lathering her satiny length with fragrant lavender soap.

Devil felt the change in his gaze. The space between them seemed charged and her nipples hardened. "Will you mate with me?" she asked huskily, an aching need pulsing through her.

"Will I mate with you?" repeated Torr thoughtfully, after a shocked pause. "I have never heard it quite so quaintly phrased," he added, rinsing himself off and stepping out of the bath, conscious that she assessed his body as openly as he did hers. "Will I mate with you?" he reiterated, tying a towel about his loins and sitting, uncomfortable with her direct gaze. He surveyed the generous platters of Christmas fare and poured himself another glass of wine. "Would you like some?" he offered, and she shook her head impatiently awaiting his answer. "Roast goose? Mincemeat pie? Fruit cake?" he asked hopefully, needing to change the subject, too fatigued for an emotional scene. "Come here," he sighed, opening his arms invitingly to her, but she just sat her dark eyes full of misery. "Will I mate with you?" he repeated resignedly.

"I'm sorry. I have obviously said something wrong," she answered haltingly.

"I want you more than I have ever wanted another woman . . . but you are too important to me," he pronounced carefully.

"More than you've ever wanted another woman?" echoed Devil, thinking of her stallion who had covered many mares. Her grandfather's biblical ravings about all women being whores rang in her head, and she remembered all the gossip about her mother, Catherine, who was reputed to have had many lovers—nearly the whole of the West Country, if rumour was true. "I want you more than I have ever wanted another man," she stated pensively. He was so startled he spilled some wine, and the red liquid splashed down his lean brown stomach.

"I beg your pardon!" he choked.

"I said 'I want you more than I have ever wanted another man,' " she obediently repeated, standing up in the tepid water and provocatively dabbing the beads of water from her firm breasts. Torr glowered as pain and rage thundered through him at the thought of another man so much as touching her. Devil's small nostrils flared victoriously knowing he was as hurt and jealous as she had been when he had mentioned other women.

Torr caught the wicked gleam of triumph, and he leaned back in his chair. He sipped his wine and surveyed her speculatively over the rim of his glass. He calmed his rage, remembering when his lips had first touched hers. He knew no one had ever kissed her before and so the possibility of her being intimately possessed by another man was extremely remote. The devilish little imp was playing a most seductive game, he decided, helping himself to a leg of goose. He settled back to the enjoyable pastime of watching her take a bath before the blazing hearth.

Devil's acute sensitivity felt the change in the lounging blond man. She was mesmerized by the strong white teeth that tore into the succulent flesh and the lazy blue eyes that caressed her naked body. Suddenly she felt unaccountably shy under his steady scrutiny. She leaped out of the nearly cold water and without even bothering to dry herself, she dashed across the room to scramble into the large bed. She gasped, thinking she was caught in quicksand as her wet limbs tangled in the sheets and she sank, nearly smothered by the thick feather bed.

Torr blew out the candles and hastily followed her into the

bed, dropping his towel on the floor. He held out his arms
and without hesitation she curled into his chest. They lay
naked, peacefully watching the magical caves and mountains
that were formed by the glowing embers in the hearth. Very
gently his broad warm hand stroked the curve of her silky
spine. She tucked her small nose into the velvet hollow
beneath his ear and her slim arms encircled his hard chest.

"Sleep, my love," he murmured and she snuggled closer
curling one leg intimately across his thighs.

Devil awakened several hours later. She breathed happily
of his clean male fragrance and pressed her tingling skin
against his firm warmth delighting in the feel of him. The fire
glowed, bathing the room in a subdued light. Carefully she
sat up, wanting to see his sleeping face. The harsh chiselled
lines were softened, and he looked relaxed and boyish, the
scar on his cheek was just a healed wound and not the
sardonic punctuation mark that often matched the cynicism of
his alert expression. His thick blond hair caught the reflection
of the hot embers like a golden halo, and she touched her
fingertips to the vibrant ends expecting to be burned by the
fiery strands. Her eyes followed the curves of his stubborn
jaw, and she pulled back the bedclothes, wishing to see all of
him. His body had been indelibly etched upon her mind for
the last two years, ever since she had first seen him helpless
and naked in the cave. What had he said to her on the ketch?
Something about the fates prophesying their union? Something about having his seal branded upon her flesh forever?
She looked at the crescent scars on her hand and then at his
lips. She ached to kiss him but feared waking him. Slowly
she ran her eyes down the long length of him, following the
planes and ridges of muscles to the relaxed centre of him.

Torr opened his eyes and watched her appraisal. For a few
moments he was shocked. Young women of breeding would
never think of examining a male's anatomy—not even in a
painting or statue, let alone in reality. He lay still, wrestling
with his emotions and then he saw her face. It was full of
loving wonder and their eyes joined and she kissed him, her
breath spiced with desire. He lay still, trying to temper his
rising passion as her curious little tongue impudently poked
and her inquisitive hands explored his body, coming to rest
wonderingly at the hard core of him.

Torr prided himself on his prowess as a lover, but he had to admit that his wild young love's uninhibited innocence was more tantalizing than any of the worldly women of his experience. He followed her lead, learning from her, taking nothing for granted, exploring, tasting, touching, delighting in her, from the tip of her toes to the top of her head. The very moment that she opened to him and he knelt poised at the virgin portal of her arched body, he felt fear.

Devil sensed his terror and their eyes locked, full of wonder; they were totally vulnerable to each other.

"I love you," he whispered, not able to plunder her, but she reached out and guided him into the depths of her. He thrust and she rose to meet him and there was no more thought. Devil cried out as every possible feeling culminated into one tremendous painful pleasure, exploding into a new world of exquisite sensation.

They lay intimately joined, clasping each other tightly, feeling their racing hearts beating as one.

"Did I hurt you?" asked Torr, gazing lovingly into her nearly black eyes that seemed smokey from passion. She grinned mistily and shook her ebony head. She made a small sound of lamentation as she felt him slip from her and then an outraged squawk when he bounded off the bed.

"I need sustenance," he growled, pouring a generous goblet of wine and piling a platter high with food. "You start on this while I feed and stoke another fire," he quipped, depositing the tray on the bed.

Devil sipped the earthy wine pensively and watched him naked before the fire, the flames reflecting off the long strong planes of his body. She revelled in his beauty, delighting in his wide shoulders and tapering waist, his lean buttocks and straight strong legs, the way his golden muscles fluidly moved as he bent over his task. She committed each beloved inch to memory, knowing that happiness was unsubstantial and fleeting, hoping that when it was inevitably snatched away, part of him would be imprisoned in her mind, emblazoned on her heart to warm her in the cold solitary times.

Torr coaxed the fire back to a roaring blaze and turned to see Devil kneeling anxiously on the bed, staring fixedly at him.

"What is it?" he asked. Devil shook her head and smiled tremulously; there were no words to explain his beauty. He faced her in all his glory, a healthy, virile young male . . . sleek and spare. She grinned at a certain precious portion of him and cocked her head mischievously.

"It is magic. One moment so awesome, so mighty . . . and the next . . ." She stopped, mulling through her mind for a suitable adjective.

"And the next?" prompted Torr, her very direct gaze at the pride of his anatomy causing him to stiffen, much to her gurgling delight. Devil had no chance to answer. He plucked her from the bed and placed her by the hearth, where once more they claimed each other, their passion flaring, reflecting the consuming flames.

Devil drifted off to sleep in Torr's arms, thoroughly sated and depleted. She felt deliriously happy and complete for the first time in her young life, but her sleep was disturbed by a dream in which Angelica shielded her unborn child from the black rage of Tremayne of Taran. The nightmare scene was played out in the reflection of a distorting mirror, lit by the frigid blue of a winter moon. Angelica's sea-green eyes reflected the stern, uncompromising figure of her husband, his murderous fury making him larger and larger until the pregnant woman was blinded by the heavy shadow.

"No! Don't hurt her! 'Tis my fault! I'm to blame!" screamed Devil, trying to run to Angelica's assistance, but she couldn't move. She was firmly held.

"Hush," Torr sleepily comforted the restless girl in his arms.

"I'm to blame!" Devil cried, desperately trying to free herself "Don't hurt her," she ranted, feeling at her waist for her weapons but finding just naked skin. She clawed wildly and was shocked by a muffled oath.

Devil opened her eyes, remembering where she was. She was pillowed on a strong bare chest. She released her painful grip and stared ruefully at the nail marks that raked his smooth skin.

"I'd not let any harm you," he crooned, kissing her damp forehead. She avoided his tender, questioning gaze and buried her nose in the safe scent of his body, clasping him tightly.

She knew she had to return to Taran to face her father before she could be free to choose a life with Torr Pendarves. "Go back to sleep," he murmured, and Devil obediently closed her eyes, listening to the steady beat of his heart as she wondered about Angelica and Iris. She hoped they had had as wonderful a Christmas as she had. She smiled wistfully, recalling the little cockney girl's indignation at being locked out of the Scot's bedchamber, and now she understood. Why had Angus Dunbar rejected Iris's loving advances? she puzzled. It was obvious that the dour man cared for the freckled girl. Then why didn't he express it the way she and Torr had done? she worried. "No more frowns, my darling," reproved Torr, and she was startled to find him watching her intently. "And no more bad dreams. Share the nightmare with me, and it'll not dare return," he urged.

"I can't remember," she lied, closing her eyes and nestling against him. He tucked her into the curve of his hard belly and soon she knew from his steady breathing that he slept.

The sky had barely started to lighten when Devil managed to extricate herself from his possessive embrace. Swiftly she donned her trews and his shirt. She rolled up the too-long sleeves, and letting the shirttails flap about her knees, she wrapped his heavy cape about her slight shoulders. She hesitated for a moment, remembering her weapons. But she did not want to risk waking him by feeling under the pillows, so she quietly unlocked the door and sidled into the corridor.

Devil's bare feet were stung by the frosty cobblestones as she ran through the darkness to the harbour. The town slept soundly after the ribald festivities of Christmas, so she encountered no one. It was very easy to find a small ketch and quietly cast off. Luckily there was a brisk breeze and soon she was sailing towards the southwest coast of Cornwall. She refused to let herself think of Torr and what he would do at finding her gone as she concentrated on getting home to Taran. She had promised she would return so there would be no reprisals to Angelica; she hoped she wasn't too late.

Angelica had tried to keep a cheerful smile despite her disappointment. She had so anticipated Benedict's return that

Devlyn's absence didn't penetrate her consciousness until nearly noon on Christmas Day. Devlyn's empty place at meals and Iris's agitation had somehow washed over her. But when her natural disgust at self-pity had overcome her bleak outlook, she faced Christmas Day with earnest zeal only to find her stepdaughter truly missing. Maybe her husband's absence was a Christmas blessing.

"She said not to worry and to give everybody 'er presents and she'll be 'ome in a coupla days,' whined Iris miserably with her thin arms full of little wrapped packages, painfully conscious of Angus's disapproval. "I tried to stop 'er, but she wouldn't pay no mind. . . . said she'd leave 'er great big 'orse so you'd know she'd be back."

Angelica silently took the wrapped presents and placed them on the piano in the small salon where she had planned an intimate family Christmas. The baby moved and her arms instinctively embraced her belly, trying to hug the new life that stirred strongly within her. She wanted to howl her misery like a child. The unshed tears ached unbearably, but she was conscious of Angus's and Iris's concerned stares. "Merry Christmas," she said too brightly; her voice trembled and her green eyes brimmed. Iris reached blindly for Angus's large hand and looked so guilty that Angelica determined no more unhappiness was to be spread.

"I 'ate to make everythink even worser," wailed Iris. "But Peg 'atch is back . . . got the sack she did, and now she's 'ere visiting her dad, but she's bin snooping about the big 'ouse, Mrs. 'itchins says."

"Then invite her for Christmas dinner," declared Angelica expansively. "In fact, we shall all eat together," she decided, not relishing the thought of sitting at a nearly empty table, hearing the revelry from the servant's dining hall.

"All?" echoed Iris.

"Everyone at Taran."

"Everyone? Even Peg 'atch?" repeated Iris, dismayed that her new position now was to be shared by all.

"It's Christmas and I'll not celebrate at an empty table," stated Angelica firmly.

Christmas dinner was a dismal failure. Fieldhands, grooms,

ostlers, gardeners, cooks, gamekeepers, upstairs and downstairs maids, and their families gathered in the enormous
formal banquetting hall dressed in their Sunday best. Each
looked more miserably uncomfortable than the next. They all
wished they were in familiar surroundings, able to talk and
laugh freely, not having to mind their manners and sit stiffly
in prickly starched clothes before the ominous rows of cutlery
in the intimidating presence of their employer's wife. Angelica gazed about, realizing her disastrous mistake. She smiled,
trying to relax the tense atmosphere, but there was no reaction. Everyone was too quiet, even the tiny children whose
inquisitive little hands were sharply rapped when they reached
out to touch the sparkling crystal or trace the rose pattern on
the damask tablecloth. Eyes were fixed downward to laps,
where fingers were nervously entwined—except for Iris and
Peg Hatch, who glared spitefully at each other across the
laden table, doing little to spread Christmas cheer.

"Merry Christmas," Angelica declared, hoping for a festive response.

"Merry Christmas, your ladyship," was the dull dutiful
chorus. Angelica shook her head sorrowfully at the long rows
of scrubbed dispirited people whose vibrant voices were usually heard happily singing or good-naturedly arguing. Those
same rosy-cheeked folk were now as stony and blank as the
grey granite on the barren winter moor. It was a wake, not a
joyous celebration.

Angelica graciously excused herself, pleading a headache,
hoping that free of her presence, the people of Taran would
relax and enjoy their Christmas goose. Fortunately she was
deaf to Peg Hatch's snide remark about the reason for Sir
Benedict's absence. Angelica slowly and wearily mounted the
wide staircase, trying to hold back her tears until she reached
the privacy of her rooms. She had just climbed to the first
landing when a furious hubbub erupted, punctuated with cheers,
crashes, shrieks, and laughter. She smiled ruefully and was
about to continue her ascent when the doors to the banquetting
hall burst open. Angus Dunbar strode out carrying a furiously
kicking and screaming Iris.

"Let me at 'er," she snarled. "I'll shut up 'er poison gob
fer ever," she promised. "Saying them rotten things about 'is
lordship and 'is mistresses!"

"But Pa, look what she's done to my new frock," wailed Peg Hatch, who was propelled from the hall by her one-legged father, Hezekiah. Angelica gasped at the girl's appearance: gravy and breadsauce dripped thickly off her lank red hair.

"New frock?!" blustered her enraged father. "Wait 'til I'm through with thy backside and head, you spiteful, ungrateful baggage, ee'll be needing a whole new body."

"Take yer pegleg to her, Hezekiah!" yelled Iris. Angus gave her a sharp slap on the rump, but the gruff old miner laughed.

"Damn good idea, Iris, maybe et'll knock some sense into thet red head," he agreed.

"Whatever is happening?" called Angelica. Iris, still in Angus's arms, stared up with dismay at the tall woman.

"I dedn't do nothing, yer ladyship, when thet slut threw your good food at me," whined Peg Hatch. Angelica winced as the girl's father lost his temper completely and backhanded his daughter. She slithered across the hall, splattering breadsauce and gravy. Iris gurgled with delight and Angus sighed with exasperation.

"Merry Christmas, your ladyship," said Hezekiah, respectfully touching his cap before hauling his mucky daughter to her feet and propelling her out by the scruff of her neck. Angelica gaped with disbelief, listening to the sound of the man's pegleg recede into the distance. Then she sagged limply against the bannister overcome with hysterical laughter. Tears streamed down her face and she wasn't sure whether she laughed or cried.

"Are you all right, Miss Angel?" asked Iris anxiously just as the front door was flung open and Taran strode in.

"Are you hurt, Iris?" he snapped, raising a quizzical eyebrow at the picture of the freckled-face girl cradled in Angus's strong arms.

"Merry Christmas, Sir Benedict," greeted Angus, ignoring Iris's struggles. "If you'll both excuse us," he added, inclining his head towards Angelica, who gazed down on her husband's gleaming dark head. Iris stared up at Angus's firm jaw as he strode with her towards his rooms.

Benedict stood motionless, filling his eyes with the vision

above him. He was unaware of the cheerful clatter emanating from the formal banquetting hall, of Mr. and Mrs. Smithers, who discreetly shut the wide oak doors muffling the revelry before they bustled back to the kitchens. Keeping his dark eyes pinned to the graceful figure of his wife, Taran slowly walked up the stairs. He frowned, seeing the tears on her pale cheeks.

"What is this, my love?" He traced the wetness with a gentle finger, and she shivered at the caress. "For me?" he asked huskily when she couldn't answer. She smiled brightly through the tears that she couldn't control. "Oh, my Angel, I have missed you more than I ever thought possible," he admitted, cupping her face between his broad hands and gazing lovingly into her brimming green eyes. "I know it is Christmas . . ."

"What's left of it," she interrupted.

"The best part is left, and I'll not share it with anyone but you until I've slaked this burning need," he growled.

Angelica laughed happily as he swung her into his arms and carried her up the rest of the stairs. She rested her head against his chest, listening to the strong beat of his heart. She reached up and laid her hand against his bristly cheek.

The fire blazed brightly, reflecting along Angelica's long graceful legs and across her swelling belly and ripening breasts. Benedict gazed upon her as the full realization of her pregnancy dawned upon him. She had never looked so beautiful and serene.

Angelica reached out eagerly for Benedict, her hungry eyes devouring every inch of him. She yearned to be crushed against his hard muscles, to give in to the dominance of his mouth, to be thoroughly claimed by him. But he made no move to touch her. He just stood in all his aroused naked glory staring fixedly at her full breasts and swollen belly. She was confused and then to her horror she saw evidence of his desire wane. She took an involuntary step backward, wishing desperately she hadn't so rashly stripped off her clothes.

"I didn't believe it possible that you could grow more beautiful."

"You are not disgusted?" she whispered, instinctively covering her stomach with her arms.

"Disgusted? Oh, my Angel, what ever makes you think that?" Angelica glanced at his relaxed manhood and then beseechingly up at his face unable to answer. "Oh, my love . . . I am in awe and that has taken precedence for the moment," he reassured, gently removing her arms and placing his large hands on her belly. "It is amazing to realize that there is a child within my span."

Angelica looked down at his splayed fingers encompassing her stomach, and she covered his brown hands with her own. "Our child," she said tearfully.

"I find it somewhat intimidating," he confessed, picking her up in his arms and laying her on the fur rug by the blazing hearth.

"You, the great forbidding Lord Taran, find something intimidating?" she teased, but he didn't share her laughter. He just surveyed her firm belly broodingly. "Shame on you, Sir Benedict, intimidated by a tiny baby no bigger than your hand," she chided. He nodded somberly and she kissed his stern mouth, trying to soften its harsh line. "I have ached for you these past cold months, and I'll not let any little Tremayne brat thwart me!"

"Speaking of little Tremayne brats, how is Devlyn?" He almost pounced on the subject.

"I repeat, I will not allow *any* Tremayne brats born or unborn to thwart me!" she stated a little too loudly as unease stabbed through her. "Please Benedict?" she pleaded, thrusting her full breasts towards him and writhing sensuously not wishing to think of any unpleasantness for a while. She wanted to be totally submerged in him, blocking out the rest of the world.

Benedict was bemused. This was his reticent, serene wife?

"Lusty wench," he murmured, his dark eyes smoldering with desire. She grinned wickedly, feeling his arousal. "I am all yours," he invited, lying back on the soft furs and opening his arms expansively to indicate his submission. "Do with me what you will, woman," he groaned, afraid to lean his weight upon her for fear of crushing their child.

Much later they sat beside the fire sipping wine and sharing a late Christmas supper. Benedict stared into the fire deep in thought.

"What is it?" she asked, stroking his lean cheek. He wrapped an arm about her shoulders and drew her close without answering.

"Seems strange and inhibiting to make love to my wife with a third person present," he confessed ruefully, running a hand over her smooth belly. "My God! Is that what I think it is?" he exclaimed when her belly contorted.

"Your child is kicking," she laughed. " 'Tis another very spirited Tremayne," she added without thinking. She instantly regretted her words.

"How is Devlyn?"

"She's wonderful. I have so much to tell you, but it can wait until tomorrow," she responded, hoping her agitation didn't show.

"I have presents for you both."

"And they can wait for tomorrow because you are the only present I desire," she said, detaining him when it seemed he would rise.

"You are insatiable, madame," he chuckled. "And bye the bye, what is going on between your harem-scarem maid and Angus Dunbar?"

Angelica stopped his questions by capturing his mouth with her own, not thinking the time appropriate to inform him that Iris Wilkins was no longer a servant but on a par with his daughter. She prayed that Devlyn would return before morning and that Benedict wouldn't insist on looking in on his dark daughter only to find her bed empty.

Iris sat chastely on a straight-backed chair in Angus's small sitting room, gaping with stupefaction at the engagement ring that he had reverently placed on her finger.

"Yer gullin' me, ain't you?" she accused, not daring to believe what was happening.

"Will you marry me?" he repeated.

"But it ain't right," she wailed, suddenly bursting into tears.

"And what isna right?" he soothed pulling her on to his lap and smoothing back her hair.

"Me and you, that's what ain't right. I'm just common and everything and you are nearly like one of them," she sobbed, availing herself of his proffered handkerchief and blowing her nose loudly.

"I love you and want to take care of you," he informed her gently, and she cried even harder. He sat patiently rocking her until she quieted. "Now, my kelpie, why all these tears?"

"Because I love you and want to take care of you, too, but I can't," she explained, her words punctuated by hiccoughs.

"And why not?" he probed. "Is it because I talk funny?" he teased broadening his brogue.

"It's because it won't work. It don't matter that you was found in a workhouse like me. It still don't make us the same. You are educated like 'is lordship . . . like the nobs and it don't matter 'ow much I learn to read and write and play music . . . I'm still common Iris Wilkins."

"You'll be my wife, Iris Dunbar."

"I don't speak right no matter 'ow 'ard I try."

"It doesna matter," he soothed.

"It bloody well does!" she shouted. "The day'll come when you'll be ashamed of me."

"Never!"

"Listen to me, Angus Dunbar!" she demanded, struggling to get off his lap, but he held her tightly. "Please let me go so I can really talk to you," she begged. He released her and she sprang away to stare blindly out of the window at the dark night sky. "You can go anywhere and talk to anyone about 'is lordship's business. Solicitors, bankers, lords, and ladies. Save for a bitta Scotch in your voice, you sound as good as them and that's ever so important. You don't need a wife what'll drag you down. I'll sleep with you . . . be your whore . . . but I ain't going to be your wife and make you a laughingstock."

"Have you quite finished?" he asked brusquely, and she nodded truculently. "If I wanted a whore, I'd go into Falmouth and avail myself of one."

"You're cross with me?"

"Aye, I'm very, very cross with you! Tis not easy for a mon to ask a woman to marry him, especially a woman he loves . . . and to be spurned hurts. Aye, it hurts and then to be further insulted when she offers to be his whore," he stated.

"You have a whore in Falmouth?" Iris asked in a very small voice, her eyes widening at the thought and pain restricting her breathing.

"And what's so surprising about that? I am a mon with a mon's needs!"

"You have a whore in Falmouth!" she repeated, her tone sharpening as her rage and indignation built. "Why? Why?" she sobbed, beating his chest with her small fists. Angus tried to smother his grin as he captured her hands in his.

"Why did you go to Falmouth for a whore when I was right here?" she cried brokenly.

"Because, my lass, you're no whore. You're my love. You're my life," he proclaimed, enfolding her tightly. "And we'll sail for America where everyone talks in a different way. We'll carve out a wonderful future for our sons and daughters."

"America?" breathed Iris. "Sons and daughters? You want me to be the mother of your children?"

"I want you to be my wife and the mother of my children." Iris scrutinized his rugged face.

"You know you're a madman, don't you? A bloody lunatic madman and no mistake," she muttered. "It would just serve you right if I said yes and you was stuck with me for ever and ever."

"Are you saying yes?" he laughed.

"Yes," she admitted before bursting into tears again. Angus threw back his head and bellowed with joyous laughter as she clung to him, wetting his shirt front. "Do you really have a whore in Falmouth?" she wailed, increasing his delighted mirth.

CHAPTER 20

SILAS QUICKBODY'S weatherbeaten face was creased with worry. He stared up at the clear night sky, his breath misting the sharp frosty air. Not a cloud existed in the arced expanse to eclipse the icy stars. The sea was coldly serene, mockingly innocent of the violent tempest that had raged for most of Christmas Day. The muted *whoosh* of the surf gently lapping against the cliff below seemed hollow and infinitely lonely to his ears, and Silas felt fear gnaw into his old aching bones. A terrible vision of a small body limply floating in and out with the tide, long dark hair entangled with the seaweed, tore into his mind and he shuddered. Pushing the nightmarish thought away, he comforted himself with the sight of the Carrack peacefully munching oats. The black stallion and the wild child of the moors were so very close, surely the animal would sense if she were in peril and kick up a rumpus. Nevertheless, Silas settled himself for another long night's vigil, hoping she would return before her father discovered her absence. He glanced up to the windows of the master suite, seeing the passionate glow of the hearth reflecting on the leaded panes before diffusing into the frigid air. A smile touched his pleated lips as he wistfully recalled his own lusty youth. He grinned broadly, remembering Iris's excitement earlier. She had dashed in, her freckled face radiating absolute joy to proudly show her engagement ring. Angus had stood in the shadows, his rugged Scottish face mirroring the same exultant happiness. Who would have imagined the stolid, steady Scot falling in love with such an unlikely scamp?

Silas snorted cynically as the words of a Christmas carol

repeated in his head. All was calm and all was bright, but for how long? It was the dangerous tranquility before the storm . . . a storm that could possibly rage more bitterly than any conjured by the elements, he mused miserably, snugly tucking a blanket about himself and resting his back against the wall of the Carrack's stall.

Boxing Day dawned grey and dismal, and Angelica slowly awakened. She stretched lazily, feeling a sensuous glow throb through her well-loved body. She reached out, hoping to entangle her relaxed limbs with Benedict's. She opened her eyes with surprise at finding herself alone in the large bed. She sat up and looked sleepily into her husband's thunderous face.

"Good morning, my darling," she greeted, her words sounding forced. Her sunny mood abruptly clouded, knowing there was an impending storm.

"Where is my daughter?" he demanded.

"I don't know."

"How long has she been gone?"

"Since before Christmas Eve."

"Three days?" he roared, and she nodded unhappily. "Three days!" he thundered.

"And she will be home soon. She left the Carrack to show her intention to return," explained Angelica, feeling lacerated by his searing scowl and pulling the covers over her bare breasts.

"She informed you of this?" challenged Benedict. She didn't answer, not wanting to lie nor to incriminate Iris. "She actually told you of her intentions?" he probed, infuriated by her silence. "I am demanding answers!" he raged.

"And I have none," she replied quietly, trying to summon up her courage to swing her legs out of the bed and rush into her connecting bedroom so she could dress. It was obvious there was to be a violent altercation, and she felt at a decided disadvantage in her naked state. She forced herself to meet his smoldering glare, noting he was dressed for riding in tight britches and high boots. He had a short quirt in hand, which he slapped impatiently against his muscular thigh, and she hoped in his fury it wouldn't be used against her. "There is a

lot to discuss, but I refuse to do so when you are in such . . .
a . . . bad mood." She could have bitten off her tongue for
finishing so lamely.

"In such a bad mood?" he repeated sardonically. "What
the hell is this, Angelica? Have I not the right to know what
is happening beneath my own roof and with my own child?"

"She is not a child, Benedict. She is a woman!" shouted
Angelica, her own rage igniting and giving her the courage to
contemptuously throw back the covers, leap from the bed and
stalk across the room in all her naked pregnant glory. She
reached her door and wrenched it open, but it was slammed
shut before she could escape. She didn't turn. She stood,
staring blankly at the wooden panels and his hands. She was
within his arms though untouched by him, and the space
between them vibrated with tension. She was unable to face
him, unable to face the blind fury that hardened the features
which such a short time before had been softened with love.
Despite her resolve she cringed, expecting harsh hands to dig
into her shoulders and twist her about.

Benedict fought to control his anger. His wife stood within
his arms, naked and pregnant. He saw her cower and he
stepped back, his hot rage turning to cold, steely anger.

"Do you really believe I would strike you?" he muttered,
and she shook her head, her arms crossed about her naked
belly and breasts, but she didn't face him.

"I should like to get dressed," she whispered.

"Look at me!" he demanded, and he watched her back
muscles tense before she slowly turned to face him, her face
white and drawn, her green eyes enormous and full of tears.
"Why the hell are you so afraid of me!" he shouted, pain
filling his own eyes and mixing with his fury. Angelica didn't
answer, but suddenly she realized the ridiculousness of the
situation and started to giggle. Benedict was startled at the
sudden change. Then it just further fanned his temper.

"I'm sorry," choked Angelica, trying to stop her mirth,
but the formidable picture of him with whip in hand, his face
black with fury, swearing at her for being afraid of him was
just too much. She could either continue laughing or burst
into uncontrollable tears.

"I don't like being made a fool of in my own house," he

stated coldly. "Neither do I relish being laughed at," he
added warningly, but she just shook her head helplessly
unable to stop. Her green eyes brimmed, pleading with him
for compassion and understanding. A sharp slap across her
face shocked her into silence. "I am also averse to hysteria."

Angelica made no movement to touch her burning cheek.
She kept her arms protecting the unborn child. "I am sorry to
have incurred your displeasure, my lord. I have done what I
felt was correct. I shall inform you of it when I have dressed
and composed myself," she stated, trying to control the
tremor in her voice. "If I might have your permission to go to
my room?"

"Angel?" The raw pain in his voice was evident. The fiery
imprint of his hand on her smooth cheek, the way she valiantly protected their unborn child from his wrath, her innate
dignity all served to melt his rage. All he wanted was her love
and forgiveness. "Angel?" he pleaded, opening his arms to
her, terrified of her rejection.

"I have deliberately gone against your wishes. I have
disobeyed you," admitted Angelica stiffly, making no move
towards him, although she longed to be enfolded in his arms.
She shivered violently suddenly feeling bereft and afraid of
his reaction to what she had to tell him.

Benedict scooped her up and tucked her snugly back into
their bed. He gently stroked her cheek, trying to erase his
handprint, but she pushed him away and struggled to sit up.

"No, you must hear me first, because if Devlyn doesn't
come back I won't expect your forgiveness . . . nor will I
ever forgive myself." Benedict lay beside her on the bed, but
as she haltingly recounted the events of the past months and
of the arrangement she had made with the dark wild girl, he
started to pace back and forth in front of the bay window, his
gaze pinned to the surging sea, his emotions seething.

"Continue," he barked harshly when she came to a stop
after describing Devlyn's hurt at having to hide herself away
whenever visitors came to Taran.

"There's not much more except to say . . . your daughter
is a beautiful, sensitive woman . . . and I know she thinks
that you are ashamed of her, that she's your guilty secret."

"Where is she?" he demanded roughly.

"I don't know. I think maybe she went to find Jonty Pengelly. I understand why you sent him and those poor old people away, but they were her only family for more than sixteen years. Those people are as much a part of your daughter as she is of your seed," she strove, intimidated by his broad back silhouetted against the bright window. "Devlyn told me that she would never stop searching for Jonty Pengelly," she confessed resignedly.

"And yet you still gave her her freedom?" he probed, spinning on his heel and pinning his dark eyes on her.

"Yes," she sighed, too weary to start a debate about freedom not being hers to give or take.

"I'm glad," he replied softly. Angelica gaped at him, not sure if she was hearing correctly. "I have had a lot of long lonely nights to think about my wild daughter and my own selfish need to harness and mold her. It was not the way to build love and trust, was it?" Angelica shook her head in agreement and tears splashed down her cheeks. "Jonty Pengelly will be here this afternoon. That is why I was so late and nearly missed Christmas . . . that and the abominable weather. I was attempting to be Saint Nicholas."

"I don't understand."

"I made a detour to collect my daughter's Christmas present," he confessed, sitting on the bed and pulling her on to his chest. "Jonty Pengelly, a rival for my child's affections. I admit to great jealousy."

"Where is he?"

"At High Tor trying to convince poor Jago that he is not an apparition induced by too much rum. I was surprised to find the house dark and gloomy. No Christmas festivities there, just Goodie carping away at Jago. Not much of a hero's welcome for young Ajax Pendarves."

"Ajax is home!" exclaimed Angelica. "Is he well?" Benedict morosely shook his head. "He's injured?"

"He lost an arm. It's ironic, isn't it? It's almost as if the fates wanted a Pendarves limb. They were thwarted by Torr's leg so they settled for Ajax's right arm."

"It pains me to think that if we have a son, he might have to fight in a war. To think of him dead or maimed on some strange battlefield so alone and far from home . . ." whispered Angelica, holding his hands over her belly as though to keep the child safe from harm.

"Where are the Pendarveses?"

"Felix is spending the holidays with my brothers, because Torr had to go away on business for several days. Granny-Griggs is also at my parents' cottage helping Maizie and Caleb Skinner with the holiday celebrations. I wanted to invite everyone here . . . but . . . well . . . I didn't."

"Because you didn't want to incur any more of your dictatorial husband's displeasure than was truly necessary?" he probed, and she smiled ruefully. "I am so very sorry, my darling. What a truly untenable position I placed you in."

"Benedict, if you had changed your mind about things, why didn't you write and tell me?"

"I wanted to undo my own autocratic mistakes. Each week I prepared to do so, but something came up and I was called to court or to the admiralty. But now I am home for a while and we must plan the most wonderful way to introduce my daughter to not only the country but . . . the world," he declared expansively.

"If she ever comes back."

"She left Carrack, so she'll be back," he stated confidently.

"What if she's hurt?" worried Angelica, the news about Ajax Pendarves filling her with dire thoughts. "I had thought she had found where Jonty Pengelly was and had gone to spend Christmas with him. He would have told you if he had seen her, wouldn't he?" Benedict silently nodded. "So then where is she?"

"You said yourself that she would return in a few days," he reassured.

"That's what I was told, but she has never stayed away so long before . . . she's always back by morning."

"Perhaps it was my company at Christmas she wished to avoid. You say she is most perceptive and sensitive? Well, maybe she wanted to keep things harmonious at Taran. You say she had presents for everyone, including the Smithers?"

"They're still unopened on the piano in the small salon. I felt she should be here to give them in person. I wanted you to hear her play. Through music, I thought you two might reach each other. She is a magical, wonderful, brave young woman, and I pray to God she is safe," sobbed Angelica, unable to stop the torrent of tears. "Oh, Benedict, I am so sorry about all this hysteria, but I can't seem to stop it. Father says it is very usual with pregnant women. That's why men leave them alone so much during their confinement, because we are so very tiresome . . . but I don't want to be left alone," she wailed, and Taran held her tightly. "If anything happens to Devlyn, I shall never forgive myself."

"Hush, my love. Don't fret so. You forget she's a Tremayne. She's the Devil-Child of the moors, used to defending herself. . ." His deep voice trailed away and unease dug sharply. "What I would have paid to witness those shooting lessons and Iris's attempts at riding," he laughed, pushing his fears for his daughter's safety aside and trying to lighten the somber mood. Angelica giggled, but her fingers clasped his arms too tightly. "Get dressed, woman. I have a notion to see young Iris's table manners. I cannot for the life of me even attempt to imagine that little hussy being able to behave with one whit of decorum."

"You mustn't laugh at her, because she tries very hard," she warned.

"I solemnly promise I will not laugh."

"Or make any sardonic remarks?"

"When have I made any sardonic remarks?" he asked indignantly. Angelica leaned on his chest and gazed adoringly into his dark fathomless eyes, her tears wetting his snowy shirt front. Her elbows dug into his pectorals. "Move those sharp joints, my darling," he growled. She obediently moved her arms and started nimbly undoing his buttons so she could rub her naked breasts against his warm flesh.

"I don't think we should wake the baby," he protested halfheartedly, making no move to thwart her assault on his most willing body.

"Then stop talking," she answered roguishly before kissing him.

Iris anxiously paced the carpeted corridor outside the master suite, wishing something would happen, as the suspense was tying her stomach into knots. She had expected to be awakened by loud roars and furious screams, but everything was too calm, too quiet, and she was mortally afraid that Lord Taran had become so incensed he had actually throttled his wife.

All night she had tossed and turned listening for Devlyn's return, and despite her firm resolve she had fallen asleep in the predawn hours. It had been a long lonely night, her thoughts and feelings fragmented. She had wished to be within Angus's arms, yet when he had left her at her bedroom door with just a chaste kiss, she had felt cherished. He would not allow her back in his bed until they were married, and although she gloried in his quiet strength, she also fought against it. She resumed her frantic pacing with a wistful smile on her face. She was loved and revered and it was almost too much for her to comprehend.

The door to the master bedroom was quietly opened, and Benedict and Angelica stood arm in arm gazing pensively at the muttering girl, who furiously stalked up and down the corridor.

"Iris?" called Angelica, and the girl froze on the spot and gaped at them.

"You're alive!" she gasped with a loud sigh of relief. She fanned herself and patted her chest trying to slow her pounding heart. Obviously from the master's benevolent expression, he was unaware of his daughter's absence.

"Is anything the matter, Iris?" asked Benedict, humour twinkling his eyes and deepening his voice.

"No, no, nothing. I just come to tell you that yer breakfast is ready in the small dining 'all, yer lordship, sir," gushed Iris awkwardly, bobbing a curtsey and turning red with embarrassment at being caught outside their bedroom door.

"Well aren't you going to join us?" he replied.

"What me?" she squeaked.

"Angelica informs me that you are now one of the family."

"Oh, no, that ain't really true, yer lordship. I know my place, honest I do, sir. It was just to keep Miss Devil 'appy. I mean Miss Dev*lyn* 'appy," she stammered, miserably twisting her ring.

"What a pretty ring, Iris!" exclaimed Angelica, taking the girl's hand.

"An engagement ring, too," added Benedict.

"No, no, it ain't . . . just don't fit no other finger, yer lordship. It ain't true. I know my place, honest I do," wailed Iris. "It was just to keep—"

"Angus Dunbar happy?"

"Oh, please sir, I won't marry 'im if you says not to. I know my place, honest I do."

"Stop being so silly, Iris," laughed Angelica.

The first half of breakfast was a disaster because Iris tried so hard to show off her good manners that she knocked everything over within reach. Benedict behaved impeccably and pretended to notice nothing, and Angus nodded reassuringly, hoping to show that he had complete faith in her ability to cope.

"Well, yer lordship, there ain't nothing left to drop or spill, so now you can stop staring at me and let me chew," Iris sighed. "I told you I would shame you," she snapped at Angus.

"Can we plan the party for Devlyn?" urged Angelica. "When shall it be?"

"It's 'er birthday next week."

"That's right. On New Year's Eve," intoned Benedict, thinking of the gravestone on the moor.

"Do you think we could have everything ready in five days? Invitations? Food? Clothes?" worried Angelica, sensing that her husband had drawn away. He smiled into her anxious eyes and reached for her hand.

"With the four of us and the indispensable Smithers we can accomplish anything we set our minds to," he stated positively. "That is, if my unpredictable daughter decides to return by then," he added whimsically.

"Crikey! You mean you know she ain't 'ere!" squawked Iris, her eyes as round as saucers and the freckles standing out on her white face. Benedict nodded. "Cor, well, don't that beat everything? Shows 'ow wrong a person can be, don't it? I was so sure you'd bust a gut when you knew, and 'ere you is all soft and purry like a nice old pussycat."

Angelica went into gales of delighted laughter seeing Benedict's expression, which in no way resembled a complacent old pussycat. Instead, he appeared to be more like a panther tensed to spring, but he kept his smile genial and calmly ate.

Boxing Day passed in a whirl of excited activity as lists were made of all the things that had to be done and the guests who were to be invited. Invitations were to be personally delivered that very evening and every available man, woman, and child on the estate of Taran was pressed into service with the promise of a handsome holiday bonus. Benedict solved Angelica's worry about appropriate party clothes by opening the door to his study, revealing an enormous pile of packages all wrapped in pretty paper and tied with bows.

"We'll open nothing until Devlyn returns," decided Angelica. Then as worry gnawed at her again, she flung herself into the whirlwind of planning.

Devil wearily steered the stolen boat between the perilous fangs of Wolf Rock. Her thoughts drifted back through the years to the night she had stood on the shore in the raging storm watching the two dark shapes swim out of the shining sheets of rain. Two beautiful ebony animals who had filled an aching lonely void, the Bucca-Dhu and the Carrack. Her eyes brimmed with tears and she felt the searing loss of her hound join with a painful new ache. Every place on her body where Torr's hands had touched felt abandoned, and she wondered miserably if she would ever feel whole again. She was so wrapped in her own memories that she was unaware of the two old people who pranced happily on the cold sand outside the cavern at Pendarves Point.

"Wait a bit, awd man, ted'nt the Devil-Child's ketch," hissed Granny-Griggs, and the two old people ducked furtively into the cave to watch the approaching vessel. "But there ent any other thet can guide a vessel with such ease through the reefs save Jonty Pengelly," she whispered. "Maybe tes the awd man hisself."

"Tes the Devil-Child," observed Caleb, watching the dejected little figure clamber out of the boat.

"Where's the boy?" demanded Granny, fear clutching at her boney chest. "Where's young Torr Pendarves?" she called, her voice echoing across the still dark water and bouncing off the cold rocks.

"Safe," Devil answered. Just hearing his name pronounced caused her pulses to race. "He'll return soon."

"What the dickins is thee wearing?" fussed Granny-Griggs, staring at the girl's feet that were bound with blanket rags and twine. "Lose thy boots, did thee? We near lost our minds worritting ourselves sick about thee, what with thet great Christmuz storm and all. Oh, my dear heart and soul, we thought thee wuz at the bottom of the sea, dedn't we, Caleb Skinner?"

"Get thyself back to Taran, Devil-Child. Thy father's home," growled the old man. "Best take my awd Queenie cuz thee look fair steeved ter death weth the cold. Leave the awd nag weth Silas Quick and I'll fetch him on the morrow."

Devil nodded silently and mounted the swaybacked Queenie.

"Ded them admiralty men get there safe?" queried Granny, uncomfortable with the bleakness in the dark eyes. Again there was a silent nod. "And the Pendarves man is safe and sound?" she probed. Devil didn't acknowledge the crone's last question. She just whirled away into the darkness. Soon the old couple heard the sound of hooves crunching the cold pebbles and then splashing through the foam at the water's edge.

"Something happen 'tween them two youngens?" asked Caleb, and Granny just pulled on her loose lips thoughtfully.

"I ent walking, awd man, so tes either two on a nag or thee'll trudge beside," she stated, uneasy with the Devil-Child's remoteness and wishing to change the subject. "And ef'n et's two on the nag, I'll ride aft. I'll not hev Maizie getting jealous seeing my fine body twixt thy spindly shanks," she nattered.

Devil welcomed the plodding gait of the swaybacked nag, feeling too fatigued to balance on a more spirited animal. She also welcomed the shrill bitter wind that cut through her damp garments, chilling her to the bones, because it kept her awake. She wound her numb fingers into the stringy mane and clamped her aching legs to the heaving girth of the patient old horse.

Silas saw the slow-moving horse top the rise of the cliff, both animal and rider hunched against the striated sky. He kept his rheumy eyes pinned to the approaching figures, not knowing if he imagined the sight. He was unaware of the tall man beside him.

"Get to your bed, Silas," murmured Benedict. The old man was startled for a moment.

"Tedn't nice to sneak up on a person," he scolded. "And I ent going nowhere," he added, setting his bandy legs stubbornly apart and glaring up at his master. "I'll not hev thee hurting thet wondrous lass of thine, Master Benedict! Ef'n thee knew the half of et—"

"Silas, I'm glad my child has a champion in you, but there are things between a father and child . . . that are between a father and child," he said softly.

"And thee'll keep thy temper on a tight rein? Thy'll not roar and terrify her? Not hurt her weth cutting words or the like?"

"I'll not hurt her, Silas," promised Benedict. "Don't you believe me?" he added when the old man still glared suspiciously.

"Is the gentle boy still within the man?" challenged Silas, and Benedict nodded, unable to speak for the emotions that constricted his throat. The old man caught the glint of tears in the dark eyes of the hawklike face above him and nodded. His gnarled hand squeezed Benedict's arm before he hobbled into the dim recesses of the stable.

Devil instinctively knew who loomed, staring intently at her as she entered the stable-yard. The tired old nag obediently clopped across the cobblestones and halted right in front of the tall dark man. Although exhausted, Devil stiffened her back, lifted her chin stubbornly, and summoning her last ounce of reserve energy, glared defiantly into her father's shadowy face. She frowned with confusion seeing him smile tenderly, tears streaking his chiseled face.

"Welcome home, my Devil-Child," he greeted. Devil didn't know how to react. She blinked, trying to awaken from a dream, but the vision of her father was steadfast.

"You're home!" Angelica's voice cut joyfully through the chilly night, and Devil toppled into her father's open arms too numb in body and spirit to cope.

Devil allowed herself to be undressed, bathed, and tucked into bed by Angelica, Iris, and Mrs. Smithers. She was dazed and confused, barraged by their overwhelming excitement about parties, birthdays, engagements, and Christmas presents. She let everything wash over her like a smothering wave, closing her senses and submerging herself in sleep.

"She's asleep!" exclaimed Benedict indignantly when he was at last allowed into his daughter's room.

"Yes, she's asleep. It doesn't look as if she's slept for days," whispered Angelica, gently tracing the dark circles under the girl's eyes. "So give her a kiss and tiptoe out," she ordered. He dutifully placed his lips to his daughter's clear brow and quietly left the room.

"Torr? Torr?" whispered Devil feverishly, and Iris and Angelica exchanged shocked looks.

"Crikey! Now what? Is that 'oo's shirt she was wearing?" mourned the freckled maid. "If it ain't one thing it's another! 'ere Miss Angel, you go to 'is lordship, I'll stay with Dev. Go on, I ain't missing out on nothing. My man ain't interested in me body 'til we's wed," she sighed. "Do you think they was together? Miss Devil and Torr Pendarves?" she hissed, and Angelica shrugged unhappily. "Torr Pendarves wouldn't 'ave done nothing to Miss Dev, 'er being 'is lordship's daughter and all. But 'e wouldn't know that, would 'e?" she ended miserably. "Well, it's a bloody good job 'is lordship didn't 'ear or the cat'd be among the pigeons!"

Devil slept soundly and awakened with the bright winter sun streaking across her bed. She lay still, sensing she was being watched.

"It's only me," comforted Iris, seeing the girl tense and feel about for a weapon. "Blimey, I didn't think you was ever going to wake up. It's nearly teatime, yer know. Guess what? I'm engaged to be married. Really I am. See me ring?" she chattered, blowing on it noisily and rubbing it briskly on her dress before extending it for approval. But the dark girl ignored her and leaped out of the bed. "You shouldn't jump up like that, it ain't good for yer brain," she warned, trotting after Devil into the dressing room and perching herself on a trunk. She silently watched the girl tear off her nightdress and stand naked, rifling through the armoire. "What are you looking for?" But Devil didn't answer; she searched diligently and then pulled out the burgundy-coloured riding

habit her father had sent from London. " 'Ave you been with
Torr Pendarves of High Tor?" probed Iris suddenly.

Devil's reaction was answer enough. She froze with the
habit in hand, unable to look at her friend. "How did you
know?" she whispered. Iris saw the colour rise on her neck,
flushing her cheeks.

"You talk in yer sleep, luvey," replied the maid, watching
Devil regain her composure and quickly dress. "Just a word
of warning, Dev. Don't let yer dad know or the fat'll be in
the fire and no mistake . . . and then poor Miss Angel. It
ain't good fer the baby, yer know . . . all this aggravation can
warp its bones and all," she pronounced direly.

"Where is my father?"

" 'In 'is study . . . 'e 'as surprises for you—ain't never seen
so many presents! 'e wants to know the minute you wake up.
You know 'e ain't such a bad sort and 'e's going to be ever so
'appy to see you dressed in that 'abit and all," chattered Iris,
following Devil out of her room and along the corridor.

Devil had no idea how incredibly beautiful she looked in
the perfectly cut habit that seemed molded to her exquisite
figure. The rich red velvet was a brilliant foil for her black
flashing eyes, and the dusky pink of her cheeks.

Benedict looked up and caught his breath at the glorious
picture of his daughter as she stood poised at the threshold of
his study. Angelica caught his rapt expression and gently
touched Angus's arm. They quietly left the room, leaving
father and daughter together.

Devil had rehearsed what she would say to him throughout
the long cold hours she had spent alone on the stolen boat,
but now face to face with him she could find no words. In her
imagined encounters he had towered intimidatingly, his thick
brows satanically raised, a diabolical sneer twisting his thin
lips. Then it had been easy to battle him. But it was not easy
to confront this tenderly smiling man who regarded her so
lovingly. She opened her mouth to speak, but he silenced her
with a slight movement of his hand.

"I want to apologize to you, daughter. I have no excuse
except I am very new at being a father. May I please have
another chance?" he said huskily. Devil's heart hammered
painfully. He was so very vulnerable. She knew how incredi-

bly powerful she was at that moment and the knowledge terrified her. How could she hurt him? How could she tell him that it was too late? How could she tell him that she was fully grown and had no need of a parent? How could she tell him that she was leaving?

Benedict stared at his daughter's masklike face. Her dark eyes were hooded and her small chin raised haughtily. He was hurt and rejected. He had not known what to expect, but now he realized that in some fanciful corner he had hoped to have his loving child in his arms. But this was no loving child, no child at all but a woman—a strange unapproachable woman.

"Before you reply, there is someone here to whom I'm sure you will be more effusive," he pronounced, his voice cynical and his eyebrows set in a forbidding line.

Devil recoiled as though slapped at his caustic tone, but she kept her back stiff and her expression arrogant, silently watching him stride from the room. She sagged against the wall, willing her tears to stay hidden, fighting to keep her composure.

Angelica groaned seeing Benedict's stormy face as he strode into the library, where she sat quietly talking to Jonty Pengelly. "Oh, darling, you didn't let loose that awful Tremayne temper, did you?"

"She didn't say a word—just haughtily stared through me."

"That's fear, my lord," informed Jonty.

"Fear? She was poised, Pengelly. I was the one quivering like a callow stripling! Go to her, old man, she wants none of me!" he shouted, uncorking a decanter and pouring himself a glass of brandy.

"You are her father, let her talk to you the way she does best," urged Jonty.

"With a dagger and gun? I hear she is very adept in archery also," seethed Benedict.

"With music," said Angelica gently.

"I cannot approach her. She is a very possessed young woman . . . a stranger. An incredibly beautiful and strange female . . . my daughter," he explained brokenly, draining his glass. "And what do you find so amusing?" he growled, glaring at Angelica's wide grin.

"According to my father it is a universal malady," she giggled.

"What is? Don't talk in riddles!"

"Daughters growing into strange women. Would you like me to go with you?" she asked and was surprised when he nodded eagerly. She had supposed his male vanity would keep him from admitting to the need for moral support.

"No!" Benedict changed his mind abruptly, and Jonty Pengelly tacitly nodded his approval.

Devil was just about to leave the study and go for a comforting ride around Taran Park when the door burst open. Her father strode in and took her firmly by the hand. Her eyes widened, but she was too surprised to fight free of his grasp. He led her to the small salon on the second floor, where she had spent many happy hours playing the pianoforte for Angelica and Iris as they sewed baby clothes. He sat her at the instrument and she stared with bewilderment.

"Tell me of yourself, my Devil-Child?" he begged gruffly.

Haltingly, Devil started to play, her fingers touching each key softly as though to ground herself before daring to fly freely into life. Her nose quivered, smelling the delicate dew on the heather and the frost on the sheep-cropped grass. The music swelled confidently and Benedict learned of the beauty and overwhelming loneliness of the moors and the many moods of the merciless sea that had helped fashion his mercurial child. He closed his eyes and saw Devlyn grown from a tiny babe to a solitary elfin toddler, treading through the white horses on the deserted shore. He wept for what had been denied them both. He was unaware of Angelica and Jonty quietly standing in the doorway, but he heard the sudden joyful lilt that skipped lightly through the bittersweet melody when Devlyn looked up to see Jonty Pengelly's wizened face. He opened his eyes and saw the tender connection that flowed between the old man and his daughter. His jealousy fled and he fervently thanked the powers that be for having provided some comfort and love to his unknown child.

Devil played, recalling the shapes and colours of the clouds and rocks through each season of her life. She rode the Carrack through the purple swirling mists of the past and slept pillowed on the Bucca-Dhu's sleek blackness. Her joy soared with the birds, bats, and butterflies of the air and her sorrow pulsed beneath the cold earth where her hound was buried. Bleak mourning winter gave rise to exultant spring and the gold of Torr Pendarves's hair, and the hot touch of his brown hand claiming each inch of her awakening woman's body.

Devil recollected her surroundings and the swelling music came to an abrupt stop on a crashing discord. She sat still with her chin high, staring straight ahead, her face flaming with embarrassment for sharing so intimate and private an experience.

" 'Ow come I can't 'ave such pretty tunes come out of my fingers?" moaned Iris, breaking the tense moment and releasing everyone from their stunned immobility. Jonty blew his nose loudly and brushed the tears from his eyes, knowing his young charge was no longer an untouched maid but a passionate woman. He wondered who the young man was and how Benedict Tremayne would react to sharing his newfound daughter.

Benedict quietly approached Devlyn. He had no words to give her. Anything he could say would be grossly inadequate. He wanted to embrace her, but he had also seen how she held herself apart, uncomfortable with being touched. The night before she had been virtually unconscious when she toppled into his arms, and the same was true when Jonty Pengelly had brought her to Taran all those months ago. The only other time he had held her, she had fought like a wild animal, biting and kicking as though her very life depended on it. Benedict pinned his dark eyes to the ones so much like his own and held out his arms.

Devil gazed back silently. She was afraid that if she walked into his arms he would never let her go. She stood and allowed him to embrace her. It was a painfully awkward moment, and Benedict's arms quickly dropped away.

"When can we open the presents?" asked Iris, uncomfortable in the strained silence. "We didn't open yours, Dev, cos we was waiting for you, and yer dad brought a bloody great pile all the way from London, too." Iris's cheerful chatter soon had everyone relaxed.

Benedict marvelled at Devlyn's delicate yet whimsical carvings. Each bird was reminiscent of the person for whom it

was made. For Angelica there was a graceful, regal swan; for
Iris a swallow soaring to new heights; for Angus, a ruffed
grouse firmly rooted to the ground; for the Smithers, perky
house wrens; and for Silas Quickbody, a wise old barn owl.
Benedict sat with his unopened package in his large hand. He
was afraid to unwrap it for fear of what he'd find. How had
she depicted him? He had been so harsh and restrictive. He
imagined a merciless bird of prey.

"Ain't you going to open it?" urged Iris. Benedict slowly
unwrapped the tiny parcel and stared down with amazement.
"Well, what is it?" asked Iris impatiently. He didn't answer
but just gazed mistily at his surprising daughter. Angelica
looked over his shoulder and caught her breath at seeing the
delicate ebony swan nestled in his hand, the mate for her
own. Devlyn knelt beside her father and taking both swans
entwined their graceful necks so they were balanced in a
loving courtship dance. Benedict cupped his daughter's face
between his palms and gazed silently into her eyes. What an
amazing young woman, able to surmount her own problems
and see beyond his faults to find what was truly beautiful
about him . . . his love for Angelica.

The rest of the day passed happily. Presents were opened
and Jonty sat back enjoying the shy reserve between father
and daughter. Still, worry gnawed at him. Who was the man
who had stolen the Devil-Child's vulnerable young heart?

Torr Pendarves arrived back at High Tor via Falmouth in a
foul mood. He had not only awakened to the wrenching pain
of his desertion but also to the embarrassment of his alleged
wife's theft. He had spent several awkward hours convincing
the local constabulary that he would not only replace the
vessel but also pay handsomely for the inconvenience and the
night's lodging. Learning that he had lied about his identity,
that he was Sir Torrance Pendarves of High Tor and owner of
the Pendarves mines on the mainland, several men decided to
accompany him to prove his allegations.

Goodie and Jago were impatiently thrust aside, their excited chatter about Ajax and Jonty ignored, as Torr and four
hefty Guernsey men strode past and into the study. The door
was firmly slammed. Several minutes later the Guernsey men

left, patting bulging pockets and sporting wide smiles, and
Torr roared for Granny-Griggs. He was stunned when Ajax
walked silently into the room. So stunned he didn't notice the
empty sleeve. All he noticed was the bitterness that prematurely aged his brother's young face.

"Ajax!" he cried joyfully, shaking free of his inertia and
extending a hand in friendship.

"Season's greetings," returned the youth caustically, picking up his limp right sleeve and offering it to Torr.

"Oh, my God, no!" Torr reached out to embrace his
brother, but Ajax broke free and pushed angrily away.

"Oh, my God, yes!" he spat. "There were no healing
witches and devils for me! I am a cripple!" He picked up a
decanter, wrenched the cork out with his teeth, and poured
himself a large glass of spirits.

"You are alive," breathed Torr, painfully aware of how
inadequate the words were.

"But useless! I cannot ride a horse, write a letter, wrap my
arms about a wench, fence, or do innumerable other manly
deeds. So I am home, dear brother, to be taken care of," he
proclaimed, draining the glass and pouring himself another.
"Aren't you impressed?"

"With what?" queried Torr.

"Me? Here I am limbless, but I am not lying in my bed
full of self-pity," he stated drunkenly. "As you did. You
drove our father to an early grave," he accused. Torr didn't
reply, knowing rational communication was impossible. He
left his younger brother to drown his pain, realizing a time for
grieving was necessary. On learning that Granny-Griggs was
in Penzance with Felix and the Carmichaels, he had Jago
saddle a horse.

"You ent surprised to learn thet my brother Jonty is alive?"

"No, Jago, it seems to be the season for the dead to rise
from their graves and prodigal brothers to return to haunt,"
he answered. "Where is Jonty?"

"He just up and left day after Christmas and I ent heard
since. Sir Benedict Tremayne brung him along weth Master
Ajax . . . which brings to mind there's an invite for thee.
There's to be a grand 'To-Do' at Taran on New Year's Eve . . .

a grand ball just like the good old days when the old lord was alive and Master Michael hadn't drowned,'' informed Jago.

The good old days and a ball were the last things of interest to Torrance Pendarves. He swung his long leanness into the saddle. If he could locate either Granny-Griggs or Caleb Skinner, he would find his Devil-Woman.

"What is Granny doing in Penzance at the Carmichaels'?'' he demanded.

"Avoiding my bride,'' confessed Jago glumly. "I wish to heavens I could avoid her, too. Marriage ent what et is set up to be! A female is the bane of a good man's existence! There ent no peace on this earth weth them,'' he lamented as Goodie's voice screeched from the house. "I wish to hell we could live without them!'' he added fervently. Torr nodded his agreement before kicking his horse into a brisk canter across the wild winter moor.

Every solitary cairn of grey granite, each curl of sea-mist, each stark stunted tree silhouetted against the surging waters joined with his pain, reminding him of his elusive elfin love. He slowed his rapid pace when Pendarves Chapel loomed into view, but there was no haunting melody melding with the wind. What would he do if he ever found her, he seethed, knowing his emotions were raw and tangled. A violent fury raged with his pain and passion. What would he do if he never found her, came the unbearable thought.

Granny-Griggs peered out of the Carmichaels' kitchen window at Torr Pendarves conversing with Caleb Skinner. Her rheumy eyes narrowed with apprehension. She knew what the young man asked, and she sighed with relief at Caleb's shaking head, knowing she would be the next interrogated. Two minutes later she stared innocently into the intense blue eyes.

"Where is she?''

"She?'' she repeated vacantly.

"No games, Granny,'' he hissed, a warning tick beating in his lean tanned cheek. "Where is she?'' The old hag silently shrugged and splayed her gnarled hands.

"I hear that your brother Ajax is home from the war and the poor nestling's lost a wing?''

"Where is she?" repeated Torr, ignoring her effort to change the subject.

"Thee are here to fetch Master Felix home? Leave him be weth young fellers his own age. I hear how Master Ajax is still mourning bitterly for his lost arm. Your home ent a fit place in this joyful season for an awd witch nor a young lad home from school for just a few weeks," chattered the old woman, avoiding the cold piercing eyes.

"Don't tempt me, old witch! I am wound so tight I should dearly love to do violence to someone," he threatened. "Now, where is she?"

"Do thee think I'd tell thee even ef I knew when thee has such murder in your eyes?"

"I love her," admitted Torr.

"Tesn't a very loving tone I hear in thy voice," snorted Granny-Griggs.

"Where the hell is she?" he shouted, his rage igniting. Fortunately for the old woman, whose boney shoulders were suddenly caught in a cruel vise, Simon entered the room. Torr's clenched fists dropped harmlessly to his sides.

"Is everything all right with Ajax?" the plump doctor enquired, frowning at the young peer's thunderous expression.

"You've examined him?"

"Benedict brought him down from London and sent word to me. The poor lad has healed well but has not taken too kindly to his condition. I warned him about drinking so heavily. It can thin the blood," stated Simon, tactfully refraining from remarking on the Pendarves's trait of morbid self-pity. Granny-Griggs shrewdly seized the opportunity to sidle from the room.

Torr rode out to Pendarves Point, hoping to find the dark girl in the vast cavern beneath the Norman fortress. Save for the stolen Guernsey ketch stranded forlornly on the beach, out of reach of the high tide, there was no sign of life. Impatiently he searched through the cold dismal rooms of the castle, but nothing stirred except the cumbersome ravens and twittering bats.

Recalling Jago's claim that it had been Benedict Tremayne responsible for Jonty Pengelly's miraculous reappearance, Torr rode on to Taran. Angelica welcomed him effusively, offering refreshments, but upon learning that her husband was away from home and not expected until evening, Torr curtly declined, knowing he was not fit company. Angelica watched him leave, disturbed by the flinty detachment in his blue eyes and the ruthless expression that marred his handsome features. She sensed suffering beneath the apparent cruel rage and correctly surmised the cause, yet she feared for Devlyn. Torr Pendarves had much growing to do before he became a seasoned, reasonable man. She shivered, envisioning the painful conflict that could wound the dark girl of the moors, who was just learning to trust.

Torr returned to High Tor, where he locked himself in his study with reports and accounts from the mines, unable to deal with the drunken taunting of his maimed brother. Although he ached with exhaustion, he could not bear to lie alone in bed, tormented by dreams of his phantom Devil-Woman.

Devil rode beside her father, her thoughts full of the Living-Dead. They were snugly housed in white-washed cottages with sheltered gardens, but they were afraid of the sunlight. They were terrified of bright colours and sat in dim parlours with the shutters closed, waiting for the dusk when they could shuffle outside in their black robes and blend with the shadows. They had recoiled from her, not recognizing their Devil-Child in the elegant red riding habit, and she had noticed that the manacles still encircled their emaciated wrists.

" 'Tis too late for them," Jonty had sighed. "But they are happier than before. They are warm and well fed," he had attempted to comfort.

"I shall visit again," she had whispered, and the old man had nodded. They both knew that her presence would make no difference to the Living-Dead, who, forced to brutally murder Rebecca Peller, had sacrificed the last vestiges of individuality and had crossed into a numb limbo of grey, waiting for eternal darkness. "You cannot stay here, Jonty! You are not as they!" she had protested, and he had agreed to return with her to Taran at least until the new year to help celebrate her seventeenth birthday.

Not a word passed between father and daughter on the long

ride back to Taran. Benedict watched Devlyn's proud profile, respecting her grief. He had been profoundly shaken by the empty shells of once vital beings. Jonty Pengelly, hunched low in his saddle, the keen wind tearing at his black robes, rode at a respectful distance behind the dark couple. He sensed that the Devil-Child's misery was caused by something beyond Curate Pomfrey's blank stare and the Three-Marys' mute inertia.

"Thank you for making such generous provision for my friends," Devil intoned stiffly before dismounting from the Carrack. Benedict nodded, knowing words were inadequate, and along with Jonty and Silas Quickbody, he silently watched the proud young woman cross the dark courtyard to the house. They all felt her sorrow, despite her graceful carriage. Later they all heard the eloquent expression of her tumultuous emotions; listened breathlessly to the anger, fury, and frustration that throbbed through her fingers. The music drifted through the sleeping house, joining with the pulses of the earth; joining with the ebb and flow of the tide and the sweet breath of the woman carrying an unborn child that Benedict held within his arms.

The last days of 1793 passed in a kaleidoscope of laughter, decorations, and breathless anticipation. Benedict couldn't believe the wonderful transformation. The gloomy halls and chambers of Taran rang with love and happiness. Gone was the dolorous aching that had shrouded him for so long, and his eyes hungrily and possessively followed his radiant wife who spread such warmth, joy, and understanding wherever she went. He was enchanted by his daughter and each day was surprised and delighted to discover yet another side to her character. It was as though he were witness to a butterfly tentatively emerging from the dark, imprisoning cocoon; the trembling wings sparking with iridescent colours that constantly changed, catching the many moods of the world, each change more wondrous than the next. He was perturbed by the poignant sadness that still seemed to cling, muting her sparkling presence. She refused to ride the Carrack and confined herself within the walls of Taran, busily helping Angelica, yet somehow detached from the mounting festivities. At first Benedict thought she still mourned for the pitiful Living-Dead, and he had offered to accompany her to their cosy cottages, but she had silently refused. She has appeared to be almost afraid to venture outside the gates of the estate. Several times he had observed her in the stables and knew that she yearned to be on the Carrack's powerful back, releasing the conflicting emotions that furrowed her brow and clouded her eyes. Several times she had caught his concerned gaze, and he had felt that she was about to impart something important. But when their eyes met, he saw fear and indecision. Her mouth would close and she'd smile tremulously.

Devil ached to be on the Carrack's high back, racing out the turbulence that seethed within her. How could she explain to her father? What could she explain to her father? Was she a whore? Would her father tell her she was a whore? What had seemed so natural and beautiful was now suspect. The wonderful memory of her Christmas night of loving had become tarnished after Iris's excited chatter about her engagement to Angus Dunbar. Devil was confused and frightened; no longer sure of anything except her need to be with Torr Pendarves. As she learned more about the dos and don'ts of acceptable society outside the grim walls of Pendarves Castle, she understood that she had given something away that could never be taken back. That very something could label her in the same shameful way as her mother; it could guarantee her the same disgust and rejection.

"Angus honest ter God respects me and that's why 'e won't 'ave me 'til we is man and wife. 'E says anyone can 'ave an 'ore and you isna an 'ore, Iris me lassie, 'e says," recounted Iris dreamily. "Decent ladies save theirselves, yer see."

Devil's plan of confronting her father and then riding out to High Tor to give herself to Torr Pendarves suddenly seemed dangerous. What if everything had changed and he no longer wanted her? Jonty watched her sadly, wishing she would confide in him but also knowing she needed a mother figure at that perilous moment in her life, not a doddering old man.

"What is it, Skilliwiddens?" he had asked softly.

"I wish I was still Skilliwiddens. Everything was much simpler then," she had replied.

"Would you really change back?" Without hesitation she had shaken her head. "Would you really like to be free of the pain of loving?" and her eyes had filled with tears.

"I cherish the pain; 'tis maybe all I'll ever have," she had whispered.

"Talk to her ladyship, she'll understand," begged Jonty, but Devil's expression had hardened and she had vehemently shaken her head.

"I'll put no more secrets between loving people," she had hissed, and then fleetly ran from the room.

The night before her seventeenth birthday, Devil could not sleep. She stood at the window watching the sea ripple to the horizon, hearing it rhythmically wash against the bluffs. Ignoring the warning that rang ominously in her head, she donned the dark trews and cape and furtively slipped out of the house and made her way to the stables.

"Are thee going to say goodbye to thy childhood?" asked Silas, leading the Carrack out into the cobbled yard, and Devil didn't answer. How could she confess to the old groom that she had no vestige of innocent childhood left. In fact, she was her mother's daughter, a whore!

Devil rode the Carrack across the high moor to the desolate stone chapel. Leaving the stallion to graze, she entered and sat at the old organ. She lit a candle, and without pumping, she fingered the yellowed ivories, not daring to feel her inner tempest for fear she would be rent to pieces. She was so immersed in her protective numbness that she didn't hear the approaching footsteps until a slurred voice rang mockingly from the pulpit.

"Good God! Could it be the Devil-Child of the moors? The demon who runs with the Bucca-Dhu mounted atop a monstrous fire-breathing steed?"

Devil gasped, seeing the moonlight on the bright Pendarves hair. She saw the chiselled cheekbones against shattered stained-glass window. It was Torr and yet it wasn't his voice.

"The Bucca is dead and buried in the dirt outside these doors," she stated softly. "A part of me is buried with him," she added. It didn't occur to her to run away from the strange yet familiar man. Ajax staggered down the steps from the pulpit and walked toward her.

"Part of me is buried heaven knows where," he informed bitterly, flapping his empty sleeve.

"You must be Ajax Pendarves."

"Yes, I am Ajax! Ajax the warrior, who killed himself because his armour was given to another!"

"You'd not do such a terrible thing!" Devil exclaimed, an icy hand clutching her heart.

"Maybe if I was brave enough," sighed Ajax, slumping into one of the front pews and unscrewing the lid of his flask with his teeth. "Just need some courage. Brandy?" he offered, and she shook her head. "Best quality French brandy. Would seem that my oldest brother is into smuggling. Our cellars are well-stocked."

"Does it hurt?" asked Devil, not wanting to think of Torr.

"This?" he laughed, picking up his empty sleeve and twirling it about. "Or my lack of courage?" Devil look silently at the coat sleeve. "Sometimes there are phantom pains and often my palm itches but there is no hand. I wonder if it's the insects beneath the French dirt eating my flesh."

Devil found herself examining her own palm, softly caressing the blue-white scars on the heel. "It shall pass, I think. It must pass. The pain must lessen," she attempted to comfort.

"How do you know? You have all your limbs!" he retorted angrily.

"I don't know. I'm sorry. I was selfish, just thinking of the Bucca and other . . . losses. It cannot be the same."

A silence fell and they sat dejectedly, absorbed in their own misery. After a while Devil blew out the guttering candle and quietly got up to leave. She assumed that Ajax slept, but he followed her out into the graveyard. Devil stood looking at her mother's tombstone, and he staggered up to her, peering drunkenly down at the crooked, weathered slab.

" 'Beneath this moor forsaken, wild . . . lies a whore and her bastard child,' " he read ponderously. "Delightful relatives I have, don't you think? A whore, a pitiful bastard, and the spiteful monster who made this cruel epitaph!"

"I am the pitiful bastard child and if it is past midnight, it is my birthday!" she announced with bravado, but her voice broke and she ended with a sob. Ajax stared into the upturned face. For a moment he wasn't sure if it was the brandy or if he actually did gaze upon the impish spirit of the moors. The enormous eyes brimmed with tears.

"Happy birthday, little cousin," he said huskily. The small figure abruptly whirled away and leaped agilely onto the back of an enormous black horse. Ajax swayed with the wailing sea-wind as he listened to the hoofbeats pound and fade over the moor before taking another fortifying swig of brandy, hoping to conjure more diversion.

Torr found his brother there an hour later as he wearily returned from a long day at the mines. He had thrown himself into work rather than impotently wait for his Devil-Woman to appear. The last days of 1793 had passed gloomily at High Tor where it seemed the only words exchanged were between Goodie and herself, as she desperately tried to penetrate Ajax's bitter drunkenness, Torr's grim industry, and her own husband Jago's laconic dejection. Luckily Felix was spared such glumness, during what was supposed to be a Christian season of good cheer by spending the Christmas holidays with the Carmichaels. Torr was oblivious to everything, yet he couldn't resist stopping by the graveyard, hoping to find his wild woman of the moors; hoping to hear the soul-touching music swell. Instead, he found his brother sitting on Godolphus Pendarves's tombstone, staring morosely at Catherine's epitaph.

"Pendarves curse the house of Taran . . . may all Tremayne wombs be barren!" declared Ajax. "Our curses aren't too potent, are they? I hear Angelica Tremayne is huge with child!"

"Come along home, Ajax," sighed Torr.

"I met a little dead relative tonight. A dear little chap about . . . so big," informed Ajax, thoughtfully measuring to his chin. "A most engaging imp. Must've been given a holiday from the grave because of his birthday. It's after midnight, so it's his birthday today, see?" he pointed to the date on the gravestone. "Our cousin Catherine's little bastard son born December thirty-first, that's now . . . 1776. Tiny little fellow didn't seem to be seventeen years old . . . didn't sound so old, either, but that's probably because he was just a spirit. Beautiful face and eyes so large and expressive I could have drowned in their painful depths."

"Enormous nearly black eyes?"

"That's right! By Jove, I forgot! You've also met the Devil-Child. I wish to God he'd been around to save my arm as he did your leg! Maybe you're not Torrance but Odysseus and the Devil-Child is my protection," muttered Ajax drunkenly. "Oh, well, too late now . . . arm's gone and its bloody sad to think of that lonely little ghost having to drift about in limbo for all eternity."

"When was the Devil-Child here?" demanded Torr, and Ajax shrugged and vaguely flapped his empty sleeve.

"I say, would you give me a ride home? I walked here, I think, but our ghostly little cousin has given me the courage to sit a horse again."

"Think, Ajax . . . how long before I arrived was the Devil-Child here?" Torr shook his brother, but Ajax just giggled and staggered, nearly toppling them both.

"By Jove, I think I shall grace Taran with my presence . . . well, nearly all my presence. . . . It shall be a fitting tribute to our phantom cousin's birthday," planned Ajax excitedly, accepting his resigned brother's help and adeptly mounting Torr's horse despite his inebriation and missing arm. "You know, big brother, you're getting stuffy and grim before your time. It would do you a world of good to kick up your heels a bit. No one'll notice your limp . . . and if they do they'll be too well-bred to stare or remark, I'm sure," he chattered. "By the way, I hope you didn't take any of my drivel to heart?"

"Drivel?" blankly repeated Torr, scanning the shadowy graveyard, hoping to see a small fleet figure.

"Goodie really took me to task, you know. Told me that father had been having heart trouble for years . . . and that you and he made up your differences before. . . . Do you forgive me for my . . . ungenerous words?"

"Of course," sighed Torr absently, mounting behind his brother. He assumed that the brandy had mellowed the truculent youth, who in the morning would be as sullen as ever. Why couldn't it have been he at Pendarves Chapel when the elusive female had made her visit? he seethed. Maybe his Devil-Woman had been there waiting for him, he thought hopefully.

"We'll begin the new year of 1794 as the best of brothers, starting with the festivities at Taran!" proclaimed Ajax.

"I'm not really the best of company these days."

"Who is she, Torr?" asked Ajax after a long silence filled only by the sounds of the bleak cold night—the weary plodding of the overburdened horse through the frost-crisped bracken; the ever-present wailing wind and the rhythmic surge of the winter sea. "Is any female worth it?" he probed when there was no answer. "Learn from poor Jago Pengelly! Was ever a man so henpecked?"

"I don't know if she's worth it, but I shall shake her within an inch of her life when I find her," confessed Torr savagely.

"Then I sincerely pray the poor wench stays well hidden," laughed Ajax, leaning back into his brother's strength. "Tell me about her?" he invited, but Torr adamantly declined. He was fiercely possessive of the precious memories of his elusive love. They were all he had of her, and he'd share them with no one.

CHAPTER 21

DEVIL SLEPT unusually late. She didn't want to wake and fervently wished that she could magically avoid her seventeenth birthday and the evening celebration planned in her honour. She awoke thinking of "honour." Did she have "honour"? she pondered. She was very aware of how much her father treasured Angelica's purity and despised her mother, Catherine's, lack of it. Her grandfather's censorious words about women droned in her head along with Iris's reveries about being chastely cherished by Angus Dunbar. Devil felt a clutch of terror when she admitted that she would hate to be chastely cherished by Torr Pendarves . . . or anyone else for that matter. Obviously her grandfather had been incorrect in his assumption that all women were whores. It was evident that only some, herself and her mother included, were guilty. Sins of the mother be visited upon the child, Godolphus's voice echoed in her mind, and she concluded that the dishonourable trait was inherited. What would her father do if he knew? He would probably cast her out of the gates of Taran, just like he had done to Catherine. At the thought, she was surprised to feel a wrenching sorrow.

Her birthday passed in a mounting frenzy of colour, scent, and sound, but Devil remained in her protective shroud. Iris's constant animated chatter flowed over her, making no impression.

"She just ain't 'erself, Miss Angel," worried the freckled girl, unable to resist a pirouette in front of the mirror so that her new ballgown swirled gracefully. "I look like a real lady," she whispered, her eyes round with awe.

"Is she dressed?"

"Yeah, and she looks a treat, but she's just staring out at the sea and 'er eyes 'ave that sad look like an 'ungry puppy's."

Angelica rapped softly on Devlyn's door and, when there was no answer, quietly entered. For several moments she stood, watching the beautiful girl who was breathtaking in a simple dusty pink gown that was draped about her exquisite figure in a casual Greek style.

"Is it all too much for you? Have we been selfish just thinking of our own pleasure in giving and insensitive to your need for solitude?" she asked gently, disturbed by Devlyn's numb detachment and hollow haunted eyes. "I know there is too much noise and bustle, but there is no need to be afraid. We've only invited kind, comfortable people like my father, whom you already know . . . and my mother, who is rather eccentric and shall probably hide amongst the orchids in the hothouse. You can join her there if it all gets too much. Then there are my two younger brothers, Owen and Evan, and their friend Felix Pendarves." At the mention of the Pendarves name, Devlyn started. "Ajax and Torr Pendarves sent word this afternoon that they will also be attending," stated Angelica, suddenly surmising why the girl might be so fearful. "Does he love you?" she asked softly.

"He doesn't know who I really am."

"Then it is time he does . . . and tonight your very proud father will introduce his beautiful daughter, Devlyn Tremayne. . . ."

"I am also Devil Tremayne, Catherine's daughter," interrupted Devil savagely. Angelica stepped back as if she had been slapped, but then she nodded thoughtfully and smiled approvingly before laughing at the incredible transformation. The glossy ebony head was no longer shamefully bowed but triumphantly raised, the eyes no longer hollow and haunted but flashing proudly. Gone was the numbing shroud. A vibrant woman had emerged, her very presence magnetic and challenging. Devil's own laughter joined Angelica's at the feeling of heady relief. It was as though an enormous weight had been lifted and there was no part left hidden . . . no secrets. Two essential halves of herself had joined and both were equally acceptable.

Benedict stood unnoticed in the threshold. He had heard his daughter's defiant declaration and had recoiled, but he also had seen the remarkable transformation.

"So Devil Tremayne, daughter of Catherine and Benedict, and my Angel are you quite ready to meet our guests?" he asked gruffly, holding out his arms to both his women.

Torr and Ajax arrived at Taran a little later than was fashionable, due in part to Ajax's whimsical desire to stop by Pendarves Chapel in order to place a birthday cake by Catherine's tombstone for the ghost of the Devil-Child. He had insisted that Goodie bake it and had then enlisted Torr's help in covering it with festive decorations. There had been a silly space in the dreary grey days for both Pendarves men, which had caused Goodie to shed nostalgic tears. They had cluttered her fragrant kitchen just as they had done as little tots, earnestly and messily daubing mounds of marzipan and icing onto the sagging cake until their fingers were glued together and their hair and faces sticky.

Now bathed and dressed in the height of fashion the two young men rode toward Taran, Torr on horseback and Ajax in a curricle. The wrought-iron gates clanged shut behind them. They entered the park and went up the winding driveway toward the enormous house on the cliff. Each window was ablaze with light and happiness; music drifted on the chill sea-breeze.

"I am not at all sure I am in the mood for all this jollity," sighed Torr, dismounting and handing his reins to an ostler. He and Ajax strode up the wide stone steps of Taran, and the doors were flung wide. They were announced, but their names were drowned out by the hubbub inside. Nodding politely to acquaintances, they made their way through the clusters of gaily dressed people. Torr's head ached from the constant noise. He was just about to leave quietly and return to his glum solitude at High Tor to pour over mine accounts when Angelica grasped his arm.

"At last! I was about to give up on you two," she chided. "I have incurred my husband's displeasure because of you! I refused to allow him to make his announcement until you were here," she informed, steering Torr through the conversing crowds and into the ballroom.

"An announcement? But it is not yet the New Year," laughed Ajax, grabbing a full glass from the tray of a passing footman and following.

"I shall not say one more word, but I want your solemn promise, Sir Torrance Pendarves, that you will remain right here until Benedict has made his announcement."

"What is this about, Angel?"

"My lips are sealed," she repeated. "Do you promise?" Torr shrugged and nodded. She gazed at him earnestly, searching for warmth and humour in his icy blue eyes.

"What is this about?" asked Ajax. Torr just frowned and watched Angelica disappear into the rejoicing throng.

They stood sipping wine and nibbling tiny canapes, obediently waiting for Taran's announcement.

"You are free to wander, Ajax; the promise was wrung from me not you," said Torr curtly, chafing against his confinement.

"Here's Taran now," remarked Ajax. "My God, what a beauty! Who the hell is she?" he ejaculated as Benedict and Angelica mounted the dais escorted by a vision in muted dusty pink. Torr turned bored, disinterested eyes towards the platform and then every muscle in his body stiffened with shock. "Who is she, Torr? There is something familiar about her."

Devil had never been the object of so much scrutiny. Her cheeks stiffened hotly, but she kept her head proudly raised as her eyes skimmed coolly over the sea of upturned expectant faces. She wanted to see Torr's expression when he learned who she was. Panic fluttered at not being able to find him. Angelica covered her mouth with her gracefully moving fan.

"He's to the right of the main doors," she furtively whispered as Benedict cleared his throat and raised his hands, demanding silence.

"Friends and neighbours, welcome to Taran. This house has been shrouded with sorrows and discordancy from the past for too long . . . and now it will be alive with joy and hope, peace and harmony for the future. There shall be no more painful secrets, and that is why with great love and even greater pride I present to you my daughter . . . Devlyn Tremayne,'' stated Benedict. There was a rousing cheer from Iris, who clapped enthusiastically, then an audible gasp from the assemblage before a furious mutter swept like a surging wave.

Benedict waited, expecting his defiant child to correct her name, but she stood aloof staring across the room.

Devil's heart hammered painfully, belieing her haughty demeanor. She was too far away to see Torr's expression, but she knew by the rigid set of his bright head that he was angry. She kept her eyes pinned achingly to him, not knowing if he was about to leave, never to be seen again, or else advance furiously on her. None of the seething, chattering crowd existed, and she was deaf to the remainder of her father's speech. There was an anticipatory hush when he finished. Everyone looked up at the exquisite dark girl, waiting for her to acknowledge them, but she stood like a statue oblivious to everyone except the tall blond young man whose icy blue eyes blazed.

''I think we should take our partners and go in to dinner,'' suggested Angelica brightly. She shrewdly noted Benedict's scowl at his daughter's preoccupation with the approaching Torrance Pendarves, who was followed by his slightly inebriated, grinning brother Ajax. ''I find I am extremely hungry, darling,'' she urged, taking her husband's arm, but he was immovable. ''Take your partners for dinner,'' she announced gaily. ''Follow the footmen to the great banquet hall,'' she added, waving the curious but unmoving throng in the right direction. ''Aah, Sir Torrance and Ajax . . . how wonderful that you both could be here,'' she chatted, her nervousness mounting at the sight of Benedict's flashing black eyes. She felt his muscles harden beneath his sleeve. ''Sir Torrance, I hope it won't inconvenience you to escort Devlyn to dinner,'' she added, trying desperately to avoid a scandalous altercation.

The tall golden young man glowered at the equally incensed girl.

''It will not inconvenience me in the slightest to escort the young . . . lady,'' pronounced Torr, pointedly stressing the word *lady*. ''I am certain we shall contrive to find much of an inconsequential nature to converse upon,'' he added, his tone heavily laced with sarcasm, his blue gaze cold and contemptuous. "Madam?" he offered his crooked arm.

"What the bloody hell!" swore Benedict. "What is this about, Pendarves?"

"Oh, please," begged Angelica, not feeling strong enough for what promised to be a very loud public quarrel. "Please?" she pleaded, casting her eyes about at the attentive crowd. Maybe she should cause a diversion and swoon. It would be attributed to her delicate, unmentionable condition, she planned frantically.

"It is quite all right, Father," purred Devil through gritted teeth, her temper thoroughly fired by Torr's boorish, insulting manner. "You and Angelica lead the way," she ordered, taking the coldly proffered arm and resisting the temptation to pinch it childishly. "I assure you, Father, I am quite adept at handling the most unbridled and crudest of animals," she added when Benedict hesitated. Angelica groaned inwardly, noting how Torr's chiselled features hardened ruthlessly and Devlyn's poignant face curved in a triumphant grin. Her worst fears about a painful collision between the uncompromising young couple appeared inevitable.

"Why, if it isn't our little devil cousin from the graveyard on the moor," rejoiced Ajax, enjoying the sparks that crackled between the gloriously handsome pair. He stepped back to better appreciate the fascinating contrast of the petite dark beauty and his tall golden brother. Crystal blue and glinting jet eyes silently and eloquently battled. "Yes, big brother, there certainly are some females well worth such aggravation," he chuckled, raising a roguish eyebrow conspiratorially at Benedict. Recognizing Taran's formidable expression, he prudently edged away. "So much for peace and harmony," he muttered.

"We shall lead the way," declared Angelica too loudly, fumbling for Benedict's clenched fist and purposefully descending the dais, determined to continue with the festivities.

Arm in arm, Devil and Torr sedately followed, nodding politely. Arm in arm, they crossed the vast ballroom, their fury masked by brittle smiles, their eyes blinded by the pulse that throbbed between them. Arm in arm, each ready to explode, they dutifully followed Benedict and Angelica toward the banquetting hall—but once in the marbled central hall, Torr swung Devil into his arms. Ignoring her struggles, he strode swiftly up the circular stairs and down a dark quiet corridor away from the noisy throng. He kicked open a door and entered a small salon that was lit by a cosy fire.

"Put me down!" spat Devil, and he roughly complied by tumbling her onto a sofa before slamming the door, ensuring his privacy. For good measure he turned the key in the lock and shot the bolt. Devil sprang to her feet, and he turned slowly to face her.

Torr glared silently, unable to formulate a word. When he had seen her standing beside Benedict Tremayne on the dais in the ballroom, everything had receded except her. He had felt caught in a current that whirled him about, deafening him with a rushing roar, and in the very centre of the maelstrom was his Devil-Woman . . . aloof and disdainful. His fury had erupted, and he wanted to reach out a savage hand and rip at her mocking elegance. He had wanted to tear at her contrived coiffure. How dare she attire herself like every other female? How dare she harness her glorious mane of hair into prim ringlets that jangled his stretched nerves and seemed to jeer at him.

Devil was unprepared for his assault. Pins and ribbons flew in every direction, his large hands tugging and pulling painfully until her hair was wild and free. In shock she stood docilely, allowing him to undo what had taken several hours to accomplish.

"There," he panted, stepping back and surveying her. Her dark eyes positively smoldered with suppressed rage, and her firm breasts rose and fell with her laboured breathing. She looked glorious. The yards of dusty-pink gossamer that reflected the heightened flush of fury on her cheeks seemed almost carelessly molded to her sensual body. Torr's anger and passion welded, and he flexed his hands, wanting to crush her roughly to his heart; wanting to brutally punish her for the pain that pulsed through him. "As you can see I am equally adept at handling unbridled and unprincipled creatures," he stated cuttingly, recognising the answering sparks of rage and desire in the depths of her dark eyes. The space between them crackled. "So you are Lady Devlyn Tremayne?" he pronounced hoarsely after a long silence.

"I am Devil Tremayne," she stated.

"Nevertheless . . . a Tremayne of Taran. Why didn't you tell me?"

Devil shrugged. She wrenched her smoldering gaze from his and walked to the piano, needing to put something between them besides the unbearable tension. "It was not my intention to deceive you," she said awkwardly, wishing he would vent his anger instead of creating such friction.

"And what was your intention?" he snapped. Devil shrugged unhappily, not knowing how to put her scattered thoughts into words. "To make a fool of me?" he challenged.

"To make a fool of you?" she repeated questioningly. "One can only make a fool of oneself," she battled, remembering one of Jonty Pengelly's wise sayings. Devil's response adroitly robbed Torr of a retort. His fury simmered, yet he had no way to vent it unless he resorted to childish hurtful words. He turned his back, blocking the tantalizing sight of her lest it goad him to make a complete idiot of himself. "I had no intention except to come to you . . . when I was free to do so."

"Free to do so?" he queried sarcastically, refusing to be seduced by her vulnerable voice, refusing to look at her.

"I didn't want Angelica to be hurt," she confessed, watching the firelight play through the golden hair.

"But it was quite all right to hurt me and embarrass me with your immorality?" he accused, turning to face her. Devil recoiled and stepped back. "Do you feel victorious? You owe me for a stolen fishing boat and a night's lodging!" he continued. "Christ, listen to me! Where is my pride? I sound like a callow, moonstruck, spiteful youth!" he stormed at himself, striding to the window and staring blindly out at the winter darkness. "What have you done to me?" he muttered, making a great effort to calm himself. He stared pensively at Devil's reflection in the window. She seemed so small and lost in the frosty whorls of glass, lost and drowning. Her image reminded him of the moment when he fished her out of the stormy sea and she hung dripping in his hands. "Why didn't you trust me with the truth?"

"It was not my secret," she repeated. Her anger was fired at the insulting sight of his broad back. "There is much I can now share with you, but not like this. Not when you are only aware of your own hurt. I'll not even try and explain when you are so muffled in cold fury. I am not ashamed and I make no excuses for myself. I love you and it is very sad that you are hurting . . . but so am I. And so was I. I had to hide my love away just as I have been hidden away all of my life . . . but no more!" she shouted, willing her tears to stay locked inside. "I shall be nobody's guilty secret ever again! Do you hear me?"

Angelica gently removed Benedict's hand from the salon door. She reached up and tenderly touched the tears that wet his cheeks at hearing his child's anguished avowal.

"Come, my love, our guests are waiting and Devlyn is quite capable of handling unbridled creatures . . . herself included," she whispered. "Especially herself," she added, steering her husband back along the quiet corridor toward the happy chatter below.

Torr watched Devil's sensitive fingers gently caress the closed piano. Not a word had been spoken since her vehement declaration. She was his cousin Catherine's child, hidden for a whole childhood in that inhospitable fortress on the desolate moor. The full realization surged into his head, and he was ashamed. He recalled the haunting music that had swirled with the sea-frets, softening the sorrows that tightly bound him.

"Play for me?" he begged softly. Devil looked at him for a long moment. The cold hard blue of his eyes had softened and deepened to the warm winking blue of the summer sky; of summer flowers, mischievous and sparkling bird's eye and forget-me-nots.

"Not here, not now." she declined shyly, unable to expose her vulnerability with so many strangers milling through the halls and rooms of her home. What if, in the middle of her most intimate confession, the salon door burst open and her father's guests politely applauded?

"I know where there's a birthday cake for a Devil-Child and a wonderful wheezy old organ," he offered.

"A birthday cake for a Devil-Child?"

"A birthday cake for a Devil-Woman," amended Torr. "Ajax and I left it by Catherine's grave on our way."

"I've never had a birthday cake before. Let me change my clothes and fetch the Carrack!" she cried excitedly and Torr grinned fondly as she transformed from a poised woman to a rambunctious child.

"Whoa, my love. I think it advisable that we behave ourselves and first put in a decorous appearance at your father's table. It is essential that I curry favour if I mean to ask Taran for his daughter's hand in marriage."

"Marriage?" Devil was confused by her discomfort at hearing the claiming words. She was just finding herself, just tasting her freedom, just revelling in her emerging womanhood. "No, I think it advisable that first you hold me and kiss me," she contradicted, reaching out and encircling his neck. She stood on tiptoe and pressed herself urgently against the most intimate part of him, trying to resolve her conflict.

"Oh, God!" groaned Torr, clasping her tightly as his passion flared. Devil grinned with satisfaction, feeling his arousal through the soft fabric of her clinging gown. They kissed hungrily and she writhed against him.

"Mate with me," she whispered against his lips and was surprised to be abruptly set aside. "What is it?" she whispered, watching him stride stiffly across the room, putting as much distance as possible between them.

"You are Lady Devlyn Tremayne."

"I was Lady Devlyn Tremayne before."

"But, my little demon, I was unaware of that very pertinent fact," he stated.

"Are you saying that if you had been aware of that fact, you wouldn't have lain with me?"

"That is precisely what I am saying," he confirmed.

"But I am the same person," she protested. He didn't answer and made no move toward her. "Who or what did you think I was? What was the difference between who you thought I was and who you now know I am?" she struggled. "If I was just a female, if there is such a thing as 'just-a-female' because it seems to me we are all the same—able to laugh and cry, with the same breasts and cleft between our legs—but if I was just a female like Iris and Peg Hatch, poor, having to work hard for shelter and food, then it would be all right for you to mate with me?"

"It cannot be so simply put," returned Torr evasively, at a loss because he had never given much thought to certain conventions but just accepted them as fact.

"I knew that you were Sir Torrance Pendarves and I still lay with you," she continued stubbornly.

"Nice, well-born young ladies don't—"

"But I am not nice nor am I well-born. I am the whore Catherine's daughter, so I cannot be chastely cherished," she stated roguishly, relishing the way the alliteration twisted her lips.

"Chastely cherished?" echoed Torr, totally perplexed and equally horrified.

"Angus Dunbar 'chastely cherishes' Iris . . . locks her out of his chamber . . . refuses to share his bed until they are wed," informed Devil, fixing her mischievous eyes to the front of Torr's tight britches, fully aware that he was as desirous of her as she was of him. "Can't you pretend that you don't know who I am?" she asked hopefully.

"Absolutely not and most certainly not under your father's roof! That would be decidedly bad form. Now, avert your immodest eyes and make yourself presentable because it is high time we put in an appearance. It is essential that Taran looks favourably upon my suit and accepts me as a son-in-law," he stated sternly.

"Poor father, he's getting inundated with offspring! Maybe we should give him time to adjust," she sighed. "Lots of time to adjust," she added pensively, staring at her reflection in the mirror. What was the matter with her? She loved Torrance Pendarves. Just the sight of him, the sound of him, the scent of him, the thought of him quickened her pulses. Yet the thought of being bound in marriage for the rest of her natural life terrified her. Maybe they should have a very long courtship, which would allow her space to fly free for a while, she planned, avoiding the word *engagement*, which conjured up entanglements. She pursed her lips seductively and shimmied her gown off one shoulder to expose a pert breast.

"It is amazing the change in your father! The court couldn't credit Taran's transformation. His reputation as a rakehell is legendary," declared Torr with a bark of laughter.

"Rakehell?" mouthed Devil. Why wasn't a man called a whore? she pondered.

"In the space of one short year, Angelica has transformed the rakehell into a veritable paragon," he chuckled, finally controlling his passion and straightening his cravat. "Are you presentable, my pet?"

Devil winced at the word *pet*, determined never to be so docile as to deserve such a name. She winked at her reflection before twirling about and posing seductively before him.

"Am I presentable enough, Sir Torrance?" she challenged huskily when he stood stunned, shaking his blond head in despair at the scandalous yet tantalizing spectacle. "Am I presentable, your lordship?" she repeated, wickedly tweaking an aroused nipple and watching with undisguised fascination how the blatant evidence of his rampant desire destroyed the fine line of his elegant evening britches.

"You are aptly named, Devil Tremayne," he croaked hoarsely, absolutely determined to observe all the proprieties of civilized courtship.

CHILDREN OF THE MIST

Aleen Malcolm

When fiery, emerald-eyed Kat MacGregor left France for
the mist-mantled shores of her native Scotland one fear
haunted her above all others – that she and her family
would be discovered by their traditional mortal enemies,
the clan of Campbell. At the crumbling grey mansion
where unwilling kinsfolk were forced to house them they
existed as best they could. Their identity achingly hidden,
they seemed to be truly

CHILDREN OF THE MIST

Dressed as a boy, Wild Kat accompanied her father on his
shady card-sharping exploits. Then a shattering twist of
fate propelled her into the arms of magnificent hawk-faced
Darach Campbell, Lord Rannoch, from whom her true
name must forever remain secret.

Out of terror and blood feud would be born, unwillingly,
dark irresistible rapture.

FUTURA PUBLICATIONS
FICTION/HISTORICAL ROMANCE
A TROUBADOUR BOOK
0 7088 3164 8

RENEGADE LADY

Kathryn Atwood

A victim of her brother's gambling debts, lovely Theone
Danvers had to choose between the hell of debtor's prison
– and the lecherous arms of the Marquis de Juliers. But
Theone had no mind to submit meekly to her fate.
Dressed as a lad, she took to the highroad with smoking
pistols and stole herself a fortune in gold.

Then, in the green depths of the forest, she met a rival – a
highwayman with haunting emerald eyes, a price on his
head, and a noble secret in his past. They joined forces,
only for the disguised Theone to ride headlong into the
greatest danger of her renegade career: the unquenchable
passion of first love.

FUTURA PUBLICATIONS
FICTION/HISTORICAL ROMANCE
A TROUBADOUR BOOK
0 7088 3604 6

All Futura Books are available at your bookshop or
newsagent, or can be ordered from the following address:
Futura Books, Cash Sales Department,
P.O. Box 11, Falmouth, Cornwall TR10 9EN.

Please send cheque or postal order (no currency), and
allow 60p for postage and packing for the first book
plus 25p for the second book and 15p for each additional
book ordered up to a maximum charge of £1.90 in U.K.

B.F.P.O. customers please allow 60p for
the first book, 25p for the second book plus 15p per
copy for the next 7 books, thereafter 9p per book

Overseas customers, including Eire, please allow £1.25
for postage and packing for the first book, 75p for the
second book and 28p for each subsequent title ordered.